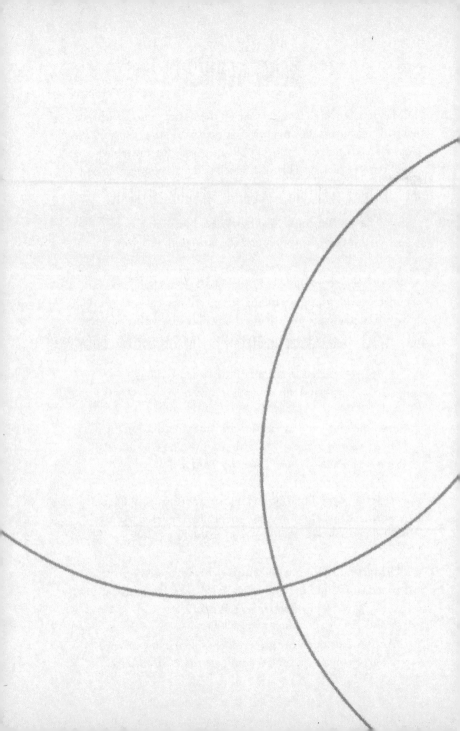

MICHAEL DANTE DIMARTINO

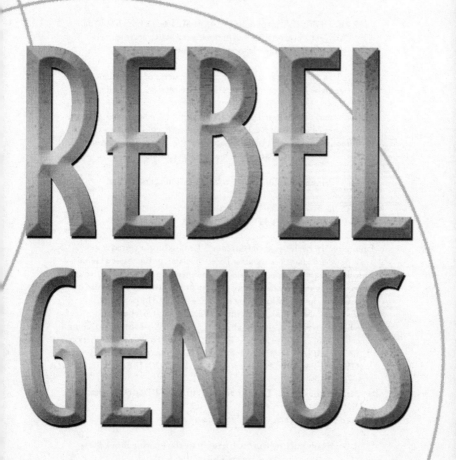

REBEL
GENIUS

SQUARE
FISH

Roaring Brook Press
New York

SQUARE
FISH

An imprint of Macmillan Publishing Group, LLC
175 Fifth Avenue
New York, NY 10010
mackids.com

REBEL GENIUS. Copyright © 2016 by Michael Dante DiMartino.
All rights reserved. Printed in the United States of America by
LSC Communications, Harrisonburg, Virginia.

Square Fish and the Square Fish logo are trademarks of Macmillan and are
used by Roaring Brook Press under license from Macmillan.

Our books may be purchased in bulk for promotional, educational, or business
use. Please contact your local bookseller or the Macmillan Corporate and
Premium Sales Department at (800) 221-7945 ext. 5442 or by e-mail
at MacmillanSpecialMarkets@macmillan.com.

Library of Congress Cataloging-in-Publication Data

Names: DiMartino, Michael Dante, author.
Title: Rebel genius / Michael Dante DiMartino.
Description: New York : Roaring Brook Press, 2016. | Series: Rebel genius |
    Summary: "In twelve-year-old Giacomo's Renaissance-inspired world,
    art is powerful, dangerous, and outlawed. Every artist possesses a Genius,
    a birdlike creature that is the living embodiment of an artist's creative spirit.
    Those caught with one face severe punishment, so when Giacomo discovers he
    has a Genius, he knows he's in big trouble"—Provided by publisher.
Identifiers: LCCN 2016004881 (print) | LCCN 2016031116 (ebook) |
    ISBN 978-1-250-12974-1 (paperback)   ISBN 978-1-62672-539-3 (ebook)
Subjects: | CYAC: Creative ability—Fiction. | Magic—Fiction. | Art—Fiction. |
    Fantasy. | BISAC: JUVENILE FICTION / Action & Adventure / General. |
    JUVENILE FICTION / Fantasy & Magic. | JUVENILE FICTION / Art &
    Architecture.
Classification: LCC PZ7.1.D564 Re 2016 (print) | LCC PZ7.1.D564 (ebook) |
    DDC [Fic]—dc23
LC record available at https://lccn.loc.gov/2016004881

Originally published in the United States by Roaring Brook Press
First Square Fish edition, 2018
Book designed by Andrew Arnold
Square Fish logo designed by Filomena Tuosto

1 3 5 7 9 10 8 6 4 2

AR: 5.3 / LEXILE: 730L

For Shoshi

Though I have succeeded in my quest to map the lands and borders of all three empires, I now see that my pursuit was folly. My work will stand as nothing more than one man's feeble attempt to chart this physical plane.

For after climbing the tallest peaks, sailing the widest seas, and scouring the darkest forests, I am forced to conclude that one lifetime is scarcely enough to understand all the mysteries of this world.

It has become heartbreakingly apparent that what I believed I could touch is merely an illusion.

—Poggio Garrulous
(1050, age of the pentad)

CONTENTS

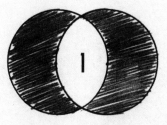

LOST SOULS

Giacomo cradled the chunk of charcoal in his hand and lightly pressed it to the paper. Faint lines circled the dirty page, darkening into the shape of his oval head. He added a shadow, carving out his round chin, then moved on to his thick eyebrows, followed by the nostrils of his bulbous nose. Before long, his face emerged. As he drew, Giacomo glanced up and down between the shard of mirror leaning against the wall and his sketchbook. He used quick strokes to build up his hair, which fell in ratty waves to his shoulders. With a fingertip, he rubbed more charcoal under his lower lip, on the side of his nose, and under his brows to give dimension to his features. Giacomo paused and examined his latest effort. He shook his head and sighed. Over the past few years, he'd filled sketchbook after sketchbook with self-portraits, but was never satisfied with the results. The boy who stared back at him from the pages always looked like a stranger.

For the finishing touch, he surrounded his portrait with black

strokes, but he pushed down too hard and his last piece of charcoal shattered. Giacomo groaned and slammed his sketchbook
shut. *Time for a supply run.*

Giacomo wiped his dust-covered hands on his tunic, which was
so filthy he couldn't tell what was dirt, what was charcoal, and

what was sewer muck. They all blended together into a brownish-green grime.

The light from his lantern flickered, creating dancing shadows on the curved stone wall. As he tucked his worn sketchbook into his burlap satchel, the flame vanished and his hideout plunged into darkness.

He slung the satchel over his shoulder and grabbed the lantern's thin handle. Reaching out, he touched the edge of the low archway, then ducked, careful not to bang his head.

In the main tunnel, rats skittered and squeaked. The stench of urine burned his nostrils. As his feet splashed through shallow water, Giacomo slid his hand across the protruding stones, using them as signposts to navigate through the cramped aqueducts.

He counted a hundred paces and turned left into another passageway. Two hundred more paces. A right. He felt a familiar mossy area—his signal to head to the surface.

Climbing a spiral staircase, he came to a narrow storm drain. Moonlight streamed through and his vision began to return. Giacomo crouched and peered out, the street at eye level. As he expected, the city looked empty. But any moment, a soldier might march by, patrolling for curfew breakers. Or worse, a Lost Soul could be lurking in the shadows, waiting to lunge at an unsuspecting victim.

Giacomo gazed up at the specks of light blanketing the heavens. On nights like this, he sensed the Creator's presence. But it was like a scent of lavender in the breeze—there for a moment, then gone.

The clomp of footsteps snapped him back to earth. As he'd

feared, two soldiers headed his way, their hands on the hilts of their swords. He ducked down and waited for the men to pass. Once the rattling of their armor faded, he counted to fifty. *Can't be too careful,* he reminded himself.

Giacomo wriggled his skinny torso through the storm drain. Knowing the soldiers would loop back around in a while, he had to move fast. But for now, this area of Virenzia was his.

He inhaled a lungful of the cool, fresh air and darted down a backstreet. On either side of him, the looming houses were stacked so precariously high it looked like they could topple over and crush him.

Rounding the corner, he spotted his target—Beppe's Bakery. Above a faded red door hung a weathered sign, the image of a plump man with a bushy mustache carved into the wood. As Giacomo caught his breath, hunger kicked him in the gut.

He snuck around back, where he was met by a pair of locked shutters. He took a palette knife from his satchel and eased the blade between the two wooden panels, lifting the handle until he heard the clink of the latch coming unhooked. The shutters swung open with a slow groan. He hoisted himself through the window and pulled the shutters closed.

Prowling past fat sacks of flour, Giacomo vowed that one day he'd retire his palette knife from its life of crime and use it for what it was meant for—mixing oil paint.

Under the baker's rolling table he found a tin bucket full of burned, stale bread. When Giacomo was first living on the streets, he had discovered that Beppe the Baker had a morning ritual of strolling down to the river and feeding the previous day's discards to the ducks. Giacomo had decided if the bread was good enough for them, it was good enough for him.

He rummaged through the baker's scraps. Most were as hard and black as coal. He dug to the bottom, where he found a few squishy hunks. Giacomo stuffed one in his mouth and packed the rest in his satchel.

While the stale bread stewed in his saliva, he crept over to a vat of olive oil and dunked a ladle into it. He poured a cupful of the thick liquid into the base of his lantern, enough to give him light for a couple of nights. Lastly, he reached into the brick oven and picked out a few pieces of charcoal.

Giacomo slipped out the way he had come in, offering Beppe his silent thanks. One day, he would pay back the baker for his unwitting kindness.

By the time his feet met the cobblestones, the bread in his mouth was soft enough to swallow. He scampered into the shadows and headed to his final stop.

He emerged from a side street and hid behind a column at the edge of the city's central square—Piazza Nerezza, named for the "Supreme Creator." He scowled. *What isn't named for her?* Over the years, Supreme Creator Nerezza had slapped her name on every major street, building, and monument in Virenzia, as if people really needed reminding that they were living in her domain.

Technically, Nerezza was the emperor of the Zizzolan Empire, like her father before her. But years of absolute power had made her delusional and she renamed herself the Supreme Creator. Giacomo fumed at her arrogance. *Who is she to put herself on a pedestal, above the true Creator of this world?*

Giacomo dashed from pillar to pillar, keeping his eyes and ears out for more soldiers. A black marble obelisk towered in the center of the square. Shapes and symbols were carved into each of its four sides. Ten times as tall as Giacomo, it was capped with a pyramid that pointed to the heavens. He recalled his mother's soft voice describing how the Creator had placed the needle of his Compass on the spot where the monument now stood, and drew a circle, bringing the world into existence. His parents also told him stories about Zizzolan heroes who protected the weak from the powerful during a time long ago when artists and their Geniuses didn't have to hide. In the tales, the heroes' belief and trust in the Creator always got them through whatever challenges they faced, which probably explained why Nerezza had burned all the books containing the old myths. Even the memory of heroes past seemed to threaten her.

At the far end of the piazza was the Supreme Creator's palace. From its towers hung flags emblazoned with the Zizzolan Empire's symbol—a black triangle pointing down, inside of which was a white triangle pointing up. The pattern repeated itself, the shapes shrinking until there was only a white dot. Just seeing the symbol made Giacomo sick to his stomach.

The buildings next to the towers were draped with two monumental tapestries, each an identical depiction of the Supreme Creator. She stood tall and proud in her black robes, her mouth bent into a conceited smirk. Perched on the palace's triangular pediment was a stone gargoyle of her Genius—a horrifying winged creature with a long tail, a beak full of fangs, and two twisted horns that sprouted from the center of the crown on its head. *What a crime,* Giacomo thought, *that the only Genius allowed in the world is that monstrosity.*

Giacomo turned away from the palace and approached a three-story building with boarded-up windows. He wedged himself between the chained double doors and shimmied through.

Then he lit his lantern, casting a warm glow through the cavernous room, and walked past the broken tables and chairs, kicking up a plume of dust with each step. Long abandoned, the space had once housed a cultural center and artists' studios. He liked to picture himself arriving for class as eager students ran up and down the halls.

Painted across one side of the main hall was a long fresco, cracked and faded. As he did every time he visited, Giacomo blew the dust off the bronze plaque embedded in the wall next to it.

GENIUSES OF ZIZZOLA
COMMISSIONED BY EMPEROR CALLISTO,
IN HONOR OF OUR EMPIRE'S GREAT MEN,
WOMEN, AND GENIUSES WHO BROUGHT
BEAUTY TO LIGHT THROUGH THEIR ART,
MUSIC, WRITING, THEATER, AND DANCE.

Engraved underneath was the artist's name:

PIETRO VASARI

A few years ago, when Giacomo first stumbled upon this room, it was like he'd discovered a cavern of hidden treasure. He found a stash of sketchbooks and drawing supplies in a locked cabinet, long forgotten. And the fresco had become his main source of inspiration. Each scene was a chance to study the human figure in different poses, wearing a variety of clothes, at all ages, from babies to hunched old couples. Had Pietro Vasari known these people? Did they all stand in this room and model for his mural? Although the artist had died—rumor was, at the Supreme Creator's hands—studying his painting was the next best thing to being a real artist's apprentice.

He found a familiar vignette, one that always brought comfort: a young girl, probably three or four, reaching for her Genius. The tiny creature's wings were spread as if it had just floated down from the sky to meet her. Nearby, her smiling mother and father held each other, grateful for the arrival of their daughter's Genius, which would become her muse and guardian.

Before Nerezza made it illegal for artists to have Geniuses, this kind of scene, while not common to all children, would've been celebrated. But now, if a Genius flew into a child's life, it meant a death sentence for both.

Giacomo took a few steps forward, studied the fresco up close, then began to draw the girl. After a few minutes, he paused, comparing his work to Pietro's. He rubbed his eyes, frustrated. How come his figures always looked stiff and awkward, while the ones in the painting looked like they could step right off the wall? Pietro captured lively gestures and natural expressions with only a few pigments and some wet plaster, and made it look easy.

Giacomo often wondered why the Supreme Creator had allowed this fresco to survive. After all, she'd wiped out Geniuses and stripped the city of any works of art that weren't her own. Did she secretly admire Pietro's work? Or maybe because her father commissioned the fresco, she didn't have the heart to paint over it? *Yeah, right,* Giacomo thought. *Like the Supreme Creator has a heart.*

Giacomo was putting the finishing touches on the Genius's feathers when he was startled by the rattle of a metal chain. He dropped his charcoal and whirled around, expecting a soldier to step from the shadows. No one came.

Unnerved, Giacomo packed his materials, picked up his lantern, and made for the doors.

But the way out was blocked.

Standing in front of him was the silhouette of a hunched figure. Unmoving.

He stopped breathing and stepped back.

The silhouette lurched closer, feet dragging. It was a woman. Gray matted hair hung in wild strands, covering most of her face.

A Lost Soul.

Giacomo tried to run, but he was frozen in terror.

A thin hand, more bone than flesh, rose out of the woman's cloak and pointed at Giacomo. She crept closer, into the lantern's light. Still, he couldn't move.

Her eyes stared not so much at him as through him. Her hollow gaze looked exactly like his mother's and father's in the weeks after their Geniuses had been taken away. He was five at the time, and their haunting expressions had been seared into his memory.

The Lost Soul's mouth opened and let out a long groan that eventually formed a word.

"Foooood . . ."

Trembling, Giacomo held out some bread to the woman. "Here. Take it."

The woman snatched it from his hand and pointed to his lantern. "Fire . . ."

"No, I need it."

"Fire!" she shrieked, her whole body vibrating.

Giacomo wasn't about to give up his only source of light. Finally, sensation returned to his legs. Confident he could outrun the Lost Soul, he made a break for it.

He arced around the woman, but she lunged and her sharp fingernails grazed his shoulder. He pulled on the door and stuffed his head and torso through the opening. The splintered wood scraped his back. To his horror, another Lost Soul waited for him outside—a man with black greasy hair pasted against his sunken cheeks. He snarled. The few teeth he had were yellow and crooked, jutting like shards of glass from his gums.

Before Giacomo knew what was happening, the man made a grab for his lantern.

"Let go!" Giacomo yelled. Despite his bony arms, the man was strong. He yanked the lantern, dragging Giacomo the rest of the way through the doors. They stumbled into the piazza, continuing their tug-of-war. Giacomo threw his weight back and pulled with all his strength, wrenching the lantern from the man's grip.

But before Giacomo could run, he felt the woman's spindly arms wrap around his neck, choking him.

As Giacomo struggled to free himself, he saw the man reach into his tattered coat and pull out a rusty blade. He rushed forward, jabbing with the knife. An icy pain stabbed into Giacomo's left side, right below his ribs. The lantern dropped from his hand and clattered onto the ground.

The woman released her hold and Giacomo collapsed to his knees, clutching his side. The world began to spin.

The Lost Souls made off with the rest of the bread from his satchel and his lantern. By the time his head hit the ground, they were gone.

As blood oozed through Giacomo's fingers, he thought, *At least they didn't take my sketchbook.*

THE TULPA

The past few days were a blur. There had been a fight, Zanobius vaguely recalled. But the memory of what had happened was gone.

This wasn't the first time he'd awakened in a new place with few clues as to how he'd gotten there or what time of day it was. He felt like a rowboat caught in a squall, tossed up and down as he fought to find the shore. He'd come to dread the blackouts.

A dark gray cloak covered his arms and legs and a hood hung low over his eyes. "A precaution," he faintly remembered his master telling him. "It's better if they don't know who you are." But whether that conversation happened a few minutes ago or a few hours ago, he couldn't be sure.

Wool fibers scratched his neck, his back, his arms. He wanted to tear off the cloak and let his skin breathe. Who cared if people saw what he was? Was his master ashamed of him?

He was standing outside a thick wooden door. Torches stuck out of the packed-dirt walls, lighting the narrow passageway.

Beams lined the ceiling for support. Between the torches hung painting after painting. The beautiful, colorful works seemed out of place in a dank tunnel that threatened to crumble any moment.

The muffled yells of two men came through the door. One of the voices belonged to his master. He shouted something about sacred tools.

The Creator's Sacred Tools.

Of course. His master, Ugalino, had been searching across the Zizzolan Empire for the Compass, Straightedge, and Pencil, but for what purpose, Zanobius couldn't be sure. Maybe Ugalino had never told him. But he did know why they had come here—to meet a black market art dealer who had information about the Tools' whereabouts.

The door swung open and a squat-nosed guard with scruffy hair stepped out. Zanobius sized him up: he was equally as tall as Zanobius, broad through the shoulders, and his muscles pulled his tunic taut. A rapier hung from his belt, its point nearly touching the ground. A poor choice of sword for close-quarters combat. The art dealer's guard was hardly a threat.

Through the open door, Zanobius glimpsed his master's wavy black hair and short beard. A white cloak draped over his wide shoulders and he gripped an ivory staff in his right hand. He faced a man with long black hair and an unkempt beard who leaned back in a chair with his feet stacked on a thick oak table. Crowds of statues, stacks of paintings, countless colorful vases, and roll upon roll of tapestries filled the room.

"Your employer doesn't know when to shut up." The guard pulled the door shut.

"He's my master," Zanobius corrected.

The guard leaned against the wall. "Well, your *master* started going on about a compass and some kind of pencil, then had the nerve to tell me to leave so he could talk to my employer alone. Like that's going to get him anywhere." The man spat on the ground. "We get collectors like him down here from time to time. Thinks he's doing Rocco a big favor by taking some art off his hands. But just because the high-and-mighty Supreme Creator has her art hounds sniffing around for contraband doesn't mean Rocco's gonna roll over and give his paintings away for a song."

Zanobius held the guard's gaze, watching his puffy pink lips flap, barely listening to the words coming out of his mouth. He was like most humans he'd encountered. Talked a lot, without really saying anything.

Not like his master. When Ugalino spoke, it was purposeful and direct. He didn't waste words on complaints or small talk. Zanobius preferred it that way.

"You okay, pal?" the guard asked, peering under Zanobius's hood. "You're pale. You're not going to pass out on me, are you?"

"It's a permanent condition," Zanobius said.

The guard took a step back, a nervous look on his face. "Not contagious, is it?"

"Not as far as I know."

Zanobius, I need your assistance. Come in here. His master's voice beckoned in his head.

"Excuse me, my master is calling," Zanobius said.

The guard looked at his employer's door, then cocked an eyebrow. "I didn't hear anything."

Zanobius knew his ears were working fine. He just didn't need them to hear Ugalino's voice. He walked past the guard and pushed the door open.

The guard grasped the handle of his rapier. "Hey, don't go in there unless Rocco gives you the go-ahead."

Zanobius ignored the warning and marched into the room. Rocco rose to his feet and drew a small dagger, pointing it at Ugalino. "You told me our guards would stay out of this." He called into the hall: "Bruno, get in here!"

Bruno rushed in, drawing his rapier. Its blade caught the edge of the door frame, causing him to stumble. "You want me to escort them out?"

Ugalino's eyes stayed fixed on the art dealer. "All I require is a name," he said calmly. "Provide it to me or I will destroy every last piece of art in here."

Rocco flung the dagger at Ugalino, while Bruno lunged at Zanobius, his sword stabbing through the air.

Four arms shot out from under Zanobius's cloak. His front two hands grabbed the blade, his back two wrapped around Bruno's neck. Bruno fought for breath, eyes wide with terror.

Ugalino dodged Rocco's flying dagger and spun his staff in one fluid motion. The fist-sized diamond on top of his staff glowed. A circle of white light shot out and hit Rocco in the chest. The force sent him crashing through a stack of canvases against the wall.

Ugalino towered over Rocco and shoved the point of his staff into his shoulder, pinning him down. Rocco winced.

"Ready to give me your collector's name now?" Ugalino dug his staff in deeper.

Rocco let out a pained yelp. "Yes, yes, it was Duke Oberto! He has a castle north of here, in Paolini."

Ugalino glowered. "I'm familiar with the duke." He drew back his staff. Rocco clutched his shoulder, sweating.

Let the guard go, Ugalino's voice commanded. Zanobius released his grip and Bruno dropped with a thud.

"What . . . what are you?" Bruno asked, rubbing his neck.

"He's a Tulpa." Rocco spat out the words like they tasted sour.

"His name is Zanobius," Ugalino proclaimed. "And he is the greatest work of art ever created."

They climbed a flight of rickety stairs and emerged on the outskirts of a small walled city. The nearly full moon hung between two jagged mountain peaks. Stars dotted the sky. Zanobius located the brightest of them all—the Guiding Star. Relieved to be aboveground again, he focused on the point of light and inhaled deeply. The fog cleared from his mind.

Ugalino whistled and an enormous, silver-feathered creature dove out of the sky. Zanobius jumped back before he remembered what this creature was—Ugalino's Genius, his companion long before Zanobius. He racked his mind, trying to recall its name.

"Ciro, to me," Ugalino hailed.

Of course. Ciro. He knew that.

The Genius flapped its wings and landed, kicking up dust. When it lowered its head, Zanobius noticed his reflection in its black, lifeless eyes. Ugalino gripped the edge of Ciro's tarnished crown and hoisted himself onto the creature's neck.

Zanobius climbed on after his master. "It happened again."

"Another blackout?"

"They seem to be occurring more often."

Ugalino twisted to face him. "But you still remember who you are?"

"Yes."

"And who I am?"

"You're my master. You created me."

"And what is our mission?"

"To find the Creator's Sacred Tools."

Ugalino nodded and turned away, apparently satisfied that Zanobius was all right. But he didn't feel all right.

"It's strange," Zanobius said. "I can remember all the important things that make me who I am, but the details of where we've been or who we've seen are completely gone."

"It's an unfortunate downside of being a Tulpa," Ugalino explained.

"Can't you fix it?"

"I've tried. But it's something you're going to have to live with. I'm sorry."

Zanobius nodded. Had they talked about this before? He couldn't recall.

Ugalino tapped the Genius's side with his staff. Ciro heaved his massive wings and they rose into the air, the ground rushing away. Tensing, Zanobius grasped a handful of feathers and held on tightly. Of all the memories erased by the blackout, why couldn't he ever forget his fear of flying?

THE GENIUS

Giacomo fought to stay conscious. With his remaining strength, he lifted his head and dragged himself across the ground, gathered his satchel and sketchbook, and crawled out of the piazza. Grasping the edge of a building, he pulled himself to his feet, but every step felt like another knife being plunged into his body. Doubled over, he leaned against a wall. His hands and tunic were red and wet. He shuddered. A coldness spread from beneath his ribs, up through his chest. Each breath was more punishing than the last.

He had to make it back to his hideout. But then what? Bleed out in the sewers? Was that how his short, insignificant life was going to end? He could find a soldier. He'd take him to a doctor. But once he was fixed up, they'd send him back to the orphanage. *Forget it,* Giacomo thought. *I'd rather die.*

In front of him, a small orb of bright white light floated down from the rooftops. It hung in the air, like the afterimage from staring at the sun. *Great. Now I'm seeing things.* He shut his eyes.

Opened them again. The orb was still there. It swelled and pulsated, growing larger and larger.

Giacomo's legs wobbled, then gave way. The hard stone street shot up and slammed into the side of his face.

With a groan, he rolled onto his back. The orb expanded around him, filling his vision until his entire universe was aglow.

Streaks of red, blue, and green cut through the light, followed by a tremendous thudding that vibrated his skin.

More colors shredded the orb, whirling into a storm of purples, greens, and yellows that whipped him with stinging strikes. Giacomo winced. He struggled to sit up, but a streak of violet slammed into him like a fierce gust of wind, knocking him flat again. The cobblestone street had vanished, replaced by roiling waves of every hue and shade.

He squinted, trying to get his bearings, but there was nothing solid to fix his eyes on. With his arms, he shielded his face as the maelstrom pelted his body like a million tiny pinpricks.

The thudding intensified, evolving into a thunderous pounding that reverberated in Giacomo's head. Fearing his eardrums might burst, he covered his ears, but his hands barely muffled the sound.

A horrid smell, a thousand times worse than sewer poop-sludge, invaded his nose. His stomach heaved and the few scraps of bread he'd eaten threatened to come back up.

Senses overloaded, Giacomo could barely form a thought. He rolled onto his side, tucking into a tight ball. The relentless pounding shook him, inside and out.

Just end it. Stop the agony. Please.

As if the Creator had heard his plea, the banging quieted, the whipping winds ceased, and the disgusting odors wafted away.

Giacomo peeled open his eyes, never so happy to see the stars. They twinkled their assurance that everything was going to be all right.

But something else floated above him too. A tiny hummingbird with orange and blue feathers cocked its head and stared at Giacomo. It darted from side to side, its wings fluttering so fast they practically disappeared.

Startled, he pushed himself up on his elbows and shuffled back. The bird dove, its long, pointed beak aimed straight at his head.

"Get away!" He swatted the bird and knocked it into a brick wall. It let out a high-pitched *skreee*. At the same moment, a hot pain shot through Giacomo's shoulder.

The bird zigzagged through the air as it tried to recover. *Aou aou aou,* it chirped angrily in a way that matched Giacomo's "Ow, ow, ow."

"Sorry," Giacomo said, "but you shouldn't fly directly at people's heads."

The bird stabilized and zipped up to his face, the tip of its beak barely an inch from his eyes. Giacomo flinched.

"You don't listen, do you?"

Now that it was practically perched on his nose, Giacomo felt foolish for mistaking it for an ordinary bird. It had ears. Pointy ones that were pierced with round earrings. A tuft of feathery hair sprouted out of a tiny gold crown on its head. And in the center of the crown sat a red oval gemstone.

"You're a Genius," Giacomo said in awe.

The bird chirped happily and backflipped in the air.

"But that's impossible." He rubbed his eyes and looked again.

Yes, that's a Genius, all right. He should know. He'd grown up around two of them.

His parents' Geniuses had been much bigger and looked more like doves, but they also wore crowns with colored gems, which was the source of their power. They had lived in his cramped house, like part of the family, always by his mother's and father's sides when they painted or sculpted. The last time he saw his parents' Geniuses, soldiers were hauling them away in cages.

What was this Genius doing here? As far as Giacomo knew, there weren't any Geniuses left in Virenzia, except for the Supreme Creator's.

"You need to get out of here. Go back to wherever you came from," he said.

The Genius landed on his shoulder and rubbed its head against his neck. Giacomo's heart skipped a beat. Maybe the reason it was there was to find him. *Could this be my Genius?*

As soon as the thought formed, he wiped it away. *Don't be crazy.*

Giacomo remembered asking his parents over and over to get him a Genius like theirs for his fourth birthday. They lovingly broke the news that he was already too old. "If the Creator had wanted you to have one, it would've already come," his mother said. Giacomo was crushed, but as he got older, he accepted his fate. In a way, it had been for the best. If he'd had a Genius, it would've been dragged away in a cage too. But if the Creator hadn't intended for him to have a Genius, why was one sitting on him now?

Giacomo rubbed his temple. *It doesn't matter. I can't keep it.*

"Don't get too comfortable," Giacomo said, scooping the Genius off his shoulder. "You need to fly as far away as you can. It's not safe for you here."

The Genius chirped brightly and spun in the air.

Giacomo sighed. "I don't think you understand the danger you're in." To make his point, Giacomo acted out each phrase with hand gestures. "Supreme Creator, bad. Lock you in cage. You die. I die." He ended his bravura performance with hands wrapped around his throat and tongue dangling from his mouth. Surely the Genius would get the gist of that.

It let out a delighted *whoo, whoo, whoo,* and circled Giacomo's head.

"Okay, I guess you didn't get the message." Giacomo waved his arms. "Go on, shoo!"

But the Genius refused to leave.

Giacomo got up and swung his satchel wildly, trying to drive the Genius away. "I'm serious. Get lost!" It zigged and zagged, avoiding the attack.

Giacomo hung his head in defeat and that was when he noticed the stinging in his side had been reduced to a dull cramp. He'd been so preoccupied with the Genius, he'd forgotten all about his injury. He peeled back his bloodstained tunic, surprised to see a two-inch-long pink scar had formed. It didn't make any sense. How in the world could a knife wound heal up in only a few minutes? He looked back at the Genius.

"Did you have something to do with this?"

The Genius chirped.

"Is that a yes or a no? Sorry, I don't speak Genius."

A booming voice interrupted them. "Hold it right there, young man!"

Giacomo spun around. Two black-armored soldiers with pointed helmets rounded the corner, marching toward him with their swords drawn. "You're out way past curfew," the taller of the two said.

"Tell us what you're up to," the shorter, muscular one demanded. "What was that bright light? Were you playing with fireworks?"

So they saw the glowing orb too, Giacomo realized. He looked around for the Genius, but it was gone. Maybe it had finally understood the danger it was in and had flown away.

"No fireworks, I swear," Giacomo said, trying to stall.

He heard a quiet *cheep* and felt a poke in the middle of his back. He reached behind him and touched the Genius's soft belly with his fingers. It was either brave or clueless, Giacomo wasn't sure which yet.

"Stay close," he whispered. "I'm going to get you out of here."

The soldiers closed in, the points of their swords leveled straight at him.

Giacomo bolted, but the Genius didn't follow. Instead, it hovered higher in the air. *I'm definitely leaning toward clueless,* he thought.

The soldiers spotted it and froze. "Is that—?" the tall one said.

"A Genius," the short one finished. His eyes narrowed. "It must belong to the boy."

Giacomo watched as the Genius flew right between the soldiers, who swung their swords. Their blades missed and clanged against each other's armor. They stumbled back.

"Come on!" Giacomo shouted. The Genius zipped past him

and down the street. Giacomo pumped his legs as hard as he could, but couldn't keep up. "Wait for me!"

The Genius banked and turned down an alley. Giacomo followed, assuming it knew where it was going. But then it flew up a winding staircase that led onto a balcony.

"This is the wrong way!" he yelled, taking the steps three at a time. "We need to go under the ground, not above it!"

"He's up there!" one of the soldiers hollered.

It was too late to turn back. Giacomo jumped onto a stone railing, wobbling as he ran. Reaching the end, he leaped over the alley, landing hard on an adjacent balcony, then scurried up to the top of the building. He raced across the rooftops, tiles clacking under his feet, the Genius soaring beside him.

Up ahead, a bearded soldier climbed a ladder, blocking his path.

Giacomo dropped down and slid across the tiles, crash-landing on a balcony. He scrambled back to his feet and barreled up another set of stairs, which spilled out at the top of a wall overlooking the city. He scanned the street below and spotted an opening back to the aqueducts. "Down there!" he alerted the Genius.

He sprinted toward the end of the walkway, but the two soldiers who'd first found him clambered up the stairs in front of him.

Turning back, Giacomo was met by the bearded soldier, his sword raised. With both exits blocked, Giacomo glanced from side to side. To his left was a sprawling marketplace, on his right, a street that was too wide to jump over to reach the next rooftop.

"There's nowhere to go," one of the soldiers barked. "Turn over your Genius. You're under arrest."

"It's not mine," Giacomo explained. "I never saw this thing before in my life." The Genius squawked, sounding offended.

The three soldiers closed in, swords at the ready. Giacomo considered his options again. *Forward or back, I'll be impaled. Left or right and the fall will break all my bones.*

There was one other possibility. He glanced at the red gem on the Genius's tiny crown. If the bird really was his Genius, then he might have a chance of escape.

He pulled a hunk of charcoal from his satchel.

"Drop it!" the bearded soldier ordered.

"Get ready," Giacomo whispered to the Genius. He sank to one knee and swiped the charcoal along the stone in quick, violent strokes.

The gem on the Genius's crown glowed and three red beams shot out. Giacomo had intended to distract the soldiers with a bright burst of light. Instead, the beams hit the walkway in an explosion of stone and dust. A wave of energy knocked the soldiers onto their backs.

Giacomo leaped to his feet and bolted past the stunned soldiers. He bounded down the stairs, and dropped into the sewer opening, the Genius close behind. He tucked his arms in tight and slid down a pipe only slightly wider than he was. He was now covered in cold muck, but he'd never been so happy to smell the foul stench.

The pipe spat him out into a bigger tunnel. A dim red light pulsed from the Genius's gem, bathing the aqueducts in a warm glow.

He huffed and puffed. "I wasn't sure that would work . . . My parents used to create light shapes with their Geniuses, but I didn't realize it would be so . . . destructive." The tiny creature chirped softly and landed on his shoulder. "Anyway, it's true! You *are* my Genius."

Elated, Giacomo scratched under the Genius's ear and it let out a contented trill.

Back at his hideout, Giacomo collapsed into the hay-covered corner he used as a bed. For the first time in hours, his heartbeat slowed and his body relaxed.

His Genius hopped around, curiously inspecting the alcove.

"This is your home now. I know it's a little smelly and dark, but no one comes down here, so you'll be safe."

It flew up and pecked at the ceiling, letting out a long string of frustrated chirrups.

"You'll get used to living down here. It's the most free you can be in Virenzia, if you ask me. No one tells you what to do, where to go, what to draw . . ."

Apparently reassured by Giacomo's explanation, his Genius chittered and then nestled in the hay next to him. Maybe it was able to understand him when it really wanted to.

Within seconds, his Genius was asleep, its head tucked close to its body, its translucent wings wrapped around itself like a blanket. Its gem had dimmed, but still emitted enough light to see.

Giacomo rolled onto his side and tried sleeping too, but the excitement of the night hadn't worn off yet. He was thrilled the Creator had finally given him what he'd always dreamed of, but his joy was mixed with dread. He knew that if given the chance, Supreme Creator Nerezza would take his Genius and he'd become a Lost Soul, like his parents had.

Restless, he dug out his sketchbook and charcoal and began to draw.

Without a doubt, Virenzia was the worst city in the world to have a Genius in. But it was the only home Giacomo had ever known. Even if he mustered the nerve to leave, where would he go? Taking refuge in the forest or farmland outside the city wasn't a great option—he didn't have the first clue how to live off the land. Not to mention the countless wild animals stalking the countryside, hunting for easy prey. Fleeing to another state in the Zizzolan Empire wasn't any safer. They were all under the Supreme Creator's rule. Sooner or later, someone would spot his Genius and turn him in. He considered heading north to Katunga. From what his parents had told him, people there had Geniuses too, only they looked like cats instead of birds. Maybe his Genius would be welcomed there? But the Katungan Empire was over a thousand miles to the north, through forests rumored to be guarded by hairy, headless monsters who had eyes and mouths on their torsos. *Not interested,* Giacomo thought.

Sailing west to Rachana was out of the question. To hear the longshoremen at the pier tell it, those warmongers would kill any Zizzolan the second he stepped on their soil, peace treaty or not. Virenzia was bad, sure, but his chances beyond its borders were no better.

Besides, the aqueducts had been his home for almost five years, ever since he ran away from the orphanage. They had kept him safe all this time, so would he really have the courage to leave now?

After his parents died, the authorities carted Giacomo away to Augustine's Orphanage for Wayward Youth, an overcrowded, decrepit house at the farthest edge of the city. He bided his time, hopeful that a kind couple would adopt him before too long. But a couple of years passed, and no potential parents ever visited. One day, an older boy named Marco told him the truth.

"No one here ever gets adopted."

"Why not?" he asked.

"Because we belong to her," Marco said ominously.

Giacomo had to think for a moment. "You mean the Supreme Creator?"

"That's right. She's never had kids of her own, so she takes the ones no one wants and makes them hers. I have less than a year until I turn ten, then I get to start training for her army."

Giacomo began plotting his escape. Even though he was only seven at the time, he knew he never wanted to serve the Supreme Creator, especially not as a soldier. A year later, while Marco and the other boys learned to sword fight in the courtyard, Giacomo pretended to lie in bed sick, then made a break for it. He scaled the wall surrounding the orphanage and snuck away into the sewers. He never looked back.

But now he had to think about what was best for his Genius. And although he didn't know a lot about taking care of one—that had always been his parents' job—he was pretty sure it wasn't going to love living underground. But being cooped up in a one-bedroom house hadn't stopped his parents' Geniuses from inspiring them. At least the sewers had space for low flying and enough room for his Genius to stretch its wings, even when it grew bigger. It was decided, then. He'd stay put. At least for now.

At some point, Giacomo must have drifted off because the next thing he knew his Genius's beak was waking him with a *tap, tap, tap* on his forehead. He opened his eyes and stared up. The gem's red light shone brightly in his face. Giacomo shooed the Genius off and it flew around the alcove, obnoxiously chirping at him to get up.

"Let me guess, you're hungry?" He rolled out of bed and brushed off the straw stuck to his clothes. His stomach rumbled and groaned. "I am too. I'll find us something. But you have to wait here."

His Genius let out one last chirp and darted down the tunnel.

"I said wait!" Giacomo snatched up his satchel and took off after it.

It flew toward a bright area of the sewer, where a beam of sunlight shone into the tunnel through a clay drainage pipe. The city would be abuzz with activity by now and if anyone saw his Genius . . . Well, he wouldn't let that happen.

"Don't go in there!" Giacomo reached out but his Genius slipped through his hands and into the pipe.

Giacomo still had the advantage. He knew the sewers' every

stinky twist and smelly turn, and from what he'd seen last night, his Genius had no sense of direction. Giacomo headed up a narrow staircase to the surface.

He poked his head up through a drainage opening, then quickly ducked down again as a horse-drawn cart wheeled right over him. Once it passed, he popped out of the sewers and mixed into the crowd.

He weaved between men and women who trudged through the streets with vacant expressions. Armored soldiers holding spears stood on every corner, keeping an eye on the passersby. When a one-legged man on crutches hobbled to the corner and began begging for coins, a soldier immediately dragged him off. People looked the other way, as if the man didn't exist, unwilling or too afraid to help. Giacomo felt ashamed for not going to the man's aid, but like everyone else, he had his own problems to deal with.

He hurried over to a dry fountain filled with dead leaves and peered into the drain. He spotted a red glow growing brighter, and covered the hole with his open satchel. A second later, his Genius hit the satchel with a muffled squeak. Giacomo pulled the flap down, trapping the creature, which threw itself against the sides of the bag.

"Stop fighting me," Giacomo whispered. "I'm trying to protect you."

The Genius chirped loudly. A soldier across the street looked around, trying to figure out where the sound was coming from. His gaze stopped on Giacomo. Giacomo leaned against the wall, acting nonchalant, but his satchel swung wildly, yanking him back and forth. He grabbed the bag and tucked it tightly under his arm.

Giacomo waved to the soldier. "Good morning, signor! Beautiful day, isn't it?" He smiled innocently.

The soldier snarled. Giacomo hustled down the street, whispering to his Genius, "Be quiet, or it's off to the Supreme Creator's dungeon for both of us."

His Genius seemed to get the gist of that, and calmed down.

Farther up the street, Giacomo spotted an elderly man in a shabby green tunic pushing a cart full of fruit. He licked his lips. "I think I found our breakfast."

He waited for the fruit seller to turn his back. When the man began haggling with a red-cheeked woman about the price of some moldy lemons, Giacomo sidled up to the cart and deftly lifted three apples. By the time the fruit seller finished his deal with the woman, Giacomo was gone.

Back in his hideout, Giacomo took a huge bite of an apple, which turned to mush between his teeth. But since he was starving and hadn't paid for it, he wasn't about to complain. He devoured his meal, then licked the remaining juice off his fingers. On the ground next to him, his Genius pecked at another apple, already riddled with holes. He kept the third apple tucked away in his bag for later.

"See? I can take care of you," Giacomo bragged. "But don't fly off like that again."

Belly bulging, Giacomo's Genius let out a satisfied chirp.

Giacomo spent the rest of the day alternating between drawing and napping. Thankfully, his Genius didn't try to escape again. For dinner, they shared the last apple. When night arrived, Giacomo prepared to head out to Beppe's Bakery.

But as he was about to leave, he heard footsteps splashing from down the tunnel. Giacomo froze and cocked his head. His Genius mimicked his movement and let out a tiny chirp.

"Shh. Did you hear that?" Had the soldier who spotted him earlier tracked him down here? Or was it another Lost Soul? Whatever it was, he wasn't going to stick around to find out.

He scooped up his Genius, clamping his hand over its gem to block the light. He tiptoed out of the alcove, shifting away from the footsteps. Giacomo ducked behind an archway and glanced back the way he'd come. A lantern's yellow light filled the tunnel. He was surprised to hear children's voices.

"Let's at least go up for some air," a raspy-voiced boy said. "I'm seriously about to throw up and I'd hate for you girls to see that."

"As long as you don't get any vomit on my dress, it doesn't bother me," a girl's voice shot back.

"It won't be that much longer," a second, younger-sounding girl said. "I think we're getting close."

Giacomo relaxed a bit. At least they weren't soldiers or Lost Souls. Maybe they were other street kids like him? Still, he had to be careful. But before he could get a look at the intruders, Giacomo's Genius squirmed out of his hands and flew toward the voices. He cursed its recklessness.

Giacomo peered out from his hiding spot and helplessly watched as his Genius's red light moved closer to the yellow glow. He braced himself for the worst.

"Look," the boy said. "It's a Genius!"

"See, I told you we'd find it!" the youngest voice proudly shouted.

They didn't sound surprised at all. Giacomo's mind spun. *How did the girl know my Genius would be down here?*

The children rounded the corner and Giacomo's breath caught in his throat. It wasn't a lantern creating the yellow light, but a circular gem in the crown of a round, purple-and-orange-plumed Genius only slightly bigger than Giacomo's. Gliding behind it were two others, over twice the size of his Genius. One was white, with a thin, curved neck and a long beak like a crane; the other resembled a falcon, with brown and tan feathers, a hooked beak, and beady black eyes. Giacomo's Genius made a high-pitched *zheezheezhee* as it happily circled the others.

Giacomo watched with a probing gaze, his heart racing. *Who are these kids and how do they all have Geniuses?*

THE BLIND ARTIST

Once the shock of seeing other Geniuses wore off, Giacomo focused his attention on the three children with them. The boy wore a blue cloak so dark in hue it was nearly black, while the girls were each draped in olive. Made of wool and tailored to fit their bodies, the cloaks were similar to the outer garments of Virenzia's upper class. There was no way this trio was from the streets. But where would three kids with Geniuses be able to live without being caught?

"Where's your artist?" the youngest girl asked Giacomo's Genius, gently holding out her hand. Without hesitation, his Genius landed on her finger. Her brown skin was at least three shades darker than the skin of the other girl and boy. A thick black braid hung over each shoulder, down to her waist. The purple and orange Genius, which looked like a robin, circled her and landed on top of her head, nestling in her hair.

"Anyone down here?" The boy's voice echoed. His black hair

was cropped short, bangs cut in a hard line across his forehead. In his right hand he held a pencil. "You might as well come out now, otherwise I'll have to drag you out."

"Don't be such a bully, Savino," the girl with the braids said. "He—or she—is probably just scared."

Savino waved his arm dismissively. "Aaminah, I got this." He whistled and the falcon Genius landed on his shoulder. The gem on its crown shot out a beam of blue light that glimmered across the wet stones. It only took a few seconds for Savino to spot Giacomo's hideout. "Nice work, Nero." He fed the Genius a piece of food from his pocket and marched toward the alcove. "Milena, over here. I found something."

The older girl hiked up her cloak and dress to avoid dragging them through the muck and caught up to Savino. Her smooth brown hair was pulled tightly into a bun and tied with a ribbon. A band of gold with inlaid beads crowned her head. She cradled a paintbrush in her left hand. The Genius with the curved neck glided gracefully behind and landed on her shoulder.

"I can't believe someone actually lives here," Milena said as she looked into the alcove.

Giacomo felt embarrassed, then immediately offended. *Who is she to judge how I live?*

"We know you're down here," Milena called out. "And we're here to help. We can take you and your Genius somewhere safe. But you have to stop hiding."

She sounded sincere, but Giacomo had no way of knowing whether he could believe her.

Savino emerged from the hideout with Giacomo's sketchbook. He flipped through its pages. "I've seen worse."

Giacomo clenched his hands. *Stupid!* He'd forgotten to take his belongings.

Savino held up a drawing for the girls to see. "Check out this portrait. You think it's who we're looking for? He's kinda grumpy-looking, if you ask me."

Without thinking, Giacomo ran out and hurled himself at the

boy. "That's mine, give it back!" He tried to grab the sketchbook from Savino, but he held it over his head, out of Giacomo's reach.

"Guess it *is* him. And he looks even more cranky in real life!" Savino teased.

"That's mine!" Giacomo yelled, fist shaking. His first instinct was to throw a punch, but now that he was toe to toe with the boy, he thought better of it. Savino stood several inches taller and his broad shoulders stretched his cloak tight. Giacomo poked him in the chest instead. "What are you doing down here?"

"Better get your finger off me, sewer-boy, or we're going to have a problem," Savino threatened.

"Sorry to show up like this, but we had to find you," Aaminah said, trying to smooth things over. "Is this your Genius?" Above her head, Giacomo's Genius chirped and playfully chased Aaminah's robin Genius.

"Depends who's asking," Giacomo said.

Savino tilted his head. "Just answer the question."

"Why should I? I don't know who you people are."

"There are a bunch of drawings of that Genius in your sketchbook," Savino said. "Are you telling us it's not yours?"

Giacomo stared at the ground, avoiding Savino's harsh gaze. "I didn't say it was or it wasn't."

"One way to find out for sure." Savino whistled rapidly three times. "Nero, attack." Nero's wings unfurled and he pushed off Savino's shoulder, soaring straight toward Giacomo's Genius. Nero's talons slashed and nicked the Genius's side. It let out a pained chirp.

"Ow!" Giacomo cried, clutching his forearm. Blood trickled down his arm as if Savino's Genius had clawed at him too. How come every time his Genius got hurt, he felt it too?

Savino crossed his arms with a self-satisfied smile. "Guess you two *are* connected."

Giacomo burned with anger. He charged Savino and shoved him toward the wall. *Bad idea.* Savino felt solid as brick.

He seized the back of Giacomo's tunic and effortlessly flung him to the ground.

Aaminah rushed to Giacomo's side. "Savino, what's wrong with you? He wasn't doing anything."

Milena shot Savino a dirty look. "Was that really necessary?"

Nero flew back onto Savino's shoulder. As a reward, Savino fed his Genius another treat. "He came at me."

"Only after your Genius attacked me first!" Giacomo snatched his sketchbook out of Savino's hand. "You're a jerk, you know that?"

"I've been called worse, usually by these two," he said, nodding toward the girls.

"*Much* worse," Milena sniped.

Aaminah knelt down and took Giacomo's wounded arm in her small hands. "Let me see." She inspected the cut, then reached into her cloak and pulled out a wooden flute. "Just relax."

"I'm not really in the mood for music," Giacomo said. The scratch stung, but wasn't too painful. Giacomo's Genius flew to him, its left wing torn from Nero's talons.

"She's going to treat the injuries," Milena explained.

Aaminah's Genius landed on the back of Giacomo's hand. He flinched.

"It's okay. Luna's a sweetheart." Aaminah raised the flute to her lips and gently blew across the mouthpiece. A low tone filled the tunnel. Luna's circular gem glowed yellow. With each ascending note, waves of light pulsed from the crown, washing over Giacomo's and his Genius's wounds.

It felt like the music was seeping into his arm and vibrating inside it, soothing his soreness and calming his frazzled nerves. The bleeding stopped and the cut sealed up, leaving only a faint red welt. The torn flaps of his Genius's wing mended too. Was this how his stab wound had healed last night? He didn't remember hearing any music, just the roar of that crazy storm.

"I didn't know Geniuses could heal like that," Giacomo said. "Thanks."

Aaminah studied him with a curious stare, as if he'd spoken gibberish.

"What is it?" Giacomo asked.

Aaminah shook her head. "Nothing." She smiled sweetly. "What's your name?"

"Giacomo."

"I'm Aaminah, this is Milena and her Genius, Gaia, and that's Savino."

Giacomo gave them perfunctory nods.

"What's your Genius's name?" Aaminah asked.

Giacomo swallowed. "Uh . . . I don't have one for it yet."

"How have you gone through your whole life without naming your Genius?" Milena asked.

"See . . . the thing is, I only found it last night. Or it found me. I'm still trying to figure out where it came from."

The three kids looked at one another, mouths slack.

"You've only had your Genius for one day?" Milena asked.

"That's right."

She eyed him with suspicion. "And what were you doing when it showed up?"

Last night's chaos rushed through Giacomo's memory—Lost Souls attacking him, his agonizing vision, his Genius appearing out of nowhere, nearly being captured by soldiers . . . Where to begin? He was better off keeping his story simple.

"I was just walking down the street, minding my own business, and it flew up to me."

"What a steaming pile of horse manure. You're hiding something." Savino pointed an accusing finger.

Aaminah spoke up. "All that matters is Giacomo and his Genius are connected. Who cares when he got it?"

Milena sniffed the rank air. "How about we get him back to the villa and keep talking somewhere less . . . pungent."

"Fine by me." Savino grabbed Giacomo's arm and pulled him to his feet.

Giacomo yanked his arm from Savino's grip. "Why should I go with you? I've survived fine on my own this long."

Milena leaned in, looking serious. "You're more than welcome to keep trying your luck down here, but if the Supreme Creator hears even a whisper that there's a new Genius flying around, she's going to have soldiers searching every nook and cranny of Virenzia, including the aqueducts. We're offering you a chance to go somewhere safe, where the Supreme Creator can't find you."

Giacomo stared at her skeptically, unable to imagine such a refuge actually existing.

"Our teacher is amazing," Aaminah added. "You'll learn so much from him."

"A teacher?" Giacomo said, intrigued.

"Assuming you're worthy of being taught," Savino piped up.

"And you'll get a hot bath and all the food you can eat," Aaminah said. "Milena's right, the best way to keep your Genius safe is to come with us."

A safe place with food *and* an art teacher? It almost sounded too good to be true. Which probably meant it was.

"Thanks for the offer," Giacomo said, turning away, "but I'm going to pass. I can take care of myself. Come on, uh . . . little Genius guy." He tried to get his Genius to follow, but it ignored him and stayed cuddled next to Aaminah's Genius in her nest of hair, cooing peacefully.

"You need to come with me," Giacomo said, scooping his Genius off Aaminah's head.

His Genius squawked and pecked his hand.

"Ow!" Giacomo rubbed the aching spot.

His Genius flew back to the hair nest.

"He's welcome to visit as long as he likes," Aaminah said. "If I could have a whole Genius sanctuary in my hair, I would."

Giacomo had no doubt he could continue to survive on his own, but apparently his Genius had other ideas. The little guy had really taken a liking to Aaminah. Maybe he should follow his Genius's instincts. Plus, washing all this grime off him would give him a welcome break from his own stench. He found himself fantasizing about a meal that didn't consist of stale bread.

"Fine. I'll come," he grumbled. "But the first sign of trouble, I'm gone." He picked up his satchel and stuffed his sketchbook into it.

"Smart choice, sewer-boy." Savino intentionally bumped into Giacomo's shoulder as he marched past. Nero let out a rattly squawk. Milena, Aaminah, and their Geniuses followed.

As he trailed the others, Giacomo looked back at the dank alcove he'd called home for so long. With each step, it faded farther into the darkness.

A short time later, they emerged from a tunnel outside the city walls. Above the mountains, the faint glow of dawn rose to meet the stars, erasing them one by one.

Savino scanned the area for soldiers and signaled the all clear. The children's Geniuses flew up ahead, staying close to the hillside. Giacomo was relieved to see his Genius following their lead. Savino led the group up a steep slope that curved back and forth, the steps nothing more than grassy indentations.

The dirt crumbled beneath Giacomo's foot and he reeled backward. Luckily, Milena was behind him, holding out an arm to keep him steady.

"And you thought you could take care of yourself," she said with a slight smile.

"I didn't need your help," Giacomo replied, pulling away. He'd been cut off from real human contact for so long her touch felt strange, but also comforting.

Milena continued on as Giacomo took a short break. He looked

down the enormous hill he'd just climbed. In all his years of living in Virenzia, he'd never seen the city from this high an angle.

By the time the sun peered over the mountains, they'd arrived at their destination, a two-story villa built on the hillside. Giacomo had often noticed the building from far below and always wondered who lived in it. Now walking in its shadow, he was overwhelmed by its size. Built from immense gray stones, the structure was as wide as an entire city block, its face lined with repeating archways and columns. Only the Supreme Creator's palace was bigger.

"You all live here?" Giacomo asked in disbelief.

Savino shushed him and ducked behind a row of hedges. Giacomo walked behind, greenery to his right and a wall to his left. He didn't see any sign of a door.

Savino ran his hand along the wall, then pressed one of the stones. A portion of the wall retracted and slid open, revealing a secret passage.

The blue gem on Savino's Genius lit up, illuminating a stairway that spiraled down. As he was about to cross the threshold, Giacomo hesitated.

"No turning back now," Milena said, then gave him a gentle nudge.

The stairs spilled out into a cavernous, shadowy cellar. Savino lit several candles. Their flames flickered, casting the children's shadows on the walls.

"Is this a joke?" Giacomo complained. "You take me from one underground hideout into another?"

"At least this one doesn't stink as bad," Savino said.

Giacomo couldn't argue, but he stayed on his guard while he took a look around.

Wooden barrels lined the wall to his right. To his left, several empty bottles of wine were tucked between the cushions on a worn bench. In the center of the room stood two easels and a long worktable. Half-finished sculptures sat on it, along with numerous brushes, pencils, pieces of chalk and charcoal, and stacks of paper. His Genius darted through the room, chirping excitedly. Giacomo's mind raced with the possibilities of the drawings he could make.

Savino opened his cloak and unbuckled a belt that held sculpting tools. He threw it on the table with a clunk.

Giacomo leaned in to get a closer look at one of the sculptures— a bust resembling Savino. He could see fingerprints where Savino had pressed holes for eye sockets and shaped the angular nose. "Self-portrait?"

Savino's frown matched the one in clay. "Obviously. What about it?"

Giacomo rolled his eyes. *I can't win with him.*

On a nearby table, Milena tidied up an arrangement of grapes in a basket and a wine bottle with a melted candle sticking out the top. "Savino, did you take the skull?" she called out.

"What skull?" he said.

"The human skull that was sitting right next to the grapes."

Milena's painting sat on an easel in front of the still life. Other than the skull that was missing from the table, the two scenes were indistinguishable. Milena's technique was so perfect and flawless, her paint strokes were only visible up close.

"Why do you always blame me when something goes missing?" Savino said.

"Because you're usually responsible," she jabbed back. She

caught Giacomo inspecting her painting and spun the easel away from him. "It's not done yet."

"It looks amazing," Giacomo complimented her. "I've always wanted to learn how to paint. Think you could show me sometime?"

Before she could answer, a gravelly voice spoke from the darkness. "So you found him, did you?"

Aaminah skipped across the room. "You were right, Pietro! Once we were down in the city, my Genius led us right to him."

It took Giacomo a second to process the name Aaminah spoke. His heart raced. "Did you just say his name was Pietro?"

"She did," the gravelly voice answered. Out of the shadows shuffled a hunched man carrying a wooden cane. He had a long gray beard and scraggly hair that ringed his bald-on-top, wrinkly head. "And what's your name?"

"Giacomo," he said nervously. "Giacomo Ghiberti. But you can't be the actual Pietro Vasari, can you?"

"And why in the world not?"

"Because you're . . . dead."

Pietro chuckled. "Sure, that's what Nerezza has taught you to believe. Yet here I stand before you, still drawing breath."

It felt like the old man had slapped him across the face. How was it possible that all this time, his idol was living right up the hill from him? "How . . . How are you here?"

"By the good graces of the Creator, just like you." As Pietro stepped into the candlelight, Giacomo noticed the man stared straight ahead. His pupils were covered in a foggy haze.

"You're blind," he realized.

Pietro touched Giacomo's face. His fingers felt like pieces of bark.

"And you're old." Pietro sounded dismayed.

"Old? I'm twelve."

"And he's only had his Genius for a day," Savino added snidely.

Pietro stroked his long beard and furrowed his brow in concern. "I see . . ."

Giacomo's Genius let out an intense, shrill whistle. "What's wrong?" he called, rushing from the main room into another section of the cellar.

Giacomo stopped short as he came upon his Genius hovering before a wide arched recess in the wall. Inside, a gnarled black beak poked out from a hulking mass of blue and gray feathers. A square orange gem glowed dimly from a crown, highlighting the creature's giant, round head; long, flowing wings; and claws as thick as tree branches.

"That's . . . that's your Genius," Giacomo whispered.

"His name's Tito," Pietro said, shuffling up to him. "And he's very friendly, just a bit wary of newcomers."

Tito stuck his head out of the alcove and let out a slow, deep-pitched hoot. Giacomo stepped back, startled. His Genius ducked behind him. Tito lifted his claw and scratched his neck, shedding dozens of feathers in the process. On his body were empty patches where his plumage had molted, resembling Pietro's bald head. And where his eyes should have been were two gaping holes. Giacomo thought back to how he had felt pain when his Genius was hurt. Had Pietro's blindness been caused by someone taking Tito's eyes? The idea sent shivers through him.

Heavy footsteps stomped down a second set of stairs. Giacomo followed Pietro back to the main room, where a pink-cheeked man with pursed lips and a brown bushy beard strolled in. He wore puffy-sleeved silk nightclothes that were cinched under his enormous round belly.

"Where have you three been?" he bellowed at Aaminah, Milena, and Savino. "And don't pretend you've been down here all night. Enzio just told me he saw you coming back from the city." The rotund man eyed Giacomo suspiciously. "And who might you be?"

"Settle down and relax." Pietro's cane clacked across the floor until it touched a table holding bottles of red wine. He felt for a glass and filled it. He passed it to the man, who despite the early hour took a healthy swig. "I sent them out because Tito sensed there was a new Genius in the city. He was right again. Meet Giacomo Ghiberti and . . . What is your Genius's name?"

"He doesn't have one yet," Giacomo answered sheepishly.

His Genius flitted around the portly man's head, as if it knew to put on a good show. The man's irate expression washed away, replaced by a smile so big it threatened to burst his plump cheeks.

"Another Genius in our midst? How wonderful!" The man clapped Giacomo hard on the back. "Welcome, young man. I am Signor Baldassare Barrolo, proud patron of the arts and owner of this villa. Whatever you need will be provided. My home is your home."

"Thank you," Giacomo said.

"There is a slight problem," Pietro said. "Concerning Giacomo's age? He only recently connected with his Genius. I'm not sure what I'll be able to do with him."

Giacomo was annoyed that Pietro had brought up his age again. So what if he had just gotten his Genius? He'd work hard to catch up to the others.

Baldassare noticed the frown on Giacomo's face. "Being a late bloomer is hardly something to worry about." He patted Giacomo's shoulder reassuringly. "We'll get you up to speed. Now, what do you say to a delicious breakfast? I imagine you must be famished."

Giacomo's stomach rumbled, responding before he could. He smiled. "You imagined right, signor."

Baldassare ushered Giacomo toward the stairs, but after getting a whiff of him, added, "First, how about a nice hot bath?"

Before they headed up, Baldassare pulled a small whistle from his pocket and blew into it, creating a flutter of high-pitched notes, similar to a birdcall. The Geniuses perked up and flocked around Baldassare, who held out a handful of dried fruit that they ate from his palm. Giacomo's Genius dove into the throng, eagerly devouring its share.

"Looks like your Genius will be right at home," Baldassare said.

Once everyone emerged from the stairwell, Baldassare shut the door, which was actually a large painting framed in gold. Giacomo wondered how many other secret passages Signor Barrolo was hiding in his villa's walls.

As the painting hinged closed, Supreme Creator Nerezza's giant face swung into view. Giacomo jumped back and that was when he noticed the long hall was lined with the flag of the Zizzolan Empire—the same black and white triangles that hung from the Supreme Creator's palace.

Giacomo clutched his Genius close and backed away. "I knew I shouldn't have trusted you!" he wailed at the other children, then directed his rage at Baldassare: "What is this place? Who are you really?"

"Like I told you, my name is Baldassare Barrolo." He paused. "And I'm one of the Supreme Creator's Council of Ten."

Giacomo turned and ran down the hall.

"Wait!" Milena shouted. "It's not what you think!"

Artwork after artwork depicting Zizzola's leader whizzed past: portraits, marble busts, tapestries. Any minute, he expected the real thing to appear and snatch his Genius from his arms.

"Giacomo, stop!" Pietro's voice was strong and commanding.

Against his better judgment, Giacomo did as he was told. He whirled around, still flushed with panic.

"My Genius and I have been here seventeen years and never been found," Pietro assured him.

"How do I know you're not working for the Supreme Creator too?" Giacomo said.

"Pfft," Savino huffed. "That's the stupidest thing I've ever heard."

Baldassare clapped his palms together, like he was giving thanks to the Creator. "I understand how unsettling all this is. But you are absolutely safe here. And Pietro is on your side, I promise."

Aaminah backed him up. "If it hadn't been for Signor Barrolo's protection, our Geniuses probably would have been taken away a long time ago."

"I live in two worlds," Baldassare explained. "When I'm not serving as Supreme Creator Nerezza's loyal Minister of Culture, I find and collect art from the black market, protect Geniuses, and work tirelessly to foster a revolution that will one day depose Nerezza and her ilk."

Giacomo thought Baldassare's story sounded genuine, and the fact that the other Geniuses were alive and well seemed to back up his claim, but something still didn't feel right.

"Then what's with all this?" Giacomo said, gesturing to the art and flags on either side of him.

"I have to keep up appearances," Baldassare stated. "If anyone suspected I wasn't loyal to the Supreme Creator, she would raze this place to the ground, and destroy everyone in it."

"After you've lived here awhile, you don't really notice them anymore," Aaminah said.

"I hope so," Giacomo muttered, then walked sheepishly back to the group, embarrassed by his outburst. Maybe he'd overreacted. Obviously Geniuses were safe here and Baldassare's explanation of why he had the flags made perfect sense. He opened his hands, freeing his Genius. Wings aflutter, it took to the air, gliding down the hall. Giacomo peered up at Baldassare. "Sorry I bolted like that."

Baldassare gave him a warm smile. "It's quite all right. I know it's a lot to take in."

The tour of Signor Barrolo's villa left Giacomo speechless. The place oozed luxury. He walked across marble floors as reflective as mirrors, past rooms the size of entire houses, and under stone archways carved with intricate patterns. Giacomo made sure to keep his distance from the upholstered chairs, cushioned benches, cabinets, and tables; he feared if he accidentally touched anything, one of his many layers of filth would rub off and tarnish it.

At the bottom of a wide stairway stood a tall, thin woman in an elegant purple robe. She smiled at them as Baldassare gave her a peck on the cheek.

"Good morning, dear. I want you to meet our new artist-in-residence, Giacomo. Giacomo, this is my wife, Fabiana."

"Nice to meet you, signora," Giacomo said.

"He needs a bath," Baldassare told his wife. "The hotter the better."

"Of course, dear," Fabiana replied. "Lovely to meet you, Giacomo. Right this way."

She led him to an outdoor bathhouse with a round wooden tub. Through the open ceiling, puffy clouds floated across the sky. Fabiana filled the tub with steaming water from a cauldron over the fire, then handed Giacomo a towel, along with a fresh dark red tunic, a black leather belt, and brown pants. "My son outgrew these a while ago, but they should fit you perfectly," she said with a kindness that reminded Giacomo of his mother.

"Thank you, signora." His Genius looped into the air, then dove, splashing into the water.

"When you're done, come down for breakfast." Fabiana exited, her robe gracefully cutting a curve behind her.

Giacomo peeled off his grimy clothes and slipped into the hot water. The icy chill that had embedded in his bones over the years began to melt. With a soapy brush, he scrubbed every inch of his body, and within minutes the water became murky. Annoyed, his Genius squeaked and hopped out.

Giacomo dried himself and tried on his new clothes. He tightened the leather ties down the front of the tunic and pulled the pants over his skinny legs. A little baggy, but they'd do the trick. He dragged a brush through his long, tangled hair and looked into a full-length mirror, hardly recognizing this unsoiled version of himself.

After a few wrong turns, Giacomo found his way to the dining room, where Savino, Milena, and Aaminah sat on one side of a long table, their Geniuses perched on the backs of their chairs. Baldassare sat at the head, shoveling forkfuls of noodles into his mouth.

"Take your pick." Baldassare gestured to the twenty empty chairs around the table.

Giacomo sat opposite the other children, who had shed their cloaks. Milena, holding herself with elegant poise, was now clad in a green velvet dress with embroidered sleeves, the bodice laced tightly. In contrast, Aaminah slouched and appeared much more casual, wearing a loose, pale yellow shirt with a boy's pants, opting for bare feet. Savino looked ready to do battle in a black short-sleeved leather tunic covered in metal buckles and a padded white undershirt. From loops on his belt hung his various sculpting tools, resembling an armory of tiny weapons.

Giacomo gazed across the table piled with platters of thick noodles, roasted meats, and pastries. He stuffed a tart into his mouth. The cinnamon sparked his long-dormant sense of taste back to life. A warm, gooey melon-and-cheese filling erupted from the dough and dripped down his chin.

Aaminah leaned over the table and whispered, "You know what's really good? If you suck out the insides first." She jabbed a hole in a tart and made a loud sucking noise as she drained it dry. She signaled her satisfaction with a tiny burp. Giacomo laughed, accidentally snorting cheese filling from his nose, which made Aaminah giggle.

Milena shot them both disapproving looks and rolled her eyes. She probably thought he was disgusting, but Giacomo didn't care, not when his mouth was full of something so sweet and delicious.

While they ate, the sounds of stirring, pounding, and chopping spilled from the kitchen. Fabiana swept in, holding a bowl of steaming soup.

"Thith ith amathing," Giacomo told her, his mouth full of tart.

"You're so very welcome," Fabiana said, setting the bowl on the table, then gliding away to create another masterpiece.

Giacomo's Genius hopped off his shoulder and sucked a noodle from his plate like it was a long, meaty worm.

"No Geniuses on the table, please," Baldassare said firmly.

Giacomo glanced at the other three Geniuses, sitting obediently, and realized he had to get his Genius in line. He first tried shooing it off the table, and when that didn't work, he picked it up and put it in his lap. But his Genius hopped right back onto the table and kept eating off his plate. Giacomo put on his most serious face and gave it a stern *no* while pointing his finger. His Genius blissfully ignored him and continued gobbling food.

Savino looked to Baldassare. "What do you expect when he just got his Genius last night?"

"I'm so sorry, Signor Barrolo. I'm still trying to figure out how to communicate with it."

"I'll let it slide for now," Baldassare said. "At least until Pietro can give you a few pointers. For the time being, please keep a close eye on your new friend here. An untamed Genius is a recipe for disaster."

To emphasize his point, he tossed bits of food to the other Geniuses, who snatched them out of the air with their beaks.

Giacomo nodded. "Understood." He felt a pit in his stomach, and it wasn't from all the rich food. Something had been bugging him ever since the others showed up at his hideout. "There is one question maybe you could answer for me?"

"I'll do my best," Baldassare said.

"If Pietro's Genius knew where to find mine, how come the Supreme Creator hasn't raided your villa looking for all their Geniuses?" Giacomo gestured across the table to the others.

Baldassare wiped his mouth with his napkin. "Nerezza's Genius is powerful, but thankfully, it never developed the ability to sense others. In this arena, Pietro and Tito have an advantage. If not for them, I never would have found Savino, Milena, or Aaminah."

"How can Pietro's Genius find another one miles away?"

"Geniuses are mysterious creatures, as you've no doubt discovered," Baldassare said. "A rare few possess the ability to sense their own kind. It's believed they emit some kind of vibrational signal through the air, in order to communicate. Others think it has more to do with the emotional bond between artist and Genius. But no one knows for sure."

"Someday Aaminah's Genius will be just as powerful," Milena said, sounding like a proud older sister.

"Maybe," Aaminah said doubtfully. "Right now Luna can only sense a Genius if it's really close by. She picked up your Genius's trail once we went into the aqueducts."

So that's how they found me. But as soon as that question had been answered, another popped into Giacomo's head: "What happens if a member of the Council of Ten decides to stop by? You all hide in the cellar?"

"Our Geniuses do," Milena said. "But we get to meet whoever visits. Signor Barrolo introduces us as his adopted children."

"But how about you?" Baldassare said, leaning forward. "How does a boy like you end up living in the sewers beneath the city?"

"Not a fan of orphanages." Giacomo stuffed another tart in his mouth, not wanting to get into the details.

A morose boy with curly black hair wearing a black tunic shuffled into the dining room, carrying a human skull. Milena fumed.

"See?" Savino nodded at the skull. "Told you I didn't take it."

Milena whistled. Her Genius took flight and extended its long neck, plucking the skull out of the boy's hands with its beak.

"Keep that thing away from me," the boy complained.

"Then don't steal my stuff, Enzio," Milena retorted. Gaia

dropped the skull in Milena's lap and returned to the back of Milena's chair.

Enzio noticed Giacomo and glared at him with eyes nearly as lifeless as the skull's. Giacomo looked at the other kids, expecting an introduction, but they stayed silent.

The boy walked over to Giacomo, sizing him up. "Great, another leech eating my food. And are those my old clothes?" He snatched a piece of bread off Giacomo's plate.

"Hey, I was about to eat that," Giacomo said.

"Enzio. Respect our guest," Baldassare scolded.

"Dad. Leave me alone." Enzio stuffed the bread in his mouth and left.

"That's my boy. A true blessing from the Creator, isn't he?" Baldassare said, with a joking smile.

"Does he have a Genius?" Giacomo asked.

"No," Aaminah said. "And he hates the fact we all do."

Giacomo made a mental note to stay clear of Enzio.

Giacomo spent the rest of the day exploring the villa and the lush gardens. Then, after another unbelievable feast of mouthwatering and stomach-filling pastas and cakes, he and his yet-to-be-named Genius headed up to their room, where he sketched from memory everyone he'd met since his arrival.

His first day in Baldassare's villa had been one of the most exciting and exhausting of his life. After finishing a particularly gloomy portrait of Enzio, he tossed his sketchbook on the bedside table. He fell back onto the soft mattress and buried himself under a mountain of blankets.

Although he was safe for the moment, Giacomo felt uneasy. He didn't deserve this. Any of it. A Genius, the never-ending piles of food, the cozy bed. Not when there were one-legged beggars on Zizzola's streets struggling to survive. What made him so special?

He tossed and turned, jealous of his Genius, who was nestled into the pillow next to him, sound asleep.

Finally, he flung off the blankets and curled up on the floor next to the bed. The hard, cold stones offered a familiar comfort. Within seconds, his eyes felt heavy and his thoughts drifted off, making way for sleep.

SACRED GEOMETRY

That night in his dreams, Giacomo was lost, walking down one of the many halls in Villa Barrolo. Every turn brought him back to the exact same place. His heart raced. Then, to his surprise and relief, his mother and father stepped out of a doorway and waved to him.

"It's so good to see you," his father said in his baritone voice.

His mother hugged him and told him how much she missed him. Giacomo burst into tears. She wiped them away and told him not to cry. "We're here now."

"Has your Genius arrived?" his father asked.

"You know about that?" Giacomo said.

"Make sure you keep him safe," his mother said.

They kissed Giacomo on the head and walked back down the hall and through the doorway.

Giacomo rushed after them. "Wait! Don't go!"

He bolted into the room, but they had already vanished.

Suddenly, he was back at his sewer hideout. The ceiling cracked. Chunks of stone broke off and smashed down onto his head. Then the entire structure ruptured and the tunnel flooded. When he opened his mouth to scream, his lungs filled with water.

Giacomo woke, gasping for air, a bright light assaulting him. The sun blazed through an opening in the curtains, shining right into his eyes. He ducked under the covers, trying to hold on to the reunion with his parents. But the moment was gone.

He peeled back the blankets, letting his eyes adjust. He didn't remember getting into the bed. He must've done it in the middle of the night. Giacomo looked at the other pillow, but his Genius wasn't there. He jumped up and searched the room.

"Hey, little guy, you here?" *Little guy?* Giacomo sighed. *I really have to come up with a name. As soon as I find him.*

He pulled on his pants and tunic, then checked behind the wardrobe, under the piles of blankets, and behind the furniture. No luck.

He headed down the hall toward the kitchen. Maybe his Genius had gotten hungry and left to find breakfast. Through a large hallway window, he noticed that the sun was already high in the sky. Everyone was probably already up. Why hadn't anyone woken him?

He descended the stairs, struck by the villa's eerie quiet. The kitchen and dining room were deserted, as were the library, the sitting area, and ten other rooms that may or may not have had a specific purpose. Where were the servants, the cooks, the maids? A place this size seemed like it would need a small army to keep it running, but so far the only person he'd seen doing any cooking or cleaning had been Baldassare's wife. He guessed that to keep the Geniuses a secret, Baldassare couldn't employ any outside help. In Virenzia, you never knew who you could trust.

"Hello? Anyone here?" Giacomo's voice echoed through the villa.

At the end of a hall, he spotted a familiar face passing by.

"Enzio!" Giacomo called out, waving to him.

The boy shot him an annoyed look and kept going.

"Hold on, I want to ask you something!" Giacomo caught up to Enzio and stopped in front of him.

Enzio tapped his foot impatiently. "Yeah? What?"

"I was wondering if you know where Aaminah or Milena or Savino are?"

"You check Pietro's studio?" Enzio shoved Giacomo aside.

"The cellar. Of course!" He should've looked there first and saved himself the awkward interaction with Enzio.

Walking away, Enzio muttered, "You have your own Genius and you couldn't figure that out? Pathetic." He rounded the corner and vanished.

Giacomo didn't know who he liked less—Savino or Enzio. But he was sure they were two of the most disagreeable people he'd ever met.

He found the gold-framed painting of the Supreme Creator and swung it open, revealing the passageway he'd come through yesterday.

When he reached the bottom of the stairs, he came upon Milena and Savino standing in the center of the room, Gaia and Nero perched on their shoulders. Pietro sat on a chair in the corner, a glass of red wine cradled in his hand. Giacomo was relieved to see his own Genius sitting with Aaminah and Luna at the table. When Aaminah spotted him, she gave him a friendly grin and waved. Giacomo smiled back.

"Brushes up," Pietro instructed.

Milena and Savino raised their paintbrushes in front of them as if they were about to lay the first strokes on a canvas, except they weren't standing in front of easels.

"Picture a hexagon," Pietro continued. "Visualize each of its six sides. Can you see it?"

"Yes," Milena said.

"Got it," Savino quickly followed.

"Now, bring it to light."

Savino and Milena both brushed six short strokes in the air, signaling their Geniuses to illuminate their gems. A brilliant blue light shot out of Nero's crown and projected Savino's hexagon into the center of the room. At least five feet tall, the hexagon's bold, rough lines hung in the air as if cast against a wall. At the same time, Gaia projected a green light, forming an equally large hexagon, but with a thin, delicate outline. Both colorful shapes hummed with energy, their edges vibrating; their centers were translucent, like a section of a stained glass window.

When Giacomo was very young, his parents had used their Geniuses to create similar glowing shapes. When he lay restlessly in bed, his mother would draw little stars in the air and her Genius would project them on the ceiling and walls. Floating among the stars always calmed him down and helped him fall asleep. Now that he had his own Genius, he couldn't wait for Pietro to teach him how to master the technique.

Giacomo stepped into the room, catching Milena's attention. She glanced at him and immediately her hexagon's precise form wavered; its gentle, low hum became a high-pitched buzz.

"Milena. Focus," Pietro said brusquely.

She gripped her brush tighter, trying to bring her hexagon under control, but it shifted sideways and collided with Savino's. A wave of heat and light surged through the studio, knocking Savino and Milena off their feet. Their Geniuses squawked and scattered.

Savino picked himself off the floor. "Quit messing up my work, Milena."

"I got distracted," Milena complained. She dusted off her dress and gave Giacomo a look. "Thanks a lot."

"What did I do? I was just watching," Giacomo said, offended that she was blaming him.

Giacomo's Genius flew over and landed on his shoulder, greeting him with a buoyant chirp. "Good morning to you too," Giacomo said. "You should've let me know you were coming down here."

"Is this how you wanted to begin your first day of lessons?" Pietro said gruffly. "By being late and disruptive?"

Giacomo's cheeks burned. "Signor Barrolo didn't tell me what time to come down and no one woke me up, so—"

"Your excuses don't interest me. Are you serious about mastering your Genius?"

"Of course I am."

"You're not acting like it."

"I want to learn," Giacomo said firmly. "That's why I came here."

Pietro pulled a long piece of black silk off the table and dangled it from his fingers. "Savino, would you blindfold Giacomo?"

Savino smiled. "Absolutely." He snatched the blindfold from Pietro.

"Hold on a second—" Giacomo started, but Savino ignored his protest and wrapped the fabric around his eyes. His vision plunged into darkness. "I can't see anything."

"That's the point, idiot." Savino cinched the blindfold extra tight, yanking back Giacomo's head.

"We'll start with the basics," Pietro began. "You're going to draw a circle."

"A circle?" Giacomo chortled. "I don't need a Genius to do that."

"Then please, demonstrate your inspiring circle-drawing abilities for us." Pietro's voice was tinged with sarcasm.

"I'd love to, but I can't draw anything with this stupid blindfold on." Giacomo tugged at the knot, unable to loosen it.

"Leave it," Pietro commanded. "To form a deeper connection with your Genius and unlock its true potential, you need to change your perception of reality."

Giacomo dropped his hands to his sides and groaned. "Fine. So how do I do that exactly?"

"There's a piece of charcoal lying on the edge of the worktable. Pick it up, take it to the paper on the easel, and draw a circle with it."

Giacomo remembered the table with the art supplies was about twenty paces to his left and the easel stood just beyond. If he could find his way through Virenzia's aqueducts without a light, this should be easy. He took a couple of tentative steps forward, feeling the area in front of him. His arm knocked into someone.

"Watch it!" Savino shoved him. Giacomo spun around and caught his balance. But now he had no idea which way he was facing.

"Try using your Genius as a guide," Aaminah offered.

"Don't help him," Savino said.

"I can do this." Giacomo stumbled around the room, grasping at nothing. He imagined Milena and the others shaking their heads at his foolishness.

"You're doing an amazing job so far," Savino said, adding to Giacomo's already growing insecurity.

He swallowed his pride and took Aaminah's advice, calling out to his Genius. "Help me find the charcoal, little guy."

"You really need a name for him," Milena commented.

"I know, I know . . ."

His Genius emitted a slow, steady chirp.

Chi . . . chi . . . chi . . .

Giacomo moved to his right, following the sound. The staccato notes got faster. He turned left, and the noises slowed again. It was a game of hot and cold. The closer he got to his goal, the faster his Genius chirruped.

Chi-chi-chi—

He reached his arm out and touched the edge of the table.

Chichichichichichi—

He dragged his palm across the rough wood surface, wincing as a splinter pierced his skin.

Chiiiiiiiiiiiii—

The shrill note told him he was right on top of the charcoal. *Why can't I feel it?* He patted the table for what felt like an eternity, until his fingers grazed the stick of charcoal.

"Found it!" Giacomo announced triumphantly.

"Not bad," Pietro said. "But try to make it to the easel a little faster."

Giacomo's Genius started the game again, beginning with slow, even chirps. Charcoal in hand, Giacomo felt his way around the corner of the table. The chirps sped up. He held his arm straight out in front of him until it contacted the edge of the wooden easel. Clipped to a board were sheets of rough-edged paper. Giacomo carefully sketched the outline of a circle, but without being able to see what he was drawing, he kept losing his place on the page. Somewhere behind him, Savino snickered. Giacomo guessed his circle wasn't looking so good.

His arm finished its loop. "All done. Can I take the blindfold off and see how it looks?"

Savino didn't even try to hold back his laughter. "Don't bother. It looks terrible."

Giacomo lifted the bottom edge of the black silk and his heart sank. The start and end points of his line didn't come close to meeting. His circle looked like a long, hairy worm that curled in on itself.

Pietro's cane clacked against the easel's leg. He ran his fingers across the paper, leaving behind smudged trails of charcoal. "Keep the blindfold on," Pietro ordered. He tore down Giacomo's first attempt, revealing a fresh piece of paper. "Try again."

Giacomo lowered the blindfold and raised the charcoal. He was about to start drawing, when Pietro grabbed his wrist. "To draw a circle, you must first center yourself. Relax."

"I can't when everyone's watching me," Giacomo said.

"Don't concern yourself with what others think. This is between you, your Genius, and that piece of paper." Pietro let go of his wrist. "All circles begin with a single point. Visualize that point on the paper."

Giacomo concentrated, imagining a single shining star. "I see it."

"Good. That point is going to become the center of your circle. Use it as your anchor. And this time, I want you to draw the shape with a continuous stroke."

Giacomo held the imaginary point of light in his mind and put his hand directly above it. He moved the charcoal in one long loop. As he drew, he began to see a bright red line cut through the darkness, forming the circumference of a circle.

"Giacomo, look at your Genius!" Aaminah said with awe.

He peeled up the blindfold. His Genius hovered over his right shoulder, shining a red beam from its crown. It projected a glowing ring on the paper, matching his charcoal circle exactly.

"How did I . . . ? How did my Genius . . . ?"

The light from his Genius's gem dimmed and the red circle faded away.

"What was different for you that time?" Pietro asked.

"I could see the circle as I was drawing it."

"Good. It means you're getting better at picturing a shape."

"No, I mean I could *actually* see it," Giacomo said. "It was like I was looking through the blindfold."

"Fascinating . . ." Pietro murmured.

"I thought you said you only got your Genius the other night?" Milena said accusingly.

"I did."

"Then how did he help you create a sacred geometry shape already?"

"Sacred geometry?" Giacomo replied, puzzled.

"It was probably just a fluke." Savino crossed his arms and challenged Giacomo. "Bet you can't do it again."

Even though Giacomo had triggered his Genius's power the other night to escape the soldiers, and again to draw the circle, he had no idea how he had done it or whether he could repeat it. But his desire to prove Savino wrong outweighed his self-doubt. "Bet you I can."

He ripped the paper away and began fresh. With the blindfold covering his eyes, he visualized the pinpoint of light, then put charcoal to paper, moving his hand with a bold confidence. His Genius chirped in his right ear, then he heard the faint hum of energy. The same red light appeared in the blindfold's blackness, matching the movement of his hand.

"Unbelievable," Milena said softly.

"You're a natural!" Aaminah burst out.

Excited, Giacomo pulled down his blindfold, letting it hang around his neck. He'd drawn a perfect circle.

Savino scowled. "You're such a liar. How long have you really had your Genius?"

"I told you, he showed up the night before you guys found me."

"He's telling the truth," Pietro said. "Otherwise, Tito would have sensed his Genius sooner."

The glowing circle faded away and Giacomo's Genius flew to his shoulder. Milena and Savino glared at him as if he'd just pick-pocketed them. At least Pietro believed his story.

"Giacomo, usually an artist has to work for many years with a Genius to be able to use sacred geometry like you did." Pietro showed no emotion, but Giacomo sensed a hint of surprise in his voice. "Clearly, I was wrong about your age being a problem."

"But how am I using sacred geometry when I don't even know what it is?"

Pietro felt for the wine bottle and refilled his glass. "Can you count to ten?"

Giacomo rolled his eyes. "Yes, of course."

"And you're familiar with different shapes—the circle, the triangle, the square, and so forth?"

"Yes."

"Then you already have a basic understanding of what sacred geometry is. Different numbers correspond to different shapes. It's like a language the Creator invented to tell us about the underlying patterns that make up all existence."

Giacomo stared at the circle he'd drawn. "So that red circle my Genius projected . . . That's the Creator talking to me?"

"In a manner of speaking."

"So what's he saying?"

"That's between you and the Creator."

Frustrated, Giacomo threw down his charcoal. "You're really not helping."

"Maybe I can." Milena stepped to Giacomo's side. "Shapes are like numbers you can see. Sort of how the written word makes speech visible. You can't see the words I'm saying unless you write them down. And you can't see numbers until you draw them as shapes."

Pietro smiled proudly. "Couldn't have made it any clearer myself. Giacomo, the circle you drew is a symbol of the number one, also known as the monad. It represents creation, unity, and perfection."

Milena nodded knowingly. "The numbers one to ten and their corresponding shapes are the original patterns for everything that exists. Sort of like an architect's model for a building."

"Precisely," Pietro said. "Sacred geometry can be found in mathematics, art, and music. Anyone can recognize the patterns, but only an artist or a musician with a Genius can transform those patterns into energy."

"Is that why Savino and Milena got knocked down when their hexagons smashed into each other?" Giacomo asked.

"For the record, hers ran into mine," Savino interjected. "But yes, sacred geometry can cause some serious damage if you're not careful."

Like when I shot the light at the soldiers and the stones exploded, Giacomo recalled.

He turned to Aaminah. "But it seems like it can repair damage too, like when you fixed that cut on my arm." It might also explain how his knife wound had healed so quickly.

"That's right," Aaminah said. "It's taken me a lot of practice, but I've figured out how to use music to release healing energy. It all depends on what notes I play, and in what order."

"Sacred geometry can be used to create *or* destroy," Pietro said. "It rests on the artist's intentions."

Everything was starting to make some sense. Sacred geometry must be the blueprint the Creator had used to build the universe. Now, with the help of his Genius, Giacomo had the key to that blueprint—and to the energy that could affect the world around him.

"But how come Milena and Savino were able to draw their shapes in the air, and I had to use paper?" Giacomo asked.

"Because we've been down here studying for years," Savino said bitterly.

"You have to learn to crawl before you're ready to walk. So for the time being, you will need the aid of drawing on paper," Pietro explained. "But over time, you'll get better at picturing sacred geometry in your mind. And once its shapes become second nature, you won't need the paper anymore."

"Is that why you blindfolded me?"

Pietro nodded. "Sometimes our eyes deceive us. The blindfold removes distractions so you can focus on visualizing the shape. I want you to learn to trust your own inner vision. Learning sacred geometry is a way to tap into your deepest nature and unlock the knowledge within."

Giacomo stayed in Pietro's studio all day, drawing circle after circle until his hand felt permanently stuck in a clawlike grip and every piece of charcoal was worn to a nub. He even skipped dinner, which his Genius wasn't too happy about. But if he wanted to catch up to Milena's and Savino's level, some sacrifices had to be made; Fabiana's mouthwatering fennel and ricotta lasagna was one of them.

At some point, Giacomo realized he had lost all track of time. Pietro was snoring on the bench and Giacomo could barely keep his eyes open, so he guessed it must have been long past dark. Calling it quits, he trudged up the stairs, his tired Genius swaying behind him.

He passed through the kitchen and took a plump pear from a basket on the counter, devouring it on the way to his room. From down the hall came the soothing sounds of harp music.

He followed the melody to a parlor, where Aaminah sat holding a tall golden harp between her knees, her eyes closed. Each time she plucked a string with her tiny fingers, a luminous yellow circle sprang from her Genius's crown. The circle wiggled and vibrated in the air. Each dancing shape floated up, then faded away as the next note took its place. Giacomo's Genius perked up and flitted around his head, delighted. As the notes washed over Giacomo, the cramp in his hand eased and his grip relaxed.

"You play beautifully," he said. Aaminah's eyes snapped open and she stopped. The wiggly circles of light popped like soap bubbles. "Sorry, I didn't mean to interrupt." He backed out of the room.

"It's okay. Stay." Aaminah waved him over. "I didn't hear you come in. Sometimes I get lost in the music and it's like the world around me disappears."

Giacomo nodded. He knew what that was like. Sometimes he became so absorbed in drawing that hours felt like minutes.

He plopped down on a long cushioned bench across from Aaminah, not expecting to slide down the silky fabric. He caught himself before falling on the floor. Aaminah giggled.

"What's the point of a seat you can't sit on?" Giacomo complained.

"I know. I grew up in a tiny farmhouse in the countryside, playing in mud and running through fields. I've been here three years and I'm still not used to all the fanciness."

A silence filled the room. Aaminah looked at Giacomo expectantly. He sat on his hands and stared at the floor, suddenly uncomfortable with talking.

"Don't get me wrong," Aaminah continued. "I'm so grateful to Signor Barrolo for taking me in, but sometimes I wish I could go into the city and play for people on the streets and let my Genius fly free. You ever feel like that?"

"Uh-huh," Giacomo answered, then fell silent. In the sewers, the only conversations he had were with his own reflection. Giacomo looked at his Genius, hoping it would inspire him with something smart to say. But it was busy cleaning its feathers. Aaminah picked up on his awkwardness and tried another question.

"Did you figure out a name for your Genius?"

Giacomo forced himself to open his mouth. "No. Not yet."

"Maybe I can help. I'm really good at naming things. I used to have a doll I named Serafina Santorini, the Mermaid Princess of Acquarone."

"That's an impressive title for a doll."

"She was a princess, but also a mermaid who fought pirates," Aaminah said proudly. "So what's your favorite thing about your Genius?"

Giacomo looked at his Genius, curled up on a pillow with his eyes closed. "He's really cute when he sleeps."

"Sleepy!" Aaminah burst out. "No, that's a terrible name, sorry."

Giacomo laughed. "I thought you said you were good at this?"

"I need to work through the bad names to find gold. Don't make fun of my process." Aaminah squinted in concentration and tapped her finger to her pursed lips. "What's your Genius's personality like?"

"Hmmm . . . He's annoying, loud, never listens to what I tell him, and always wants to eat."

"Buzzer? No. Munchie? Aw, forget it." Aaminah shot down the names before Giacomo had a chance to respond.

"He's loyal too. I feel like he's always going to have my back, so I want his name to sound respectable." Giacomo scratched the tuft of hair on his Genius's head, then raised his finger, proclaiming, "I've got it! Signor Ludovico Aurelius Francesco the Third!"

Aaminah stared at him flatly. "It's a bit of a mouthful."

"Well, Serafina Santorini, the Mermaid Princess of Acquawhatever doesn't exactly roll off the tongue."

Aaminah shrugged. "I'm just giving you my opinion."

Giacomo let his arm drop. He slumped back into the cushion. "You're right. This is hard."

"Keep thinking about it. It'll come to you."

While Giacomo mulled over other possible names, Aaminah put aside the harp and picked up a viol and a bow. She propped the long-necked instrument between her legs and gently ran the bow across one of its six strings, creating a low, mellow note that resonated through the room.

"How many instruments can you play?" Giacomo asked.

"Let's see . . . harp, flute, bass viol, treble viol, harpsichord, dulcimer, the drum, lute, and recorder."

"That's all?" Giacomo teased. "Seriously, who taught you to play all those?"

"No one. I taught myself. I only had a flute growing up, but once Signor Barrolo took me in, he gave me every instrument I could imagine, and some I'd never seen. You ever hear anyone play the bladder pipe?"

"No. What does it sound like?"

They walked to the back of the room, where Aaminah picked up a long, wooden instrument with a translucent bag attached to it. She blew on a pipe sticking out of the top. A horrid sound escaped and her Genius projected erratic waves of light that bounced around the room, then coursed through Giacomo. It felt like his eyeballs were vibrating and he was overcome by dizziness.

"All right, enough!" he shouted, bracing himself against the wall.

Mercifully, Aaminah stopped. Giacomo's Genius poked out from under a pillow, squawking its disapproval.

"It sounded like a sheep and a cow yelling at each other," Giacomo complained. "My vision was all blurry. I thought I was going to pass out."

"Whoops," Aaminah said. "Certain harmonics have that effect. Sorry."

Giacomo and his Genius weren't the only ones put off by the bladder pipe's cry. Enzio glared at Aaminah from the doorway, hands covering his ears. "I'm going to bed. Music time's over."

"If you have a problem with it, talk to your father," Aaminah said. "He told me I could practice whenever I want."

Enzio pulled the doors shut with a slam. Giacomo flinched, as did his Genius. "What's his deal? He seems to hate everyone."

"I've tried to be nice to him, but after a while, I gave up. He's not interested in making friends."

Aaminah seemed so nice and caring. If she couldn't find a way to get along with Enzio, Giacomo didn't stand a chance.

"Well, it is late," Aaminah said. "I guess it's time for—"

"Mico!" he declared out of nowhere.

She jumped back. "What do you mean, 'time for Mico'?"

"No, the name. For my Genius. You were right, it just sort of came to me."

Aaminah said the name slowly. "Mee-coh. I love it!"

Mico chirruped and hopped onto Giacomo's lap. Giacomo smiled. "He seems to like it too."

The next morning, Giacomo rose before the sun. Sketchbook in hand, he hurried down to Pietro's studio, itching to try out all the new art supplies and get in some extra drawing time before the day's lesson. As Pietro's snoring echoed from somewhere in the back of the cellar, Giacomo lit the candles and stared in wonder at all

the different drawing tools lying on the table. Living in the aqueducts, he had been limited to whatever rough chunks of charcoal he could scrounge up. They were imprecise and smudged
with the slightest touch. But now he had his pick of graphite
pencils and powder; sticks of red, white, and black chalk; quill
pens and bottles of ink; and jars of colored pigments. Plus countless pieces of paper and sheets of canvas. It was an artist's paradise
and Giacomo and Mico had the run of the place.

He tested each material, getting a feel for it on the paper. The
pencil was a revelation to him. He'd never been able to control his
lines so easily. The chalk had a nice smooth feel, and the pens
would be perfect for detailed work.

Mico was hardly the perfect model. He was always twitching
his head from side to side and hopping around. But Giacomo got a
few sketches he was happy with.

"Good morning," Pietro said from the shadows.

Startled, Giacomo jumped, dropping the pen. "I was just trying out all your amazing supplies," he said, picking up the pen.

Pietro shuffled toward him, his cane sliding on the floor in front of him. "Experimentation. That's good. But remember, it's your vision, not your tools, that will make you a great artist."

"Where'd you get so much wisdom?"

Pietro wearily rubbed the bridge of his nose and took a seat on the bench. "I've been at this a long time." His cloudy eyes stared straight at Giacomo, though Giacomo knew he couldn't see him.

What would it be like to be able to draw and paint anything you can see and then have that sense taken away? He hoped he'd never have to find out.

"Do you know you've already been my teacher for a while?" Giacomo said.

"And how's that?"

"I spent a lot of time in the old cultural center, copying parts of your fresco."

"It's still there?" Pietro said, sounding surprised. "Baldassare never told me . . . I always assumed Nerezza had destroyed it."

"You must've been pretty young if Emperor Callisto hired you to paint it."

"I was twenty when he held a competition for it," Pietro said. "The best design would get the commission. Guess who I had to compete against to win it?"

Giacomo had no idea. "Who?"

"Nerezza."

That was the last name Giacomo had expected to hear. "Emperor Callisto picked you over his own daughter?"

"He had a habit of not giving her what she thought she deserved."

"So . . . you knew her?"

"Painted next to her in the same classes growing up. Our Geniuses were inseparable." His voice got quieter. "For a while . . ."

Giacomo had a hard time imagining Tito hanging out with the Supreme Creator's grotesque Genius. "Was Nerezza always as awful as she is now?"

"No, not always . . ." Pietro stroked his beard, lost in thought.

"Can I ask . . . When did you lose your sight?"

Pietro sat silently for a moment before answering. "About fifteen years ago."

"How did it happen?"

Pietro let out a long, heavy exhale when he was interrupted by the soft patter of footsteps coming down the stairs. He leaned against his cane and pushed himself up. "Sounds like Fabiana is here with breakfast."

"But you were just about to tell me—"

"That's enough about my past for now," he said, abruptly ending the discussion.

As Pietro had predicted, Fabiana arrived with a platter piled with breads, fruit, and meat. "Good morning!" she sang warmly. "Sustenance for your morning lessons!"

"Thank you, signora," Giacomo said, impressed by her cheerfulness. Being the only one keeping the villa running must have been exhausting, but she didn't show it.

"It is my pleasure." She placed the food on the table and headed back upstairs.

Pietro took a heaping handful of meat and tossed it into the darkness, where it landed with a squish. An orange beam lit up and scanned around, finding the food. Tito's head emerged from an alcove and scooped up the meal with his gnarled beak, swallowing it all at once. Then he tucked his head under his wing and went back to sleep.

Giacomo and Mico ate their fill, while Pietro gnawed on a piece of bread. It wasn't long before Savino and Milena made their way downstairs.

"Today we'll be studying the dyad," Pietro informed them. "It is the second sacred geometry shape and embodies the idea of twoness."

Savino groaned. "This is simple stuff, Pietro. Can't you go over it with Giacomo when we're not around?"

"It never hurts to refine your basics," Milena said.

Savino groaned again. "I'll be over here if you need me." He grabbed a hunk of clay and began forming it into a human figure, his Genius watching intently.

Giacomo waited impatiently as Pietro uncorked a bottle of wine. After the headway he'd made yesterday, Giacomo was eager to discover what incredible new skill he'd unlock after his next sacred geometry lesson.

The wine glugged as Pietro filled his glass. "The circle is the most important shape, for out of it, all other shapes are created. But with the dyad, things start to get interesting. Tell me, Giacomo, if the circle represents the number one, what shape represents the number two?"

Pietro's inquiry hung in the air. Giacomo glanced at Milena, hoping she would enlighten him with the answer, but she stayed silent.

"It's a real question," Pietro said, growing impatient.

Giacomo's hands started to sweat. Why couldn't Pietro have asked him about the number three? That one was easy. A triangle.

Four? A square. Five? A pentagon. All the other numbers had shapes with the same number of sides. He racked his brain, trying to imagine a two-sided shape. He drew a blank. He glanced at Mico, hoping his Genius would give him a clue, but it was preoccupied with sucking a grape dry.

"It's a line," Savino called out without looking up from his sculpture. "Obviously."

"A line?" Giacomo repeated. "A line's not a shape, Master Pietro. That was a trick question."

"You think I'm trying to deceive you?" Pietro sounded offended.

Giacomo sheepishly scratched the back of his head. "No . . . I just . . . Never mind."

He thought the questioning was over, but then Pietro asked, "So how do we construct a line from a circle?"

Savino said, "First you draw a—"

Pietro cut him off. "Let Giacomo answer."

Giacomo shrugged. "I don't know." He drew a circle in his sketchbook, but couldn't figure out how to make a straight line from a curved one.

"Look at it another way," Pietro said. "If you wanted to make a copy of yourself, how would you do that?"

Giacomo thought about it for a second, then flipped the pages until he found one of his self-portraits. That was a copy of himself, wasn't it? And how had he drawn it? "With a mirror!" he blurted out.

Pietro smiled. "Very good. Milena and Savino, why don't you demonstrate."

They walked into the center of the room and stood several feet apart, their Geniuses on their shoulders. Using her brush, Milena traced the shape of a circle in space. The gem on Gaia's crown lit up, then projected a large, green, shimmering disc into the center of the room, its outline thin and smooth.

"To make a line from a circle, we must first create its mirror image," Pietro said. Savino waved his brush and his Genius projected a blue circle into the air. Like Savino's sculpture, the style of his lines was thick and rough. "Now what?" Pietro asked Giacomo.

"Connect their center points?" Giacomo said, unsure.

"Yes," Pietro confirmed. "But you're getting ahead of yourself. First, the circles must overlap."

Savino and Milena dragged their brushes through the air; their Geniuses mimicked their movements. As the circles came together, the differing styles clashed, erupting in sparks of energy. When the edge of each circle touched the other's center point, Milena's and Savino's styles unified. Giacomo sketched their overlapping circles, which created an almond shape in the middle.

"Meet the mandorla," Pietro said. "It is the medium of creation, from which the line, and all geometric forms, are born. Believe it or not, this shape is the basic building block for the entire universe."

Giacomo had a hard time wrapping his head around what Pietro was telling him. "So that eye-shaped thing in the middle can make a ten-sided shape or a twenty-sided shape?" he asked.

"The possibilities are infinite." Pietro took a sip of wine.

"Okay, but how?"

"One shape at a time," Pietro cautioned. "First, we need to create a line."

Milena took Pietro's cue and waved her brush. A shining green horizontal line connected the center point of her circle with Savino's.

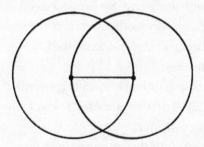

"The line symbolizes energy, force, and tension," Pietro said. "Tension is at the root of all creation. You can't have black without white or a creature without a creator. How is it possible to know light, without darkness? For any being to grow, it must confront its opposite."

"Is that why Milena's and Savino's different styles evened out when they came together?" Giacomo asked.

"Yes. The mandorla symbolizes a merger of opposing forces. It shows us it's possible to create harmony out of conflict, to overcome differences, and to find oneness." Pietro nodded to Milena and Savino. They waved their brushes, separating their two circles.

Once apart, the glowing shapes returned to their original styles before fading away.

Pietro raised his wineglass as if giving a toast. "Master the mandorla and you are on your way to mastering your Genius." He swallowed the rest of the wine in one gulp.

Creation out of conflict? It was an interesting idea, but Giacomo wasn't entirely sure what it meant. He was more excited to try creating his first mandorla.

"Milena, why don't you help Giacomo practice," Pietro said. "Savino, you're with me."

"Have fun with sewer-boy." Savino snickered, elbowing Milena. He followed Pietro into another section of the studio.

"You like that nickname?" Milena asked.

"No, of course not."

"Then why do you let him keep calling you that?"

Giacomo walked to the worktable. "I don't know. I'd rather not start something with him."

Milena shrugged. "If that works for you."

"What's that supposed to mean?"

"It sounds like you'd rather let Savino walk all over you than stand up to him."

Giacomo took a piece of charcoal, then dragged the easel into the center of the room. "I'm not afraid of Savino."

"Then don't act like you are. He likes to pretend he's tough, but deep down, he's actually pretty nice."

"Yeah? *How* deep down?"

Milena cracked a smile. "Let's get to work."

Giacomo stood in front of the easel, to Milena's left. "Don't be too hard on me. A lot of what Pietro said kind of went over my head."

"I'm not cutting you any slack, Signor I-just-got-my-Genius-and-I-can-already-do-sacred-geometry. You'll figure it out."

Giacomo stared at the blank page. "If you were trying to help me feel confident, you failed." He ran his hand down the paper, smoothing it out. "Okay, ready."

Milena crossed her arms and tapped her toe. "Who's failing now?" she muttered.

"What? I have charcoal, I have paper, I'm ready."

"So you don't need your Genius? Wow, you're more gifted than I thought."

Mico! Of course! Giacomo wanted to slap himself for being so foolish. Mico was right where he'd been all morning, gorging himself from the breakfast platter. Giacomo whistled. Mico raised his head, stared at Giacomo, then went back to eating.

"Oh come on, don't do this to me." Giacomo stomped over, picked up Mico, and placed him atop the easel. "Sit."

"Geniuses don't like to be ordered around, it's much better if you—"

"Can we just start?" Giacomo said, embarrassed by his inability to control his Genius.

"Fine. I'll go first." Milena raised her brush. She swung her arm in a graceful loop and Gaia projected a green circle in the air. "Now you."

Giacomo pictured the circle in his mind like Pietro had taught him, then drew it on the paper. Mico's gem glowed, projecting a wobbly red line that eventually took the shape of a translucent circle. If Giacomo had to describe his style, he would say it reminded him of a wet, floppy noodle. Which was really no style at all.

As Giacomo dragged his hand to the right, Mico turned his head and the red circle stabilized, moving closer to Milena's green ring.

"Brace yourself," Milena cautioned.

Giacomo tensed. "Why? What's going to happen?"

As the two circles intersected, their energies clashed and strands of white light sparked. Milena's circle grew larger, but Giacomo's shrank. It vibrated, then shattered into a million specks of light.

"Why'd you do that?" Giacomo demanded.

"I didn't *do* anything. You were holding back. Draw like you mean it."

"So you're the teacher now?"

Milena pointed her brush at him. "Pietro wanted me to help you. That's what I'm trying to do."

Giacomo sighed. "Sorry. I know. Let's try again."

On his second attempt, Giacomo's circle stayed together for longer, but Milena's still overpowered his. He drew circle after circle, while Mico projected them over and over. But no matter what he tried, his energy shape broke apart every time Milena's circle came in contact with it. And every time, Giacomo groaned in frustration.

Finally, Milena said, "You're too tense. Try to relax."

"I am relaxed!" he yelled, throwing his piece of charcoal onto the floor. It broke into shards.

Milena shook her head, turning away. "If you're not going to take this seriously, I'm not going to help you."

Giacomo took a breath and unclenched his hand, which had been balled into a tight fist. "No, wait. I know what to do." He grabbed a new piece of charcoal off the worktable. "One more time."

Milena returned and raised her brush. As Gaia projected her circle, Giacomo closed his eyes. The blindfold trick had helped him yesterday. There was no reason it couldn't work again.

Without looking, he drew the circle on the paper as he pictured it in his mind's eye.

"Good, much better," Milena said.

He kept his eyes closed. As Milena's circle moved closer to his, the low hum grew louder. The sound spiked into a high-pitched buzz, then dropped into a hum again.

"You got it!" Milena sounded impressed.

He opened his eyes. His red circle and Milena's green one overlapped, creating the mandorla. With a flick of her brush, Milena connected the two center points with a glowing green line. Mico chirped with excitement.

But Giacomo's breakthrough was short-lived. First came an ear-splitting screech. Then the almond shape in the mandorla glowed bright white.

Milena took a step back, looking uneasy. "Uh ... I've never seen that happen before."

Inside the glimmering mandorla, a storm of color brewed and sounds wailed. Wind like tiny needles shot out and lashed Giacomo's face. Milena cried out, feeling it too.

Giacomo flung the charcoal across the room, but his circle didn't vanish. "Mico, make it disappear!"

His Genius's wings fluttered frantically as it tried to fly away, but its ray of light was stuck to the mandorla, like clothing caught on a nail.

A tremendous boom rocked the room. Stones dislodged from the wall. The floor cracked and split.

The sensations felt familiar: swirling colors, deafening sounds, freezing cold air, foul scents that burned his nostrils. *It's just like the other night!*

If that was true, maybe he could stop it the same way. He closed his eyes and called on the Creator.

Please, make it stop. I didn't mean for this to happen.

He opened his eyes, but the storm still raged. Through the swirling haze, Giacomo spotted something in the eye of the mandorla. It looked like an upside-down V. Its golden outline smeared and blended into the swirling colors around it.

"Do you see that?" he shouted.

"See what?" Milena hollered back.

Pietro and Savino ran in, shielding their faces. "Sever the link!" Pietro yelled.

"Our circles won't come apart!" Milena frantically waved her brush while her Genius squawked in distress.

It only took a second for the room to turn from numbingly cold to blazing hot. It was like they'd been thrown into a blacksmith's forge.

When Giacomo looked back at the mandorla, the mysterious shape had transformed into a whip of fiery golden light. It lashed out, straight for him. He dove and the yellow flames arced over his head, singeing his hair. As the whip retracted, it swung back toward Milena. Giacomo watched in horror as the blaze engulfed her left arm. She screamed. Her brush incinerated.

Savino dashed over and pulled her away.

Giacomo wiped the sweat from his eyes. His insides boiled. *What have I done?*

Pietro hollered, "Tito, to me!" and his massive Genius lumbered into the room. Running his hand across the table, Pietro found a brush, then waved it toward the mandorla. Tito opened his beak, releasing a piercing screech. A beam of orange light shot out of his crown's square gem and into the heart of the mandorla.

To Giacomo's relief, the almond shape narrowed. The whipping winds gradually died down, the deafening sounds silenced, and the temperature dropped to normal.

The mandorla sealed shut, like a wound closing. Milena's and Giacomo's circles split apart, then exploded, the force of the blast hurling everyone to the ground.

Giacomo dragged himself to his feet and held a hand to his head. He put his other hand against the wall to steady himself, trying not to faint.

Savino knelt next to Milena. She leaned against him, cradling her injured arm. Tears streamed down her cheeks.

Giacomo staggered over. "Milena, are you all right?"

"Of course she's not!" Savino's face burned with anger. "You could've killed her!"

"I didn't mean—"

"Savino, take her upstairs to Aaminah," Pietro urged. "Now!"

"I'm . . . I'm fine," Milena said as Savino helped her up. Giacomo caught a glimpse of her injury. Deep slashes ran the length of her forearm. Her skin blistered purple.

What did I do to her? Giacomo thought in a panic.

Savino hurried Milena up the stairs, their Geniuses close behind. Giacomo kept his gaze on the floor, which was scarred with fissures and littered with broken stones. He waited for the well-deserved lecture Pietro was about to give him.

Once the cellar door slammed shut, Pietro asked, "Do you realize what you just did?"

A lump welled in his throat. Giacomo's voice trembled. "I didn't mean to hurt her. It was an accident. What's wrong with me? Why does this keep happening?"

"What do you mean? Giacomo, have you experienced something like that before?"

He dreaded to speak about the other night, but maybe if he told Pietro, the master could shed some light on what was going on.

Pietro must have sensed Giacomo's hesitation. He placed a comforting hand on his back. "It's important you tell me."

Giacomo took a deep breath. "The night before I came here, I had a run-in with a Lost Soul. Two, actually. When I tried to get away, one of them stabbed me. I didn't think I was going to survive. But then I was swallowed up by some kind of storm, like the one that just came out of the mandorla. At first, I thought I was hallucinating. But the pain was definitely real. It was so bad, I wanted to die. And then suddenly the storm passed. I woke up back on the street, and my wound was mysteriously healed. That's when my Genius showed up." Once he had finished, the lump in his throat dissolved and he felt more at ease.

Pietro stroked his long beard, considering Giacomo's explanation. "I don't understand how, but I believe you've accessed the Wellspring."

"What's that?"

"A dimension of sensation. Every color, sound, smell, flavor, and texture originates in the Wellspring. It is the universe's source of creative energy."

"You make it sound like a good thing, but it feels horrible. Savino was right, I could've killed Milena, or collapsed the villa on top of all of us."

"Creative energy is wild and untamed."

"Obviously! And I have no idea how to control it!"

"With practice, you can learn."

"So *you've* mastered the Wellspring?" Giacomo asked hopefully.

Pietro shook his head. "I wish I could tell you I had. But even the most talented artists only harness its power every now and then, in moments of pure focus. That's when ideas and creativity flow effortlessly and masterpieces are created." Pietro scratched his bald spot. "However, that's strictly a *mental* experience, you understand. What's puzzling is how you've been able to tap into the Wellspring on a *physical* level."

"I'd rather not tap into it again on *any* level." Giacomo searched for Mico and found him hiding in the space between two casks of wine.

"You're scared," Pietro said. "I understand. But don't let that fear stop you from exploring your creative power."

"Even if it might kill me, or someone else in the process?" Giacomo snapped. He took his Genius in his hands and pulled it out. "Come on, Mico. We're leaving."

"Wait—"

But Giacomo was already halfway up the stairs.

"Step into the fear!" Pietro called after him. "Or someday, you might regret not taking that journey."

Giacomo raced along the main hall, Pietro's words still lingering in his head. Aaminah's healing viol music streamed through the villa. Part of him wanted to check on Milena, but he was too ashamed to face her right now.

He careened out the front door and stumbled into the courtyard, the breeze cooling his sweaty skin. Mico jumped from his hands and flew loops, chirping happily. After being confined in the cellar, the open air was a relief to them both.

Giacomo had his hand on the front gate when Aaminah caught up to him.

"Where are you going?" she asked, a concerned look on her face.

"I don't know," Giacomo said. "Back to the sewers, I guess."

"Why?"

"Because of what I did."

"Milena's going to be fine, I promise."

But Giacomo wasn't so sure. He slumped against the gate. "She's never going to forgive me."

"Of course she will."

"Even if she does . . . I think coming here was a mistake."

Aaminah twirled her braid with her finger. "You know . . . when I first got to the villa, I felt the same. Like I didn't belong. For days, all I could think about was running away, back to the countryside."

"What stopped you?"

"Luna did. She loved being here. And when she met Milena's and Savino's Geniuses, it was like she'd been reunited with long-lost relatives. I realized she needed other Geniuses to thrive. And I needed other people."

"If I left, everyone would eventually forget I was ever here," Giacomo said. "Savino and Milena would never miss me."

"I would." As soon as Aaminah said it, her eyes darted away. "It wouldn't be the same without you."

Giacomo softened. She seemed to have the skill of knowing the perfect thing to say.

Aaminah's gaze followed Luna and Mico as they wove through the air, playfully chasing each other. She smiled, exposing her crooked front tooth. "Plus, our Geniuses seem to be hitting it off. You can't tear them apart now."

Giacomo gave a halfhearted nod. "Okay . . ."

Aaminah held out her hand. "Come on." He took it and let her lead him back inside.

"But I'm taking a break from all this sacred geometry stuff," Giacomo said. "I'm sticking with charcoal and paper. It's a lot safer."

DUKE OBERTO

The wind whipped Zanobius's face. He grasped huge handfuls of silver feathers with all four fists, his cloak flapping like a ship's sail in a storm. He kept his gaze up and resisted the impulse to look down. If he focused on the star-filled sky, he wouldn't fall. At least that was what he told himself.

In front of Zanobius, his master straddled Ciro's neck, staff tucked securely in the crook of his arm. He looked from side to side, studying the ground far below.

Duke Oberto's castle should be close, Ugalino's voice said.

When they had first made camp, after leaving the art dealer, Zanobius had asked his master about the duke.

"You said you were familiar with him. Have I met him also, but don't remember?"

"No, I visited him nearly twenty years ago, when I was still searching for how to create you. His collection of esoteric knowledge proved crucial. But I haven't spoken to him since. I should have known he was after the Sacred Tools as well."

"Is he a friend?"

"He's a greedy man who refused to accept his station in life," Ugalino said bitterly. "I didn't leave his castle on pleasant terms."

"So he won't be happy to see you again?"

"Doubtful. But he will be pleased to see you, I'm sure."

"Why?"

Ugalino didn't provide an answer and Zanobius didn't press any further. If his master wanted him to know, he would tell him.

For the next several nights they flew north. Ugalino preferred to travel after the sun set. There was less chance of being spotted, and Ciro needed the days to recuperate.

Zanobius's thoughts were interrupted by his master's voice. *We've arrived. Get ready.*

"Ciro, dive!" Ugalino shouted.

The Genius plunged, letting out an ear-piercing screech. Zanobius's stomach heaved.

Before they could land, a streak of flaming light shot past Zanobius, inches from his eye—a fire-tipped arrow. A second one embedded in the Genius's side. Ciro screeched again. At the same time, Ugalino let out a pained groan and rubbed his thigh.

Careful not to fall, Zanobius reached down and dislodged the shaft, patting Ciro's feathers to put out the flames.

Ugalino pushed his Genius into a full dive, forcing Zanobius to look down, where a dozen more fiery arrows shot toward them. Ciro heaved his massive wings and flapped them, generating a powerful gust that batted the projectiles off course.

Ciro accelerated toward the castle, a pentagonal stone fortress sitting atop a pillar of raised earth, ringed by a moat. On two corner towers, archers dipped their arrowheads into barrels of black pitch and touched them to standing torches. They nocked the arrows and launched another volley.

Flames whizzed past Zanobius on both sides. One shaft thunked into his shoulder. His cloak burned, but he didn't even wince. He yanked out the arrow like it was an annoying splinter and tossed it away.

Ciro swooped low and Ugalino leveled his staff at the first tower. The diamond mounted atop the weapon's handle glowed. Ugalino made a series of short, sharp strokes, as though the staff were his paintbrush and the sky his canvas; sparkling strands of white light launched from the diamond. They spiraled through the air and erupted where the archers stood, throwing them off the tower.

Ugalino targeted the second corner, but this time the archers knew what was coming. A split second before the tower exploded, they leaped away and dove into the murky moat.

Ugalino steered Ciro over the open courtyard. The Genius flapped its giant wings and slowed its descent. Before they touched down, Zanobius jumped off Ciro's back, eager to meet the ground below. His four bare feet smashed into the stone slabs with a sharp crack. Helmed swordsmen, draped in chain mail and covered in plates of armor, fenced in Zanobius, their blades ready to cut him down. He whipped off his cloak. Beneath it, he wore only a swath of red linen around his waist. He saw no point in hiding what he was from these men.

Zanobius raised all four arms and took a defensive stance. Through the slits in their visors, he saw the swordsmen's eyes swell with fright as they took in his hulking white form: his four arms and four legs and the tattooed purple circular patterns across his chest and back.

"Monster!" a man to his right called out.

"Freak!" yelled another.

"Abomination!" hollered a third.

Zanobius snarled, their words wounding him more deeply than their blades ever could.

Ignore their insults, his master whispered. *They will never appreciate how truly unique you are. They don't deserve to exist in the same world as you. End them.*

Zanobius lunged at the nearest man and seized his gauntlet, crushing his wrist. The sword clattered to the ground as the man's painful howls mixed with the crunch of metal and snap of bone. With one arm, Zanobius hurled the man across the courtyard, where he fell in a heap against the wall.

Three swords slashed; three of Zanobius's hands reached out, catching the blades. He disarmed his attackers, then flung their weapons back at them. Two of the men dove out of the way, but the third took steel to the leg.

Though the cuts Zanobius sustained were painless, a thick, gray liquid oozed from his palms. His skin squeezed itself together and the wounds instantly closed.

The last two guards circled him, one striking from behind and the other at his chest. Zanobius dodged and turned, clamping his massive hands around their helmets. The metal buckled in his vise-like grip as the men screamed for mercy. He knocked their heads together and let them drop with a thud.

Ugalino strode past the mound of bodies and struck the heel of his staff on the stones. A luminous white cone formed above the diamond on the handle. He thrust his staff at the castle's doors and light spiraled out, boring a large hole through the thick wood.

Zanobius followed Ugalino into the castle and down a wide

hallway, where he gazed in wonder at all the wealth. Each room he passed was filled with ornate furniture, giant glazed vases, and tapestries so big Zanobius looked like a child next to the monumental figures woven into them. Humans seemed obsessed with collecting material things, he observed. Especially rich ones. But for what purpose? How many gold-framed mirrors did a man need before he got sick of looking at himself?

Zanobius glimpsed his reflection in one of the mirrors, his uniformly pale skin punctuated by his piercing blue eyes. He moved on, breezing past painting after painting, until one caught his attention. As his master continued down the hall, Zanobius looked fixedly up at the canvas.

What he noticed at first was all the stars. It looked like an exact replica of the sky Zanobius gazed at night after sleepless night. In his head, he drew lines connecting a group of stars, making the shape of a tiger. Another grouping took the form of a bear.

At the top of the image, a man with long gray hair hovered in the clouds, looming over the earth below. With his right arm, he reached toward the earth, holding a large drafting compass. The tip of its long leg touched the earth and several bright circles spread out, like ripples in a pool of water. In his left arm he held a long straightedge and a pencil.

His master's voice called to him: *Zanobius, I have someone eager to meet you.*

Ugalino approached, along with a man whose face was covered in wrinkly skin—Duke Oberto, Zanobius assumed. Over his hunched back, he wore a long red cloak embroidered with gold and silver thread that sparkled in the torchlight. As he came closer, Zanobius realized the man's wrinkles were actually scars that cut deep grooves across his face, like he'd been horribly burned in a fire.

"You should have sent word you were coming," the duke said to Ugalino. "I would have ordered my men to stand down and—" His voice dropped away as soon as he laid eyes on Zanobius.

The duke stared, but not with the horror and anger Zanobius was used to. No, this man's eyes looked hungry. Like he'd been starved for weeks and Zanobius had just arrived with a platter of roast duck.

"I'd heard you were successful, but to see your Tulpa with my own eyes . . ." The duke turned back to Ugalino. "May I?" he said, gesturing toward Zanobius.

Ugalino nodded. "Of course."

Let Duke Oberto observe you, his master instructed. *He is weak of mind and spirit. Make him feel important, and he'll give us what we want.*

Zanobius stood like a statue as Duke Oberto circled him, examining his flesh up close. The duke dragged a withered finger across his chest, tracing one of the many circles designed into his body. The duke poked and prodded him, murmuring, "Mmm," and, "Ah, I see . . . ," as if he were reading from a letter. The duke stared up into Zanobius's eyes. He was so close now, Zanobius could see that he was missing most of his teeth. The few that remained were so decayed they looked like they might fall out at any moment. His body was so ravaged, it was impossible to determine his true age.

"A bit roughly hewn and the extra limbs look rather tacked on, but this Tulpa is truly a masterpiece," Duke Oberto said.

Ugalino seemed to ignore the duke's backhanded compliment. Zanobius tried to listen in on his master's thoughts, curious to know if the duke's critique had offended him, but he found only silence. When Ugalino didn't want to be heard, Zanobius was left in the dark.

"No wonder the Supreme Creator saw your Tulpa as a threat," the duke said. "Imagine an army of creatures like this one, marching on Virenzia . . . She wouldn't stand a chance!"

"My intention was never to build an army."

The duke raised one of Zanobius's arms and pressed on his biceps. "A mistake, if you ask me."

"Zanobius isn't just some creature," Ugalino said, his voice growing more intense. "He is a work of art, crafted with care and skill. He can't be copied endlessly. Now, if we could—"

"A million gold *impronta*," the duke interrupted.

Ugalino's hand tensed around his staff. "I'm sorry?"

The duke spun around. "I'll pay one million for your Tulpa. Far beyond what even the finest paintings command on the black market."

"He's not for sale," Ugalino said firmly.

"Two million," the duke countered. "Now don't be a fool, Ugalino. I'm sure you can whip up another if you want to."

Ugalino glowered. "As I've been trying to explain, one does not merely 'whip up' a Tulpa. Zanobius is one of a kind." He leaned in and jabbed the duke's chest with his staff's diamond handle. "No amount of money will make me part with him."

"If you didn't come looking for a buyer, then what are you doing here?"

"I wish to acquire three rare objects, and the word is, you have black market connections across all three empires."

Duke Oberto smirked. "True. I can get you anything you want. Assuming you have the money."

Ugalino looked at the painting of the Creator. "I want those," he said, pointing to the Compass, Straightedge, and Pencil.

"Like your Tulpa, the painting's not for sale."

"Don't pretend to be clueless. I want the actual Sacred Tools."

Duke Oberto scowled. "I deal in the tangible world. The Creator's Tools are a myth. I think our business is done. You can see yourself out." The duke pushed past Ugalino and marched down the hall.

Seize him, Ugalino ordered.

Zanobius took hold of the duke, picking him up with all four hands. The man felt fragile, like his bones would shatter with even the slightest pressure.

"Release me!" the duke demanded.

"Do you take me for a fool?" Ugalino shouted. "I know you've been searching for the Sacred Tools."

"I haven't, I swear." Sweat beaded across the duke's forehead.

"Then if you can't be of service, what use are you?"

Ugalino glanced at Zanobius. *Crush him.*

Zanobius removed his two front hands from the duke's shoulders and wrapped them around his head.

"No, wait! I . . . I can help you!"

The wealthiest always cave the quickest, Ugalino's voice whispered. *They have the least amount of courage and the most to lose.*

Zanobius eased his grip.

"There's a man in Virenzia . . ." the duke confessed. "A collector . . . He's bought dozens of old maps, parchments, ancient tomes . . . He never outright said what they were for, but I'm sure he must be looking for the Sacred Tools too."

"What's his name?"

"Baldassare Barrolo, the Supreme Creator's Minister of Culture."

Ugalino ran his staff down the duke's scarred face. "You look much worse than the last time we met."

"The tragedy of aging."

"I'd wager age has nothing to do with it." Ugalino narrowed his eyes. "You never abandoned your experiments like I bid you to."

"Please, tell your Tulpa to let me go," the duke appealed. "I gave you a lead on the Sacred Tools."

Ugalino shook his head. "I warned you what would happen if you insisted on pursuing this reckless, self-destructive path."

The duke's frightened expression became defiant. "The Well-spring's power shouldn't be available only to those with Geniuses."

Ugalino took a step back. "Consider this an act of mercy. I'm saving you from yourself." He turned and strode toward the door.

Zanobius waited for the word to let the duke go, but instead his master ordered him to end Duke Oberto's life.

It was as simple as snapping a twig.

THE WELLSPRING

The day after the incident with the mandorla, Giacomo skipped his lessons, preferring instead to try out the softness of all eighty-six cushioned benches and chairs throughout the villa. But he couldn't get comfortable. He asked Signora Barrolo to bring his meals to his room, where he and Mico ate alone. But no matter how much food he stuffed in his mouth, he never felt full.

He still couldn't face Milena after what he'd done to her. He kept replaying the accident over in his mind—the blazing heat, the strange whip of fire, her tormented scream.

Aaminah stopped by to check on him, the first time to let him know that Milena's arm was healing up nicely, which he was glad to hear, though it did little to ease his guilt. Later, Aaminah burst into his room, full of wonder and amazement. "Pietro told us you opened the Wellspring! How did it happen?" She wanted to know more about his unique new power. Giacomo avoided her eager but annoying questions by saying he wasn't feeling so good, which was half true. He had no words to explain how he'd summoned the

Wellspring, and he wasn't sure he wanted to find them. Part of him believed if he ignored what he'd done for long enough, it would be like it had never occurred.

But two things prevented Giacomo from going into full denial. The first was his Genius. Every time Giacomo lounged on a new cushy seat, Mico chirped in disapproval and pecked him on the head. Geniuses thrived when an artist drew, painted, or sculpted. Without a creative outlet, Mico grew restless.

The second and harsher of the two was Baldassare Barrolo. That evening, a pounding on Giacomo's door awoke him from a nap. Baldassare marched in and stood at the foot of the bed, arms crossed and brow furrowed.

"Pietro told me what happened. Is it true you haven't been to the studio all day?"

"Yes, signor."

"Having access to the Wellspring is something most artists would embrace," he lectured. "You should be jumping at the chance to learn more about it."

"I'm not most artists." Giacomo pulled the covers over his head.

Baldassare yanked them back off. "I'd like you to come with me. There's something you need to see."

Giacomo wasn't in the mood for an argument, so he begrudgingly rolled out of bed. "Fine."

Baldassare led him through the maze of hallways, finally stopping in front of an immense wooden door secured by a thick iron bar. Baldassare rotated a series of numbers and symbols on a cylinder built into the lock, triggering a metallic *clunk*. He lifted the bar and pushed the door open. He took a torch off the wall and led Giacomo inside.

Giacomo's eyes widened and his mouth went slack. The light flickered through the cavernous room, falling on stacked paintings, burlap-covered sculptures crowded together, and piles of rolled-up tapestries.

"This is a small sample of the art the Supreme Creator has banned," Baldassare said. "I've purchased these pieces little by little over the years in . . . well, what you might call 'unusual' ways and places."

"I've heard rumors of a black market. I didn't know it was real."

"Very real, if you know the right people. Which I do. And this is what I've amassed over the years."

Mico flew in loops, making excited whirring sounds. Giacomo would have done the same if he had wings. His sour mood gave way to excitement. He ran from painting to painting, barely looking at one before another caught his eye.

The heroes in these artworks weren't mythic figures, emperors, or the Supreme Creator, but ordinary people: a young girl holding bright yellow flowers, a group of colorfully dressed musicians playing in a piazza, a hunched farmer and his horses plowing a green field. It baffled Giacomo that the Supreme Creator was threatened by these. And it wasn't fair that all this amazing art was covered up and hidden away.

"People should be able to see your collection," Giacomo said.

"I completely agree with you. But as long as Supreme Creator Nerezza is in power, these masterpieces will remain here."

Giacomo bristled at the mention of her name.

Baldassare stepped toward two paintings covered with white sheets. "But the real reason I brought you in here was to show you these."

He pulled back the sheets, unveiling two portraits: one of a mother and her baby, the other of a father with a young boy. A chill shot through Giacomo. He recognized his face in theirs. He shared his mother's large brown eyes and full lips; his wavy brown hair and bulbous nose were both thanks to his father.

"I imagine you thought you'd never see these again," Baldassare said.

Giacomo nodded, his eyes still on the paintings. "When Nerezza's soldiers took my parents' Geniuses away, they took all their paintings too. How did you get these? I always assumed Nerezza had them destroyed."

"As far as she knows, they were," Baldassare said with a smug smile. "Being Minister of Culture has allowed me to secretly divert illegal art from the palace's furnaces to my vault. When Pietro mentioned your family name, I knew it sounded familiar, so I checked the arrest records. Sure enough, Amera and Orsino Ghiberti's names were inscribed there. Finding their paintings among my collection took a little digging, but here they are."

The paintings once hung over the hearth in Giacomo's house. His father must have painted the one of his mother when Giacomo was only a few days old. His mother had painted the other one a couple years later. He had a vague memory of being four and pointing up at the portraits, yelping, "Me, me, me!" His parents were delighted that he saw himself in their work.

"The tragic part is, your parents might have been able to save their Geniuses," Baldassare said.

"What do you mean? How?"

"The Supreme Creator made them an offer: if they helped her, she would let their Geniuses live. But they refused."

Giacomo could hardly believe what he was hearing. "Helped her with what?"

Baldassare didn't answer his question. He flung the sheets back over the paintings, covering Giacomo's parents. "You could be a part of bringing this art into the light of day again."

He escorted Giacomo out and closed the door, then locked the iron bar back in place.

"I know you must have many questions. Meet me in my study in an hour, and I'll help you find some answers." Baldassare returned the torch to its stand and walked away.

Giacomo lingered at the door, thinking about his parents' paintings, locked away with so many others, like they were the Supreme Creator's prisoners. They seemed destined to decay in the dark.

But maybe it didn't have to be that way.

Curious to find out why his parents had refused to help Nerezza, Giacomo made his way to Baldassare's study later that evening. Baldassare greeted him at the doorway with a big smile.

"Glad you could make it!" Baldassare ushered Giacomo and his Genius in.

To Giacomo's surprise, Pietro, Aaminah, Milena, and Savino were present too. He had thought it was going to be a private meeting, so why were they all there? He was about to turn around and leave, but Baldassare had already shut the doors.

The study was paneled in dark wood. Shelves of books and scrolls towered along each wall, floor to ceiling. A gold stand in the corner held a globe so large Giacomo doubted he could wrap his arms around it.

Mico swooped through the room and landed on the back of a chair next to Gaia, Nero, and Luna, who all welcomed him with happy chirps. Giacomo wished he felt as accepted by the group. But after deliberately avoiding everyone all day, what did he expect? To be greeted with cheers and hugs?

Aaminah looked up at him and smiled, which helped relax him a bit. But Savino stayed slumped on the chair, refusing to make eye contact. Pietro leaned against Baldassare's massive desk, which was covered with stacks of books and piles of parchments. Milena glanced at Giacomo coldly, cradling her left arm, which was wrapped in translucent cotton. He guessed the damage done by the Wellspring was beyond Aaminah's skill to fully heal it.

"We are faced with a serious predicament," Baldassare said, pacing around his desk. "I received word from an art dealer I do business with, in the north of Mardovino. He was recently attacked by two men, one of whom had eight limbs."

"Impossible!" Pietro exclaimed.

"It seems Ugalino has finally come out of hiding." Baldassare leaned forward. "And my guess is he's making a play for the Sacred Tools."

"But we're not ready," Milena said, looking unnerved.

Nothing Baldassare and Pietro had said made any sense. How could an eight-limbed man exist? Who was Ugalino? Why was Baldassare talking about the Sacred Tools as if they were real? And what did any of it have to do with Giacomo?

But before Giacomo could voice any of his questions, Baldassare continued: "We all knew this moment would come. It is the reason you've all been studying and training so hard. I had hoped we would have a lead on the Sacred Tools before Ugalino, but no matter. It simply means we'll need to move more quickly."

Savino stood up. "I'm ready, just give us the go-ahead."

"But we still have no idea where to start," Milena argued. "We can't randomly wander around Zizzola, hoping one of the Sacred Tools will magically reveal itself. The key to finding them is buried somewhere in those, I'm sure of it." She gestured to the books and parchments on the desk. "We're close. We must just be overlooking something."

"Burying your head in books hasn't helped us so far," Savino said. "What makes you think it will make a difference now?"

With a wave of his hand, Pietro silenced Savino. "Enough. Milena's right, we can't send you off without a plan. Especially if Ugalino is on the offensive."

"I'm with Savino," Baldassare said. "We can't afford to sit back any longer. We need to make a move now."

"Only a fool would journey without a destination!" Pietro shouted.

"I'm not in the mood for your wise quips!" Baldassare shot back.

"Excuse me, Signor Barrolo?" Giacomo interrupted. "But I thought you had something important to tell me about my parents. Did they have anything to do with this Ugalino guy? Who is he anyway?"

Everyone fell silent. Pietro reached out, his hand finding the back of a chair. He fell into the seat as if the weight of his bones was too much to carry. "Ugalino could have been one of the greatest artists ever to live," he said bitterly. "But seventeen years ago, he created a work of art so menacing, Nerezza ordered him to destroy it."

"So even back then, she was threatened by what artists painted," Giacomo commented.

Pietro's expression turned grim. "Ugalino's creation wasn't an ordinary work of art. It was a Tulpa."

Giacomo drew a blank. "What's a Tulpa?"

"A living, breathing, thinking statue," Pietro explained. "Ugalino's Tulpa has skin as white as marble, four arms and four legs, and the strength of twenty men. He even gave it a name—Zanobius."

Giacomo couldn't wrap his mind around the concept. "That's impossible. Artists can't create living things . . . can they?"

"Throughout history, artists have experimented with infusing life into statues," Baldassare said. "But compared to what Ugalino accomplished, they were like children playing with clay."

"Making a Tulpa was arrogant and misguided," Pietro complained. "Ugalino should have left the work of creation to the Creator."

Sounds like Ugalino and Nerezza have a lot in common, Giacomo thought. *They both think they're better than the Creator.*

"Nerezza believed the Tulpa was a challenge to her authority," Baldassare continued. "She feared Ugalino might create an army of Tulpas to overthrow her, so she and her soldiers attacked and destroyed Zanobius. But weeks later, he rose again, as strong as ever. Ugalino had used his knowledge and power to rebuild him, proving his Tulpa could not be killed by ordinary means."

"Nerezza redoubled her efforts and went after Ugalino and Zanobius again, finally driving them out of the city," Pietro said. "But in the course of the battle, many lives were lost at the hands of that creature. Some were Nerezza's soldiers, but others were innocent civilians, in the wrong place at the wrong time." Pietro took a deep breath. "Nerezza chased them through Zizzola for years. Everywhere the Tulpa went, it left behind death and destruction."

Baldassare picked up the story. "After a while, the Supreme Creator lost their trail and abandoned the hunt. She assumed they had found refuge in one of the other empires. But she's always been on alert, waiting for the moment when Ugalino and his creature would show their faces again."

"So that's why Nerezza began killing off Geniuses," Giacomo realized.

Pietro nodded. "She began to see every artist as a potential threat. As the Geniuses were wiped out, their artists started losing their minds, becoming Lost Souls."

"And a gloom has clouded Virenzia ever since," Baldassare added. "Like a painting that's faded."

Sadness and anger swirled within Giacomo. He looked to Baldassare. "Is that what Nerezza asked my parents to do? Help her fight Ugalino and his Tulpa?"

"That's right," he said. "But they refused to use their Geniuses against another artist."

Giacomo's first thought was, *Good for them*. The fact that his parents had stood up to the Supreme Creator only made him more proud. Of course, if they hadn't stuck their necks out, maybe someone like Baldassare would have taken them in and protected their Geniuses. He felt a twinge of sorrow. In standing up for their beliefs, his parents had sacrificed their family.

Giacomo changed the subject to something less upsetting. "The Sacred Tools Ugalino wants—are you talking about the Creator's Compass, Straightedge, and Pencil?"

"The very ones," Baldassare declared.

"But I thought they were just a myth to explain how the world was created. They're not real . . . are they?"

"Are they not?" Pietro said. "Over the ages, philosophers, alchemists, and artists have delved into the myth's origins and found clues indicating that the Sacred Tools are in fact physical objects."

Physical? Giacomo wondered. His mind flashed back to the Wellspring. The upside-down V he'd seen inside the mandorla was the same shape as a drafting compass. That had to mean something.

"Each Tool possesses a unique power," Baldassare explained. "The Compass controls light; the Straightedge, energy; and the Pencil, matter."

"The Compass can create a portal that lets you travel thousands of miles in an instant," Milena said.

"However, its power limits you to only places you've been," Pietro added. "You must be able to form a clear picture in your mind's eye of where you want the Compass to take you."

Milena continued: "Now, the Straightedge will allow an artist to—"

"What does the Compass look like?" Giacomo blurted out.

Milena looked annoyed.

"Sorry I cut you off, but I really need to know."

With a sigh, Milena picked up a book and flipped through its pages.

"It's a Compass," Savino said. "Hinge at the top, two pointy legs . . ."

"Here." Milena shoved an open book into Giacomo's arms. The page showed an illustration of the Creator's Compass.

The Compass in the image had long legs that tapered to points and a short handle at the top. Giacomo was deflated. "I'm not sure if it's the same as the one—"

"The same as *what* one?" Milena interrupted.

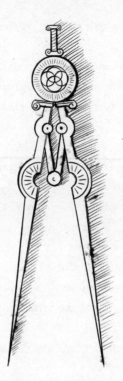

"I saw something inside the mandorla. It had the shape of a compass, but things were so chaotic and hazy I couldn't make it out clearly. I thought maybe it was the Creator's Compass."

"Why didn't you tell us this before?" Baldassare said excitedly. "Milena, did you see it too?"

"No. I just remember Giacomo yelling about something."

Baldassare whooped and slapped Giacomo on the back. "You may have just given us the break we've been waiting for!"

"How is this going to help us?" Savino scoffed. "Giacomo said he saw *a* compass, not *the* Compass."

"I suspect they are one and the same," Pietro said. "Because here's what I do know: in a life-or-death moment, Giacomo somehow tapped into a source of energy and was healed. When he came to, his Genius appeared. Then, when that very same Genius helped form the mandorla, the channel of energy opened again."

"You mean the Wellspring?" Milena asked.

"Yes. So this is no coincidence. Giacomo is meant to help us find the Sacred Tools."

Milena, Savino, and Aaminah stared at Giacomo with a mix of awe and skepticism, as if Pietro had proclaimed him the boy who would save all of Zizzola. Giacomo looked fixedly at the floor.

"When we found you, all you told us was that your Genius just showed up," Savino said. "You didn't say anything about nearly being killed or that you could open the Wellspring."

"Yeah, you might've mentioned you could tap into the ultimate force of energy in the universe," Milena said, with an edge in her voice.

Giacomo wrung his hands together. "I didn't know what happened that first time . . . or that it would happen again . . . I don't understand any of it!"

"The important thing now is that you work with Pietro to hone your skills," Baldassare said, trying to calm Giacomo. "My hope is that the Wellspring will tell you more about where the Compass might be located."

Giacomo backed away from Baldassare. "I don't want to open it again, not after what happened to Milena." He approached her, his emotions spilling out. "I'm so sorry. I've been avoiding you because I felt horrible about hurting you."

Milena ran her fingers across her bandage, her expression softening. "It was an accident."

"If I could take it back or make it right, I would."

"It's too late to change what happened." She pursed her lips, thinking. "But I know one way you can make it up to me."

Giacomo's heart sprang in his chest. "How?"

"You're going to help us find the Compass, Straightedge, and Pencil," she said with authority. "Whatever it takes."

His first instinct was to grab Mico and rush back to his room, but then Giacomo remembered how he'd ignored the one-legged beggar in the street. For so long, Giacomo had convinced himself he couldn't help people in need because he had nothing to offer—he was poor and weak and starving too. But now he had the ability to tap into enormous power. And besides, he owed Milena after what he'd done to her. If he turned his back on everyone now, how could he ever feel worthy of his Genius?

Step into the fear.

He met Milena's gaze, the candlelight glimmering in her brown eyes.

"I'll help you."

Following a night of restless sleep, Giacomo returned to Pietro's studio. His teacher was already up, feeding Tito. Milena stood at the table, poring over a dozen open books. Savino proceeded to work on his sculpture, which now resembled a fierce warrior swinging a sword. Aaminah tightened the strings of her viol. The dissident notes warbled into tune.

"Finally, you're up." Milena flipped a page.

Giacomo yawned. "Good morning to you too."

"I could barely sleep," she said. "I've been reading everything I could find in Baldassare's library about the Wellspring. Listen to what this artist wrote hundreds of years ago: 'For I hath witnessed it with mine own eyes. One moment it is calm and beautiful, the next, a harsh, unyielding land that burns skin from bone.'" She held up her wrapped arm. "Pretty accurate, don't you think?"

Before he could answer yes, Milena opened another book on top of the first. "And check out this map. It dates back over five hundred years and was drawn by Poggio Garrulous."

"The explorer?" Giacomo vaguely recalled learning his name from one of his teachers at the orphanage.

"And cartographer," Milena added. "He mapped the whole world."

Giacomo peered over her shoulder at a depiction of the three empires. Unlike most maps, this one showed the world split into two: in the left circle lay Rachana, the western half of Katunga above it; the other circle contained Zizzola and the eastern part of Katunga. Garrulous had drawn it as if two planets were colliding, with rays of light shooting out. Around the map were illustrations of the Creator's Compass, Straightedge, and Pencil.

"It looks like the mandorla," Giacomo remarked.

"I know. And here's what he wrote: 'From the void of the Wellspring, the Creator used his Sacred Tools to bring into being the three great empires. With his Compass, he created the light of the sun, so that the world could see; with his Straightedge, he created the Genius, a living force that bound the world together; and with his Pencil, he drew the mountains, the rivers, the forests, the animals, and the people, so the world could come to know itself.'"

"That's the creation story," Giacomo said dismissively. "Every kid in Zizzola has heard that."

"But not this next part." She kept on reading. "'Should humankind seek to possess all three Tools, be forewarned: misused, the Compass, Straightedge, and Pencil could undo the Creator's work. Like unraveling the thread from a tapestry, the Sacred Tools have the power to rip apart the fabric of reality.'"

"That makes it sound like the Tools could permanently open the Wellspring and allow it to spill out into our world." Giacomo shivered at the thought. "Everything would be wiped out. No one would survive."

Pietro took a seat with them at the table. "That's my fear too. Which is why we can't let Ugalino or Nerezza find the Tools first."

"But I can't believe either of them would actually use the Tools to destroy the world," Giacomo said. "It seems like a terrible plan. I mean, if the world falls apart, they'll be dead too."

"Correct, but simply the threat of using them could give Nerezza the upper hand. From what Baldassare has learned, she has her eye on taking over the other empires and spreading her rule across the world, starting with Zizzola's old enemy, Rachana."

"And what's Ugalino's plan?" Giacomo asked.

"He would use the Tools to overthrow Nerezza."

"Wouldn't that be a good thing? Isn't that what we're trying to do too?"

"The difference is, if Ugalino were to defeat her, he'd take power for himself," Pietro complained. "And an Ugalino-led empire would be equally as harsh and oppressive as what we have now. I wouldn't be surprised if he used the Tools to raze this city and build a new one of his own design. We'd be trading one tyrant for another."

Aaminah looked up from her instrument. "Signor Barrolo told me Ugalino took the gem out of his Genius's crown and carries it around on his staff. Is that true?"

Pietro nodded gravely. "The man has no respect for the sacred, or for the artist-Genius bond. Removing the gem may have given Ugalino more independence and power, but he's turned his Genius into nothing more than an empty, spiritless creature. And if he became the ruler of Zizzola, he'd do the exact same thing to its people."

Mico hopped back and forth on the table, chasing a bug. Giacomo couldn't imagine taking the gem off his crown. It seemed so cruel, like pulling someone's heart out of their chest.

Pietro stood and paced around the table, his voice becoming more and more emphatic. "In order for society to go through a true revival, whoever becomes Zizzola's new leader must allow everyone to express their voices. For decades, our empire has been controlled by just one vision—Nerezza's. It's as if people have been allowed to drink only from one well—a well that dried up long ago. Zizzola is dying of thirst, and it's up to us to bring it some new sources of water."

"This might sound dumb," Giacomo said, "but what do we do with the Compass and the other Tools once we find them?"

Savino chortled. "You're right, that did sound pretty stupid. We take out Nerezza and her army, obviously."

"That's only half of it," Pietro said. "We've recently discovered information suggesting that a Tulpa can only truly be destroyed with the Tools' combined force. Without the might of his Tulpa, or the power of the Sacred Tools, Ugalino would likely abandon his quest for domination."

His parents had once refused to attack the Tulpa. Would Giacomo make the same choice if given the opportunity? He wasn't sure, but for now, he wanted to help Pietro and Baldassare any way he could.

Giacomo looked over Milena's shoulder at the book. "What else did you find about the Wellspring?"

Pietro clapped his hands. "Enough reading! Giacomo, you're not going to discover the insight you need in any book. It's time to look within. That's why this morning we're going to learn about the triad."

"I thought you were going to teach me how to use the Wellspring to find the Compass," Giacomo said.

"The truth is, I can't teach you anything—"

"Then what am I doing here?"

"You didn't let me finish." Pietro rose to his feet with the help of his cane. "I can't teach you anything because the knowledge is already inside you. All I can do is guide you to recall it."

"How?"

"By reaching beyond the five senses. You've stepped onto the path of sacred geometry and the only chance you have at gaining control over the Wellspring is to continue on that journey. So here we go!" Pietro rapped his cane against the table leg to get everyone's attention.

"The triad—represented by the triangle—is the merging of three." Pietro motioned to Savino and Milena. "Could you two please demonstrate?"

With a grumble, Savino traded his sculpting stick for a pencil and joined Milena in the center of the room. They traced arcs in the air; Nero and Gaia each projected a glowing circle, and the two overlapped, creating a mandorla. Savino and Milena each made another stroke. From the top point of the almond shape, two lines extended down at angles, passing through the circles' center points.

"Two lines have emerged through the mandorla," Pietro continued. "But in order for them to create a triangle, they need a third factor to bind them. Aaminah, you're up."

Aaminah plucked a short string on her harp, creating a high-pitched note. Luna projected a yellow horizontal line that connected Savino's blue line and Milena's green line. A triangle came to light.

"From this unified form," Pietro said, "any number of other triangles can be created."

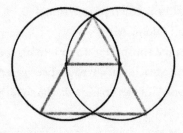

Aaminah plucked a flurry of notes. Multiple lines extended from different points on the triangle, illuminating a series of smaller and smaller triangles.

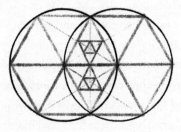

Pietro must have taken Giacomo's silence for confusion. He picked up a half-melted candle from the worktable. Its flame reflected in Pietro's cloudy eyes. "Here's another way to think of it: what is this candle made of?"

"A wick and a bunch of wax," Giacomo said, not sure what point Pietro was trying to make.

"And . . . ?" Pietro prompted.

Giacomo had to think about it for a second. "Fire?"

"Correct," Pietro said. "Only when you add that third element—the flame—do you have a candle."

"Or you can think of it like Aaminah's braids," Milena added, holding up one of Aaminah's long ropes of hair. "You can't make a braid out of two separate lengths of hair. You need a third length to tie them all together."

Pietro nodded approvingly. "Excellent example, Milena. When two opposites are unified by a third element, a new entity is created."

"Let me see if I understand," Giacomo said. "When I was living in the sewers, there was only me and my pencil. I could draw regular pictures that way, but I wasn't able to create sacred geometry shapes until my Genius showed up, which was the third element?"

"I think you're catching on," Pietro complimented.

Giacomo smiled proudly, then noticed that Mico was pecking at the table, still looking for the bug. Giacomo gave his Genius a nudge. "Pay attention, you need to know this stuff too."

Nero, Gaia, and Luna stopped projecting and the kids gathered around the worktable. Pietro opened a drawer and pulled out a small metal drafting compass that held a pencil.

"Now that you're familiar with the first three sacred geometry shapes, you have the basic formula for all creation." With his right hand, he planted the compass on a flat piece of paper and rotated it, drawing one circle, followed by another. The tips of his left fingers trailed behind, feeling the line as it created the mandorla. "The Compass generates the circle's center point." He took a long wooden straightedge and placed it over the circles' center points, then used a pencil to draw a line between them. "The Straightedge connects the points and the Pencil links them with a line. And from that line, an artist can create every shape in the universe." He finished by drawing the triangle.

Giacomo watched in amazement as Pietro drew without the aid of his Genius or his sight.

Pietro handed Giacomo the compass. "I want you to practice the first three shapes for the rest of the day, on paper."

"How is that going to help me find the Creator's Compass?"

"There are no easy answers, I'm afraid. The only way I know to find inspiration is to put in the time and effort. Art doesn't appear in the world as a finished masterpiece. It always begins like a lumpy mound of clay."

Like Savino's sculpture, Giacomo thought.

"But as you mold it, the clay begins to take the shape of something recognizable. If you want to create a work *of* art, you must work *at* art. Embrace the lumpy phase, and you may find what you're looking for."

"The lumpy phase . . ." Giacomo mumbled. "Great."

For the rest of the day, he spun the compass and used the straightedge and the pencil to draw lines and triangles. Circle, line, triangle. One, two, three. Circle, line, triangle. One, two, three. He repeated the process until his vision blurred and his hand cramped from clutching the compass's tiny handle.

When he had finished, he didn't feel any closer to finding the Creator's Compass, but Mico had become noticeably calmer. When he'd first started, Mico was hopping all over his paper, pecking in Giacomo's ear, and fluttering around his head. As Giacomo drew his last triangle, Mico sat obediently on his shoulder, watching Giacomo's every movement, as though he'd been pulled into a trance.

"The more you're able to internalize the sacred geometry shapes, the easier it will be to get your Genius to work with you," Milena explained when Giacomo asked her about Mico's improved behavior.

Giacomo yawned. "I think I've had enough internalizing for

one day. Good night." Aaminah and Savino had already gone to their rooms. Milena drooped over the books, seconds away from slumber. Gaia was curled up on the table, her long neck wrapped around her body, her head tucked under her wing. "You should get some sleep," Giacomo urged Milena. "The books will still be here tomorrow."

"I know," she said. "Only a few more pages."

"Come on, Mico." Giacomo's Genius followed him upstairs.

Giacomo lay in bed staring at the green velvet canopy above him. He'd drawn the mandorla and the triangle so many times, it looked like the fabric was embroidered with the pattern. He shut his eyes, but he could still see the glowing outline of the shapes.

After what felt like hours, the lines of the pattern shifted and rearranged, taking the forms of his father and mother.

They appeared in the villa's hallway again, this time hovering a few inches off the floor. When Giacomo approached, they floated away, as if they hadn't noticed he was there.

"Wait!" he called out. "Tell me why you didn't help the Supreme Creator. Why didn't you try to stop the Tulpa?"

His parents vanished through a door that resembled the one to Baldassare's art vault. A moment later, they reappeared in a painting on the wall. They drifted into the frame, holding hands.

"The Compass is within you," his mother told him.

"Let Garrulous be your guide," his father said.

Suddenly, the painting fell off the wall, hitting the floor with a thunderous crash. The frame split, tearing the canvas in half. The images of his parents smeared, then dripped onto the floor in a puddle of colors.

Waking with a start, Giacomo shot out of bed, casting off the covers. Before he realized what he was doing, he had his sketchbook in hand. He flung the door open, then stopped himself.

"Mico, sorry, I almost forgot—"

His Genius zipped past his head, already awake and ready for action.

Giacomo ran downstairs and bolted into the studio. "Master Pietro, wake up! I think I know how to find the Compass!"

Minutes later, everyone was gathered in the courtyard, looking groggy and annoyed that Giacomo had roused them from the comfort of their beds in the middle of the night. Giacomo figured the courtyard would be the best place to try his idea—if things got out of control, at least he wouldn't bring down the villa on top of them.

Giacomo convinced Savino to help him carry the globe from Baldassare's study. Savino cradled the top, while Giacomo struggled with the heavy base. By the time they made it outside, Giacomo's arms felt ready to rip off. He dropped the metal stand with a clang, its heavy base cracking one of the stones on the ground.

Baldassare cringed. "Careful, please!"

"Sorry!" Giacomo righted the globe, then spun it until Zizzola faced him.

"So sewer-boy thinks he can crack a millennia-old mystery in one night?" Savino said. "This I have to see."

Pietro shuffled over to Tito. Freed from his cramped alcove, Tito stood nearly ten feet tall.

"How are you going to find the Compass with the globe?" Aaminah asked.

"Not only the globe," Giacomo said. "I'm going to combine it with the Wellspring to create a kind of location device."

"Inspired thinking," Baldassare complimented him. "Where did you get this idea?"

"It sort of came to me while I was asleep. I guess what Pietro taught me about the triangle sank in." *When two opposites are unified by a third element, a new entity is created.* Pietro's words, seeing Garrulous's map, his vision of the Compass inside the mandorla, the dream of his parents: they all must have been swirling around in his brain until something sparked.

"With Tito, I'll be able to keep the Wellspring's energy contained," Pietro said, relaying the details he and Giacomo had discussed before waking everyone. "Once we get it stabilized, I'd like you to man the globe, Savino."

Giacomo and Pietro had agreed that Savino would be best suited for the job. Giacomo selfishly didn't want Milena in harm's way again. Or Aaminah, for that matter.

As expected, Savino embraced the danger. "Tell me what you need me to do."

Milena, Aaminah, and Baldassare backed away, retreating to the edge of the courtyard. Giacomo and Pietro stood with their Geniuses facing the globe, Savino behind them.

"Ready?" Pietro asked.

"Ready," Giacomo answered.

Pietro nodded and drew a circle in the air with his brush. Tito's gem projected an orange ring, matching it perfectly to the circumference of the globe.

"Bring it to light," Pietro instructed.

Holding his sketchbook in his left hand, Giacomo arced his

pencil across the page. Mico projected a red circle and moved it closer to the globe. As Giacomo's circle overlapped Pietro's, he braced himself for the Wellspring's onslaught.

Bright light filled the almond shape of the mandorla and beams of light shot out from the top and bottom, like in Garrulous's map.

Freezing air streamed out, sending a shiver through Giacomo. Thankfully, the intensity of the Wellspring's energy was kept in check by Pietro's and Tito's combined power.

Step into the fear.

Giacomo held his circle steady and moved closer. Swirls of color cascaded inside the Wellspring. Periodically, an orange or blue burst pelted Giacomo in the face. He pressed forward.

"Are you all right?" Pietro hollered above the howling wind.

"I'm okay!" Giacomo put his face as close to the mandorla as he could withstand and stared into the Wellspring. The glow dissipated slightly, the temperature evened out, and the colors vanished. He started to make out an image—a magnified, bird's-eye view of Virenzia, with the Piazza Nerezza at its center, similar to the view he'd seen looking down from the hill.

"It's working!" Giacomo exclaimed. "Savino, you're up! Turn the globe."

Without hesitation, Savino spun it. Virenzia vanished and the landscape blurred past Giacomo's vision.

"Not so fast!" he shouted.

Savino slowed the rotation and the image came into focus. Giacomo was now looking over the rolling hills of the countryside. "It's amazing. Like I'm flying over Zizzola."

"Do you see the Compass?" Savino asked.

"Not yet."

They kept at it for nearly an hour, with Savino tilting and rotating the globe as Giacomo scanned the magnified landscape. The problem was, he didn't know exactly what he was looking for. Would the Compass just be floating in the air? He swept over the peaks of Rapallicci in the north, all the way down to the chain of islands off Mardovino's southern tip. After searching across the whole empire, Giacomo was beginning to fear his idea was a failure.

But as he circled back through central Zizzola, something caught his eye—a glow from behind a rushing waterfall.

"I think I see it!" he said through gritted teeth.

"Where?" Baldassare demanded. "We need to know exactly where!"

Instinctively, Giacomo reached into the mandorla. It felt like sticking his hand in a fire. He steeled himself and fought past the discomfort. His view zoomed down, past an ancient-looking tree, through a waterfall, and into a cave. A glowing shape hovered above the floor. It looked like two pyramids stuck together at their bases. Inside it floated the Creator's Compass—the same one he'd seen in Baldassare's book.

He reached out again, his fingers grazing the sacred geometry shape. A burning pain shot up his arm. He screamed and jumped away from the mandorla, falling to the ground.

"Tito, shut it!" Pietro commanded. The orange ray faded. The mandorla split apart and the Wellspring vanished.

Aaminah hurried to Giacomo's side. "Are you all right? Let me see." Giacomo kept his eyes shut tight, afraid to look at his injury. "It's . . . it's not that bad." She sounded surprised.

Giacomo checked his arm. The sleeve of his nightclothes had

been burned away and his skin was swollen and red. But compared to what had happened to Milena, he'd come away relatively unscathed.

"Maybe it's because Pietro was keeping things under control," Aaminah speculated.

Baldassare came up behind him and yanked him to his feet. "So did you get a good look? Do you know where it is?"

"I think so," Giacomo said. He pointed to an area on the globe in central Zizzola. "It was around here, near a tree that had a twisted trunk and bare branches. And there was a river that led to a waterfall. The Compass was hidden in a cave behind the falls."

"Ring any bells?" Pietro asked Baldassare.

He stroked his mustache. "I'm afraid not."

"Can you draw what you saw?" Milena asked.

"Sure. I think so."

They went to Baldassare's study, where Giacomo sketched the location of the Compass. Milena sat next to him, bouncing her knee anxiously. While they waited, Enzio shuffled downstairs, hair askew, looking particularly disgruntled.

"You woke me up with all that racket outside," he said. "What's going on?"

"Giacomo and his Genius may have located the Creator's Compass," Aaminah said. "Isn't that incredible?"

Enzio shrugged. "If you say so." He slumped into a chair.

Giacomo completed the drawing and handed his sketchbook to Milena.

She jumped up. "I've seen a place like that in one of these books!" Milena rushed to the shelves, scanned the spines, and pulled out a thick tome. She frantically flipped through the pages until she found what she was looking for. "This is it!" She held open an illustration of a tree, river, and waterfall that looked remarkably similar to the ones Giacomo had sketched. His heartbeat quickened.

"It's called the Cave of Alessio," Milena said, then read from the book: "'In the fifth century, age of the tetrad, Alessio the Archer saved the Zizzolan Empire from the invading Rachanan barbarians, but was mortally wounded in the battle. He was laid to rest outside the cave. A few days later, a stalk sprouted from his burial site, eventually growing into a tree that still stands, three thousand years later.'"

"If that place is so legendary, how come nobody ever noticed a giant compass lying around?" Enzio asked. Giacomo was surprised he was showing any interest, but he had raised a good point.

"It is curious . . ." Pietro mused. "I suspect it's somehow hidden in plain sight. Perhaps Giacomo's ability to harness the Wellspring has allowed him to see what's invisible to the ordinary eye."

"The Cave of Alessio is here," Baldassare said, pointing to a spot in the middle of the map spread out on his desk. "It's just south of Terra della Morte, nearly seven hundred miles from Virenzia, as the Genius flies."

Savino nodded as he looked over the map. "The best route would be to cross the Calbrini Range, then head west. I bet I could get us there in a month."

"You'll have plenty of time to plan the journey," Pietro said. "You're not leaving quite yet."

"Why not?" Baldassare said. "Every hour that passes gives Ugalino a chance to find the Compass before us."

"The plan was to locate all three Tools, then send out a search party," Pietro argued.

Baldassare's cheeks burned red. He looked at Giacomo and the others. "If you'll excuse us, Pietro and I need to speak privately."

Pietro grimaced and crossed his arms.

The group filed out and Savino closed the door behind them.

Enzio slunk back to his room, while Giacomo waited in the hall with the others. Through the doors, he heard Baldassare's and Pietro's muffled voices yelling at each other, but he couldn't make out what they were saying.

Savino paced. "They have to let us go."

"We're not ready," Milena said. "We need time to prepare, gather supplies."

"We've been preparing ever since Signor Barrolo brought us here," Savino argued.

"It would be nice to let our Geniuses get out and really spread their wings," Aaminah said. "Luna hates being inside all the time." Her Genius whistled in agreement.

"I'm with them," Giacomo said to Milena. "I think we should get the Compass first, then regroup to find the other Tools."

"Who says you're even coming?" Savino said.

"Why wouldn't I? I'm the one who found the Compass."

"You just started your lessons. You're not ready."

"Why do you have such a problem with me?"

Savino stepped close. "Look, you might have some special Wellspring power, but I've been working my butt off for years. Milena and Aaminah too. We earned this."

"And I haven't?"

"You've been hiding out in the sewers, like a coward."

"I was surviving! I'd like to see how long you'd last down there."

"Longer than you, I bet!" Savino jabbed him in the shoulder. "You're not coming. End of discussion."

Giacomo knocked Savino's hand away. "You don't get to tell me what to do!"

The doors to the study swung open, putting an end to their shouting match. Pietro came out first, his cane clacking on the floor. By the scowl on his face, it looked like he'd lost the argument.

"You'll leave in two days' time" was all Pietro said as he passed them, on his way to the cellar.

Baldassare emerged a moment later, a satisfied look on his face. "In the meantime, get some rest. You four will need all your energy for this journey."

Savino shot Giacomo a dirty look. "He's going too?"

"Of course," Baldassare answered.

Giacomo smirked, making sure Savino saw it.

"Why?" Savino whined. "Giacomo hasn't even finished his training. He just got his Genius!"

"You sound like Pietro. Giacomo's going. And I won't hear any more about it." As Baldassare headed back upstairs, Savino stomped away in a huff.

Milena looked at Giacomo sternly. "You really think you're ready for this?"

"Absolutely." Giacomo's voice cracked and he cleared his throat. "Why wouldn't I be?"

Because I have no idea what I'm doing.

With a feeble wave good night, Giacomo retreated to his room.

THE CHASM

By the next morning, everyone was in preparation mode. Baldassare told them to travel with only what they could carry on their backs. For Giacomo, that meant a change of clothes, a waterskin, a bedroll, his sketchbook, and pencils. When he asked Baldassare about food and cooking supplies, he replied with a curt "It's being taken care of." He wouldn't provide any other details, but Giacomo couldn't imagine he'd send four children across the Supreme Creator's realm alone.

When they all gathered in the studio, Pietro confirmed as much, but he was also uninformed about Baldassare's plan.

"My instructions were to prepare you to release the Compass. So that's what I'm going to do." He still sounded bitter about losing the argument with Baldassare.

"What's there to know? Nero and I can handle it," Savino bragged.

Pietro whacked Savino's foot with his cane. "This isn't a joke!"

Savino jumped back. "Okay, okay . . ."

Pietro proceeded. "The Compass is locked inside one of the most impenetrable shapes of sacred geometry—the octahedron."

Giacomo glanced at Pietro. *So that double pyramid does have a name.*

"How do we open it?" Milena asked.

"The ancient texts say that only the Creator's living force can break the shield."

"A Genius!" Milena said. "In the creation myth, the Genius is called a 'living force.'"

"Precisely," Pietro said, then addressed only Milena, Savino, and Aaminah. "Ugalino will be able to release the Compass with his Genius alone. Luna, Nero, and Gaia are young and their gems are still quite small. However, by combining their powers, you should create enough energy to crack the octahedron. Then you must pry it open, like a knife opening an oyster's shell."

"Mico can help too," Giacomo offered.

"The three of them will be able to handle it," Pietro said firmly.

Giacomo shrank back. "If you only need three Geniuses, why am I even going?"

"Good question," Savino muttered.

"I told Baldassare the same thing," Pietro said. "You're not ready."

"Thanks for the vote of confidence."

"But then he reminded me there is a grim reality we must face. Should one of you . . . fail to arrive at the destination—"

"You mean die," Savino said.

"Yes. Should that happen, you will still have three Geniuses."

"So I'm only valuable if one of them gets killed?" Giacomo couldn't believe what he was hearing.

"It's not like that," Aaminah assured him.

Pietro felt for a chair and took a seat. "You four are likely the last generation in Zizzola to have Geniuses. If I had it my way, none of you would go. But I can't keep you hidden in my studio forever. I've been here too long as it is. It's time for Geniuses to be out in the world again. Is it dangerous? Absolutely. But anything worth doing requires risk."

Giacomo realized he'd been thinking selfishly. This mission was bigger than him, bigger than all of them. He should be proud to take on the responsibility of helping his fellow students.

"Let's do this for the next generation of artists," Giacomo said. "For everyone in Zizzola."

Milena and Aaminah smiled. With a curt nod, Savino agreed.

The evening of their departure arrived. The night sky looked the same as the hundreds that had come before, but to Giacomo it felt different, like the air pressed a little heavier against his skin. Following Baldassare's instructions, Giacomo headed to the courtyard at midnight, when the group would set off under cover of darkness.

With Mico on his shoulder, Giacomo walked out of the villa and found thirteen scruffy, armored men and women waiting. *These were their escorts?*

They didn't look like soldiers, exactly. Their armor was made up of a hodgepodge of metal shoulder, forearm, and leg plates, tattered leather jerkins that had seen more than a few battles, and skirts and sleeves of chain mail. A few of them wore helmets of various shapes, some visored, others open-faced with angled neck protectors. They were armed with a mix of crossbows, swords, and polearms.

Baldassare spoke to a dark-skinned, muscular man who Giacomo assumed was the leader of the group. The tip of his left ear had been shorn off, along with the hair above it. A nasty scar started from the bald spot, ran across his jutting cheekbone, and ended at the corner of his mouth. What hair remained hung in tangles past his right shoulder. He stood in a wide stance. In his meaty hands, he held the thick hilt of his sword, its long blade pointed down, piercing the ground by his feet.

Giacomo shuffled closer so he could hear what they were talking about.

"You still think we might run into that monster out there?" the man asked.

Baldassare nodded. "Ugalino and his Tulpa are on the move. Is that going to be a problem?"

"Not at all," the man replied.

Giacomo walked over to Milena, Savino, and Aaminah, who each carried a canvas bag packed full of supplies. They all wore cloaks over their regular clothes, and Milena had traded her long dress for a pair of brown breeches and tall leather boots.

Aaminah was clad in instruments. A smaller version of her viol was strapped across her back and her flute was tucked into her belt. She slipped a handheld harp into her satchel and closed the flap over it.

"So I guess this is Baldassare's plan to keep us safe?" Giacomo commented.

"Mercenaries," Savino said, disgusted. "I can't believe Signor Barrolo is putting our lives in their hands."

"Why? What's wrong with mercenaries?" Giacomo asked. "They look pretty tough."

"They're just hired muscle," Savino complained. "They're not going to care about this mission, only about getting paid."

Baldassare shook the brutish man's hand and headed toward the children, smiling.

Savino fastened a hatchet to his belt, next to his sculpting tools. "You really think we can trust these guys?" he asked Baldassare point-blank. "The second we leave the villa, they might turn us over to the Supreme Creator."

Baldassare dismissed the notion. "Mercenaries are only loyal to one thing—money. And I'm paying them a small fortune, far more than Ozo Mori could ever hope to collect from the Supreme Creator.

"Ozo Mori?" Savino said. "Sounds like a Rachanan name."

Baldassare nodded. "He has a few in his ranks as well."

"You're sending us off with the enemy?" Savino said accusingly.

"Rachana and Zizzola haven't been at war for a long time," Milena reminded him.

"Still, I don't like it," Savino muttered.

"Now, I've instructed Ozo to stay off the main roads and avoid villages and cities," Baldassare explained. "We can't risk anyone spotting your Geniuses. But it means you'll be roughing it for a while."

"Dirt between my toes . . . sounds perfect to me," Aaminah said.

Giacomo realized he'd lost track of Mico. He spotted his Genius buzzing around Ozo's head, chirping curiously. Ozo spit at Mico, who darted back to Giacomo's side. Giacomo wanted to yell at the man, but took one look at his massive sword and kept his mouth shut.

"Ozo isn't exactly an art lover," Baldassare admitted, "but he's worked for me before and always comes through."

Enzio emerged from the villa, carrying a heavy-looking trunk. He dropped it at Ozo's feet and went back inside, without even acknowledging the fact that Giacomo and the others were leaving.

Baldassare led Giacomo and his companions over to Ozo, who was busy opening the trunk of money. Countless gold and silver coins were piled to the brim. It was more *impronta* than Giacomo had ever seen in his life. The rest of the mercenaries gathered around, ogling the loot.

"This is the first half of the money, which I'm giving to Ozo to distribute," Baldassare told the soldiers-for-hire. "You can all claim the rest once you return—with the children *and* the Compass."

Ozo nodded. "Fair enough." He sized up the group of children. Giacomo tensed as Ozo's severe stare landed on him. Up close, he noticed how the man's scar pulled the left side of his mouth into a permanent frown.

"I have three rules," Ozo said in a deep, gravelly voice. "Follow me. Stay close. And do everything I say." He walked down the line of mercenaries. "Now meet the men and women I've entrusted with your safety."

Ozo slapped the shoulder of the first man, a towering mass of flesh and hair. He held a long wooden crossbow across his right shoulder. A thick silver ring hung from his nose. "This is my second in command. You can call him the Bull."

The Bull flared his nostrils and snorted his hello.

To his right was a second crossbowman with intense bulging eyes. "This is Accosius." Standing next to him were two archers, each carrying a bundle of arrows tied at their waist. One was a tall woman with an eye patch, the other a man, short and stocky. "Next up—Malocchio and Baby Cannoli," Ozo said, before moving down the line.

"I'm Old Dino and these are my boys, Big Dino and Little Dino," said an elderly man clutching a polearm with a curved, jagged blade. His two sons, one heavyset, the other bone thin, each held similarly frightening-looking scythes.

Ozo kept going down the group. "And these three are the finest individuals to wield swords across all three empires, next to me of course. Sforza, Spike, and Sveva."

Sforza snarled, exposing yellowed, rotten teeth. Spike adjusted his round helmet. Attached to it was chain mail that covered his face, except for two black, beady eyes.

Sveva looked around, distracted by a fly buzzing near her head. Before Giacomo knew what was happening, Sveva's blade whipped through the air and the two halves of the fly fell to the dirt.

Giacomo flinched. "Stay clear of her, okay?" he whispered to Mico.

Ozo arrived at the last two men in line. One wore armored gauntlets and carried a double-headed ax. "Meet Zatto the Beheader." A wide smile emerged from within Zatto's bushy black beard.

"An absolute pleasure to make your acquaintance," Zatto said in a gentle voice that didn't match his vicious looks.

"And finally, our secret weapon, Valcaro. Handgunner."

Valcaro was clad in black armor from head to toe, his face hidden behind a cylindrical helm with two slits for eyes. Over his shoulder, he held a long wooden pole with a vented metal tube attached to its end. It didn't look as imposing as the other weapons, but Giacomo knew it was equally deadly, able to fire steel balls at tremendous speeds.

With the introductions out of the way, Ozo's face hardened. "Now, I want to get clear of Virenzia before dawn and we got

149

a lot of ground to cover, so say your goodbyes and we'll get moving."

While Ozo divided up the money among his mercenaries, Giacomo and his companions gathered around Baldassare and Pietro. Savino gave the men firm handshakes.

"Thank you both, for giving me a home . . . for keeping Luna safe." Aaminah hugged Baldassare, then Pietro.

Milena gently touched the back of Pietro's hand. "You've taught me so much. We'll be back soon with the Compass, I promise."

"Watch out for one another and stay alert," Pietro urged.

"We will," Giacomo said. "Goodbye."

Pietro's expression turned grave. "Ugalino and his Tulpa are out there somewhere. Never forget that your lives and your Geniuses' lives will be in constant danger. Fail, and any hope for Virenzia's renaissance will die with you."

Giacomo felt as though Pietro had saddled him with a heavy yoke. The others stared at their teacher with wide, stunned eyes. No one knew what to say.

"I think what he means is 'good luck,'" Baldassare said, trying to lighten Pietro's bleakness. He gave a quick blow on his whistle and the four Geniuses flocked to him. He fed them pellets of food from his cupped hand. "And good luck to you too, feathered friends. May you inspire and protect your artists."

"What was rule number one?" Ozo hollered from across the courtyard, where he and his team were ready to depart.

"Follow you!" Milena replied. "We're coming!"

Giacomo slung his bag over his shoulder as he and the others hustled after Ozo and his mercenaries, who were already ascending the hill behind the villa. His nerves still rattled by Pietro's grim warning, Giacomo took one last look at Virenzia disappearing into the fog and a frightening thought struck him. *I might never see my home again.*

Ozo led the group up to the ridge, then down the other side, along a craggy trail. Half his troops marched in front of the children, the other half behind. Anytime Giacomo's pace slowed, the Bull shoved him to keep him moving.

After a couple of hours, they broke from the main route. Giacomo was about to ask where they were going, when he saw why they'd detoured. Ozo had a team of horses waiting for them, packed with supplies, ready to carry them the rest of the way.

"Mount up, everyone!" Ozo ordered.

By the time each mercenary claimed a steed, there were only two left. Giacomo was about to ask Milena if she wanted to ride with him, but Aaminah beat him to it. The girls jumped onto the back of a white horse with a brown mane, while Giacomo was forced to sit behind Savino on a spotted gray mount that seemed more the size of a pony than a full-grown horse.

"I think we got stuck with the runt," Savino complained.

They trekked all night, climbing higher and higher into the mountains that bordered Virenzia to the north. As darkness departed, the stars vanished into the dawn's pink sky. The sun crept over the mountains in the east.

"Can we take a break?" Giacomo called out.

Ozo stopped his horse and whipped around. "Oh, do you have to pee?"

"Actually, I do, thanks for asking—"

"Then hold it! We stop when I say we stop." Ozo's horse continued on.

Aaminah pulled out her flute. "How about some music?" As she played a warm, happy tune, Luna projected rolling waves of light around them.

"And no music!" Ozo barked. "You trying to call attention to us?"

"Sorry," Aaminah said, sheepishly tucking her flute back into her belt.

Giacomo leaned over to her. "I thought it sounded nice," he whispered.

"These guys seem more like captors than escorts," Savino muttered.

At least their Geniuses were enjoying themselves. No longer constrained by the villa, Mico, Nero, Luna, and Gaia glided overhead, chirping happily. Giacomo imagined himself jumping on Mico's back and being carried away into the clouds. *Maybe someday, when Mico grows bigger.*

After several more hours, and only one short break to refill their waterskins, they emerged above the tree line and picked up a rocky trail that ran along the ridge. Without any tree cover, the wind whipped the kids' faces and the sun burned hot. Giacomo squinted, trying to make out the end of the mountain range, but it seemed to extend forever.

"Time to set up camp," Ozo informed everyone.

"Finally . . ." Giacomo jumped off his horse. But then he looked back and saw why Ozo was so willing to stop—a mass of gray clouds threatened to overtake them. Thunder rumbled and a bolt of lightning shot out of the sky.

Ozo paused at a flat plateau dotted with moss-covered boulders and ringed by pine trees. A large shelf of rock jutted from the mountainside, forming an overhang.

"Gather firewood," Ozo ordered. "We'll take cover here."

While the Dino family tied up the horses, Giacomo plunked down on a fallen tree trunk and scarfed up a few salty pieces of dried meat. By the time he finished, the mercenaries had already gathered a pile of dead branches and were crowded under the rocky ledge. As the first fat drops of rain plopped on Giacomo's head, he and his companions went to join the mercenaries.

Ozo waved them off. "This is our shelter. You and your Geniuses find your own." It was clear from Ozo's tone that the matter wasn't up for discussion, but Savino didn't get the message.

"Baldassare paid you to keep us safe," he argued. "This shelter is as much ours as it is yours."

"He paid us to deliver you to the Cave of Alessio and back home, not coddle you all the way," Ozo said.

"Let us in!" Savino reached for his hatchet.

Aaminah put a hand on Savino's arm, stopping him. "Don't," she whispered. "We'll make do."

With a grunt, Savino brushed her off and stomped away.

Thunder rolled and buckets of rain poured from the sky. The Geniuses took refuge in the trees, while the horses huddled underneath them, whinnying anxiously. Savino paced back and forth, rubbing his arms to keep warm. Giacomo crouched with Milena and Aaminah between two boulders.

In the mercenaries' shelter, the handgunner, Valcaro—still wearing his helmet—lit a fire with a long match from his belt.

Malocchio tracked Savino with her one good eye. "Aw, poor little Genius-boy, feeling cold?" she called out mockingly. "Sure is nice and cozy in here, ain't it?" The mercenaries guffawed and hollered, which only made Savino redder in the face.

Aaminah stared at the boulders surrounding them and jumped up, bouncing on her tiptoes. "Who needs them? We can make our own shelter!"

"How?" Savino said, looking around. "There aren't any other outcroppings or caves around here."

"We just need to get a little creative," Aaminah said. "Savino and Giacomo, gather the densest pine branches you can find. Milena, help me collect some twigs and dead branches before they get too soaked."

While the girls scoured the ground, Savino scaled one of the trees, cutting down pine boughs with his hatchet. Giacomo stood below, catching them as they fell. Following Aaminah's instructions, he laid the boughs across the tops of three boulders, creating a thick canopy. When he was finished, it resembled a small hut with rocks for walls and an evergreen roof. Aaminah ushered everyone inside, where they huddled together in the makeshift shelter. Other than a few drips, Aaminah's structure kept most of the rain off them.

"How'd you learn to build something like this?" Giacomo asked her.

"When you grow up in the country, you learn to use what nature gives you," Aaminah replied.

Milena dropped a handful of small sticks on the ground. Aaminah held two small rocks in her hands and struck them against each other, creating a spark. After a couple of tries, the tinder lit up. She blew gently on the tiny fire, encouraging the flames to grow. The warmth dried Giacomo's damp skin.

Savino pulled a carving tool from his belt and began whittling a chunk of wood. He glanced up at the pine branch roof, which sagged in the middle. "If this thing holds up until morning, I'll be surprised," he grumbled.

"Why do you have to be so grumpy all the time?" Aaminah shot back. "We're dry, we have a fire, we're all together . . . enjoy it!"

While Aaminah tried to brighten their damp spirits by singing a song, Giacomo took out his sketchbook and began drawing. Soon though, the day's travel began to wear on him, and he fell asleep with his pencil still in his hand.

* * *

Giacomo woke the next morning to Ozo's voice booming, "Pack it up! We're moving on!"

He scrambled out of the shelter, which had kept them dry all night. Outside, he found Savino admitting to Aaminah that maybe she had some useful survival skills after all.

Giacomo devoured a cracker, washed it down with a swig of water, and hopped onto the spotted horse, behind Savino.

The group continued along the ridgeline at a slow trot. Thankfully, the skies had cleared and Virenzia was far behind them; all signs pointed to a smooth journey. In a couple of weeks, they'd make it to the Cave of Alessio and the Compass would be theirs.

For the next seven days, they traveled without incident, not counting all the times Ozo yelled at one of the children for falling behind, or for taking too long to eat, or for looking at him the wrong way. But despite his gruffness, Ozo seemed to genuinely take their safety and the mission seriously. He found a secluded path through a narrow valley that snaked between the mountains of the Calbrini Range; in order to make up for any lost time he pushed the horses to gallop for short bursts.

Then one morning, when they were more than halfway to the Cave of Alessio, Ozo called out, "Hold up, we got a problem!"

The team caught up to Ozo, who had stopped where the trail abruptly disappeared. Cut into the earth was a deep gorge with sheer cliffs, over a hundred feet wide. An imposing stone statue, more than twice Ozo's height, towered on either side of the path. The statues stood sentry, their swords forming an archway. Vines and moss covered their legs and torsos, their faces worn smooth by time. One statue's nose had broken off, while the other had lost multiple fingers.

"I passed through here a few years ago," Ozo grumbled. "And I definitely remember there being a bridge."

Milena ran her hand along the noseless statue's stone armor. "Incredible . . . Looks like it was carved from one huge chunk of rock. Savino, you should check this out."

"In a second," Savino said, busy studying the map he'd brought.

"We'll follow the edge of the gorge south and go around," Ozo said.

"But that's going to add at least another week to our journey," Savino argued. "On my map, it looks like the gorge starts narrowing just north of where we are. Maybe we can find somewhere to cross."

Ozo snatched the map out of Savino's hand and tossed it over the edge of the cliff, where a gust of wind carried it away. "I make the route. Not you."

Savino's hand shot to his hatchet. He yanked it from his belt and took a step toward Ozo. "That was my only map!"

In a flash, Zatto the Beheader drew his ax and swung it at Savino. The curved blade lopped the hatchet's head clean off its handle. Savino jumped back.

"Next time he cuts off body parts," Ozo threatened.

Zatto's fierce expression softened into a polite smile. "But I'd rather not. So please don't give me a reason to."

Savino stared in disbelief at the stump of wood left in his hand. He tossed it to the ground without another word.

"If you need to answer nature's call, now's the time to do it," the Bull called out. "We leave in two minutes."

The male mercenaries dismounted, lined up along the edge of the gorge, and emptied their bladders over the side, their streams of urine turning to mist. The women found privacy behind some shrubs. Giacomo sat at the base of the noseless statue and leaned against its moss-covered legs, relieved to be off his horse for a couple minutes.

A second later, the ground rumbled. The statue shifted, and Giacomo shot to his feet, convinced he'd accidentally toppled it.

But the statue didn't fall. *It's moving on its own!* He froze as its leg rose up, ripping away the vines that clung to it. The statue shook its head, tossing off chunks of moss and dust, covering Giacomo.

"Uh . . . guys?" Giacomo said, still not believing what he was seeing. Mico let out a *whoop, whoop, whoop,* alerting everyone. The horses got spooked and ran, tearing off along the ridge, where they disappeared around a bend.

Milena whirled around. "What did you do?"

"Nothing! The statue started moving on its own!" Giacomo stumbled away, accidentally backing into the second statue, which also groaned to life. Its left hand reached out, as if searching for its missing fingers. The two statues dislodged their crossed swords and swung at Giacomo, who stood paralyzed with terror.

He felt a meaty hand grab the back of his collar and yank him out of the path of the stone blades. Ozo hurled Giacomo to the ground, then faced the noseless statue, sword drawn. A stony fist swung down hard. Ozo met it with his steel and sparks flew. The force of the blow drove Ozo to one knee. He rolled right to avoid the next strike. Giacomo scrambled away on all fours, Mico hovering close.

"Savino, we have to cross now!" Milena shouted. "Aaminah, we'll need you too!" They hurried to the edge of the chasm and looked across.

Giacomo tried to join them, but the statues kept targeting him, knocking aside any mercenary who got in the way. Arrows pinged off the statues' torsos; swords and spears clinked uselessly against their stony skin. The Bull fired a shot from his crossbow, but before he could reload, the fingerless statue walloped him, sending him tumbling across the ground. The Bull dug his feet into the earth, slowing himself to a stop an inch away from the chasm's edge.

"Valcaro, fire!" Ozo ordered. The gun-carrying mercenary dropped to one knee, struck a large match against his armor, and lit the barrel's fuse. The gun burst with smoke and flame, causing Valcaro to recoil. A metal ball blasted away a chunk of the noseless statue's right shoulder.

"Reload!" Ozo commanded.

The mercenaries formed a wall between the statues and Valcaro, protecting their handgunner as he furiously packed powder into his gun's barrel.

Giacomo looked past the line of mercenaries to the cliff, where Milena drew brushstrokes in the air. Gaia projected a line of glowing hexagons, starting at the edge of the cliff. The shapes interlocked, forming a narrow bridge that extended partway over the gorge, its surface glimmering like green glass.

As her last row of hexagons flashed on and off, Milena yelled, "Gaia's reached her limit! She can't project any more! Your turn, Savino!"

Savino whistled and his Genius flew to the end of Milena's section. Savino swiped his pencil and Nero projected one hexagon after another, extending the interlocking pattern farther out over the gorge. His shimmering strip of blue reached halfway across before Nero's gem flickered, signaling that his power had also been depleted.

A horrifying scream snapped Giacomo's attention back to the mercenaries. Accosius was looking up at the fingerless statue, crossbow raised, his already bulging eyes swollen even wider with fear. His legs were stuck to the ground, encased in a stony skin. Like a pond freezing over, the stone crept all the way up Accosius's body. His scream didn't cease until his head was entombed in rock.

"Don't look those things in the eyes!" Ozo shouted.

The noseless statue turned in Giacomo's direction, and the boy averted his gaze. Valcaro fired off another shot. Broken rocks erupted from the statue's chest. But despite the gaping hole in the middle of its body, it whirled back around and stalked toward the handgunner.

Valcaro reloaded, but it seemed to take forever. As the statue stomped closer, Giacomo fumbled in his satchel and pulled out his sketchbook and pencil. Frantic, he flipped to a blank page and drew circle after circle. Mico buzzed overhead, targeting circular red blasts at the approaching statue. The circles hit, but only chipped away tiny shards of stone. It would take hours to do enough damage to bring it down. *We might not even have a few minutes,* Giacomo realized.

Aggravated, the noseless statue turned again and charged at Giacomo. Mico made a beeline for its head, trying to distract it. The statue stopped and swatted, but Mico dodged and landed on its forehead. He bent down and jabbed his beak at its eye. The statue raised an open palm and swung. Mico squeaked and zipped out of the way just in time, causing the statue to slap itself in the face. It stumbled backward, stunned by its own blow.

"Mico, get out of there!" Giacomo screamed. But the warning came too late. The stone monster backhanded the tiny Genius, swatting it out of the sky. Giacomo felt a tremendous force slam into him. He hit the ground hard.

Giacomo's head rang. Through his blurry vision, he saw the statue's two massive feet stamping straight for him.

Ozo roared, "Now!" He and the Bull yanked on opposite ends of a chain, pulling it taut and tripping the statue. As it toppled, a shadow fell over Giacomo. He rolled out of the way a split second before the statue slammed into the earth, shaking the ground and kicking up a cloud of dust. The stone giant lay still.

Dirt-covered and dizzy, Giacomo rose to his knees, dimly aware that Aaminah was playing her flute near the cliff's edge. With each staccato note, Luna projected yellow hexagons that attached to the blue ones, extending the bridge.

Giacomo picked up his sketchbook and staggered over to Mico. He scooped up his limp Genius and held it in his cupped hands.

"Mico!"

The Genius let out a single chirp and fluttered its wings weakly.

"You're okay . . ." Giacomo said, relieved.

"Giacomo, we need your help!" Milena yelled. He rushed to the edge of the cliff. The other three Geniuses hovered over the chasm at even intervals, projecting portions of the bridge, but there was a gap between the end of Aaminah's section and the other side. "You have to finish it," Milena said.

She might as well have asked him to fly them across. "I don't know how," he said.

"If you can project a circle, you can project a few hexagons," Savino urged.

"Mico got hit, I don't know if he'll be able to—" But then to Giacomo's shock, Mico rose out of his hands and flew over the gorge, taking his place between Aaminah's Genius and the opposite cliff side.

"He seems fine to me!" Savino said.

In his sketchbook, Giacomo drew a six-sided shape, copying the glowing ones that made up the bridge. Mico projected a few rows, but before the bridge was completed, the hexagons broke apart and hundreds of specks of light floated away, like red dust in the wind.

"It's not holding!" Giacomo glanced behind him where the noseless statue was pushing itself back to its feet. The fingerless statue grabbed Baby Cannoli by the arm and hurled him through the air, where he slammed into Old Dino.

Malocchio drew her bow, firing an arrow that pinged off the statue's back. The stone giant whirled around, but instead of catching her gaze, it stared straight at Big Dino, who was running past her.

He screamed as he transformed into stone.

Giacomo's heart beat as fast as his Genius's wings. He wasn't going to let anyone else meet the same fate. He looked at the gap in the bridge. *I can connect it. I have to.*

"Ozo, start getting everyone across!" Giacomo shouted.

Ozo deflected a wild swipe from the noseless statue and glanced at the unfinished bridge. "I'd rather try my luck with these two!"

The statue caught Sforza by his long hair, whipped him around like a lasso, and flung him into Spike.

Old Dino hugged his son's stony form, wailing. Little Dino pulled him away. "Leave him, Dad! There's nothing you can do."

The rest of the mercenaries were caked in dirt and blood from being repeatedly pummeled and tossed around. They couldn't take much more.

Giacomo locked eyes with Ozo. "I'll finish the bridge! Start crossing!" He turned back to the chasm where Gaia, Nero, and Luna held their sections. Aaminah's playing became faster and more intricate. Sweat beaded on her forehead.

Giacomo closed his eyes, visualizing the six-sided shape he needed to create.

"Hurry up!" Savino pressed.

"Let him concentrate," Milena said.

"Retreat!" Ozo called out.

Giacomo opened his eyes and put pencil to paper, sketching a series of interlocking hexagons, like tiles on a floor.

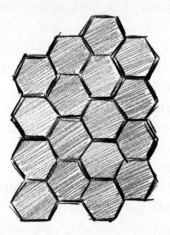

Row by row, Mico projected red hexagons from his crown, filling in the missing part of the bridge. Ozo and Valcaro held off the statues as the remaining mercenaries limped to the cliff's edge. Little Dino placed his foot on the green section, checking to see if it would hold, like it was winter's first ice and he was worried he'd fall through.

"Go! Now!" Ozo barked. Little Dino went first, followed by his father, then Spike, Sveva, and the rest. The bridge gave slightly under their combined weight, but it held solid.

Giacomo filled the page with hexagons, as Mico projected several more rows, completing the bridge. Savino stepped onto it, then Aaminah, who kept playing as she jogged across. Milena pulled Giacomo and they followed. He was careful not to remove his pencil from his sketchbook—a broken connection meant a broken bridge.

Behind them, Valcaro fired off a final shot. The fingerless statue raised its good hand to block the attack, but the metal ball blasted through its palm. The hand crumbled away, leaving a stump at the wrist. Valcaro backed onto the bridge, then ran past Giacomo, followed a moment later by Ozo.

At the other end, Little Dino and Old Dino made it safely across. Relief washed through Giacomo as his part of the structure held up.

"Go, go!" Milena urged, letting everyone pass her. The statues stomped onto the bridge, losing their balance and unleashing a wave that rippled the tiles. Milena almost toppled off the side, but caught the back of Giacomo's collar, nearly dragging him off with her. Giacomo pitched forward, pulling her back to safety.

The statues righted themselves and stalked unsteadily toward the group. Racing for the other side, Milena and Giacomo crossed onto Savino's section of the bridge. Milena lowered her brush and Gaia's projection vanished. Row by row, Milena's green tiles dissolved into specks of light, but the statues kept ahead of the widening gap.

As soon as everyone had crossed the halfway point, Savino let his pencil drop and Nero's beam flickered off. In quick succession, his blue hexagons vanished.

The disappearing tiles caught up to the noseless statue and on its next step, its foot met only air. With a loud groan, the statue plummeted into the chasm.

Ozo reached the other end and joined the rest of his mercenaries back on solid ground. With the other statue closing in, Giacomo's group sprinted across the yellow part of the bridge. When they reached Giacomo's section, Aaminah pulled the flute from her lips. The music cut off and the yellow hexagons separated, breaking into bits of light.

As the children neared the other side, the final pieces of Aaminah's section broke away. The fingerless statue slipped, but immediately found support on the red hexagons, and regained its momentum.

Giacomo waited until Milena, Aaminah, and Savino careened onto the dirt of the opposite side, then yanked his pencil off the page. Mico's gem went dark, and the last remaining section of the bridge began to fade.

He glanced back as the vanishing bridge overtook the fingerless statue. It paused in midair for a split second before plunging down toward the bottom of the gorge.

But Giacomo realized his timing had been off—he'd released his hold on the bridge too soon. Panic swept through him. *I'm not going to make it!*

The remaining hexagons gave way underneath Giacomo's feet, and he dropped. As the wind surged around him, he let out a primal scream that threatened to tear his throat apart.

Ozo ran to the cliff's edge and whipped his chain into the chasm.

Giacomo's left arm shot out to reach the lifeline. After what felt like an eternity, his fingers wrapped around the sun-warmed links. The chain pulled taut, swinging Giacomo like a pendulum. His shoulder slammed against the sheer rock, and he nearly lost his grip.

As he dangled, Mico flew to him, chirping in distress.

"I'm okay," Giacomo said breathlessly.

He began to rise, slowly at first, then faster. Mico pitched in, his tiny claws clutching a link as he strained. Giacomo appreciated the effort, even though Mico wasn't having much of an effect. When Giacomo reached the top, Ozo, the Bull, and Zatto gave one last yank, launching him over the ledge. He sprawled on the ground and let out gasps of relief. Mico flew around his head, chittering happily.

Aaminah fell to her knees and threw her arms around him. "That was so close . . ."

"I know," Giacomo said, still in shock.

Savino helped Giacomo to his feet. "You had me scared for a second."

"You had us all scared," Milena added.

"I don't think anything's broken," Giacomo said, rolling his left shoulder, which throbbed. Ozo wrapped the chain back into a loop around his belt. "Nice trick," Giacomo said. "Thanks for saving my neck."

Ozo replied with a single nod.

"What? We don't get a thank-you for saving *your* hides?" Savino griped. "Giacomo could've died."

"Two of my men *did*." Ozo spat into the dirt by Savino's feet. "The rest aren't doing much better."

Giacomo looked over at the injured mercenaries who nursed bruises, cuts, and probably a few broken bones. Old Dino howled in pain as Little Dino shoved his father's shoulder back into its socket. Tears filled the old man's eyes. Giacomo wasn't sure if they were because of his injury or from losing his oldest son.

Ozo addressed everyone. "Our horses are gone, along with all our supplies and food. But I know a castle a couple days' journey from here. We can regroup there and figure out our next move." Ozo trudged off, followed by a line of the wounded.

Giacomo started to follow. "Wait," Savino called out. He waved the children in close and whispered, "This is our chance to ditch Ozo. We'll have better luck on our own."

Milena shook her head. "We won't survive very long out here without food or supplies. If there's a place to get more, that's where I'm heading."

"I'm with Milena," Aaminah said. "Plus, these people are going to need some healing. I'll be able to help them once Luna gets her strength back. Forming that bridge took a lot out of her."

Giacomo looked at Mico, who had joined Luna atop Aaminah's head. They both looked exhausted.

Savino faced Giacomo. "What about you?"

Ozo rubbed him the wrong way too, but if not for him and his crew, Giacomo would be lying with the statues at the bottom of the gorge.

"We should stick with Ozo," Giacomo said.

Milena nodded sharply. "Then it's decided." She headed after the mercenaries, leading Aaminah and Giacomo away.

Savino kicked the dirt while Nero let out a shrill cry.

"Don't get all pouty about it," Milena called back.

Savino fell in line behind them. "I'm not. I just think we're making a huge mistake."

"You're entitled to your beliefs. But it doesn't make them right."

While Savino and Milena carried on bickering, Giacomo's thoughts turned to the two statues. Baldassare had mentioned how artists in the past had tried bringing statues to life. Could those two have been some kind of ancient Tulpas? And assuming they were, why did they attack?

Their mission had already brought about death and suffering, and they weren't even close to their destination. Giacomo didn't want to think about how much worse it could get, especially if they crossed paths with Ugalino's Tulpa.

9

MASTER AND APPRENTICE

We've arrived at the place of your birth, Zanobius. Virenzia . . .

Ugalino's voice echoed in Zanobius's head. From the sky, Zanobius glanced down at the sprawling walled city that lay nestled
between two mountain ranges, a long river winding through it to
the sea.

He struggled to recall even one moment of his life in Virenzia,
but his memory resembled a half-finished mosaic with hundreds
of missing tiles, making it impossible to determine what the full
image was supposed to look like. Once in a while, Ugalino would
fill in a gap by telling a story from Zanobius's past. But inevitably,
another blackout would hit and tiles would break off, depriving
him of the whole picture.

Ugalino's voice cut in. *Baldassare Barrolo's villa is down there.*

Zanobius spotted a vast estate on the side of a hill overlooking
the city. Ugalino dipped his Genius closer to the mountainside.
The tops of trees whipped past Zanobius's feet.

SCREEEEEE!

Zanobius's ears rang from the piercing sound. A blue-and-gray-feathered Genius burst out from behind the villa and hurtled straight at them. It was nearly as large as Ciro, but this one had a round head, a small, hooked beak, and a large gem in its crown.

Hold on! Ugalino wrapped his arm around Ciro's neck.

Zanobius's four hands gripped handfuls of feathers a second before the oncoming Genius slammed into Ciro. The impact thrust Zanobius from Ciro's back and into the air. The villa spun upside down, then right-side up. He clipped the top of a wall, then tumbled across the ground as pieces of stone rained down.

Stunned, but otherwise unharmed, Zanobius stumbled to his feet. Nearby, Ugalino caught himself by creating a glowing net between two trees. With a twirl of his staff, the diamond dimmed and the pattern vanished.

Overhead, the two Geniuses battled in the sky, swooping and snapping. Ugalino winced and grabbed his side as Ciro took a claw to his flank.

Ugalino thrust his staff toward the sky. Spiraling light struck the enemy Genius, driving it away from Ciro.

Inside, Ugalino commanded. *Quickly!*

Ugalino blasted the doors open and they raced into the courtyard. Inside stood two men—one large and portly, the other hunched and frail.

"I thought I recognized your Genius," Ugalino said to the old man. "There's actually a little part of me that's happy to see you're still alive."

His master seemed to know the old man, though Zanobius had

no idea how. "It's interesting that Nerezza chose to show you mercy. Quite unlike her."

"She might not have taken my life, but she took enough." The old man stepped into the torchlight. Zanobius could now see the man's pupils were foggy.

Ugalino let out a surprised chuckle. "Rather ironic, don't you think?"

"What is?"

"The man who lacked any artistic vision can no longer see," Ugalino said, smiling smugly. "And now I find you taking refuge with one of Nerezza's councilors." Ugalino glared at the portly man. "Rather cowardly, even for you."

The blind man raised a trembling hand and pointed his paintbrush at Ugalino. "*You* are the coward. Hiding behind that abomination of yours all these years, removing the diamond from your Genius's crown . . . You're a disgrace to every artist who's ever lived. I should have thrown you out of my studio the second you came to me wanting to create a Tulpa."

"You never were a very inspiring teacher, Pietro," Ugalino shot back.

Zanobius was surprised to hear that his master had studied with this man. Had Ugalino ever told him? Or was that information he'd lost during a blackout?

On a second-floor balcony overlooking the courtyard, a boy in black clothes and a woman in an elegant night robe ran out and gazed down at Zanobius in fright. "Baldassare," the woman shouted. "What's going on? Who are these people?"

"Go back to your rooms!" Baldassare ordered, but the boy and the woman didn't budge.

"The lives of so many great artists were lost because of you and your Tulpa," Pietro ranted. "Countless Geniuses have been destroyed!"

"Not by my hand," Ugalino said defensively. "I'm not responsible for Nerezza's tyranny."

"If not for your creature, artists wouldn't be forced to live in the shadows."

Now Zanobius was the one who felt defensive. How was he to blame?

"It doesn't have to be that way anymore," Ugalino said. "That's why I'm here, Pietro. Your patron, Signor Barrolo, has been collecting information that can help me strip Nerezza of her power and put things right."

"I'm not sure what you're looking for," Baldassare said, "but you'll be leaving empty-handed."

"You know what I want," Ugalino said firmly. "The Creator's Sacred Tools."

Pietro waved his brush. From the sky, his Genius shot orange squares of light straight at Zanobius and Ugalino. They leaped aside as the attack exploded, kicking up dirt and rock.

Ugalino spun, drawing a wide arc with his staff. A bright wave emanated from the diamond and spread across the courtyard, knocking Pietro and Baldassare onto their backs. Then he turned his staff on Pietro's Genius, striking its wing with a blaze of light. Ciro quickly followed up, grasping the wounded Genius in his talons and driving it down into the roof. The defeated Genius fell limply into the courtyard, near its unconscious master.

Ugalino created an energy swath that cut through the pillar

underneath where the woman and her son stood. The balcony crumbled and they plunged into the courtyard.

Bring the woman to me, Ugalino said.

Zanobius pushed aside a chunk of marble and found her. She had been stunned by the fall, but as soon as Zanobius lifted her, she began kicking and screaming.

Baldassare rose to his feet. "Let her go!" he demanded.

Ugalino stared the man down. "Tell me where the Compass is."

"I don't know!" Baldassare wailed. "Please . . . I swear I don't know anything!" Tears began to stream down his fat cheeks.

"That thing's going to kill Mom!" the boy cried, climbing from the rubble. "Tell him where it is!"

Baldassare's face turned red. "Enzio, stay out of this!" The man turned back to Ugalino and fell to his knees. "Please . . . My son doesn't know what he's saying. Don't listen to him."

"Then say goodbye to your wife," Ugalino said coldly.

Zanobius wrapped a hand around the woman's throat and waited for the order. She gasped for air.

"Stop!" the boy said desperately. "Let her go and I'll tell you where the Compass is."

"Enzio, don't speak another word!" Baldassare commanded.

"You'd trade her life for some stupid treasure?" Enzio said. "You're a greedy, selfish oaf!"

Zanobius stared at Enzio, surprised at how the young man had raised his voice at his father. Zanobius wouldn't consider speaking that way to Ugalino.

"Tell me what you know," Ugalino urged. "Right now. It looks like your mother is having trouble breathing."

The woman clawed at Zanobius's arms, but his grip remained firm.

"My father and Pietro . . . They've been training some kids with Geniuses."

"Not another word, Enzio!" Baldassare sounded desperate.

Enzio ignored his father. "The other night, one of them figured out the Compass is in the Cave of Alessio. You know where that is?"

Ugalino nodded. "Where are these young artists and their Geniuses now?"

"Already on their way." Enzio spat out the words. "But they just left last night, on foot. With your Genius, you can easily beat them to the cave."

Release his mother.

Zanobius dropped the woman and she crumpled in a heap, taking in huge gulps of air. Enzio rushed to her.

Take the boy instead.

Zanobius reached down and plucked the boy away from his mother.

"Enzio!" she cried out.

The boy flailed, trying to break free. "What are you doing? I told you what you wanted!"

"You're coming with us. And if I discover you're lying, my Tulpa will rip you apart and feed you to my Genius, piece by piece."

"You can't take my son," Baldassare said.

"You were willing to let your own wife perish, rather than give up the Compass," Ugalino said. "Be thankful this is all I took from you today."

He whistled and Ciro flew to his side. Zanobius climbed on, carrying Enzio over his shoulder.

"Put me down, you ugly, disgusting thing!" the boy howled. Zanobius tried to ignore his insults.

Ugalino gave Baldassare a menacing look. "And if you or Nerezza's army tracks me or tries to ambush me, your son is dead." Baldassare gaped, speechless.

Pietro regained consciousness and struggled to his feet. On the roof, his Genius shook in a wave from head to tail, sending out a flurry of gray feathers.

"Taking the Compass will only bring more suffering and misery to Zizzola," Pietro warned.

Ugalino took his position on Ciro's neck. "I will heal our empire by tearing down what Nerezza has built and creating a new world in its place. One that treats innovative artists not as criminals, but heroes."

Ciro flapped his giant wings and they soared into the sky. The boy's struggling stopped as soon as they were in the air. His anger was replaced by alarm as he stared at the ground rushing away.

"I hate heights too," Zanobius said.

"I'm not scared," Enzio replied. But his fear-filled eyes betrayed his words. Humans always acted tough, even when they were terrified. The boy was no exception.

THE CASTLE'S SECRET

"There it is," Ozo announced. "Castille di Oberto."

Atop a jutting mound of earth, ringed by a wide moat, sat a stone castle with numerous towers. A long viaduct with tall arches created a raised path above the surrounding pine trees and moat. Strips of orange peeked between the clouds as the sun fell.

"Duke Oberto hired me once to deal with some unruly peasants," Ozo said. "He has a soft spot for artists, so you'll be safe here."

As they walked along the top of the viaduct, Giacomo got a closer view of the two front towers, which were in ruins. The drawbridge was raised. In the moat below, the bloated body of a man bobbed in the water. A shiver of fear ran through Giacomo.

The mercenaries approached, swords and crossbows raised.

"Everyone wait here," Ozo said. "I'll check it out."

"We can make a bridge across," Milena offered, pointing to the gap between the viaduct and the castle.

"I've had enough of magic bridges," Ozo grumbled. "I'd rather use the real thing." He wrapped one end of his chain around a chunk of stone protruding from the viaduct. He leaned back, pulling the chain taut, then walked vertically down until he reached a lower part of the hillside.

He scaled the rocky terrain to the castle, then climbed through a triangular opening at the corner of the outer wall where the tower had crumbled.

The group waited in silence for Ozo to give the all clear. Giacomo jumped as metal chains clattered. The drawbridge fell open like a tongue lolling out of a giant mouth, revealing Ozo on the other side. "The place looks abandoned, far as I can tell," he called. "But stay alert."

They entered the courtyard, where enormous black ravens pecked at the bodies of dead guards. Giacomo looked away from the grim scene. The ravens let out a chorus of grating croaks, warning the Geniuses to stay away from their meal. Mico squawked back at them, but stayed close to Giacomo.

"Help me check the rest of the castle," Ozo commanded Zatto and the Bull, whose injuries were minor compared to the others'. "The rest of you wait out here with the kids."

The three men passed through the doors, which had been blasted into splinters, and disappeared into the castle.

The four Geniuses flew around the courtyard, circling. They all cried out with startled chirps.

"They seem agitated," Savino said.

"No kidding," Milena scoffed. "Think it has anything to do with all those dead bodies over there?"

Savino sighed. "Think you can lay off the sarcasm once in a while?"

Giacomo noticed something on the ground near the wall—a silver feather, nearly as long as his forearm. He showed it to the others. "Looks a lot bigger than a normal bird's feather, don't you think?"

Savino nodded. "The only people who have full-grown Geniuses are Pietro, the Supreme Creator, and—"

"Ugalino." Milena's voice quavered.

Aaminah looked around nervously. "What if he's still here?"

From somewhere inside the castle came a woman's terrified scream.

Giacomo tensed, his heart racing, expecting Ugalino and his Tulpa to emerge with their latest victim.

Instead, a young woman in a dark green peasant dress bolted into the courtyard, her hair flowing behind her in wild curls. Ozo, Zatto, and the Bull chased after her.

"We just want to know where the duke is!" the Bull called out.

She stumbled, falling to her knees. At the sight of the other mercenaries, she held up a carving knife, shouting, "Stay away!"

"It's okay, signora," Aaminah said, cautiously approaching the woman. "We're with these people. They're not going to hurt you. Please put down the knife."

Aaminah's soft tone calmed the woman and she lowered her trembling arm. She eyed them with suspicion. "More Geniuses? Who . . . who are you?"

"My name's Aaminah. This is Milena, Savino, and Giacomo." Then she gestured to the mercenaries: "These are our escorts."

Ozo stepped toward the woman. "And who are you?" he said gruffly.

"My name is Ersilia," the woman replied, catching her breath. "I was one of Duke Oberto's maidservants."

"The person who attacked the castle," Savino said. "Did he have a Genius too?"

She nodded, confirming their earlier suspicion.

"Was a four-armed man with him?" Ozo asked.

Ersilia looked spooked. "Yes. But it was no man. It was a monster."

"What happened?" Giacomo said.

"I was in my quarters when I heard loud booming sounds. I looked out from my room, up there." She pointed to a small window in one of the towers that overlooked the courtyard. "I saw the guards confront the monster and it went crazy and attacked them. It threw them around like . . . like they were sacks of flour." She looked at the bodies nearby, tears welling in her eyes.

"Is Duke Oberto alive?" Ozo wanted to know.

"No . . . that creature killed him too. Once they flew away, and we were sure the danger had passed, the other servants fled."

"Why are you still here?" Milena asked.

"My grandmother . . . She's ill. She's not able to travel. So I stayed with her. But the herbs, they're not working anymore. I don't know what to do." Ersilia buried her head in her hands.

"Maybe Aaminah could help her," Giacomo suggested. "She and her Genius are great at healing people."

"Really?" Ersilia looked hopeful.

"I can't make any promises," Aaminah said. "It depends on how sick she is."

"Hold up," Ozo said. "You still got half my team to get to." He turned to Ersilia and gave her a sad smile that didn't look genuine. "Sorry, signora, but your grandmother's going to have to wait."

Aaminah had started healing the mercenaries during their travel breaks. She began with the most serious injuries and was still working through the rest of the wounded by the time they'd arrived at the castle.

"I'll help her as soon as I can," Aaminah promised Ersilia. She pulled her flute from her belt and walked over to Spike, who was sprawled on the ground, clutching his side and groaning. As she played, a yellow light from Luna's crown washed over his torso and the moans died down.

"We're going to need to take some of your food," Ozo told Ersilia. "But a castle this size must have a pretty healthy stash."

"Help yourselves," she offered. "There's no one left here to eat it anyway."

"Let's get in there and start stocking up," Ozo ordered. Everyone headed inside, except for Aaminah and her Genius, who remained with the injured.

Ersilia pointed down the long main hall. "The kitchen's all the way at the end. I need to check on my grandmother and let her know everything's all right." She left, disappearing through an archway.

The duke's home reminded Giacomo of Baldassare's villa— immense and opulent. But unlike the villa, where Baldassare kept his art collection hidden, the duke's walls were covered in gold-framed paintings of past Zizzolan heroes, with not one portrait of Supreme Creator Nerezza among them. He'd probably be arrested for his collection if he hadn't already been killed.

"Watch out, dead body alert," Ozo said flatly as he led the group past a lifeless figure in a red robe lying on the floor. Flies buzzed around it. With the tip of his sword, Ozo turned the limp head, revealing an old man's scarred face, frozen in horror.

"That's Duke Oberto all right," Ozo said. "Looks a lot older than I remember . . ."

Ozo and the group continued down the hall. Giacomo caught a glimpse of the duke's frightening appearance and averted his gaze. But something made him take a second look. He leaned over the body. The duke's face was a petrified tangle of flesh that looked like it had been ravaged by fire, not old age. It reminded him of the way Milena's arm had looked after her Wellspring injury.

Realizing everyone was already far down the hall, Giacomo called for Mico and headed for the group. But his Genius stayed hovering by one of the paintings—a depiction of the Creator holding the Compass, Straightedge, and Pencil. Mico pecked at its frame, chipping off flakes of gold leaf.

Giacomo stomped down the hall. "Mico, quit it!" But his Genius only redoubled its efforts. Giacomo seized Mico. "Geniuses shouldn't deface artwork," he scolded.

Mico responded by jabbing Giacomo with his beak. "Ow! What's wrong with you?"

Giacomo let go and Mico darted back to the painting, this time trying to poke his head behind the frame.

"Why don't you ever listen to me?" Giacomo tried grabbing Mico again, but the little creature avoided his grasp and wriggled behind the canvas.

"Mico? Mico, get out here right now!" Giacomo peered behind the painting, but his Genius wasn't there. Impossible. Mico couldn't vanish into a wall . . . *Or could he?*

He grasped the edge of the frame and pulled. The painting swung open like a door. Hidden behind it was an arched passageway with stairs spiraling down. *Just like the secret passage to Pietro's studio,* Giacomo thought.

"Mico? You down there?" To Giacomo's relief, his Genius replied with a faint chirp.

The opening stood a foot off the floor. Giacomo stepped up, then slowly descended, his back pressed against the cold stone wall.

"Some light would be nice," he whispered, but the stairwell remained dark. Either Mico hadn't heard him or was purposely ignoring him.

From the depths of the castle came the sound of breathing. The smart thing would have been to have Ozo check it out, but something drew Giacomo farther into the darkness.

The breathing got louder, sounding like a man's snores mixed with a dog's growls. But the inhales and exhales also spoke to him on a deeper level, as if they were whispering to his soul, urging him closer.

A wall of foulness slammed into him. Giacomo recoiled and his stomach heaved. He fell back on the steps and coughed. That morning's breakfast threatened to come back up, but Giacomo swallowed hard and the nausea passed. After spending most of his life in the sewer, he thought he'd smelled every horrendous odor humans could make, but this was ten times worse.

He covered his nose and mouth with his collar. It barely masked the putrid odors, but made it tolerable enough for him to stand again.

"Mico, this isn't funny. Where are you? I can't see anything."

A bright red light pierced the dark and shot into his eyes.

"Not in my face!" Giacomo complained.

Mico turned, and the beam moved from Giacomo to the wall behind him.

"There," Giacomo instructed, pointing down the stairs. When Giacomo and Mico reached the bottom, the Genius's red beam glinted across a row of metal bars. As Giacomo's eyes adjusted, he began to make out a cage with a form inside, a lumpy mass that heaved with each growling breath. Whatever kind of wild animal it was, it must have been responsible for the horrible stench too.

Mico cast his light around the room, and Giacomo's pounding heart thumped even faster. There wasn't only one cage. There were ten. And huddled in each was a pale, hairless creature with shiny, whitish flesh. Scars crisscrossed their bodies. They didn't look like any animal Giacomo had ever seen.

Tentatively, he moved closer to the cages, both curious and horrified. He made out an eyeball staring back at him, but the eye wasn't on a face. It was set in what appeared to be a shoulder. Giacomo took a closer look. *Or is it an elbow?* And it had teeth too, but not where a mouth would normally be. Several jagged fangs stuck out from the top of the creature's head, near two slits that opened and closed with the growling-snoring sound. It had a tail, a rodent's paws, and arms too short for its body. It was as if the Creator had taken a lump of clay, thrown on a dog's face, mixed it with a baby's, added a rat's tail and claws, then smushed the clay with his thumb until the features became almost unrecognizable.

The others were variations of the first, some a little bigger, others smaller. A few had more than two eyes; one had none at all. The eyeless creature sniffed the air with its two gaping nostrils, though how it could pick out Giacomo's scent amid the stench, he couldn't imagine.

The creatures crawled to the bars of the cages, their paws clawing the rusted metal, their growls growing more agitated. He backed away, and was about to flee, when a baby's faint cry came from deeper in the underground chamber.

He already thought the duke was horrible for torturing these creatures, but keeping a baby down here? That was pure evil.

With Mico lighting the way, Giacomo crept toward the sound, past stacked paintings and statues draped in white sheets, like ghosts. The duke's vault of contraband art made Baldassare's collection seem tiny by comparison.

The crying got louder and louder until Giacomo found its source—a large wooden box, about six feet tall. Cautiously, he circled it and found a glass portal embedded in its side, no bigger than the palm of his hand. He peered through the foggy glass but it was too dark to see anything inside.

"Shine your light in here," Giacomo said, and Mico aimed his beam at the portal. Giacomo's worst fear was confirmed. The foggy glass distorted his vision, but there was no mistaking what he saw. Inside the box lay a naked baby, wriggling its arms and legs and wailing.

"We have to get it out!" Giacomo scrambled to the other side of the box and found a door. He raised a thick wooden bar and yanked the door open.

He charged inside and reached for the squirming baby. But he stopped short as Mico's light fell across its misshapen body—its flesh looked like waxy lumps from a melted candle.

The baby twisted around, revealing a gaping mouth of fangs where its face should have been. It snapped at Giacomo's fingers. He flinched and jumped, backing into the wall. With a creak, the door swung inward and banged shut. He heard the wooden bar fall with a thud.

Giacomo threw himself at the door, but it wouldn't budge. "No!" He charged again, slamming his shoulder into the wood. The door still wouldn't open. A paralyzing realization began to sink in—he and Mico were trapped. With that *thing*.

He became aware of mechanical clicking and whirring sounds outside the box. A bright beam of light shot through the glass portal. Projected on the opposite wall was the drawing of a man standing on a ceiling. It took Giacomo a second to realize the man wasn't hanging upside down; the whole drawing was upside down.

A whir and a click. The image was replaced by a masterful study of hands, also upside down. The drawing showed the hand in different positions, from various angles. Another whir and click. The image changed to a study of an eye. One by one, new drawings clicked into place, each depicting various parts of human anatomy. Some of the illustrations even showed humans on the inside. Giacomo had heard about certain artists who cut open dead bodies and drew the organs, muscles, and bones in order to study how the body worked. Giacomo found himself disgusted but fascinated by the imagery.

Startled by a scraping noise, he looked around. The baby creature had wandered into the corner and was gnawing at the wooden wall. *At least it's not chewing on my leg,* Giacomo thought with mild relief.

The anatomical drawings switched to a symbol: a six-pointed star inside a hexagon. Crisscrossed lines created a smaller star and hexagon inside the larger shapes and connected the center points of a number of circles. Giacomo counted thirteen circles in all.

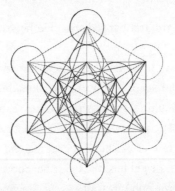

The picture changed again. The thick black outline of a cube appeared, the hexagon-star's faded image still visible behind it. Several more images followed, showing the different shapes that could be drawn from the blueprint of the original symbol.

Then a familiar shape appeared—the mandorla. As Giacomo stared at its lines, they began to waver and vibrate. Then his head pounded. His vision blurred. The temperature inside the box plunged to freezing and Giacomo shivered uncontrollably. Streams of color shot out of the mandorla's eye, slamming into him like a tempest. Deafening low booms rattled his bones and shook skin from muscle.

Giacomo kicked the door over and over, trying to break his way out, but it refused to yield. Yellows, reds, and blues swirled around him, obscuring the walls of the box. The force of the winds picked him up and spun him.

He was back in the Wellspring.

Mico whipped past, caught in the storm's grip. Giacomo reached out, but each time his fingers nearly wrapped around Mico, the wind whirled them again, and they drifted farther apart.

Another wave of color crashed over him, and Giacomo lost sight of Mico altogether. The cold developed into searing heat. Fearing he'd be lost in the Wellspring forever, Giacomo frantically tried to figure out a way to escape. But fighting the storm only made it worse. The deafening bangs transformed into a loud, droning buzz. Giacomo could barely think. His senses overwhelmed, he tried to focus on a peaceful image. Something that could ground him amid the madness.

He pictured his hideout in Virenzia's sewers, then his comfortable room in Baldassare's villa, and finally Pietro's studio. None of the places offered any relief. Then the image of the Cave of Alessio popped into his mind. He could hear the gentle rush of the river, touch the rough bark of the ancient tree, and feel the cool mist from the waterfall.

Gradually, the wind died down and the temperature evened out. The loud drone transformed into the sound of rushing water. When Giacomo opened his eyes, his feet were on the ground, and he was pushed up against the gnarled tree. He was panting and sweaty, but otherwise all right. Mico lay across a branch, feathers askew, chirping woozily.

It had worked! He'd tamed the Wellspring, at least for the moment. The storm dwindled into a fog of color, like a painter's smeared palette.

Once the immediate danger passed, the shock of what just happened sunk in—somehow the duke's bizarre box hadn't only opened the Wellspring; it had physically transported Giacomo somewhere else. But he wasn't yet sure if the Cave of Alessio was real, or another Wellspring-induced vision.

He took a step, but jumped back when he noticed the baby creature had come through with him. It crawled around, touching whatever was in its path, uttering weird wheezing sounds. Its behavior reminded him of a curious child, eager to explore its new surroundings. When it came upon a pile of rocks, the creature stuffed one into its mouth and ate it, crunching it between its sharp teeth. Then it splashed through the river and disappeared into the bushes on the opposite shore.

Giacomo walked along a path toward the waterfall, wondering if the duke had used his invention to access the Wellspring too. The scars on his face seemed to suggest so.

As the question rattled around in his head, he arrived at the mouth of the cave. He touched the damp, slick rocks. The cave sure *felt* real. He peered in, hoping to see the Compass, but the space was empty, leaving him discouraged. *Did I make a mistake? Am I leading everyone astray?* He'd barely formed the thought when a blue light shimmered, revealing the Compass floating inside the suspended octahedron. As he let the relief sink in, his fingers tingled with warmth.

But before he could take a closer look, a Genius's screech filled the skies. The call was much too loud and deep to be Mico's. Giacomo looked up. Out of the colored fog emerged an enormous silver-feathered Genius.

Giacomo pulled Mico close and hid behind a large boulder near the cave's entrance.

The Genius landed next to the tree. Giacomo spotted three figures sitting on the creature. The man on the neck dismounted first. His wavy black hair hung over his ears and down to his angular jaw, which was covered in a close-cropped beard. A long white cloak flowed off his broad shoulders. In his right hand he carried a tall staff with a diamond set atop its handle. Giacomo noticed the empty space on the Genius's crown where the diamond should've been. Giacomo shuddered, realizing the man had to be Ugalino. The man patted the Genius's feathers. "Wait here, Ciro."

Accompanying Ugalino was a huge, white, muscular figure with four arms and four legs—*the Tulpa.*

Surprisingly, there was a third person with them as well—a skinny, curly-haired boy. The Tulpa picked him up off the Genius's back and shoved him toward Ugalino. As the boy raised his head, Giacomo was shocked to see Enzio's frightened face.

I'm definitely not imagining this, Giacomo thought. If he hadn't been sure before, he was now. *This must all be happening in the real world,* Giacomo surmised, feeling his chest tighten. But if that was true, it meant Ugalino must have been at Baldassare's villa. Had something terrible happened to Enzio's parents and Pietro? It also meant the entire mission was a failure. Ugalino had beaten them to the Creator's Compass.

A TRICK OF THE EYE

Zanobius pulled Enzio from Ciro's back and pushed him toward Ugalino, relieved to finally be at their destination.

For over a week, they'd spent much of their time soaring west above Zizzola. Knowing the Compass was within his grasp, Ugalino abandoned his usual caution and they traveled both night and day. They probably would have gotten to the cave sooner if not for all the breaks. Maybe it was the extra passenger, but Ciro's strength had seemed to fade from flying for extended stretches over the long distances. So they were forced to land several times a day to give the Genius time to rest. Zanobius wondered if the Genius's weakness might be due to the fact that its source of power—its diamond—was on Ugalino's staff, not in its crown.

The thought had struck him when he witnessed Pietro's Genius in action. It seemed fully capable of handling itself, almost independent. Ciro was the opposite—reliant on Ugalino's instructions, directionless without him. Just like Zanobius.

"The Compass should be in the cave behind the waterfall," Enzio said.

Zanobius could hear Ugalino behind them as they trudged up a narrow path that passed the falls. Water misted over them. As they got closer, Zanobius noticed a blue light pulsating from within the cave.

"See, I told you," Enzio said as they walked in.

Swiftly, Ugalino marched past, heading straight for the Compass. It was as large as the one Zanobius had seen in Duke Oberto's painting, its two golden legs nearly the length of his own. It floated inside an octahedral casing that lit up the cave and cast shadows on the damp walls.

As he stepped closer, Zanobius thought his eyes were playing tricks on him. For a moment, it looked like the Compass and the blue shell around it had vanished. But a step later, it reappeared. He stopped and leaned left and right, noticing that the Compass was only visible at certain angles.

Ugalino also realized something was amiss. He circled to the opposite side and reached out. His hand easily passed through both the outer shell and the Compass.

"It's a mirage!" Ugalino marched toward Enzio, raising his staff. "I warned you what would happen if you lied to me!"

Grab him.

Zanobius took Enzio by the shoulders.

"I told you the truth!" Enzio shook with fear. He seemed just as surprised that the Compass wasn't there.

"Was this one of Pietro's illusions?" Ugalino asked. "Did he really think he could fool me with a simple trick of light?"

"No, he thought it was here," Enzio said. "Everyone did."

Drown him, Ugalino commanded. *I want him to suffer.*

But as Zanobius pushed Enzio toward the falls, he was surprised to find a part of him wanted to resist. The boy hadn't deliberately deceived them and didn't deserve this punishment, a rebellious voice told him. Zanobius had a vague notion that he'd felt this way before. In his mind, he saw the hazy silhouette of a woman. And a child . . .

What are you waiting for? Ugalino shouted in his head.

And as quickly as the thoughts formed, they were gone. Zanobius shoved the boy's head into the rushing water.

Enzio flailed, desperate to escape, but Zanobius didn't budge. Only Ugalino's command could save the boy's life now.

Out of nowhere, a rock slammed against the back of Zanobius's head. It wasn't painful, but it startled him enough that he turned, pulling Enzio out of the water.

"Where'd that come from?" Ugalino looked around in confusion.

Zanobius scanned the cave. A few feet away, the image of a boy with shaggy hair appeared for a split second, then vanished. Was it another illusion, like the Compass?

"I see someone! Right there!" Zanobius pointed where he'd last spotted the boy. Distracted, he dropped Enzio, who gasped for air.

Ugalino came to his side and the two of them stalked their invisible prey.

"There he is!" Ugalino fired a quick blast from his staff. But the shaggy-haired boy disappeared again and the dagger of light missed, cracking the cave wall instead. He kept appearing in quick flashes—there for a split second, then gone. "Is that the boy you told us about?" Ugalino asked Enzio. "The one who located the Compass?"

There was no answer, only a loud splash. Zanobius and his master spun toward the falls, but Enzio was gone. They'd only turned their backs for a moment, but it was long enough for Enzio to escape.

"Bring him back!" Ugalino shouted. "I'll keep looking for the other boy."

Zanobius jumped through the waterfall and emerged outside, drenched. He glanced around, but Enzio was nowhere in sight. Rumbling came from behind. He turned just as a boulder crashed down the slope and onto his head. He reeled, but regained his balance. Above the falls, Enzio scrambled away, kicking rocks loose as he climbed. Zanobius knocked aside the falling rocks and went after him.

Like a startled roach, Enzio zigzagged up the rock face, but Zanobius was faster, using his limbs like a spider to propel himself up the cliff side.

Enzio dove behind a large boulder and used both legs to dislodge it. The rock crunched and crashed its way down the hill. It slammed into Zanobius, knocking him back several feet. But it wasn't enough to stop him.

Zanobius made one last lunge up the hill and clutched Enzio's ankle. With his free leg, Enzio smashed his foot into Zanobius's face over and over. Annoyed, Zanobius yanked Enzio's leg, pulling him down. With his two front arms, he pinned the boy's shoulders to the rocks; his two back arms restrained his legs.

"Stop running!" Zanobius called out.

"Stop trying to kill me!" Enzio shot back.

"I don't want to hurt you."

"You were about to drown me!"

Zanobius fell silent. His thoughts felt mixed up.

"Ugalino ordered me to kill you," Zanobius tried to explain. "I . . . I didn't want to."

"I didn't hear him say anything," Enzio replied.

Zanobius didn't want to elaborate on how he could hear Ugalino's voice in his mind. The boy was already unhinged enough as it was.

"Doesn't matter," Enzio continued. "Ugalino's not here now, so how about you let me go?"

The rebellious voice returned and Zanobius found himself seriously considering Enzio's request. He could turn his back and give Enzio time to escape, then tell Ugalino that the boy had outsmarted him and gotten away. Zanobius shook off the thought—his master would know he was lying.

"Ugalino is my creator," Zanobius said. "I have to obey him."

"Even if that means killing someone innocent like me?"

Zanobius nodded gravely. He couldn't defy Ugalino, even if he questioned his master's orders. He lifted Enzio to his feet. "I have to take you back now. He'll wonder why I've been gone so long."

"The Compass isn't here. He doesn't have any use for me. What do you think is going to happen to me once we go back down there?"

Zanobius felt his grip loosen around Enzio's arms. It would be the simplest thing to let him go. But Ugalino's voice seared into his head.

The other boy is gone. Bring Enzio here. Now.

Zanobius's hands tightened again. He dragged Enzio down the

rocky slope and back into the cave, where Ugalino gazed at the false Compass.

He listened for his master's order to finish off Enzio. He didn't hear one.

Ugalino faced Enzio. "There was another boy here, with long, shaggy hair. Tell me about him."

"Giacomo?" Enzio sounded surprised. "He was in the cave?" He looked around, but there was no sign of the boy now.

"Why did your friend believe the Compass would be found here?"

"First off, he's not my friend," Enzio replied. "He just lived in my house and ate my food."

Ugalino scowled. "Don't act cute or I'll have Zanobius shove you under the waterfall again."

"Okay, okay," Enzio said. "Look, I don't know much about him. He showed up at my house a few weeks ago. He claimed he had just gotten his Genius, which is kind of weird for a kid who's twelve, right? But that's not even the strangest part. The reason I thought the Compass was in this cave is because Giacomo saw it here when he looked into the Wellspring."

"Impossible," Ugalino said.

The Wellspring? Was that a place? Zanobius had never heard of it. But his master's stunned reaction told him what he needed to know—Giacomo was powerful, much more powerful than Ugalino had expected.

Stay with him, his master instructed. *Don't let him out of this cave. I'll be back soon.*

Ugalino marched out.

"Where are you going?" Zanobius asked. His master didn't answer.

Ugalino climbed onto Ciro and took off into the sky, leaving Zanobius alone with Enzio.

Zanobius pointed to the back wall of the cave. "Sit over there. And don't move."

Enzio muttered an exhausted "Fine." He shuffled away without a fight.

Zanobius stood sentinel at the mouth of the cave and tried to listen in on his master's distant thoughts, hoping to hear what he was plotting. Instead, the rebellious voice spoke again, asking him a simple question.

How long can you go on living like this?

THE CAMERA OBSCURA

Giacomo crouched behind the bushes, watching the Tulpa stand guard at the mouth of the cave, Enzio his prisoner. Clad only in a skirt of red fabric, the muscular, round-faced Tulpa appeared incredibly lifelike. It had extra arms and legs, skin like alabaster, and short, curly hair as pale as snow, but it moved and talked and had expressions, just like a human.

While studying the beautiful markings emblazoned on its torso, Giacomo was struck by the fact that they were identical to the six-pointed star pattern he'd seen projected on the wall of the duke's mysterious contraption.

Giacomo struggled to understand what was happening. Somehow, the Wellspring had transported him to the Cave of Alessio, where he could see Ugalino and his Tulpa. But the even stranger part was that they were able to catch glimpses of him. Like the mandorla circles, it seemed as if the Wellspring and the real world overlapped and Giacomo had been able to pop between them, though he had no idea how he had done it.

The good news was the Compass in the cave wasn't real and Ugalino hadn't been able to take it. The bad news was the Compass in the cave wasn't real and they would have to begin their search all over again. But the more pressing problem was Enzio.

Giacomo tried to figure out how to sneak past Zanobius and save Enzio without being spotted again, but before Giacomo could make a move, colors began to swirl around him, obscuring the tree, the waterfall, and the Tulpa. The pounding returned and the heat flooded back. He braced himself as he and Mico were sucked away into the Wellspring's vortex. First, he felt the blistering pain, like his flesh was peeling away. Next came a suffocating pressure, like being pressed between two slabs of marble. His pounding heart slammed against his chest. He tried to inhale, but his lungs wouldn't fill; he tried to scream, but he couldn't make a sound.

Even though Giacomo had been through this before, he knew he could never get used to it.

In an instant, the pain eased and Giacomo was back inside the locked box. The light in the glass portal was now gone.

Savino's muffled voice came through the wall. "Okay, the machine is off now!"

"Giacomo! Giacomo!" Milena shouted.

He fell to his knees, too weak to respond. Mico wound dizzy circles around him, then dropped into his cupped hands, exhausted. Giacomo heard a metal scrape. The door swung open, revealing Milena, her face full of worry.

"Are you okay?" she said, kneeling next to him. "You disappeared upstairs. We found the secret passage and figured you came down here. But why?"

"Ugalino . . ." Giacomo managed to whisper. "His Tulpa . . . I saw them . . ."

"Where? Here in the castle?"

"No. At the Cave of Alessio."

Milena stared back skeptically. Savino poked his head through the doorway. "Uh, what did he just say?"

Giacomo sat up, beginning to feel like himself again. "I know this is going to sound crazy, but you have to believe me." He proceeded to tell them how he'd followed the cries of a baby to the box, was locked in, saw the mandorla projected on the wall, and got sucked into the Wellspring, which took him to the cave, where he saw Ugalino and the Tulpa, who almost drowned Enzio. As he heard himself saying it all out loud, it did sound pretty farfetched.

"Wait," Milena interrupted. "What was Enzio doing there?"

"Leading them to the Compass," Giacomo said. "Ugalino must

have shown up at the villa after we left and taken Enzio hostage. He knew where the Compass was."

"If that's true, then Pietro, Baldassare, and Fabiana might be . . ." Milena couldn't say the word. Giacomo feared the worst too.

"So Ugalino already has the Compass," Savino said, sounding defeated.

"Actually, no," Giacomo said. "When he tried to take it, his hand passed right through. It was only an illusion."

"But that means we have to start our whole search over," Savino muttered. He slammed his fist against the box. "Unbelievable!"

A curious look crossed Milena's face as her focus shifted to the structure surrounding them. "Giacomo, I think I might know how you were able to trigger the Wellspring."

"How?"

"This box is a giant camera obscura."

"What's that?" Giacomo asked.

"It's an optical device artists use to help them draw realistic scenes," Milena described. "Light from outside passes through a small hole and gets projected upside down on the wall of a dark room, where the artist traces the image."

"Pietro had us build one once," Savino added. "But it was a lot smaller than this."

"Well, I'm pretty sure the duke didn't make this one to learn how to draw better," Giacomo said.

Milena continued her inspection of the camera obscura. "You said that after you got locked in, you saw images projected on the wall?"

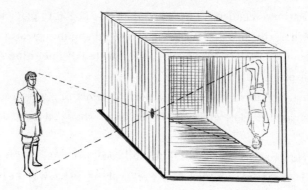

"That's right," Giacomo said. "Some were anatomy drawings, then a bunch of different shapes. The last one was the mandorla. But I don't understand how a projection of the mandorla could have opened the Wellspring."

"You triggered the Wellspring by accident before," Savino piped up. "You sure that's not what happened?"

"I don't think so," Giacomo said. "When the Wellspring opened, Mico wasn't even shining his gem."

"What if the light was coming from a different Genius's gem?" Milena suggested. She walked to the glass portal and peered closely at the hole where the light had passed through. "Look. This isn't an ordinary piece of glass."

Embedded in the wall was a faceted clear jewel. Giacomo had mistaken it for foggy glass earlier, but now he could see its resemblance to a Genius's gem.

"But I don't think Duke Oberto had a Genius, so where did he get the gem?" Giacomo wondered out loud.

"How do you think?" Savino said. "Probably stole it off a dead Genius."

Giacomo recoiled. "That's horrible." He began to piece it all together: the duke's strange scars, those disfigured creatures, a stolen Genius gem. They were all connected by one thing—the Wellspring.

Giacomo looked around and noticed something was missing. "Did you see those creatures in the cages when you came down here?"

"How could we miss them?" Savino said.

Milena's nose wrinkled. "They're revolting. What was the duke doing with them?"

"There was one in here earlier. It crossed over with me, but then it ran off."

"You think it was absorbed back into the Wellspring?" Milena asked.

"Possibly," Giacomo said. "But listen . . . I think the duke was trying to create his own Tulpa. That's what all those creatures are—his failed experiments."

Milena gasped.

"So this is some kind of Tulpa-making machine?" Savino stepped out of the doorway, putting some distance between himself and the box.

"It has to be," Giacomo said. "I got a look at Ugalino's Tulpa up close. There were tattoos on its chest and back that looked exactly like the symbols I saw projected on the wall. The duke's Tulpas have parts of the same markings too. I thought they were only scars at first."

Giacomo, Milena, and Savino stood in shock, struggling to comprehend the horror they'd uncovered. The silence was broken by a racket of urgent squawks.

They scrambled out of the camera obscura and found Nero, Gaia, and Mico atop a tall cabinet against the wall. The Geniuses pecked at the wood with their beaks, trying to break in.

"Mico, come on. We should go back upstairs." Giacomo whistled for his Genius, but as usual, Mico didn't listen to him.

"Wait," Milena said, walking toward the cabinet. "I think our Geniuses are onto something." She pulled the cabinet door, but it was locked.

Savino glanced around for a key, but didn't find one. He pulled out his pencil and sketched a triangular shape in the air. Nero projected a blue blast of energy at the lock, shattering it. The doors swung open, exposing stacks of parchment with drawings, along with several sketchbooks. Milena flipped through them, her face lighting up. "Plans for the camera obscura, notes on the Wellspring, some bizarre-looking symbols . . . I'm going to need time to study it all, but I think these might help explain what happened to you, Giacomo."

"Think they'll also help us figure out where the Compass really is?" Giacomo asked.

"I have no idea," she said. "But for now, they're all we have to go on."

They were about to head upstairs when Ozo's voice bellowed through the chamber. "What wretchedness is this?"

The Tulpas. Giacomo dashed over and met Ozo and Zatto by the cages.

After Giacomo shared what they'd learned about the duke's Tulpa experiments, Ozo's brow furrowed and his hand grasped the hilt of his sword. "We need to destroy them."

Giacomo jumped in front of one of the cages. "No! You can't."

"One of these gets out, it'll rip you limb from limb." Ozo drew his weapon.

Giacomo looked into the eye of one of the disfigured Tulpas, crouched in its prison. It gazed back with a watery stare, and its vicious growling quieted.

"But I was close to one and it didn't touch me. They're ugly and smelly, sure, but otherwise harmless." Giacomo couldn't explain why he was defending them, but the thought of Ozo running his sword through their bodies didn't feel right.

"Nothing harmless about Tulpas," Ozo snarled.

"What else can we do with them, Giacomo?" Milena said, coming up behind him. "We can't release them and we certainly can't take them with us."

"So letting Ozo slaughter them is better?"

"It might seem harsh, but it's more humane than leaving them caged up while they waste away." She took him by the arm and tried to lead him away, but Giacomo stayed put.

"Get him out of here," Ozo ordered.

Zatto wrapped his thick hands around Giacomo's shoulders. "My apologies." Giacomo tried to break free, but unsurprisingly, Zatto's grip was a lot stronger than Milena's. "We found quite a lot of tasty food in the kitchen. Maybe you'd like a snack?"

"I don't want a snack!" Giacomo thrashed and kicked as Zatto pulled him up the stairs. Milena and Savino trailed behind.

Giacomo watched helplessly as Ozo plunged his blade between the bars of the first cage. An ear-piercing squeal made his blood run cold. He looked away. A chorus of shrieks followed as the Tulpas met their end.

* * *

Back in the hallway, Zatto released Giacomo, who dropped to his knees, head in hands, trying not to burst into tears. Mico settled on his shoulder and offered a comforting chirrup.

"I don't get what the big deal is," Savino said. "Those things were monstrosities. Good riddance to them."

"At least they're not suffering anymore," Milena said, trying to make him feel better. He didn't.

Giacomo got up and trudged away, following the sound of harp music. "I'm going to see how Aaminah's doing with Ersilia's grandmother."

Flames roared in the great hall's gigantic stone hearth. Aaminah played a soothing song for an old woman who lay on a long cushioned bench, her head in Ersilia's lap. Luna projected waves of yellow light over the old woman's limp body. Almost immediately, Giacomo's tense muscles relaxed. Unfortunately, it didn't look like the music was having the same effect on Ersilia's grandmother.

"How's she doing?" Giacomo asked.

Aaminah glanced up and shook her head, a despairing look on her face. Giacomo had never seen her look so sad.

Savino and Milena came in and spread out the parchments they'd found across the long dining table. Soon after, Ozo stepped into the doorway, his sword dripping red spots on the white marble. Ersilia gasped. "What . . . what have you done?"

"Took care of an infestation in your cellar," Ozo said. "Duke Oberto ever let you go down there?"

"No, it was strictly off-limits to the maidservants," she replied.

"I figured as much." Ozo wiped the blood on his leather pants and sheathed his sword. "We're going to spend the night," he informed everyone. "Lots of nice cushy beds in the castle, so take your pick. Then back on the road first thing."

"There's one problem," Milena said. "The Compass isn't at the Cave of Alessio. We need to change course."

Savino tipped his head toward Giacomo. "*His* fault."

"It's not there?" Ozo's jaw clenched and he pressed his fingers against his scarred temple. "Then where are we headed?"

"That's the problem," Milena said. "We don't know yet."

Ozo growled and shook his head. "You got until morning to figure it out. Otherwise, I'm calling off this mission and taking you back to Virenzia. I've already lost too many men as it is." Ozo marched down the hall, the heavy clomp of his boots fading away.

Milena split the parchments into three piles. "Start going through these. Anything that seems promising, let me know." Giacomo joined them at the table and began riffling through his stack.

"How about we throw you back inside the camera obscura?" Savino suggested to Giacomo. "Maybe you can find some new clues in the Wellspring."

"I got sucked in by accident, I'm not going back on purpose. I thought I was going to die in the Wellspring. I'm staying as far away from the camera obscura as possible, especially now that Ozo turned the cellar into a slaughterhouse."

"Why are you being so weird about a few dead Tulpas?" Savino asked. "The whole point of finding the Sacred Tools is so we can use them to destroy Ugalino's Tulpa."

Giacomo kept his eyes on the papers. "I know . . . but . . . Ozo was acting cruel. It was like he enjoyed killing them."

"If he hadn't gotten rid of them, I'd have done it myself," Savino bragged.

"And I don't think Zanobius is as mindless and dangerous as Pietro and Baldassare believe," Giacomo said.

"Not dangerous? I thought you saw him try to drown Enzio."

"Yeah, I know. But I got the sense he didn't really want to."

"So now you think a Tulpa can have feelings?"

"Why not? Zanobius looks human, he moves like a human—"

"It's a Tulpa!" Savino interrupted. "There's nothing human about it!"

Aaminah's music stopped. "If you're going to yell, do it somewhere else," she snapped. "I'm trying to create a soothing mood here."

"Sorry," Giacomo said, feeling annoyed. He didn't know why he was apologizing when Savino was the one raising his voice.

"Can we focus on finding the Compass?" Milena said, trying to get them back on course.

Aaminah strummed her harp, and music filled the room once again. Giacomo's frazzled nerves settled and he focused back on the duke's papers. As he sorted through the stack, he came across a page full of different patterns inside rows of squares.

"Think these doodles mean anything?" Giacomo showed the parchment to Milena.

She glanced at the patterns. "Maybe . . ." Suddenly, her eyes lit up and she snatched the paper out of his hands. "Wait, it's a cipher! It has to be!"

Her excitement was lost on Giacomo. "What's a cipher?"

"It's a key that helps you figure out a secret message," she said, buzzing with energy. "Look, there are twenty-six different patterns. I bet each one corresponds to a letter."

Savino peeked over her shoulder to get a look at the symbols.

"But I haven't seen any other piece of paper with those symbols on it. Have you? If it is a cipher, we'd need the message it was meant to decode."

"Keep looking," Milena told him. "It must be in here somewhere."

They all riffled through the parchments, but Giacomo couldn't find anything with the same symbols.

"Got something!" Savino held up a piece of parchment. On it were rows of the same cipher patterns grouped together, like words.

Milena placed the message next to the cipher. "Now we need to figure out which letters correspond to which patterns."

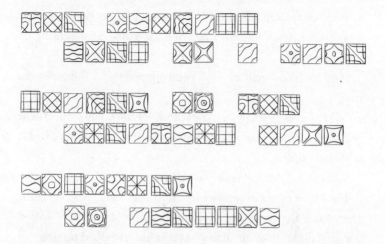

They first tried assigning *A* to the first pattern, *B* to the second pattern, and *C* to the third, but it soon became apparent that whoever had made the cipher hadn't made it that simple to figure out.

"Look at the message." Milena pointed to a box with wavy lines that angled to the right. "This is a one-letter word. It can only be *A* or *I*, right?"

"Good point." Giacomo made a mental note.

"We should focus on the two- and three-letter words too. Notice how these two are identical?" She pointed to a clump of three symbols at the start of the message and in the middle. "It's most likely *and* or *the*."

Giacomo nodded, impressed by Milena's quick thinking.

"And here," she said, pointing to two identical grid-like patterns sitting next to each other. "This has to be a double letter, like *SS*, *TT*, or *OO*."

They each copied the message into their sketchbooks and set

to work using Milena's tips as the starting point. But no matter what combination of letters he tried, Giacomo kept coming up with nonsense.

"And blomboo went to . . . A bend opened in . . . and backache lost?"

"Well, I guess we can stop the search for the Compass," Milena said sarcastically. "Turns out some guy named Blomboo's had it this whole time."

"Ignore her," Savino said. "Just keep at it."

The three of them worked late into the night, past the time when Ersilia covered her grandmother in a blanket and kissed her good night. Past the time when Aaminah stopped playing, her fingers raw and blistered. Past the time when the roaring fire diminished to a pile of glowing embers. And past the time when their Geniuses fell asleep high in the great hall's eaves.

Savino slumped over the table and put his head in his hands. His head jerked as he tried to fight off sleep.

"Lie down, Savino," Milena said. "We'll keep working."

Savino mumbled something that sounded like "good night" and collapsed in a large chair by the window. Within seconds he was snoring.

Infected by Savino's sleepiness, Giacomo yawned. In his sketchbook, the symbols blurred.

"You should get some sleep too," Milena told him.

Giacomo rubbed his eyes and the patterns came back into focus. "No, I'm okay." But as he stared at the different squiggles and lines, they all began to jumble together. He wasn't brainy like Milena. There was no way he was going to be able to figure out the message. His thoughts turned to Pietro, back at the villa.

"Do you think they're okay?" Giacomo said.

"Who?" Milena asked, not looking up.

"Pietro, and Signor and Signora Barrolo."

Milena put her pencil down. "I honestly don't know . . ." Her words trailed off. "But if Pietro were here, I am pretty sure he'd tell us to stay focused on the mission and keep going." She went back to work.

Giacomo nodded and looked at the cipher. But as he stared between it and the coded message, he began to drift off. He shook his head and slapped his cheeks to keep himself awake. He pushed the scattered parchments aside and was about to lay his head on the table, when a symbol on one of the pages caught his attention: a six-pointed star inside a hexagon. It was the same as the tattoo Zanobius had on his chest and back.

He slid the parchment out from the others. It was a drawing of a man with four arms and four legs. Surrounding him was a circle and a square, which were lined up perfectly with his hands and feet. Ringing the man was a series of three-dimensional shapes, some of which looked similar to the symbols he'd seen projected in the camera obscura.

Giacomo's heart raced. Was this a different kind of cipher, one that hid the secrets to creating a Tulpa?

"What's that?" Milena asked. She must have noticed the stunned look on his face.

"Uh . . . nothing," Giacomo said, slapping the parchment face down on the table. "I thought it was going to help me figure out this message, but it's another dead end."

"Too bad." Milena didn't press him any further.

Giacomo slyly dragged the parchment off the table, folded it, and tucked it in his satchel. He didn't trust anyone else with it for the time being, especially Ozo and Savino. They'd tear it to shreds without a second thought. Once he was by himself, he'd examine it more closely.

The discovery energized Giacomo and he forgot all about sleep, working until sunlight streamed through the window. By then, Milena was slumped over the table, arms splayed, fast asleep.

But despite staying up all night, Giacomo was no closer to deciphering the message. He peeked across the table at Milena's sketchbook. Among the scribbles and crossed-out letters she had written:

The Compass _ _es in a ca_e
s_ape_ by the Creator's _a_ _
o_sc_re_ by Alessio.

Giacomo couldn't believe it. She was so close. He shook her. "Milena, wake up!"

She jolted up to sitting and wiped drool off her mouth. "What time is it?"

Savino groggily came to and pulled himself out of the chair.

"The message," Giacomo said, eagerly pointing at Milena's notes. "Only a few letters are missing."

Milena looked at her sketchbook, like she didn't recognize her own handwriting. "Before I fell asleep, I was on a roll. But I could barely keep my eyes open."

"The last word has to be *Alessio*," Giacomo said.

"Right! Of course!" Milena filled in the letter *L*. "And if that's the case the second word begins with an *L*."

"Lies!" Savino proclaimed.

"I'm not lying, it's the same symbol," Milena said.

"I wasn't calling *you* a liar," Savino said. "The word is *lies*."

"Oh. Sorry."

"'The Compass lies in a . . .'" Giacomo read the first line, which was nearly complete.

"Case?" Savino said, trying to guess the last word.

"Cave," Milena said confidently. "'The Compass lies in a cave.'"

"The message is about the Cave of Alessio," Savino said with disappointment. "It's telling us what we already know. Or what we thought we already knew."

But Giacomo wasn't ready to give up. They still had two lines of the message to decipher. He began sounding out *S* words. "Sh, sl, sn . . ."

"Shaped!" Milena exclaimed, filling in the first word on the second line. "Shaped by the Creator's . . ."

"The last letter has to be *D*," Giacomo pointed out. "Hand!"

"'The Compass lies in a cave, shaped by the Creator's hand,'" Milena said. There was only one word missing now.

"The Creator's hand shaped every cave in the world, so not much help there," Savino complained.

Milena shot him an annoyed look. "If you're not going to help, then be quiet." She and Giacomo stared at the final word.

o _ sc _ red

"Any ideas?" Giacomo said.

"On . . . or . . . ob . . . obscured!" Milena declared in a burst of insight. She filled in the missing letters and reread the entire message. "'The Compass lies in a cave, shaped by the Creator's hand, obscured by Alessio.'"

Giacomo had expected the message to shed some light on where they should go next, but he felt more confused now than when they started.

"It doesn't mean anything," Savino said, exasperated. "We wasted the entire night!"

Giacomo folded his arms on the table and buried his head. They'd have to tell Ozo they didn't know where the Compass was and he'd march them back to Baldassare's, empty-handed. The mission had failed, and it was all his fault.

Why was Alessio even part of the message? The Compass wasn't in the cave. It was an illusion, like a projection on the camera obscura's wall.

Obscura . . . Obscured . . . The similarity of the two words couldn't be a coincidence.

Giacomo jolted upright. "The message isn't a dead end. It's a huge breakthrough!" He jumped up from his chair. "I know what we need to do!"

"Where are you going?" Milena asked.

"Back into the camera obscura."

"You said you never wanted to open the Wellspring again," Milena reminded him.

"I don't," Giacomo said. "I have a different idea. Hopefully one that's a lot less painful."

Giacomo hustled out of the room, followed by Milena and Savino. A flutter of feathers blew past them into the hall. Their Geniuses were awake, ready for a new day.

Giacomo covered his nose and ran past the Tulpas' cages, turning away from the carnage within.

Across from the camera obscura, Giacomo found the mechanism responsible for projecting the images. He'd breezed past it the first time, mistaking it for a small cabinet. He pulled open the door, revealing an unlit lantern inside. Above the lantern was a venting tube, probably for smoke. In front of the lantern was a second tube that extended out through the cabinet's wall and aimed directly at the camera obscura—this was how the light was projected. Mounted on the outside of the cabinet was a large wooden disc inset with round illustrations on vellum—these were the anatomical drawings and shapes Giacomo had seen on the wall. Ropes attached to the projector cabinet looped around a series of pulleys and counterweights suspended from the ceiling, then connected to the camera obscura's door. The rigging explained how the camera obscura automatically turned on when Giacomo had been locked inside.

He found more vellum drawings stacked next to the lantern and flipped through them until he found the image he'd hoped for—a map of central Zizzola.

"The Cave of Alessio is here." With charcoal, Giacomo marked an X next to a winding river on the vellum map. Then he slid it into the wooden disc on the projector. "Savino, I need you to stay out here and flip this map when I tell you to."

Savino took his post next to the projector cabinet. Giacomo then ushered Milena inside the camera obscura and closed the door, sealing them in. He heard the clicking and whirring of the contraption coming to life.

"It's working!" Savino confirmed.

A beam of light shot through the camera obscura's gem. The map of Zizzola appeared on the opposite wall, upside down.

A smile crossed Milena's face as she realized what Giacomo was up to. "Obscured by Alessio. Brilliant thinking using the camera obscura like this, Giacomo."

Milena's compliment sent a tingle up his neck. *Does she really think I'm brilliant?*

Giacomo marked the wall where the *X* indicating Alessio's Cave was projected. "Savino, now flip the drawing of the map!"

Zizzola vanished for a moment, leaving a wall of white. When the map reappeared, it was right-side up. With the map inverted, the *X* on the wall now marked a new location—a mountain directly to the north of Alessio's Cave.

Giacomo pointed at the mountain. "That's where we'll find the Compass."

Milena passed her left hand in front of the map, casting a shadow of her arm. "So the Compass in Alessio's Cave must've been a projection of the real Compass, like this map being projected by the lantern."

"Sure seems like it," Giacomo said.

Savino opened the door and looked in. "So did you figure out where we're going?"

With her long, shadowy finger, Milena pointed to the new mark on the map. "The Abscondita Mountains."

Savino hung his head and sighed. "Are you kidding?"

"No. Is that a problem?" Giacomo said.

"Only that we'll have to cross through Terra della Morte." He pointed to a long jagged strip that cut across the map, between the duke's castle and their new destination.

"The Land of Death . . ." Milena said hopelessly.

Giacomo wrung his hands together. They felt cold and damp. "It can't be that bad . . . Can it?"

A NEW ALLY

Zanobius reclined against a slanted rock, his four legs stretched out in front of him, and stared up at the cloudless night sky. Though relaxed, Zanobius could be on his feet at a moment's notice if Enzio tried to sneak out of the cave. But the boy had pretty much kept to himself the past few days. The most he spoke was to ask if he could leave to urinate in the bushes. For food, Zanobius collected some fruit from the nearby trees, along with handfuls of berries. Enzio gobbled them up without a word.

Zanobius also kept an eye out in case the boy named Giacomo returned. But there had been no sign of him since their initial encounter. The Compass had vanished not long after, which seemed odd. Did the boy have anything to do with it?

His attention turned back to Enzio, who snored peacefully in the cave. Zanobius longed to know what it was like to sleep, to let his mind go somewhere else, even for a few hours. He imagined it was much more relaxing than his blackouts. Every time Zanobius lost consciousness, he woke riddled with questions and fears and uncertainty. When humans rose, they seemed refreshed and not confused by their surroundings.

So he spent his nights staring up at the heavens, connecting the shining dots to form pictures of animals or people. Some were the images discovered by the ancients—Cassian's Bow, Morlok the Bear, the long tail and mane of Laterna's Lion. But if he got creative, he could also connect the specks of light to form his own pictures. Tonight he found the outline of Ugalino's angular face— its high cheekbones, long nose, and stern expression.

"You ever sleep?" Enzio stood over Zanobius and stared up at the sky, which was beginning to lighten with dawn's arrival. The stars blinked out, one by one.

Zanobius sat up, surprised that Enzio had spoken. "No. I can't. My master told me it's a downside of being a Tulpa."

"That sounds pretty awful," Enzio said.

"You should probably get back in the cave," Zanobius said, waving him away. "In case Ugalino comes back."

Enzio looked around. "He's been gone for days, I doubt he's going to show up right this second. Where is your delightful master, anyway?"

"You find him pleasant?" Zanobius asked.

"I was being sarcastic," Enzio explained. "Don't Tulpas have a sense of humor?"

"I'm not sure." His master wasn't one to joke around, so it was possible he had deprived Zanobius of the ability too.

"So where is he?" Enzio asked again.

"My master doesn't always tell me where he's going. Sometimes he disappears for days. But he always comes back, sooner or later."

"Sounds like my father," Enzio said. "Always off dealing with some Council business, or buying illegal art, or looking for more Geniuses. I barely ever see him."

Zanobius sat up and gestured for Enzio to join him, curious about what he might have to say. The boy took a seat on a rock facing him. "Your father . . . he's looking for the Compass too?"

"Finding the Sacred Tools has been his obsession," Enzio said. "It's the whole reason he started recruiting kids with Geniuses and bringing them to our villa. He and Pietro have been preparing them for this big, important mission for years. That's all he's cared about."

"Did you train with them?"

Enzio shook his head and looked off toward the river. "In my home, if you didn't have a Genius, you didn't have much of a purpose."

"Your father had a Genius?"

"No, that's the thing. I think he wished like crazy he had one. And when it became clear I wasn't going to have one either, he starting looking to other places."

"That's when he found the children who had Geniuses?"

Enzio nodded with a bitter frown. "What's with all the questions?"

"You came out to talk to me," Zanobius reminded him.

"Point taken," Enzio said with a shrug.

"I'm intrigued by humans," Zanobius went on. "Why they act in ways that seem against their self-interest."

"Like how?"

"Take your father. Rather than accept his own son for who he is, he formed a rift between him and you. He put his all-consuming passion over his own family. What if he doesn't get what he wants?

What if, after all this, my master finds the Compass first? He'll have alienated you for nothing."

Enzio snorted dismissively. "And you think you and Ugalino have some kind of ideal relationship? All he does is boss you around and order you to kill people. Humans might be messed up, but at least we have the choice to make stupid mistakes."

Had Zanobius ever attempted to do something different from what his master told him? He tried to recall even one choice he'd made on his own, but all he found in his shattered memory were the traces of Ugalino's commands.

"How did you do it?" Zanobius asked.

"Do what?"

"Speak out against your father. You called him greedy and selfish and refused to do what he asked of you."

"It had been building for a while. Pretty much my whole life. I couldn't stay quiet when he was about to let my mother die."

"Sometimes Ugalino commands me to do things I don't want to. Like attacking your mother. Maybe you could show me how to stand up to him?"

"Teach you to rebel against Ugalino?" Enzio shook his head. "No thanks. My father acts tough, but he doesn't scare me. Ugalino does."

"I understand. It was a foolish idea." Zanobius changed the subject. "Are you hungry?"

Enzio raised his eyebrows. "Starving. You have something besides berries?"

"We could catch some fish." Zanobius gestured to the river.

"Uh . . . I don't know how to. Never really had to learn. My father knew the best fisherman in Virenzia."

"Then I'll teach you." Zanobius rose to his feet and waved with his two right arms for Enzio to follow.

"I thought Ugalino told you I wasn't supposed to leave the cave."

Zanobius looked back at the boy. "I know, but I'm going to let you anyway. It's my choice."

Enzio smiled and jogged over. "See, you don't need me. Just let that rebellious side come out once in a while."

"If you try to escape, I will hunt you down and rip you limb from limb," Zanobius warned. Enzio halted in terror. A huge smile spread across Zanobius's face. "I was being sarcastic," he said proudly.

"I don't think you quite get the concept yet," Enzio remarked.

They walked down to the river. Zanobius found two branches about the length of his arm and tied a piece of twine around the end of each. He dug in the dirt and pulled out a couple of long, juicy worms.

"No fish will be able to resist these," he said, impaling the worms onto bone hooks that he had attached to the twine. Enzio looked disgusted as the bait wriggled, trying to free themselves. Zanobius handed one of the fishing lines to Enzio, who held it vertically.

"No, you need to angle it, like this." Zanobius extended his stick over the river, letting the hooked worm plop into the water. Enzio copied Zanobius's movements.

"Now what?" Enzio asked.

"Now, we wait."

Zanobius smiled at Enzio, content in the moment. Though there were many things he didn't admire about humans, he was envious of their ability to form friendships with each other. It was astounding that two people, bound neither by blood nor duty, could form an alliance.

"Tulpas can't make friends," Ugalino often reminded Zanobius, "only enemies. Humans fear what they don't understand." He had always believed this to be true, but talking with Enzio, he began to question whether things could be different. Not that he expected Enzio would want to be his friend after Zanobius had almost killed him and his mother.

The sun peeked out from behind the mountain and its rays glinted off the water's surface like a thousand shimmering candle flames. After a long silence, Enzio spoke up.

"I have to ask, did your master put those tattoos on you?"

Zanobius nodded, relieved to remember something from his past. "After he sculpted me, Ugalino drew this pattern on me to bring me to life. He told me this design connects me to the Creator and the universe, though I have to admit, I'm not exactly sure how."

"Did he tell you why he gave you four arms and four legs?"

"They're supposed to make me a perfectly proportioned man," Zanobius replied. "I never quite understood what he meant by that either."

"Seems like your master keeps you in the dark about a lot of things."

Before Zanobius could explain about his blackouts, Enzio's line tugged, splashing the water's surface.

"Pull it up!" Zanobius instructed.

Enzio yanked on the stick and an enormous green-scaled fish flung itself into the air, tugging against the twine. He let it drop on the sand, where it flopped from one side to the other. After a few seconds, the fish lay still.

Enzio's mouth hung agape. "What do I do with it now?"

"Eat it," Zanobius said. "Why do humans overthink even their basic survival?"

Zanobius brought out his knife and showed Enzio how to gut the fish, cutting a long line down its belly. He scooped out a handful of warm, slippery insides and tossed them into the water. Enzio wrinkled his nose. "I didn't realize fishing would be so . . . gross."

"It would do you good to spend some time outside that stuffy villa of yours."

"Assuming I ever make it back home."

Zanobius built a fire and cooked the fish on a spit over the flames. Once the scales became black and crispy, Zanobius handed the spit to Enzio.

"Aren't you going to have any?" Enzio asked.

"Tulpas don't need to eat."

"Another downside?"

"I suppose so."

"Then why'd you learn how to fish?"

"My master doesn't like to get his hands dirty with this kind of thing."

Enzio eagerly bit into the steaming fish, leaving only the bones and the head. "I can't eat the heads, even when my mother cooks. I hate how the eyeballs stare back at me. Creeps me out." He tossed the carcass into a nearby bush.

Ciro's familiar *caw* cut through the sky, signaling his master's return.

"Quick, back into the cave," Zanobius ordered. Enzio scrambled to his prison while Zanobius stamped out the fire and kicked the fishing lines into the river.

The Genius landed and its master dismounted, carrying a satchel that looked heavy with supplies. "Any problems with the boy?"

"None," Zanobius said.

"Bring him out," Ugalino instructed. "I have work to do in the cave."

When Zanobius emerged with Enzio, he made a show of dragging the boy out by his collar, as though Enzio had been resistant.

Ciro raised his head and looked around, honing in on something. He lumbered toward the bushes and poked his beak into the leaves, finding the carcass of Enzio's fish. Ciro tossed his head back, swallowing the leftovers in one gulp. Ugalino's eyes flashed to the smoldering ashes, then to Zanobius.

"The boy wanted to eat something other than berries," Zanobius said, covering. "I caught a fish and prepared it for him."

"He's a good cook for never having tasted food," Enzio added.

Ugalino regarded Enzio with a probing stare, then he tossed the satchel into Zanobius's arms. "Grind the pigments. I need blue, white, green, and black."

Zanobius nodded. "Of course."

"When they're ready, bring them to me." *Along with the boy,* Ugalino added so Enzio couldn't hear. He disappeared into the cave.

Zanobius emptied his master's satchel onto the ground. Chunks of green and white rock lay next to iridescent shards of a blue mineral. The remaining raw materials were animal bones, most likely the remains of Ciro's last meal.

Enzio looked over Zanobius's shoulder. "You can make paint out of all that?"

"I can show you how, if you're interested."

Enzio shrugged. "Not like I have anything else to do."

"But you have to follow my instructions carefully. My master is very particular about his pigments."

Zanobius put Enzio to work, first piling stones into a small, enclosed stove, then putting the animal bones inside. Enzio did as he was told, starting the fire and sealing off the opening. "Leave it until the bones are charred," Zanobius said.

Next, he directed Enzio to wash off the rocks and minerals in the river. Once they were clean, Zanobius ground each one against a larger rock, collecting the falling grains on a sheet of parchment. It was a slow, laborious process, but by sundown, the pieces of hard earth had been transformed into delicate piles of green, white, and blue powder.

Last, he had Enzio pull the bones, which now resembled pieces of charcoal, from the fire. Zanobius ground those too, then carefully transferred the bone powder and each of the pigments into wooden cups. Drop by drop, he mixed in water until the paint became the perfect consistency. Neither too thick nor too runny.

Enzio had turned out to be a studious apprentice, helpful and inquisitive. But a feeling of unease crept through Zanobius. Something told him Ugalino wasn't keeping Enzio around to help him mix paint. The boy had a critical role to play—but what it was, Zanobius had no idea.

"Why is Ugalino having you make all these colors anyway?"

Enzio rinsed his sooty hands off in the river. "If I were him, I'd be looking for the Compass, not wasting my time painting a cave."

"I'm sure whatever he's planning will help him on that quest." Zanobius left it at that. The less Enzio knew, the better. "Ugalino never ceases to surprise me with his creativity."

Zanobius hid his dread under a smile.

14

TERRA DELLA MORTE

"You sure about this?" Ozo asked, looking very unhappy.

Giacomo had just told him where the real Compass was located, and that they would have to travel through Terra della Morte—the Land of the Dead—to get there.

After yesterday's Tulpa slaughter, Giacomo had little respect for the mercenary. "Yes, I'm sure," he said with an irritated edge. *I can't be wrong twice, can I?*

"Do Ugalino and his Tulpa know about this new location?" Ozo asked.

"Not yet. But if we could figure it out, it's only a matter of time before Ugalino does too, so we should leave soon." Giacomo marched off, with Savino and Milena trailing behind.

"Your friend's been playing since the sun came up," Ozo called after them, commenting on the lilting flute music coming from the great hall. "Tell her to pack it up and let's get moving."

Giacomo overheard the Bull complaining to Ozo. "The others aren't gonna be happy about this."

"They all have a job to complete," Ozo said. "Those who abandon the mission give up their cut of the money."

"I'll tell 'em."

Giacomo found Aaminah in the great hall, dark circles under her eyes. Despite the beautiful music and Luna's healing waves of light, the elderly woman still lay unresponsive in Ersilia's lap, her face drained of color.

"Aaminah . . ." Giacomo said, gently trying to get her attention.

She kept playing.

"We have to go."

She pulled the flute away from her lips. The yellow light from her Genius dissolved into the air. "Maybe if I try the viol again." She reached for her stringed instrument.

Giacomo put a hand on the viol's neck, stopping her. "You've done everything you can."

"No, I haven't," Aaminah snapped. "She's still as sick as when we got here." Giacomo had never heard her so upset.

"It's all right." Ersilia's eyes were full of tears. "My grandmother's been ill a very long time. I'm sure she found comfort listening to your beautiful music. I know I did."

Aaminah snatched her viol from Giacomo and played a series of long, low notes. Giacomo and Milena shared an uncomfortable look, neither one of them sure how to convince Aaminah to leave the woman's side.

Savino pushed past and snatched the bow away from Aaminah, cutting off the music.

"Hey!" Aaminah shouted.

"Time to move on," Savino said harshly.

"Don't be a jerk about it," Milena said.

Savino stomped out of the room. "I'll be outside when you're all ready."

Aaminah covered her face and began crying. Giacomo put a hand on her shoulder and tried to comfort her.

"Sometimes the world is unfair and cruel for no good reason," he said quietly. Giacomo knew that better than anyone, but it never made the grief any easier to bear.

Milena helped Aaminah from the chair and guided her out, leaving Giacomo to collect her instruments.

Ersilia cradled her grandmother's pale cheek in her hand. "I hope you all find what you're looking for," she said, her voice quavering.

"I'm sorry about your grandmother." Giacomo gathered the flute, harp, and viol in his arms and hurried out, not sure what else to say. From the hall, he heard Ersilia's faint sobs.

In the courtyard, Savino and the mercenaries gathered around Ozo. Giacomo counted eleven. *Good, they're all still here.* Apparently, the lure of money outweighed their fear of death. For Giacomo, the excitement of being the first to find the Compass kept him motivated, though he was beginning to question whether he would actually use the Sacred Tools against Zanobius if given the chance. *Do I really have it in me to kill a Tulpa? Could I be as merciless as Ozo?*

"We'll head west along our original route, then break north," Ozo announced. "With any luck, we'll be on the other side of the Land of the Dead in a few days."

"We go through there and none of us are coming out the other side," Old Dino warned. "Isn't there a way around?"

"A detour will set us back more than a month," Ozo countered. "Ugalino and his Tulpa will have beaten us to the Compass by then. This is the path we're taking."

Old Dino shook his head. "Then I guess me and Little Dino are forfeiting our cuts. I already lost one son on this wild-goose chase. I'm not losing another." Father and son dropped their coin-filled pouches on the ground. Then Old Dino put his hand on Little Dino's back and led him away.

"I'm with them," Zatto the Beheader said, throwing his coins down too. "The Compass can't be worth the lives of all your men, can it?"

"Or women." Malocchio added her *impronta* to the pile, then hoisted her bow over her shoulder. "Good luck out there, Ozo."

The Bull slapped Valcaro on the back. "More for the rest of us!" Valcaro remained silent beneath his helmet.

Zatto, Malocchio, and the Dinos walked out of the courtyard.

Giacomo's heartbeat quickened. Had he been too eager to push on? The mercenaries were battle hardened. Giacomo doubted they ran from a fight without good cause.

Ozo looked across the remaining mercenaries: the Bull, Baby Cannoli, Valcaro, Sforza, Spike, and Sveva. "Anyone else having second thoughts?" The mercenaries shook their heads.

Giacomo wanted to raise his hand, but he couldn't bring himself to. He'd set these wheels in motion. *No stopping us now.*

They set out that morning, and by midday the sun was bearing down on them. The crunch of their footsteps in the pebbly dirt and an occasional Genius squawk were the only sounds for hours. Aaminah kept her distance behind the group, head hung, staring at the ground. Giacomo slowed his pace.

"You okay?" As soon as he said it, he knew it was a dumb thing to say. Obviously she wasn't.

Aaminah shrugged and kept her gaze down. "It just doesn't make any sense."

"What doesn't?"

"Why did the Creator give me a Genius if I can't use it to heal people?"

"But you've helped a lot of people. You fixed me up more than once. And what about Ozo's troops?"

"Surface wounds are easy. Whatever Ersilia's grandmother was sick with, it went deep. It felt like I was digging out tangled roots from the ground. I kept pulling and pulling and pulling . . ." She sounded like she was about to cry.

Milena heard their conversation and joined them. "She reminded you of your mother, didn't she?"

Aaminah nodded with a sadness in her eyes.

"I'm sorry," Giacomo said. "I didn't know . . . What happened to your mother?"

"She was sick too," Aaminah explained. "A terrible fever . . . By the end she could barely breathe. I played for her night and day, but nothing I did saved her."

"What about your father? Where was he?" Giacomo asked.

"I never knew him. My mother told me that right after my Genius showed up, he went back to Katunga, where he was from. I was only a few weeks old."

"He abandoned you when you were a baby?" Giacomo asked. "What kind of person does that?"

"No, he didn't leave me, he was trying to protect me," Aaminah explained. "My father was worried that someone would turn my Genius and me over to the Supreme Creator. So he decided to go to his homeland and find somewhere safe to move our family. But he never came back for us."

"What happened to him?"

"I don't know. Whenever I asked my mother about him, she put on a hopeful face and reassured me that my father loved me and that he'd return. But before she died, she confessed that he was probably never coming back and told me why: my father's parents had forbidden him to marry my mother because she was a Zizzolan peasant. When my father married her anyway, they disowned him."

"Do you think your grandparents stopped your father from bringing you and your mother to Katunga?" Milena asked.

"Maybe," Aaminah said with a shrug. "You know, sometimes I feel like he's still out there, looking for me . . . but other times I think I'm just kidding myself."

"There's nothing wrong with having hope," Milena said.

Aaminah's story made Giacomo realize that even though he'd been with his new companions for a few weeks now, he barely knew anything about their lives before Baldassare had taken them in.

"Milena, where did you grow up?" Giacomo asked.

"I was born in Virenzia," Milena said. "Same as Savino."

"Except her parents were loaded," Savino piped up. He'd obviously been listening. He dropped back and walked next to Giacomo.

"They were wealthy, it's true," Milena said, sounding embarrassed. "Still are, as far as I know."

"You don't talk to them?" Giacomo asked.

"Not since I left home."

Giacomo couldn't imagine not seeing his parents if they were still alive. "How did they react when your Genius showed up?"

"They didn't take it well. It was my first birthday. My parents had this big celebration all planned, but the second they saw Gaia, they canceled everything, then spent the next few years trying to get rid of her. My father locked her in a cage and sent her away on one of his merchant ships. He told the captain to release her near an island in the middle of the sea. The captain claimed he did, but somehow, Gaia flew back to Virenzia and found me again. This happened over and over."

"At least your father didn't have your Genius killed," Giacomo said, trying to find a bright spot in her story.

"My parents aren't the most compassionate people, but they weren't going to let me become a Lost Soul." Giacomo noticed Milena rubbing her left arm, where she'd been injured. "Anyway, while all that was going on, my sisters were born, a year apart. And neither one had a Genius. After that, I pretty much became invisible to my parents.

"Then one day, when I was six, Baldassare showed up at our door and offered to take my Genius off their hands. But there was one condition—I had to go with him. My father told him yes on the spot. So they finally got rid of my Genius by getting rid of me too."

Milena fell silent and looked out toward the distant mountains.

Giacomo turned to Savino. "What about your parents?" he asked.

"They were a couple of gutless fools," Savino said. "They were so scared of what would happen if someone saw my Genius, they locked me and Nero in my room. The highlight of my day was peeking through the curtains down at the street, imagining myself playing with the other kids. Baldassare showed up when I was seven and offered to take me in, but my parents lied and said I had died in a tragic accident. When I overheard that, I busted out of my room to show Baldassare I was definitely alive, and told him to get me out of there. I never looked back."

Giacomo couldn't understand how Milena's and Savino's parents could be so uncaring when it came to their Geniuses. But that was the kind of world Nerezza had created, where parents felt like the only way to save their children was to abandon them.

"What's your story?" Savino asked. "How'd you become a sewer-boy, sewer-boy?"

Giacomo bristled and shook off the insult. Milena shot him a look that said, *When are you going to tell Savino to stop calling you that?*

"Both my parents were artists who had Geniuses," Giacomo began, "so I was used to having them around growing up. Of course, my parents had to keep their Geniuses secret, but that didn't stop my mother and father from painting. I guess they weren't careful enough, though. When I was five, Nerezza's soldiers broke into our home. They stuffed my parents' Geniuses into cages and hauled them away. After that, my mother and father changed. They didn't go out anymore, and stopped drawing and painting. They'd sit in the living room for hours, just staring at the wall. When it was time for bed, they wouldn't tuck me in or tell me stories like they used to. By the end, they stopped eating. They even forgot about feeding me. I was too young to understand at the time, but my parents were becoming . . ." He felt the words get stuck in his throat.

"Lost Souls," Aaminah said, saving Giacomo from having to say it.

Giacomo took a deep breath, not sure if he could get through the end of the story. "One morning, they didn't come out of their room. Finally, I went in and found them lying in their bed . . . but they didn't wake up . . ." He wiped his eyes before his tears made a fool out of him.

"Oh, Giacomo . . ." Aaminah was misty-eyed too.

Milena caringly squeezed his shoulder. Savino gave a heavy nod. No one said anything else for a long while after that.

Ever since his parents' deaths, Giacomo had felt different, like he didn't really belong anywhere, or with anyone. But hearing the others tell their stories made Giacomo realize they had more in common than he had thought. Aaminah had lost her mother and been separated from her father, and Milena and Savino were outcasts from their own families. Giacomo's heart felt more open, knowing they all understood one another a little better. And as he watched the sun dip behind the mountain and turn the clouds a radiant orange, Giacomo knew he'd do anything for these people whom he could now call his friends.

Over the next four days, the group hiked north, through a mostly desolate part of Zizzola.

Eventually, the dirt trail tapered to a barely visible path, then vanished altogether, leaving the group in the middle of a scrubby desert with piles of boulders scattered in every direction.

"Are we in the Land of Death?" Giacomo asked.

Ozo let loose a raucous howl from deep in his belly. He had barely cracked a smile since they left Virenzia, so at first Giacomo didn't recognize the sound as laughter.

"What's so funny?" Giacomo asked.

Ozo's laugh faded. "You, kid. Believe me, you'll know Terra della Morte when you're in it."

A few hours later, the group arrived at the edge of a vast canyon. As far as Giacomo could see, jagged pillars stabbed up through the earth, the setting sun glinting off them like a thousand blades of light. He wished Mico were as large as Ugalino's Genius so they could fly right over.

"Okay, now I see why they call it the Land of Death," Giacomo said.

Ozo shook his head. "They don't call it that because it's nasty-looking. It's because of the creatures who live down there."

"The Invisibilia," Sveva said in a slow, ominous voice. She drew her sword.

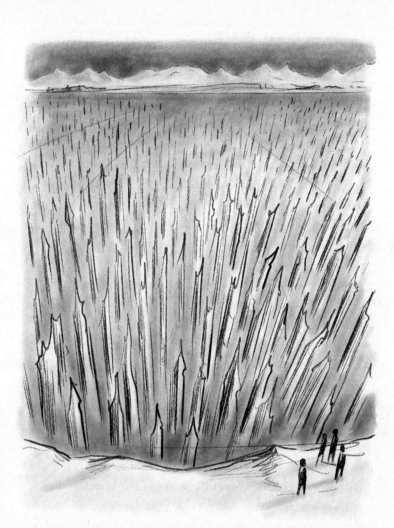

"Few have ever survived an encounter with them." Spike's intense black eyes stared out from the opening in his face guard. "The ones who have tell of giant lizards that'll wrap you up in their tongues as strong as chains. And the worst part? You can't even see 'em when they swallow you whole."

Giacomo glanced at his friends, who looked as terrified as he felt.

"You're the one who wanted to go this way," Savino reminded him. "I tried to warn you."

At least they had a night to rest before they would be forced to deal with the dangers that lay ahead. Giacomo took his satchel off his shoulder and sat down in the dirt, happy to be off his feet for the first time all day. As the sun dipped behind the horizon, a cool breeze danced through his hair. The ground was hard and rocky, but he didn't care. He could fall asleep on a bed of nails at this point.

"Back on your feet. We're not camping tonight," Ozo said.

"Wait, what?" Giacomo grudgingly picked himself up. Savino, who was sprawled out on the ground next to him, groaned.

Ozo unsheathed his sword. "The Invisibilia are only active when the sun's out, so the safest time to pass through is now."

Giacomo followed Ozo to a steep path that dropped into the canyon. Step by perilous step, the group descended single file down a narrow walkway. Mico and the other Geniuses effortlessly glided past them. By the time they reached the bottom, a canopy of stars had filled the sky and darkness enveloped them.

As they forged ahead into the heart of the canyon, Giacomo tripped on a rock. Stumbling, he went to catch himself and his palm scraped against one of the pillars, sending a stinging shock up his arm. He cried out, grasping his injured hand, which felt slick with blood.

"Are you all right?" Aaminah asked.

"No loud noises," Ozo snapped in an angry whisper.

"Maybe if we could get a little light, that would help," Giacomo complained.

"Fine. But not too bright. We don't want to wake our lizard friends."

Milena whistled to Gaia, who flew to the front of the group. The gem on her crown gave off a dim glow, casting an eerie green light on the path. Giacomo examined his palm, which had been sliced in several places.

"Of course it had to be my drawing hand," Giacomo said uneasily.

"That looks bad," Aaminah said. "I can fix it, but you'll have to wait until we're out of here."

"I'll be fine." Giacomo clamped his hand into a fist and pinned it against his waist to stop the bleeding. But if he was being honest with himself, he wasn't fine. The cuts only reminded him of that. It was thanks to him that they were all crossing this life-threatening canyon in the first place. He'd already seen two of Ozo's men perish on this mission, and he couldn't shake the thought that he was to blame. If more were killed, or if—and he hated to even consider the idea—Aaminah, Milena, or Savino met some horrible fate, he wouldn't know how to live with himself. That was assuming *he* made it out alive. The chances of which, he had to admit, seemed slim. If what Spike had said about the Invisibilia was true, they could all be killed before they even knew what hit them. *Is the Compass worth all this risk? Worth all this pain and the constant threat of death?* He didn't know, but it was too late to turn back now. He'd make sure they survived. Somehow.

The possibility of being attacked by the Invisibilia kept

everyone vigilant. They crept through the forest of razor-sharp pillars, staying close to one another.

The night passed swiftly, and before Giacomo knew it, the sky began to brighten in the east. But the end of the canyon was still a ways off.

Ozo picked up the pace. It was a race against the sun now. Giacomo's legs burned. Sweat stung his eyes. The morning light was already hitting the tops of the pillars above them. They reached a full sprint, but the canyon wall remained out of reach.

A warmth spread across his back. Normally, he would have welcomed the sun's rays after spending the night in a cold canyon. But this morning, all he could think was, *We're all about to die.*

Suddenly, he heard a scream. Giacomo spun around to see Spike yanked into the air by an unseen force. The mercenary was whipped back and forth like a helpless, floating rag doll. Spike's sword flew out of his hand and spun straight at Giacomo. He ducked as the blade whizzed over his head, planting itself into a pillar.

Ozo ran forward and swung his sword, trying to sever the Invisibilia's hold on Spike, but his blade sliced only air. Savino swiped his brush, and Nero projected a triangle at the unseen creature. The dagger-shaped blast missed and instead took a chunk out of a nearby pillar, scattering shards of sharp stone in all directions.

Mico dodged one of the fragments and lit up his red gem, shining a bright beam at their unseen attacker. By now, Spike's legs had vanished; he was just a floating torso. As Mico's light swept the scene, Giacomo caught sight of a giant, rainbow-scaled lizard with a long pink tongue wrapped around its prey.

Ozo and Sveva stood several feet away from the creature, blindly swinging their swords back and forth. The Bull aimed his crossbow and shot, but the arrow flew way off target. Valcaro fired his gun, but the shot missed by several feet, ricocheting off the pillars.

"Can't you see it?" Giacomo shouted.

"See what?" Confusion was scribbled across Ozo's face.

"The Invisibilia—it's right there!" Giacomo pointed to Mico's red beam. Aaminah, Milena, and Savino aimed their Geniuses to shine their lights in the same direction.

"I don't see anything," Milena said frantically.

"Me neither!" Savino yelled. "How about you, Aaminah?"

"No! Nothing!"

Giacomo grasped his sketchbook. In his injured hand, he clutched a pencil. Wincing, he drew a series of circles as fast as he could. Blood smeared across the page as Mico fired off a series of glowing discs that deflected off the lizard's scales and broke apart.

Spike's screams fell silent as the lizard's scaly lips swallowed his head. Then the creature turned and sped away, winding between the columns.

"It's gone," Giacomo told everyone.

"And so is Spike!" Ozo snapped angrily.

Sveva held her sword at the ready and scanned their surroundings. She glanced at Giacomo. "How come you could see that thing with your Genius, but they couldn't?" She nodded toward his friends.

Equally baffled, Giacomo looked to Mico. "I have no idea!"

"Doesn't matter," Ozo said gruffly. "You're leading us out of here."

Giacomo nodded. He whistled to Mico, then pointed at the path in front of them.

Mico hovered above Giacomo, bathing the area ahead in a red beam of light. To his horror, Giacomo spotted a slumbering Invisibilia less than a foot away. As Mico scanned farther on, Giacomo found another. Then another. Eight in total. They still lay in shadow, but in a minute, the sun would reach their bodies and wake them up. Giacomo and his friends were about to become lizard breakfast.

"How's it looking?" Savino asked.

"Uh . . . better if you don't know. Just follow me." With Mico illuminating the way, Giacomo led the group past one Invisibilia, then zigged and zagged through the pillars, avoiding the others.

As he passed the last of the creatures, Giacomo was jolted by another scream.

He whirled around. Mico's red beam revealed an Invisibilia's tongue wrapped around the Bull's waist. It was dragging him toward its gaping, fang-filled mouth. The Bull leveled his crossbow and fired, piercing the lizard's eye. It screeched, but didn't loosen its grip, pulling the Bull's legs into its throat. As the Bull struggled to grasp another arrow, Giacomo scanned the area they'd just passed through and saw scaly eyelids opening one by one. Gigantic eyeballs rotated in their sockets, and as the sun cast light on them, their huge black pupils narrowed into ominous slits. The Invisibilia lumbered to their feet.

"They're all waking up!" Giacomo warned.

Milena tugged on Savino's sleeve. "We can make a shield."

Savino nodded. "Everyone huddle in!"

When Giacomo looked back to the Bull, he was gone.

Ozo and his four remaining mercenaries trained their weapons on their unseen attackers and formed a tight clump around Giacomo and Aaminah. Milena and Savino stood opposite each other and directed their brushes toward the ground. As they painted in the air, Gaia and Nero projected green and blue strands of light, creating an elaborate interlocking pattern that built up like a wall around them.

A tongue lashed out, arcing over the top of the rising shield, right at Savino. With a flick of his wrist, he completed a star shape, severing the leathery organ in the process. The Invisibilia shrieked and backed away. The wall tapered above their heads and sealed shut, forming a dome.

The rest of the Invisibilia attacked the shield with a barrage of whapping tongue flicks, cracking its surface in a few places. But thankfully, the dome held.

"Everyone move together and we'll make it out of here," Giacomo said, trying to convince himself as much as anyone else. They shuffled slowly as a unit, the dome moving with them.

As more Invisibilia closed in, each tongue lash and claw slash shattered sections of the dome faster than Milena and Savino could replace them. A tongue snaked its way through an opening at knee level and yanked Baby Cannoli out of the shell. Valcaro shoved the barrel of his gun through the gap and fired, blasting the lizard in its side. But the metal bullet bounced off its scaly armor and skittered away. The Invisibilia threw its head back and swallowed Baby Cannoli whole. All that remained of him was a bow, which was immediately trampled.

Milena and Savino worked as fast as they could to keep their creation intact, but it seemed like the second they patched one damaged segment, another hole formed. Aaminah bowed short, high notes with her viol, and Luna sent out pulses of light wherever a section opened. But the panic on their faces said it all—they were fighting a losing battle. Giacomo urged the group to pick up the pace, but more and more Invisibilia surrounded them. By now the whole canyon was bathed in the morning sun. There was nowhere to hide.

Sforza jabbed his sword through an opening, stabbing one of the creatures in its mouth. In Mico's red beam, Giacomo saw the injured Invisibilia wrap its tongue around the sword's hilt.

"Let go!" Giacomo warned Sforza, but it was too late.

The Invisibilia pulled. Sforza, still gripping his weapon, flew out of the dome and into the lizard's maw.

Giacomo realized that out of the thirteen mercenaries who had begun the journey with them, only Ozo, Valcaro, and Sveva remained.

Then Giacomo felt a tightening around his right leg and he knew he'd be the next to go.

The tongue twisted several times, wrapping his leg from knee to hip. Giacomo pounded at it repeatedly with his fist. Its pink surface felt like leather covered in grit and mucus. The tongue jerked back and he flew out of the dome. His back slammed into the ground, knocking the wind out of him. Dirt and rocks scraped his body as he was pulled toward a gaping, fang-filled mouth.

Aaminah screamed "Giacomo!" and a burst of yellow light hit the Invisibilia right between the eyes. The creature reeled back, loosening its grip ever so slightly.

Mico swooped in, stabbing the tongue with his tiny beak. To Giacomo's surprise, the attack worked. The Invisibilia let out a screech and its tongue retracted.

Giacomo scrambled backward on elbows and feet. Mico flew to

meet him, and through the red beam, Giacomo saw the Invisibilia's tongue whip around.

"Mico, look out!" he shouted, but the tongue was too fast. It struck Mico, sending the Genius tumbling through the air. Mico smashed into one of the pillars, and pain ripped through Giacomo, like being slashed with a hundred knives. He lunged for his Genius, but his weakened right leg wouldn't hold his weight, and he collapsed. Giacomo caught sight of the Invisibilia lurching toward him just as Mico's red glow faded.

A long wave of bright yellow light streamed past and he heard a screech as the creature was hit.

Aaminah sprinted through what remained of the dome, scooped up Mico in her hands, and dashed to Giacomo's side. The last three mercenaries took up positions around them while Milena and Savino rapidly rebuilt the shield. But the end of the canyon was still far away. And with Giacomo's leg unable to carry him, running was out of the question.

"They'll pick off the rest of us if we stay on the ground," Savino said. He looked up at the towers of stone, then glanced to the cliff wall. "Aaminah, do you think you can topple that pillar?" He pointed at one to his right.

"Maybe," she said. "If I can make a low-enough note."

"I need you to crack it on the side facing the cliff."

Savino opened a small hole in the top of their shield, just wide enough for Luna to slip through. Aaminah propped the viol in the crook of her neck. Then she clunked the bow onto the bottom strings, pressing down and dragging it with all her might. The instrument let out a deep note, but then the tone dropped, becoming scratchy and grating. It reminded Giacomo of the harsh sound of the bladder pipe. Long, thick yellow waves washed over the base of the pillar, and the stone shards shattered, followed by a deafening *crack!* Aaminah dragged her bow again, causing the bottom of the pillar to rupture.

It slowly toppled, like a giant tree felled by loggers. It crashed into the one next to it, which slammed into another, causing a chain reaction of falling pillars. Shrieks from the Invisibilia mixed with the rumble of pillars collapsing. By the time the final boom rang out, a long, raised bridge had been created above the canyon floor, clearing a path to the canyon wall.

"Now!" Savino led the group up onto the nearest pillar, letting his part of the dome break apart as he ran. Ozo picked up Giacomo with one arm and continued to wield his sword with the other, cutting swaths around him in case any Invisibilia were near.

Giacomo held Mico close, carefully protecting his Genius's torn wings and chipped beak. Mico's eyes stayed shut. "Hold on," Giacomo said weakly.

With each pounding step, Giacomo found his hatred of Ozo eroding. Despite losing nearly all his companions, Ozo had still risked his own neck to save Giacomo—twice. Maybe he was more honorable than Giacomo had given him credit for. Baldassare should pay Ozo ten times what the mission cost. He had more than earned it.

Then with a startled yell, Ozo fell.

He lost his hold, and Giacomo crashed onto the shards of rock. They sliced his entire body, shredding his tunic. Behind him, Ozo slid down the length of the pillar, dragged by an Invisibilia, leaving behind a trail of blood.

"Ozo!" Sveva screamed. She and Valcaro ran after their leader.

Ozo hacked his sword at his unseen enemy as he disappeared off the side of the pillar. Valcaro ran to the edge and fired. Somewhere below, the Invisibilia screeched. Valcaro frantically stuffed more powder into the barrel.

"Go!" Sveva barked at Savino. "Get out of here!" Then she and Valcaro jumped off the pillar, back into the fray.

Giacomo heard the sound of steel clanging against scales, followed by a chorus of screams. A second shot never came.

Savino hooked his hands under Giacomo's arms and hoisted him onto his feet. "Come on, we're almost there."

Giacomo winced, mustering every last ounce of strength. He ignored his crippling aches and, with Savino's help, limped along the last two pillars and onto the cliff wall. Luna and Gaia launched an onslaught of blazing shapes toward the canyon floor. More shrieks.

As they scrambled up the steep incline, Giacomo looked down at his leg, alarmed by the sight of so much blood. On him, around him. *It's all draining away.*

He clutched Mico, whose feathers were matted with blood too. Giacomo lost his balance, but Milena was there to hold him. She and Savino heaved him up and up, toward a cloudless blue sky.

But his head felt like it was being pulled into an abyss, down and down. His skull met the hard ground with a thud, as he was hauled deeper and deeper into unconsciousness.

The last thing he heard was Aaminah shouting, "Giacomo! Giacomo, stay with us!"

AWAKENING

Ugalino stayed inside the Cave of Alessio for two days, forbidding Enzio and even Zanobius from entering. He took the added precaution of making Ciro stand guard should either of them become curious.

So Zanobius passed the time at the river, playing a game Enzio showed him. The rules were simple enough: skip smooth, flat rocks over the surface of the water. Whoever bounced his rock the greatest number of times was the winner.

Enzio was a master of the game, and on his first attempt, skipped his rock a dozen times before it sank.

Knowing he'd fail to match Enzio with one rock, Zanobius picked up four, cradling them in his hands. Using all his arms at once, he winged the rocks across the water. The ripples overlapped and expanded like one of Ugalino's sacred geometry attacks.

"Uh, I'm pretty sure that's cheating," Enzio said drily. "But I'll give you points for creativity."

Zanobius smiled. "Let's go again. I think I'm getting the hang of this."

"You'll never beat me, even with all those arms of yours." Enzio scanned the shore for another rock.

Zanobius was fascinated by how humans could be so competitive. Whether it was someone like the Supreme Creator who wanted to hold power over her people, or a simple game of skipping rocks, humans seemed to have an insatiable need to win, feeding off victories like a glutton devours food at a banquet. Over the years, he'd witnessed firsthand how his master's search for the Creator's Compass had grown from curiosity into a relentless quest. And with others now threatening to find it, Ugalino's drive had only intensified.

But Zanobius was also thankful for his master's passion and obsessiveness, because without it, Zanobius wouldn't exist. When others warned Ugalino that bringing a Tulpa into being was impossible, dangerous, and forbidden, he only devoted more energy to his creation. Zanobius wondered if he could ever be as intensely committed to anything.

Ugalino's voice interrupted. *I'm ready. Bring Enzio to me.*

Zanobius dropped his stones on the shore. "Next round is going to have to wait."

"Why?"

"My master told me to bring you to the cave."

Enzio looked confused. "I didn't hear anything."

"He speaks to me without saying a word," Zanobius admitted. "I hear his voice in my head."

Enzio's eyebrows rose in shock. "Doesn't that make you feel insane? For someone to get inside your mind like that?"

"It's how he's always communicated with me."

"Still, it's weird." Enzio looked down at the rock in his palm. "And I'd just found the perfect stone too." He tossed it into the water with a splash.

As they entered the cave, Zanobius looked around in amazement. Across the walls and ceiling, Ugalino had painted countless overlapping white circles. Within each grouping of circles, blue and green lines crisscrossed, connecting in a complex, interlaced design. The image resembled the pattern on Zanobius's chest, but on a much larger scale.

On the right side of the cave were two enormous black circles that dwarfed all the other shapes. The circles overlapped, forming an almond shape in between, which was filled in with white. On the rocky floor, Ugalino had painted a map of the Zizzolan Empire, contained within yet another circle.

"What's all this?" Enzio asked.

"It's how you're going to help me find the true Creator's Compass," Ugalino said.

Enzio cast a wary gaze across the cave walls. "And how am I supposed to do that, exactly?"

"Please stand inside the mandorla," Ugalino instructed.

"The what?" Enzio said.

Ugalino pointed with his staff to the white almond shape on the cave wall. "There."

Enzio took a few hesitant steps and stood with his back against it. His body covered the almond shape between the two black circles. His head reached just above where the outlines of the circles overlapped.

"Arms and legs out."

Enzio cautiously raised his arms and took a wider stance.

"Hands at the centers of the circles, feet directly below," Ugalino instructed.

Enzio dropped his arms. "What's going to happen?"

"Take the stance." Zanobius recognized the harsh tone in Ugalino's voice, which meant, *Don't question me.*

Enzio followed Ugalino's instructions, holding his arms out at an angle until his palms covered the center point of each circle. His feet covered the bottom of the circle, where it met the ground.

With a sudden jerk, Ugalino pounded his staff on the ground. The diamond lit up and four bright rings appeared around Enzio's arms and legs. He tried to pull away but found himself shackled to the wall.

"What are you doing?" Enzio demanded.

"You're going to help me access the Wellspring. Giacomo's not the only one who knows how to tap into the ultimate source of creative power."

"Let me go!" Enzio screeched. Ugalino made a swift circular motion with his staff and a band of light covered Enzio's mouth, pinning his head to the wall. Enzio struggled against the bonds. Zanobius felt an urge to help the boy, but held back, confident that after Ugalino got the information he needed, he'd release Enzio.

Ugalino closed his eyes and the diamond on his staff burned brightly. Then his eyes snapped open and he thrust his staff straight into the air.

The lines of the outermost circles began to glow and crackle with energy, like tiny bolts of white, blue, and green lightning.

A low-pitched hum filled the room. Enzio's frightened eyes darted around as the trails of light made their way up across the ceiling and down toward him. The sparkling glow flowed into the black circles where Enzio was bound, then lit up the mandorla. Enzio went rigid and his eyes rolled into the back of his head. As the energy coursed through him, he shook and vibrated.

The humming grew louder. Zanobius felt his body resonate with the sound. The cave, the symbols, the mandorla . . . it all seemed familiar, like this had happened before. Was it another memory lost to his blackouts?

"Is he all right?" Zanobius shouted over the noise.

"Quiet," Ugalino commanded, then he lowered his voice: "Through the power of this mandorla, I summon the Wellspring, the source of all creation. Reveal to me the true Creator's Compass so I may set the world free!"

The glow intensified. In the center of the cave, above the map, the image of the Compass shimmered into view. It appeared as it had before—floating inside the rotating octahedron.

Then in an instant, all the light and energy poured out of the interlaced designs and into the mandorla. The brightness nearly engulfed Enzio. The hum abruptly cut off and a beam of light shot out of Enzio's chest, hitting the Compass's shield, turning it from blue to white.

Enzio thrashed against his bindings. Zanobius feared the boy wouldn't survive. He refused to stay silent any longer. "Let him go!" he roared.

Silence! Ugalino called back. *You do not command me.*

A narrow shaft of light extended from the bottom tip of the

octahedron to the map on the ground. The three-dimensional shape tilted and the ray cut across Zizzola, then paused.

That's where we are now, his master said.

The octahedron leaned again, slowly drawing a line from the Cave of Alessio directly to the north on the map.

Enzio continued to writhe, his face twisted in agony. It wasn't right using the boy like this—like he was nothing more than a machine. If his master wasn't going to end this madness, Zanobius would.

As the light advanced up central Zizzola, Zanobius lunged, grabbing the staff from Ugalino's hand and hurling it against the wall. With the connection severed, the beam of light vanished from the map. It emptied from the octahedron and coursed back through Enzio's chest. The glowing mandorla faded, along with the image of the Compass.

The bonds holding Enzio also disappeared, causing his limp body to wither and fall. Zanobius caught the boy before he hit the ground. A fury like he'd never felt before welled in his chest. He whipped around and glared at his master. "What did you do to him?"

Ugalino snatched his staff off the ground and pointed it at Zanobius. "He was a necessary sacrifice."

"You knew he wouldn't survive?"

His master turned away.

"Answer me!" Zanobius demanded.

Ugalino lowered his head, his fist clamping tightly around his staff. "Humans can't withstand the energy of the Wellspring," he said. "The boy never had a chance."

Waves of heat pulsed through Zanobius. Normally, he could keep his feelings at bay, like a dam holding back water. But Enzio's death had released them. The dam hadn't just broken, it was obliterated.

"FIX HIM!" Zanobius howled with a furious intensity, surprising both himself and his master.

Ugalino spun around and marched toward Zanobius, pointing the staff's glimmering diamond at his head. Zanobius felt a stabbing jolt between his eyes, and feared his whole head might split in two.

I brought you into the world and I can as easily erase you from it. You will never command me again. Do you understand?

It took all of Zanobius's strength to nod even once. Ugalino lowered his staff. The diamond's glow dimmed and the shooting pain in Zanobius's head faded to a throb.

"Bury him in the back of the cave, then meet me outside. We're leaving." Ugalino's cloak billowed as he turned and strode out.

Zanobius looked down at Enzio's lifeless body, a feeling of heaviness overwhelming him. He wanted to shed tears for the boy, but his eyes remained dry. Another downside of being a Tulpa.

Enzio wasn't some armed aggressor, he was an innocent child who had been cast aside first by his own father, then by Ugalino. Zanobius knew how fragile human bodies were, but he hadn't truly understood how vulnerable life could be until now. One moment Enzio had been on this earth, then the next, he was gone. But his body remained. So who was Enzio? The lifeless carcass Zanobius held in his arms? Or was Enzio something more?

Zanobius found a narrow alcove at the back of the cave and lay the body inside. He covered the opening with rocks, to hide the boy from any hungry animals looking for easy prey.

He was nearly finished entombing Enzio when the boy's head jolted. He gasped, eyelids fluttering. Startled, Zanobius fell backward.

"What . . . what happened?" Enzio's voice was barely a whisper.

"You're hurt. Badly," Zanobius told him. "I'm sorry."

Zanobius dug past the rocks and pulled Enzio out, placing him next to a shallow pool of water so he could drink. "Stay hidden. I'll be back for you. I promise."

"When?"

"I don't know . . . Soon."

"Thank you," Enzio said weakly.

Zanobius left the cave and met Ugalino by the tree, where he was climbing onto his Genius's neck. Zanobius knew that if he told Ugalino that Enzio was alive, he'd order him to go back and finish the boy off. Zanobius chose to stay silent, but his face must have reflected his conflicted feelings.

"The boy is gone," Ugalino said. "Grieving for him won't bring him back."

Zanobius ignored Ugalino's attempt at sympathy and changed the subject. "Where are we going? We still don't know where the true Compass is."

"No thanks to you," Ugalino grumbled. "But before you interfered, the ray of light passed through Terra della Morte and was continuing due north. If we fly along that route, we should find what we're looking for. And if we happen to cross paths with the Giacomo boy, all the better."

Zanobius jumped onto Ciro's back, and the Genius heaved its wings. Though they soared, Zanobius couldn't escape the sinking feeling that standing up to his master would soon come back to haunt him.

THE SINGING GROTTO

Giacomo drifted in and out of consciousness. For how long, he wasn't sure. It might have been hours, maybe days.

During that time, music enveloped him, shrouding him in soft, warm notes. The music surged through his heart, sustaining him during the darker moments, when his body threatened to quit on him. The melodies soothed his angry wounds and convinced Giacomo to hold on a little longer. Just one more song, one more note might be all that was needed to pluck him from his hazy state and make him whole again.

The part of him that still clung to life maintained an awareness of what was going on around him. He heard Savino insist they keep moving, despite Giacomo's inability to walk. He saw Savino make a stretcher out of two long branches and a wool blanket. He watched with gratitude as Savino and Milena carried him while Aaminah started to play.

At some point they stopped near a creek. Milena filled her

waterskin, then held it to his mouth and poured the cool liquid over his lips. He tried to drink, but the muscles he needed to swallow wouldn't respond. Drops of water trickled down his throat. Most dribbled down his chin.

"Do you think he's going to be okay?" Milena asked.

"I'm doing everything I can," Aaminah answered desperately. And for a moment she wasn't talking about Giacomo, but about her mother.

His mind was pulled to another time and place, where Giacomo saw Aaminah, a few years younger, with Luna hovering over her shoulder. A beautiful, brown-haired woman listened to Aaminah while she played the flute, the woman's cheeks sunken and her skin white like it had been dusted with flour. Tears streamed down Aaminah's face. Her mother whispered that it was her time to leave now. She had already sent word to Aaminah's aunt in Virenzia. She would care for Aaminah now. Aaminah begged her not to go. Giacomo experienced it all so vividly: the sunlight streaming through the window above Aaminah's mother's bed, the light-filled notes that washed over her mother, the sound of her mother's breathing weakening to a near-silent wheezing, Aaminah's tortured sobs as her mother's soul left her body, the crack of the flute as Aaminah threw it to the ground and cursed the Creator.

Giacomo wanted to wrap his arms around Aaminah and tell her it wasn't her fault her mother had died, but when he tried to open his mouth it felt like it had been sewn closed.

It was so strange for his mind to still be active when his body had nearly shut down. Was this what it was like to die? Were his mental and physical sides so separate from each other that one could thrive while the other perished?

But there was a third part of all this he hadn't considered—his soul. He recalled Pietro's words: "When two opposites are unified by a third element, a new entity is created."

Our bodies and minds are opposites, Giacomo realized. *Our souls unify them and make us human.*

Floating in and out of a haze, Giacomo followed this train of thought. People inhabited a form for a certain amount of time, wore it out, and were forced to give it up, whether by disease, or violence, or old age. But when the body and mind died, where did the soul go? Was it like a circle, with no beginning or end, going around and around for eternity?

And in a feverish burst of inspiration, it hit him—*What if our souls go back to the Wellspring?* What if all the whirling and howling and stabbing was actually the cries of a billion souls spiraling through creation until a tiny crack opened, just big enough for one of them to slip out of the chaos and bind to a human body and mind?

And eventually, when the body and mind failed, whether in young age or old, the soul returned to its source.

If this was true, his parents' souls hadn't been destroyed at all. They had simply retreated into the Wellspring when life in the physical world became unbearable. Which meant, in a way, they were still alive. Aaminah's mother too.

And what was a Tulpa except a physical home for a soul? That must have been why Zanobius had seemed so lifelike. He possessed a soul, like any human. Ugalino might have taken one out of the Wellspring and placed it in a protective shell. And how was that any different from a soul finding a human body to inhabit on its own?

The parchment he'd found in the duke's castle held secrets on how to build such a protective shell. If he could decipher it, maybe he could build his own Tulpas—one for each of his parents. He could welcome them back to the physical world and they'd be a family again.

But to do that, he needed to wake up and return to his body.

Aaminah's beautiful playing wasn't enough to draw him back, though. His body wanted to give up and let his soul return to the Wellspring, but Giacomo wouldn't let it. He grasped the tether connected to his soul and held on to it with all his remaining strength. Aaminah would figure out a way to bring him back. She had to.

"The music's not strong enough on its own," he heard her say.

"I need a way to boost the sound . . ."

Aaminah's words could have been part of the same sentence or an idea she came up with the next day. Each moment weaved into the next, all separate threads that made up the tapestry of time. Giacomo was unraveling.

The next thing he heard was Aaminah's voice echoing:

"Bring him in here . . . in here . . . in here . . ."

He felt Savino lay him down and heard water drip into pools. Even though he couldn't open his eyes, Giacomo was able to visualize the water reflecting off rock walls like wiggling strands of light.

Aaminah plucked a note on her harp and immediately the music felt different. Waves of yellow leaped from Luna's crown and bounced off the cave walls, growing bigger and brighter before crashing into Giacomo, sinking into his deepest hurts.

Aaminah's Genius projected circles, squares, and triangles through the cave, creating a dancing pattern of geometric shapes all around him. A circle hit the wall, split into three more, which hit other walls and multiplied over and over. Soon, the space was filled with hundreds of floating, illuminated shapes. The pools of water rippled in wavy lines, resonating with the music. High and low notes stacked one on top of another in a swelling, soaring symphony.

The healing notes seeped into every part of his being. The tether slackened, and he pulled his soul back, where it entwined with his body and mind once again, uniting him.

But as soon as his soul returned, so did the pain. It began as a stabbing in his big toe and wound its way up his legs, into his torso, and through his neck. It felt like a thousand tiny blades were scraping his skin and muscles from the inside. The stinging passed through the top of his head, then eased to an uncomfortable throb.

Water splashed against his face and he peeled open his eyes. Mico floated in the pool next to him, fluttering his wings and kicking up droplets of water. A new layer of feathers had grown in where his wings had been torn.

"Giacomo?" Milena leaned over him, looking relieved.

Aaminah lowered her harp and the music trailed off, along with the multitude of glowing shapes. "You're okay?" she asked, like she didn't entirely believe he'd woken up.

"I think so," Giacomo said, slowly pushing himself against a rock to rise to his feet. He cautiously put his weight on his injured leg, relieved to find it could support him, though it still ached. All his cuts and scrapes had stopped bleeding. Pink lines indicated where the skin had healed. His body was tender, but it had survived.

Giacomo smiled at Aaminah. "Thank you."

She stared back with a perplexed expression, as if he were a stranger who had just wandered in.

"What?" Giacomo said.

"Nothing," she replied. "I . . . I was so scared you weren't going to make it."

269

"Yeah, we thought we'd lost you," Savino said, slapping him on the back. He looked to Aaminah. "Brilliant thinking, using the cave walls to amplify your music like that."

Aaminah looked away and nodded silently. Her thoughts seemed to be somewhere else.

Later, Giacomo rested by the warmth of the fire. He perked up when Aaminah came to check on him. She handed him a few pieces of dried meat, along with some purple berries. "You should eat. You need your strength back."

Giacomo tossed the berries into his mouth, savoring their sweetness. "I want you to know," he said, "when I was unconscious, I saw everything so clearly. You . . . your mother . . . I know you feel like you should have done more to save her, but I'm certain she'd be so proud of you right now."

"Thank you," Aaminah said softly. "I wasn't sure you could hear me when I told you the story."

"What story?" Giacomo asked.

"About the day my mother died."

"Right . . . of course. I guess it must have sunk in somehow." He'd been so convinced that what he saw was real, but his mind must not have been as clear as he'd thought. "Thanks for telling me about that."

"Catch," Savino said, and Giacomo spun around in time to see his satchel flying at him. He reached out to grab it, but missed. The satchel hit the wall and fell on the ground. His sketchbook, papers, and art supplies spilled across the cave floor. "Sorry," Savino said. "Guess your reflexes aren't fully recovered."

Milena knelt down to help pick up the mess. Giacomo limped over. "That's okay, I got it."

"No, it's fine, let me—" Her words cut off as she glanced at the one thing Giacomo didn't want her to find. In her hand she held the piece of parchment he'd taken from the castle. As she rose to her feet, her expression turned serious. "Giacomo?"

Savino peered over her shoulder. His eyes widened. "Where'd you get this?"

"I found it in the duke's papers," Giacomo admitted.

"What is it?" Aaminah asked.

Savino snatched the parchment out of Milena's hand. "Looks like instructions for creating a Tulpa."

"What are you doing with it?" Aaminah asked Giacomo. Her sweet expression turned suspicious.

"Are you thinking of trying to make one?" Savino accused.

"I don't know . . . I guess I thought it might come in handy . . ."

"Come in *handy*?" Milena huffed, her anger building. "The world's in this mess because Ugalino thought it was a good idea to create a Tulpa. And now you want to build another?"

"This is why I didn't tell any of you about it. I knew you wouldn't understand."

"You know what I do understand, Giacomo? That we're hundreds of miles away from home, the people hired to protect us are all dead, and now I can't even trust you!" Milena's eyes burned with fury.

"I'm on your side," Giacomo pleaded. "Nothing's changed."

"This," Savino said, holding up the parchment, "changes everything." He crumpled it in his clenched fist and marched over to the fire.

Giacomo hobbled over, putting himself between Savino and the flames. "Please, don't. Not until we know what it really means. I saw Zanobius up close. He was so real. So . . . human."

"It's a Tulpa. It kills people."

"I know he's dangerous, but what if you could create one that wasn't? What if you could make one that was kind and loving and caring?"

"You can't, Giacomo . . ." Aaminah said, her voice shaking.

"Can't what?" he snapped.

"Bring your parents back. You might think that's a good idea, and believe me, there were times I would've done anything to see my mother again, but nothing good can come from messing around with Tulpas."

Giacomo fell silent. He knew no argument would convince them that reviving his parents as Tulpas was a smart plan.

Savino shoved Giacomo aside, knocking him to the ground, then tossed the parchment into the flames.

"No!" Giacomo lunged for the fire, but Savino swung his leg and kicked him back to the dirt, pinning him down.

"Let it burn," he said.

But before the fire completely consumed it, Milena stuck her hand in and rescued the burning parchment. She patted out the flames. "Giacomo's right. We don't know what this means yet."

"It means more problems for us," Savino argued. "Throw it back in the fire."

"Or it might be a solution. A way to destroy Ugalino's Tulpa, in case we don't find all the Sacred Tools."

Savino took his foot off Giacomo's chest and got in Milena's face. "You want to be responsible for it? Fine. But don't let *him* get his hands on it again." He pointed at Giacomo.

"I won't." Milena glared at Giacomo as she folded the parchment and tucked it in her bag.

Giacomo rose to his feet and dusted off his shirt, shaking with emotion. He was relieved Milena saved the parchment, but furious too. They were treating him like he was some kind of deranged person, as if he were no different from Ugalino. He turned away, avoiding their angry glares.

The uncomfortable silence was broken by Luna letting out a bloodcurdling screech, followed by a raspy, clicking noise.

"That doesn't sound good," Savino said ominously.

"It isn't . . ." Aaminah's eyes filled with fear. "Ugalino's Genius must be close!"

"We need to get out of here," Milena said. "Now!"

They frantically gathered their bags while Savino stamped out the fire. They headed for the mouth of the cave, but halfway down the tunnel, it split into three paths.

Savino stopped. "Milena, do you remember which one we came in?"

"The one on the right." She paused. "I think?"

"No, it was the left one," Aaminah said.

"You don't remember how to get out of here?" Giacomo said, panicked.

"Sorry," Savino said, "we were a little busy trying to make sure you weren't dying. Maybe that was a mistake."

After a brief debate, Savino and Milena decided to try the passageway in the middle. As they ran through the winding tunnel, Giacomo found himself holding his breath, expecting Ugalino and his Tulpa to appear around every turn.

ON THE TRAIL

Ciro dropped out of the sky and hurtled toward the earth, exhausted. Zanobius clutched the Genius's feathers and braced for a rough landing.

They had been flying for hours, the landscape turning from green fields to gray stone. When they passed over a wide canyon full of giant pointed pillars, Ugalino called it Terra della Morte.

The Land of Death.

At the bottom of the canyon, Zanobius had spotted a zigzagging line of fallen pillars. Could four children really have survived such a harsh and deadly place?

Ugalino guided his Genius to land near the edge of the cliff. Ciro hit the ground hard and collapsed, dead tired. Zanobius and Ugalino walked over to a large patch of blood that had soaked into the dirt and was surrounded by numerous small footprints. The children appeared to have escaped the canyon, but at least one of them was badly hurt.

Kneeling, Ugalino touched the blood with his fingers. *Still sticky*. His eyes followed the trail of crimson, which headed toward a mountain range in the distance. *They can't be far*.

Ugalino and Zanobius climbed back onto Ciro, and Ugalino urged his Genius on. Uttering a caw of protest, Ciro took to the air once again, but glided low over the land, which transitioned from endless piles of boulders to a lush forest with a river winding through it. Soon, Zizzola's rolling hillsides returned. Zanobius was thankful to see so much green again.

Ugalino spotted something below. He steered Ciro toward the ground, where the Genius landed roughly, nearly jostling Zanobius off its back.

Ugalino slid off Ciro's neck and headed down a slope toward a mossy hillside pocked with numerous entrances. He knelt and ran his hand across a rock, then held it up to Zanobius. The tips of his fingers were bloody.

They must have taken refuge here, Ugalino said. Since they'd left the Cave of Alessio, Ugalino hadn't spoken directly to him, only in his mind. It was his way of punishing him—a reminder that his master's voice should be the only one he listened to.

"Why won't you speak to me out loud?" Zanobius complained. "Like normal people talk."

His master ignored the question and continued mind-speaking. *We'll split up. You take that tunnel, I'll take this one*. Ugalino disappeared into the darkness.

Zanobius lumbered inside, where he discovered a maze of passageways. Every so often, the tunnel widened out into a grotto where stalagmites sprouted up between pools of water. Overhead, stalactites shot down like needles. Narrow beams of light pierced through openings in the stone walls.

Zanobius passed through six of these cavernous pockets, but other than some old animal bones, he found nothing—certainly no sign of Giacomo or his companions.

As he entered another passage, he spotted a faint glow up ahead. A fire crackled. He crept quietly, not wanting to startle the children. According to Enzio, they all had Geniuses. Probably not as powerful as Ugalino's, but he still needed to be cautious.

When he got closer, he peered around the corner, but didn't see anyone. A skinned squirrel cooked on a spit over the flames. Whoever had been there couldn't have gone far. He took another step and immediately felt the pinch of steel against his throat.

"Come out. Slowly." A man's deep voice spoke to him from the shadows.

Zanobius inched out of the tunnel and raised all four hands.

The man emerged from a shadowy recess. His clothes and armor, or what was left of them, hung like rags. He was caked in blood and deep gashes ran up and down his arms and legs. His long, messy hair was also matted with blood. A ragged scar ran down the side of his face, but it looked like a wound from years ago.

"I should run this blade through your throat right now," the man threatened.

"Many have tried, all have failed," Zanobius warned.

"You hunting those kids? The ones with the Geniuses?"

"Do you know where they are?"

"Tracked them here but they moved on, far as I can tell."

The man held his gaze for a long time without pulling his blade away, like Zanobius was a riddle he was trying to solve. "You interrupted my dinner. How about you join me while I eat." It wasn't a question.

"All right," Zanobius said.

They sat across from each other, the fire between them. Behind the man, the flickering flames cast looming shadows on the wall. With his left hand, the man held his sword, and with the other, he picked up the crispy squirrel carcass. He stuffed it in his mouth and swallowed nearly the entire thing in one bite.

"I'd offer you some," he said through a mouthful of food, "but Tulpas don't eat, isn't that right?"

"Correct." So the man knew something about him. Come to think of it, the man hadn't seemed shocked by his appearance. At least, not the way most were when they encountered an eight-limbed man. A silence hung between them. The man kept chewing.

"What happened to you?" Zanobius finally asked.

"The Land of Death happened. Thought that was the end for old Ozo here. But I guess the Creator had other plans for me." He spit a piece of squirrel bone into the fire. "Like finding you."

There was that look again. A piercing stare, like he knew something Zanobius didn't.

"How did you end up following those children through the Land of Death?" Zanobius asked.

"I was their escort," Ozo corrected. "Someone paid me a whole lot to protect them."

"But all the gold and silver *impronta* in the world won't do you any good if you're dead," Zanobius pointed out, though he was aware that humans behaved recklessly when money was involved.

Ozo's hand gripped the hilt of his sword tighter. "True. Greed will get a man only so far."

Zanobius was confounded by Ozo's behavior. Why hadn't Ozo tried to kill him when he had the chance? Why the fireside chat?

It was another way humans made no sense to him. They were always carrying around secrets, their words never conveying what they truly wanted to say.

Zanobius eyed Ozo's hand on his sword. Waited for him to unsheathe it. But the man maintained his intense gaze, the hatred running deep. It was as if Zanobius's presence had dredged up awful memories.

"Have we . . . met before?" As soon as Zanobius asked the question, Ozo's eyes widened.

"You don't remember?" The fire reflected in Ozo's black pupils.

Zanobius frantically searched his memory, trying to figure out where he had met Ozo before, but he drew a blank. If he had to guess, the encounter hadn't ended well.

"My master's here too." Zanobius didn't need Ugalino's help, but if Ozo knew he was outnumbered, maybe he'd back down. Zanobius was tired of leaving a trail of bodies in his wake. "If you can help us find Giacomo, I'm sure Ugalino would pay whatever you wanted."

"You and your master are never getting near that kid, understand?"

"I don't want any harm to come to him either."

"So you're a murderer *and* a liar."

The blade came at him in a blur. Ozo had lunged over the fire, stabbing straight for the chest. Zanobius rolled left and the blade nicked his front right arm. When Ozo charged again, Zanobius used all four arms to pick him up off the ground. He shook him until his sword came loose, splashing into a pool.

He hurled Ozo into the wall with enough strength to knock him out, but not kill him. Ozo crumpled to the ground. He moaned, but didn't move. The show of power would be enough to convince the man not to mess with him again.

Zanobius backed out of the grotto and found his way through the tunnels, eventually emerging outside. His master stood on an embankment with his back to Zanobius, looking toward a distant mountain range.

"They've moved on," Zanobius said.

I know. I found tracks leading out of the tunnels and heading north. Ugalino walked to Ciro's side. He spotted Zanobius's wounded arm, which was in the process of healing. *What happened?*

"Cut myself on a stalagmite."

I see. His master didn't sound convinced, but he didn't press Zanobius on the matter. *We should be able to spot them from the sky. They can't have traveled very far on foot.*

Ugalino jumped onto Ciro's neck and the Genius screeched its opposition.

"Maybe you should let Ciro rest a little longer," Zanobius suggested.

He's rested enough. Now we fly.

With great effort, the Genius ascended toward the clouds.

Though they had left the grotto behind, Zanobius couldn't shake the feeling that he hadn't seen the last of Ozo.

THE CREATOR'S HAND

Giacomo rushed across the grass, limping behind Savino, Milena, and Aaminah. Every few steps, he glanced back to see if Ugalino's Genius had caught up to them, but there was no sign of Ciro yet. If they could stay ahead of Ugalino, they'd beat him to the Compass. But how had Ugalino even picked up their trail in the first place?

Thanks to Milena, they had found their way out of the grotto before Ugalino showed up. They had pushed through the night, with Giacomo needing to take breaks every hour to rest.

His legs burned. With each step he felt like his lungs were going to burst. Although Aaminah had brought him back to life, his body still needed time to heal. He stumbled more than once, but with the Compass so close, he ignored the pain and pressed forward. Mico chirped and circled his head, urging him on. As the morning fog burned off, they spotted jagged mountain peaks in the distance.

They ran up and down a rolling hill, splashed through a rocky riverbed, and dashed into a dense forest. The entire time, no one spoke a word to Giacomo, which was fine with him. He'd selfishly decided that finishing the mission was the most important thing right now. He couldn't waste time worrying about his crumbling friendships.

Savino barreled out of the tree line and slowed to a jog. "We're here!" he announced. Milena, Aaminah, and Giacomo emerged from the forest behind him. Giacomo huffed and puffed as he took in the sight before them. The land dipped into a valley dotted with trees, before rising again into a slope of dirt and gravel and erupting in a ridge of pointed, rocky peaks.

"The Abscondita Mountains," Milena said. "The Compass has to be somewhere up there."

Giacomo looked up. Assuming they could even scale the rocks, it would take days, maybe weeks, to search the entire mountain. They didn't have that kind of time.

"If we had full-grown Geniuses, we could fly up there," Savino muttered. Nero swooped from the sky, squawking in his ear, sounding annoyed. "What?" Savino replied. "It's nothing personal."

"We don't need to climb up there," Milena realized. "Our Geniuses can scout it out for us." Gaia landed on her shoulder. "Fly to the mountains. Give us a squawk if you see any caves."

"Or Compasses," Savino added.

Gaia rose into the air, followed by Luna and Nero.

"Go on," Giacomo told Mico. "Go with them." Mico chirruped and took off. The Geniuses grew smaller and smaller as they flew away, until they were only colorful specks against the mountain range.

While their Geniuses searched, the group descended into the valley, then climbed the gravelly slope. Savino found a flat area at the base of a rocky wall where they rested and waited.

Milena unfolded the message they'd deciphered at the duke's castle and read it again. "'The Compass lies in a cave, shaped by the Creator's hand, obscured by Alessio.'"

"Too bad it doesn't tell us which cave it's lying in," Savino said.

"Maybe we overlooked something," Milena said, riffling through the rest of the parchments they'd taken from the castle. She tossed aside the grid of various lines and wavy patterns. "Guess we don't need the cipher anymore."

Giacomo watched as their Geniuses dove out of the sky and landed on the slope next to them. Mico hopped around, pecking at the pebbles, looking for a stray bug to eat.

"I guess that means you didn't see anything useful?" Giacomo asked.

Mico chirped and went back to scavenging. The other three Geniuses huddled on a nearby rock.

"What a surprise," Savino said, shaking his head. "Giacomo was wrong about the Compass before, and he's wrong again."

Giacomo looked to Aaminah for a nod of support, then to Milena, hoping she'd tell Savino he was out of line, but they both looked away. Still, he wasn't ready to admit failure. They'd solved the coded message. He'd used the camera obscura to locate the true Compass. Everything pointed to its being here. *So where is it?*

"We never should've left Baldassare's villa until we were absolutely sure where the Compass was," Savino said.

"You're the one who couldn't wait to leave!" Giacomo reminded him.

"Because you told us you knew what you were doing!" Savino's face burned red. "Now we're stuck out here with a madman and his killing machine on our heels. We never should have taken you out of the aqueducts. Once a sewer-boy, always a sewer-boy."

"Stop calling me that!" Giacomo threw himself at Savino, tackling him. They tumbled down the slope, head over heels, fists swinging. As they slid to a stop, Savino shoved Giacomo off him.

Giacomo pushed himself to his knees and spat out a mouthful of sand. Heat flushed through him and he started sweating. "I'm sorry I led you all the way out here and we have nothing to show for it!" he yelled. "And I'm truly sorry about all the lives we lost on the way, but I swear, if you call me sewer-boy one more time I am going to take you the rest of the way down this mountain with me!"

"All right, all right . . ." Savino said, relenting. "All you had to do was say something."

Giacomo collapsed against the slope, still feeling the ache of his injuries.

Savino got up, his feet sinking into the sliding pebbles as he walked back to the girls, who wore bemused expressions. "It's getting late," he said. "We should find somewhere hidden and camp for the night."

"And then what?" Aaminah asked. "Where do we go next?"

Milena shrugged and looked out toward the horizon despondently. "Back to Virenzia, I guess."

Giacomo pulled his knees to his chest and buried his head in his folded arms. The thought of returning empty-handed to the city, where Pietro and Baldassare might or might not even be alive, was too much to bear. All the deaths, all the suffering . . . What had been the point? The Creator was probably looking down from the heavens having a good laugh at his expense.

A gust of wind caught the cipher and blew it against the rock Luna was sitting on. She hopped and chirped excitedly, then grabbed the parchment in her claws and flew it over to Aaminah, dropping it in her lap.

"What's gotten into you?" Aaminah put the cipher back in the pile with the rest of the parchments. Luna took to the air, shining her light across the cipher's patterns. Then she picked up the parchment and flew it back to Aaminah, waving it in front of her face.

"What's the big deal?" Aaminah said. "We already know what the message says—"

She gasped and snatched the cipher from her Genius. "I think Luna's trying to tell us something! What if this isn't only one cipher, but two?"

"How can it be two?" Savino asked, puzzled.

Curious, Giacomo returned to the group.

Aaminah showed the patterns to everyone. "When I played in

the grotto, the music made the pools of water ripple like these drawings." She grabbed the decoded message. "You all figured out that the symbols equal certain letters. But what if they're also musical notes?"

"You think it's a song that will somehow show us where the Compass is?" Giacomo said.

"I'm not sure, but it's worth a try."

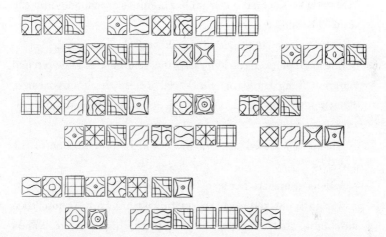

Giacomo looked around. "But how are you going to make ripples without any water?"

The slope was covered in granules of sand mixed with larger chunks of gravel. Milena scooped up a handful of loose sand and shook it in her palm. The small grains jumped and danced. "Maybe we can use sand instead of water," she said. She picked up a large round, flat stone and laid it on the ground next to Aaminah, sprinkling granules across its surface.

Aaminah sat with her legs crossed, cradling her harp in her arms.

She plucked the strings, letting each note ring out before moving to the next. Luna projected waves of yellow light into the air, but the sand remained still. Aaminah frowned. "It's not working."

"What if Luna projects directly onto the stone," Giacomo suggested.

Aaminah snapped her fingers and pointed at the sand. Luna tilted her head down and Aaminah started playing high notes.

Short waves spread out from her Genius's crown and onto the stone. The sand suddenly shifted.

Milena gasped in wonder. "Play slower," she instructed.

Aaminah plucked the longest string, sending out a low-pitched vibration. Long strands of light flowed over the tiny grains of earth. They bounced up and down, then in an instant formed four horizontal wavy lines.

Giacomo scanned the cipher. "Look! It matches one of the patterns."

Milena jumped to her feet. "Keep playing!"

Aaminah plucked her harp, starting with the lowest note, then moving up the strings, all the way to the highest note. When Luna's projection created one of the cipher patterns in the sand, Milena marked the corresponding symbol on the message.

Once the harp's last note rang out, Aaminah studied what Milena had written, committing the sequence of notes to memory. She closed her eyes for a moment, then began to play. The sand on the stone shifted with every note, each shape matching a symbol on the message.

Giacomo found the music haunting. The tune began with low, ominous tones, before gradually ascending into a higher octave, then coming down again, the end of the piece mirroring its beginning. He found himself surrendering to the melody as it surged through him, seeping into his skin and muscles, warming his heart, and strengthening his bones. Even though he was hearing the piece for the first time, he was sure he'd known it all his life, as if the song had been written solely for him. As the last note reverberated, he realized the others were staring at him.

"You okay?" Aaminah said.

Giacomo felt his cheeks, noticing they were wet. Embarrassed, he wiped the tears on his sleeve. "Yeah, I'm fine. The song was . . . really beautiful."

They gazed up at the mountain, but Giacomo didn't know exactly what they were looking for. Maybe a flash of light? At the very least, he needed some sign from the Creator that the Compass was close.

Aaminah sighed. "I don't think it worked—"

The ground shook. Sand spilled off the stone. Chunks of gravel rolled past Giacomo's feet. He dropped to all fours to keep from sliding down the slope too. Their Geniuses all shot high into the sky and flew in loops, chirping wildly.

"Wh-wh-what's ha-ha-happening?" Milena's voice vibrated over the rumbling.

Then came five thunderous explosions.

Huge chunks of rock broke free from the mountain pinnacles and crashed hundreds of feet to the ground.

The tremors seemed to go on forever. The song had unleashed a force of energy so powerful, it was ripping apart the mountainside. Boulders the size of houses rolled down the slope and tumbled straight for them.

"Get behind me!" Savino ordered.

As everyone scrambled, Savino pulled one of his tools from his belt. He hacked his sculpting blade against the air and Nero hit the boulders with pulsating blue circles. The giant stones burst and crumbled into small rocks that harmlessly rolled past.

The convulsions eased, then stopped altogether.

"The Creator's Hand . . ." Milena said. "Look!"

Giacomo gazed up through the dust, where five pinnacles rose from the mountain, past the summit. As each pinnacle locked into place, a boom echoed across the valley. The song Aaminah played had reshaped the mountainside into four tall peaks like fingers, and a fifth shorter one that resembled a thumb.

Milena's mouth hung agape. "The Creator's Hand . . ."

Giacomo spotted a crevasse, cradled between the thumb and the first finger. A dim blue glow shone from within. "There's the cave!" he shouted, pointing to the spot.

He clambered up the slope until he reached a sheer wall. Then it was an exhausting climb using precarious hand- and footholds to ascend straight up the mountain's rocky palm. His hands turned slick with sweat and his right leg ached. One slip and he'd plummet to his death, taking his friends down with him. Giacomo dried his hands on his pants and pressed on.

Finally, he crawled up to a narrow ledge where the blue glow radiated from inside the wedge-shaped mouth of the cave. He waited so they could all share the victory. Savino joined him first, followed a minute later by Milena and Aaminah. Giacomo took a deep breath. "You ready?"

The three nodded in reply.

The fissure was only wide enough for a single person to enter at a time, so Giacomo led the group into the narrow tunnel. As the light grew brighter, the air cooled.

The tunnel emptied into a cavernous room with smooth slanted walls and a sand-covered floor. And floating in the center of it, inside a rotating octahedron, was the Creator's Compass.

Giacomo savored the moment for as long as he could. *We found it.*

Luna startled them all with the same bloodcurdling screech and clicking sound she'd made at the grotto.

"Ugalino's close again." Aaminah's voice quavered.

In the excitement of finding the Compass, Giacomo had completely forgotten about Ugalino. And if he was close enough for Luna to sense him, he would have been close enough to see the mountain burst apart and the peaks rise. "He knows exactly where we are," Giacomo said.

"We need more time," Milena said hurriedly.

"We don't have it." Savino reached for the Compass. "So let's free this thing before Ugalino shows—ow!" The octahedron sent out a shock of energy that threw him to the ground.

Milena helped him up. "Why did you touch it?"

Savino stumbled to his feet. "At least we know it's the real thing."

Luna flew in frantic circles around the cavern, her squawking growing more agitated.

Giacomo's gaze darted to Milena. "I'll watch for Ugalino. Free the Compass!"

Gripping his sketchbook in one hand and his pencil in the other, he ran through the fissure to the mouth of the tunnel and scanned the orange sky—no sign of Ugalino yet. He glanced back into the cavern, where Milena and Savino brushed triangular shapes in the air, while Aaminah played her flute, the notes rising and falling. The music calmed Luna and forced her to focus her energy on the Compass. Giacomo watched as wedges of blue, green, and yellow struck the middle seam of the octahedron, trying to pry it open. The energy pulsed, but the Compass's prison remained intact.

SCREEEEEE!

Giacomo whipped around. Silhouetted by the setting sun, the

silver-winged Genius flew straight at the mountain, Ugalino astride its neck.

Flipping open his sketchbook, he furiously scribbled circles and triangles. Mico fired the shapes from his crown in quick, red bursts. They either missed their mark or fizzled harmlessly against Ciro.

Ugalino raised a staff and swung, launching a helix of white light from a gem on its handle. "Ugalino's here!" Giacomo dove into the tunnel. The attack erupted against the cliff side, shaking the cave.

Aaminah's music abruptly stopped. Milena fell back and dropped her brush. Savino stumbled against the wall. Their triangles of light vanished.

Giacomo's head rang. He tried to rise to his feet, but dizziness overcame him and he fell to one knee. He scanned the ground for his sketchbook, but didn't see it. Panic set in. Without it, he was defenseless.

Suddenly, he spotted it lying inches from the ledge, its pages flapping in the breeze. Giacomo crawled toward it. Ciro flew closer, blocking out the sun.

Giacomo reached for his sketchbook, the pages fluttering against his fingers. But another blast hit, tearing out a chunk of the ledge. His sketchbook was incinerated.

"No!" Shards of rock pelted Giacomo. The energy from Ugalino's attack pushed him back into the cavern. He slid to a stop beneath the floating Compass, the octahedron's spinning point inches from his head.

Savino and Milena sprang forward and performed a dual strike. The wedges of blue and green light shot into the fissure and collapsed the tunnel, cutting them off from Ugalino. But now they were trapped inside the mountain with no way out.

Outside, a muffled explosion bombarded the cave. The rocks filling the tunnel rattled and broke loose.

"Try freeing the Compass again," Giacomo urged.

Savino, Milena, and Aaminah took stances around the octahedron and attacked it once again with triangular projections. Giacomo and Mico joined the effort.

Another explosion. Ugalino was digging his way in.

The glowing triangles scraped the seam of the octahedron, but the shape refused to crack.

From the tunnel, white light burst through, sending huge rocks flying. One slammed into Giacomo, knocking him to the floor. His right arm stung from the impact.

Ugalino marched through the rubble, followed by his Tulpa, his four arms and four legs silhouetted by the orange sky behind him.

Panicked, Savino, Milena, and Aaminah retreated toward the back of the cavern, their Geniuses scattering in all directions.

Even though Giacomo had seen Zanobius once before, his heart still hammered.

Ugalino laid eyes on the Compass and smiled. "I'm impressed. I never imagined four children would find one of the most elusive objects in the world." He looked to Giacomo. "Or should the credit lie only with you?"

Giacomo masked his fear behind a scowl. "Where's Enzio?"

"He served his purpose," Ugalino replied coldly.

What does that mean? The way Ugalino spoke made it sound like Enzio might be dead. Caught up in his own horrified thoughts, Giacomo almost didn't notice Zanobius's face. The Tulpa stared at the floor, like his mind was somewhere else. His expression could have been one of remorse, but that was impossible for a Tulpa. *Or is it?*

Ugalino took long slow strides, circling the Compass.

"Good luck trying to get it out," Savino said. "Our Geniuses couldn't."

"Let me guess," Ugalino said. "Pietro told you only the Creator's living force can release the Compass."

Giacomo bristled at the mention of Pietro's name. "What did you do to him? Is Pietro still alive?"

"He wasn't in great shape when I left him, but he's cheated death once before."

Savino let out a wild roar and raised his pencil in a blur. His Genius shot a blue triangle, thin as a knife's blade. Ugalino speedily raised his staff, forming a shield that shattered Savino's attack. Then he shot out a white streak of light that slammed into Savino's chest and propelled him across the cave, where he landed in a heap.

"Savino!" Milena dashed over to him.

Ugalino nodded to Zanobius, who approached the Compass. "Pietro misled you when he told you a Genius's power would free the Compass. The Creator's living force can take many forms, but Pietro's too narrow-minded to understand that."

Giacomo felt a chill in his spine. What was Ugalino trying to say?

Zanobius's two right arms reached toward the octahedron. Giacomo braced himself, expecting the energy shield to hurl Zanobius away, just like it had Savino. Instead, the Tulpa's hands dipped in as easily as if he was reaching into a pool of water.

"My Tulpa is the purest expression of the Creator's living force," Ugalino said with a self-satisfied smirk.

Without warning, Giacomo felt a burning in his chest, like his heart was on fire. For a second, he thought the Wellspring had opened again, but it hadn't. He clutched his shirt and gasped for air.

"Bring it to me, Zanobius."

The Tulpa wrapped his hands around one leg of the Creator's Compass and tugged, but it didn't move. Zanobius pulled harder, but it still wouldn't budge. "It's stuck!" Zanobius called out.

Ugalino's face flashed with worry. "You have four arms, use them!"

Zanobius passed his two left arms through the octahedron and grabbed the other leg of the Compass. His four massive feet dug into the sand and he heaved, muscles pulling taut. But the Compass remained locked in place.

Air flowed back into Giacomo's lungs, though the burning in his heart remained. He tried to stand up, but couldn't hold his own weight and collapsed back into the sand.

A familiar deep voice echoed from the tunnel. "Guess your Tulpa isn't as all-powerful as you thought." Ozo stepped into the cavern, sword drawn. He was cut up and bloody but, to Giacomo's surprise and relief, still alive.

Ozo rushed Zanobius, sword raised. With a furious howl, the mercenary brought the blade down and cut clean through Zanobius's front right forearm. The Tulpa roared and released his grip on the Compass. He stumbled back, colliding into Ugalino and falling on top of him. In the crush, Ugalino's staff flew from his hands and spun across the ground.

Ozo lunged at the toppled giant, who rolled out of the way and staggered back to his feet. The Tulpa stared at the stub of his arm in disbelief. Instead of blood, it oozed a thick, gray substance. His severed limb, which lay in the dirt, crumbled into pieces.

Ozo stabbed and slashed as Zanobius dodged and swung, using his massive fists as weapons. One of the punches connected with Ozo's jaw and he dropped with a thud.

Ugalino shuffled on his hands and knees, reaching for his staff.

Milena waved her brush and Gaia fired green shards of light that exploded near Ugalino. He recoiled. Savino snatched his pencil off the ground and leaped to his feet, making cutting marks in the air.

While Milena's and Savino's Geniuses pelted Ugalino with a barrage of green and blue triangles, Aaminah hurried to Giacomo. "Are you okay?"

He clutched his chest. "Hard to breathe . . . Like my insides are on fire."

"I think it'll go away once you take the Compass," she said.

"Me?" Giacomo said, gasping. "I can't. No one can."

"Yes, *you* can," Aaminah said. "Every time I've played music to heal you, there's been something . . . different about the way the notes resonated with your body. I didn't understand it at first, but now I think I know why."

Giacomo shook his head. "There's nothing special about me."

"Your Genius showing up out of nowhere, your ability to enter the Wellspring, the way you could see the Invisibilia when none of us could . . . ? I should've realized sooner, but you're not an ordinary human."

The heat in Giacomo's chest burned hotter. He gazed at the

Compass and could've sworn it was calling to him, as if it wanted Giacomo to free it. He found himself compelled to answer.

All his life, he had felt alienated from the world. He had always blamed it on his parents' deaths and living on his own for so long. But maybe Aaminah was right. Maybe he felt so different from others because he *was* different.

He moved toward the Compass, right arm outstretched. He closed his eyes, centering himself. He was dimly aware of Ozo's sword clanging against the wall, Savino's and Milena's attacks exploding around him. But the sounds reverberated, like the fight had moved far away.

He felt a surge of energy surround his hand as it made contact with the octahedron, then slipped through. He plunged his entire arm into the radiant form, and touched one of the Compass's smooth, golden legs. A soothing coolness soaked through his feverish skin. Giacomo opened his eyes and pulled. The Compass slid from its resting place.

The octahedron broke apart and faded away, leaving Giacomo in possession of the Creator's Compass. For an object so large, it didn't feel very heavy. His breathing calmed and the burning sensation disappeared.

The cavern fell silent. All eyes stared at Giacomo holding the Compass, no one quite sure how to comprehend what they were witnessing.

Aaminah was the first to speak. "I knew it . . . You're a Tulpa!"

TABULA RASA

Zanobius gaped at Giacomo, trying to understand how it was possible for the boy to be a Tulpa like him. Ugalino had always claimed Zanobius was one of a kind—what else had his master lied to him about? And how had a child freed the Compass when Zanobius had failed to? What made the boy so special?

Ugalino scrutinized Giacomo like a collector studying a rare painting. He also seemed confounded by the boy's true nature. Ozo, hair matted and face bloodied, lay on the ground, gazing up at Giacomo with a probing stare. Apparently, no one had known the truth about Giacomo. Ozo tried to push himself up, but his arms shook and he collapsed.

Grab the girl. The one holding the flute.

Zanobius looked at the young brown-skinned girl his master was referring to, but didn't make a move. She reminded him of someone . . . But when he tried to recall who, he found only a blank space in his memory.

If Enzio were here, Zanobius knew, he'd tell him not to listen to Ugalino. "He doesn't control you," he'd say.

Grab her now! Ugalino roared in his head.

Zanobius tried to fight the command, but found himself inching closer to the girl, like his feet had a mind of their own. The girl looked up at him in horror. He gritted his teeth and mustered all his strength, forcing his legs to freeze.

Ugalino's eyes widened in shock.

"I won't hurt her!" Zanobius shouted. Everyone focused their attention on him, probably wondering who he was responding to.

"You never learn," Ugalino said, now out loud.

Zanobius stepped toward his master. "I *have* learned. I've learned I'm nothing but a tool to be used by you, a weapon to be wielded when you need one."

"The Compass is almost ours, Zanobius. Think about what you're doing."

"I am. And I'm finally able to see clearly. I don't want to be like this. I don't want to hurt people anymore."

His master shook his head, a look of disgust on his face. "You continue to bring this upon yourself."

Ugalino raised his staff and slammed its tip on the ground. The diamond glowed white, triggering the design on Zanobius's flesh to light up, starting with the outer circles, then extending inward until the entire pattern burned red. It felt like his body was on fire. Zanobius clutched his chest and staggered.

Bound to me by the power of the Creator and the energy of the Wellspring, you are a Tulpa, my creation, mine to order, mine to control.

Ugalino's words spread through Zanobius's mind. He grabbed his head and roared, trying to silence the command, but Ugalino's voice only got louder. The lines in his flesh burned deeper and deeper.

For an instant, all the missing pieces of his memory mosaic flew into place, forming a clear picture of his past.

His master had done this to him once before. No, not just once, he realized. Many times. And on each occasion, Zanobius's rebellion was silenced with a sweep of Ugalino's staff.

But as quickly as his memory mosaic came together, it began to break apart. Tiles shattered as if his master were chiseling away his mind.

On one tile he saw Enzio. Lying in the cave. Dying. He needed to remember. He'd promised to help him. He needed to hold on to that one memory, otherwise Enzio would perish. His eyes felt heavy. He had to remember Enzio . . .

Remember Enzio . . .

Enzio . . .

The past few days were a blur. There had been a fight, Zanobius vaguely recalled. He looked around and realized he was in a cavern. But the memory of how he had gotten there was gone.

Zanobius let out a frustrated growl and hung his head. He'd had another blackout.

His master stood close, the diamond on his staff dimming. A swordsman lay unconscious on the ground, bloody and battered. Had Zanobius been fighting with him? There were children too. Four of them. Two girls. Two boys. They all had Geniuses. The boy with the long, shaggy hair held tightly to a large golden compass. The Creator's Compass, Zanobius recalled. His master's quest had reached its end. But how had he found it?

His front right arm throbbed, feeling lighter than his others. He gazed down, shocked to find his forearm had been severed right below the elbow. A sticky, grayish goo covered the stump, but the wound was too severe to heal on its own. It would require a lot of work on Ugalino's part to rebuild it.

He noticed a sword lying in the bloody man's hands, with the pieces of his missing arm next to it. How could he not remember getting half his arm cut off? As far as blackouts went, this had to have been one of the worst.

Grab the girl. The one with the flute, he heard his master command.

Zanobius lunged for her and chaos broke loose. A bright green spiral blasted toward him, coming from the long-necked Genius. He ducked and light exploded against the wall. His master struck back with a white swath of energy that crashed over the older girl and the two boys like a wave, pushing them toward the back of the cavern.

The brown-skinned girl raised the flute to her lips and blew a high-pitched note. Her Genius, a tiny ball of feathers, shot a jagged stream of yellow light that hit Zanobius's left shoulder, stunning him for a moment. But the blast wasn't powerful enough to stop him.

He grabbed her with his left arms and flung her over his shoulder. The girl's flute fell to the ground and her Genius darted at his head, pecking his eyes. Zanobius swatted it with the back of his hand. The tiny creature tumbled through the air and bounced in the sand several times before skidding to a stop.

"Ahh!" the girl screamed, as if Zanobius had hit her too.

Into the tunnel, Ugalino told him.

As his master attacked the children with white whorls of energy, Zanobius lurched through the tunnel, stopping at the ledge outside. He looked down at the ground over a hundred feet below, his head spinning. He braced himself against the wall, cursing his fear of heights.

"Hand over the Compass, Giacomo. Or watch your friend fall to her death." Ugalino signaled Zanobius with a nod.

Zanobius wrapped his front left hand around the girl's throat and his back left hand around her waist, then held her out over the cliff's edge, her legs dangling in the air. She clawed frantically at his arms.

In the cavern, the other two children formed a protective barrier around Giacomo with their bodies. Now awake, the swordsman struggled to his feet.

"Let Aaminah go, and we'll talk about turning the Compass over," the older boy said.

Show them I'm serious, Ugalino commanded.

Zanobius released his grip.

"No!" Giacomo screamed.

Zanobius seized the girl's braid with his back left hand seconds before she would have plunged to her death. She cried out in pain and grasped his wrist.

"That was a warning," Ugalino told them. "Next time, he won't catch her."

"What do we do?" the older girl whispered.

Giacomo shook his head. "We don't have any choice, Milena." Giacomo chucked the Compass into the sand. "Here. Now let Aaminah go!"

Free her and bring me the Compass, his master ordered.

Zanobius walked back into the cavern, dropped the girl, and picked up the Compass. Despite its size, it felt extremely light, even lighter than the girl.

Ugalino handed Zanobius his staff and took the Compass in exchange. "Watch them." He walked out to the ledge. Gripping the round handle with his right hand, Ugalino raised the Compass, pointing its legs toward the horizon. As he opened the Compass, the circular pattern on its handle lit up. He spun it, drawing a smoldering curve into the sky. After a full rotation, the line connected, and the circle blazed like the sun. Ugalino snapped the Compass's legs closed and tucked it under his arm. He looked back at the children, who shielded their eyes from the bright light.

"Nerezza will now witness the true power of the Compass," Ugalino declared. "Tonight, her reign as Supreme Creator ends."

Come, Zanobius. Ugalino took his staff and called out, "Ciro, to me!" Then he leaped from the ledge into the circle of light. In the sky, Ciro swooped in an arc, then dove into the portal, disappearing instantly.

Zanobius looked at the children. They glared back.

"What happened to Enzio?" Giacomo asked. "Is he still alive?"

The name sounded familiar, but Zanobius couldn't picture who it belonged to. "Enzio? Who's Enzio?" He stepped off the edge of the cliff, brightness flooding over him.

THE HEART OF VIRENZIA

As soon as Zanobius disappeared, the glowing circle began to slowly shrink.

"I'm sorry we lost the Compass, Giacomo," Aaminah said, gently taking his hand in hers. "But thank you for saving me."

He tried to smile in acknowledgment, but he felt frozen. How could he be a Tulpa? It didn't feel real. *He* didn't feel real. Everything he thought he knew about himself had been thrown into turmoil. How had his parents created him? And why? He looked across at his friends. *And what do they think of me now?* Probably the same thing the rest of the world is going to believe—*I'm a monster, like Zanobius.*

"What. Just. Happened?" Savino stared at Giacomo, stunned.

"For a second it seemed like the Tulpa was going to help us," Milena said. "But Ugalino put a stop to that as fast as he could."

"After those lines on his body lit up, it was like he became a different person," Aaminah pointed out.

"Not different," Giacomo said, the shock wearing off. "I think Ugalino somehow erased Zanobius's memory. You heard him, he didn't even know who Enzio was."

"I wasn't talking about what happened with Ugalino's Tulpa," Savino said. "I mean what happened with you." He pointed at Giacomo. "How long did you think you could keep your little secret from us?"

"I swear, I never knew what I was . . . What I am. I'm as confused as you."

Savino squinted skeptically and shook his head. "How could you live your whole life not knowing what you are?"

Giacomo didn't have an answer. Savino was right. *How did I not know?*

"Did your parents even exist?" Savino asked. "Or was that just some story to make us feel sorry for you? To make you seem more human?"

"Savino, enough," Aaminah scolded.

"My parents were real!" Giacomo fought back tears. The last thing he needed right now was for Savino to see him cry.

"We'll deal with all this later," Milena interrupted. She looked toward the tunnel, where the disc of light was growing smaller by the second. "The portal's still open. If we go now, we might have a chance of stopping Ugalino."

Savino glared at Giacomo. "You and me, we're not done talking about this." He whistled and Nero landed on his shoulder.

As they crossed the cavern, Ozo climbed to his feet and leveled his sword at Giacomo.

"You three go. Leave the Tulpa with me." His eyes burned with hatred.

Mico let out an angry squawk.

"What are you doing?" Aaminah demanded.

"It's okay," Giacomo said. "Go. Get the Compass. Before it's too late."

"No," Milena said, slowly raising her brush. "Giacomo's coming with us."

"Don't be stupid, Milena," Ozo growled. "I got no problem with the three of you. It's the Tulpa that needs to be dealt with."

"Giacomo didn't do anything," Aaminah argued.

"He's not human!" Ozo shouted. "He's an abomination. A cold, heartless creation."

"That's ridiculous," Aaminah said. "Giacomo's one of the best people I've ever met."

Giacomo glanced at Aaminah. *Does she really mean that?*

"He's a *Tulpa*," Ozo repeated, as if they'd forgotten. "He might seem harmless now, but any moment he could turn on you. I'm doing you a favor." He spun his sword by the hilt, ready to strike.

Milena stood firm. "You're not laying a hand on him." Then she pointedly added, "Right, Savino?"

Savino sighed and raised his pencil. "Let us pass, Ozo. You're not getting the rest of your payment unless we get the Compass and we make it back to Baldassare. *All* of us."

Giacomo was shocked that they were standing up for him. Especially Savino. After all that had happened, he wouldn't have blamed them for abandoning him. He'd put their lives at risk, slowed them down with his injuries, and betrayed them by stealing the duke's parchment. On top of all that, they had just discovered he was a Tulpa.

The mercenary spat into the dirt. "I don't care about the money."

Ozo's blade came at Giacomo fast. Mico screeched. Savino shoved Giacomo aside, knocking him into Aaminah. Savino and Milena launched triangles of light from their Geniuses, blasting Ozo off his feet and his sword out of his hand.

Milena dragged Giacomo toward the portal, which had shrunk to half its original size. "Come on!"

Savino went first, diving off the edge of the cliff and into the narrow opening, vanishing into the light. Nero flew after him. Aaminah hastily gathered her instruments, then she and Luna followed.

Milena motioned for Giacomo to go before her, but he hesitated, not wanting to leave her behind. In the tunnel, Ozo groaned and rolled to his side. "Go. Now!" she shouted.

Giacomo leaped over the gap and plummeted headfirst into the light.

Colorful threads of energy streamed past, enveloping him in warmth. Mico flew next to him, wings spread, gliding peacefully. But then pressure built up, as if he were being sucked through a narrowing tube. It felt like his eyes were about to burst out of their sockets. A blinding flash filled his vision and he shot out of the portal, landing hard. His body bashed into stone, over and over, finally rolling to a stop. Behind Giacomo, the shrinking disc of light jettisoned Milena and her Genius. Gaia gracefully took to the air, but Milena crashed into him.

The portal began to collapse in on itself, but at the last second, it flung out one last person—Ozo. Then it shrank to a speck of light and vanished, sending out a wave of heat. Before Ozo could recover and spot them, Giacomo grabbed Milena and pulled her away. "Come on!"

As they ran, he noticed the portal had spit them out at the back edge of Piazza Nerezza. The Supreme Creator's palace loomed on the opposite end of the square. Stars filled the sky. Curfew was in effect. They joined Savino and Aaminah, who were crouched behind a pillar at one side of the piazza.

Giacomo watched Ozo climb to his feet and stumble away in the opposite direction. The mercenary kept his eyes trained on Ugalino and Zanobius, who were headed toward the black marble obelisk at the center of the piazza, seemingly unaware they'd been followed. Ugalino's Genius circled in the sky above.

"Ozo's going after Zanobius," Giacomo whispered, surprised by his concern for the Tulpa's well-being.

"Let him," Savino said. "We have to get that Compass out of Ugalino's hands."

The foursome moved from pillar to pillar, along the outer edge of the piazza. Giacomo looked across the square to track Ozo, but the mercenary was gone.

Back at the obelisk, Ugalino swung his staff in an arc. A white band of light streamed from the diamond and sliced the base of the marble monument. Zanobius charged, slamming his shoulder into the pillar. The obelisk wobbled slowly at first, then picked up speed. It crashed onto the ground, shattering into pieces, sending a rumble across the piazza.

Ugalino planted the Compass where the obelisk once stood. Its round handle came even with his waist.

"What's he trying to do?" Savino whispered.

"That's where the Creator brought the world into existence," Giacomo said, recalling the old myths.

"He's going to destroy the city!" Milena exclaimed.

"Not if we stop him." Savino raised his sculpting knife and charged, ready to strike.

Giacomo heard Ugalino shout, "Ciro, attack!" A second later, Ugalino's Genius swooped into Savino's path.

Savino moved his hand swiftly as Nero fired off a series of blue arcs, but Ciro blocked them with a sweep of his wing. Before Savino could strike again, Ciro's head shot forward with a guttural cry. His giant beak opened wide.

"Savino!" Milena shouted. A circle of green light exploded in the Genius's mouth, and it reeled back, letting out a frightful screech. Milena grabbed Savino's collar and dragged him away.

"I had things under control!" Savino complained.

"Really?" she said. "Because it looked like you were about to get swallowed whole."

As they sprinted back toward Giacomo, Ciro whipped his massive wing, kicking up a strong wind that lifted Savino and Milena off their feet and hurled them through the air. Nero and Gaia flew in dizzying patterns, fighting through the gust. Savino and Milena crashed back to earth.

Ugalino glanced their way. Satisfied Ciro had things under control, he returned to the task at hand. He separated the Compass's legs until they formed a wide A-shape. Then, with both hands grasping the handle, Ugalino spun the Compass. Its outer leg scraped along the stones, kicking up white-hot sparks.

After one rotation, Ugalino released his grip on the handle and backed away. Under its own power, the Compass spun faster and faster, becoming a blur. Spreading out from the top of its handle, a glowing white dome encased the Compass, forming a half sphere. Lines began to spread out across the ground, like illuminated veins, extending in all directions, even up the sides of buildings. Patterns of overlapping squares, rectangles, triangles, and circles flickered on, appearing over every surface. It was as if a hundred Geniuses were projecting sacred geometry shapes, bringing to light the hidden building blocks of the city. Giacomo watched in astonishment at the beauty unfolding before him.

Once the architecture's underlying patterns had been revealed, living things throughout the piazza also began to glow. Hundreds of shining lines appeared on a nearby tree, snaking up its trunk and branches, narrowing into detailed patterns on its leaves.

Shimmering triangles, circles, and rectangles illuminated his friends and their Geniuses, uncovering their sacred proportions.

"Look!" Aaminah said, pointing at Giacomo's chest. He gazed down, amazed to discover a six-pointed star and hexagon with a multitude of crisscrossing lines, identical to Zanobius's pattern. There was no doubt now that he and Zanobius had been created the same way.

With the world aglow, Giacomo understood the Compass's true power. It unveiled the Creator's blueprint, which lay hidden to the ordinary eye. Virenzia's buildings, the trees, his friends, and he and Zanobius all shared similar forms. *We're all built from the same pattern,* he realized. *We're all connected.* It was like the entire city was one big cipher and

the Compass had cracked its mystery wide open.

A feeling of peace overcame Giacomo as he realized the whole universe was contained within every single thing, and all those things were woven into the fabric of the universe. *I'm not separate from the others after all.*

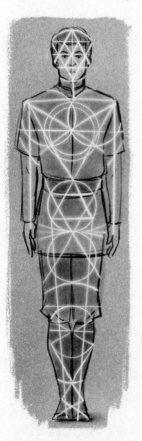

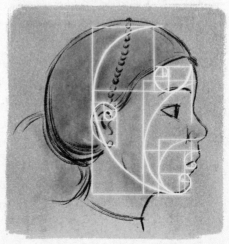

Then all of creation began to crumble.

A dozen of Nerezza's soldiers barreled out of the palace doors, armor clanging, swords and spears aglow with the same light-filled patterns that clung to their bodies.

Ugalino raised his staff, its diamond blazing. He thrust it down, driving it onto a white line between the stones. A wave of energy rippled across the piazza and up the palace stairs. The stones beneath the left flank of soldiers erupted, sending the men flying into the air. They crashed in a pile at the bottom of the steps. The remaining ones continued their charge.

With Ugalino distracted, Ozo emerged from the shadows. He drew his sword to his ear like a scorpion's stinging tail and advanced.

"Zanobius, look out!" Giacomo yelled.

The Tulpa turned and sidestepped, narrowly dodging Ozo's jabbing blade, then countered with a double punch from his two left hands, slugging Ozo in the chest and stomach. Zanobius glanced at Giacomo with a start. His confused stare took in the pattern on Giacomo's chest.

Ozo launched a second attack, driving Zanobius toward the edge of the piazza.

Meanwhile, Ugalino's staff struck more tendrils of light, sending another burst across the square, toppling the remaining soldiers. Another wave surged up the stairs and detonated the columns of the Supreme Creator's palace. The glowing geometric patterns shattered and the massive marble pillars crumbled in a shower of black dust.

"Can't say I'm sorry to see Nerezza get what she deserves," Savino said.

"You think he's going to quit with the palace?" Milena said, her voice shaking. "The whole city is in danger. Everyone's life is at risk."

"But how are we going to stop Ugalino if we can't get past his Genius?" Aaminah pointed to the huge, silver-feathered mass guarding the piazza.

"Well, we can't sit here waiting," Milena said. "One hit from Ugalino and this pillar will come crashing down on us. We have to do something."

"I think we found our opening." Savino pointed to the sky, where a second large Genius sped toward the palace, shedding feathers as it flew. When Giacomo saw the hunched figure on its back, relief swelled through him.

"Pietro!" he exclaimed.

"Tito must have sensed our Geniuses were back," Aaminah cheered.

High above, the master artist swiped his brush. A burst of orange light shot from Tito's crown and hit Ugalino's Genius. Silver feathers exploded everywhere. Ciro screeched and took to the sky, clearing a path to Ugalino.

Savino led the charge as Nero, Gaia, and Luna flew in a V-formation over their heads. Giacomo was about to follow, but stopped himself. His sketchbook had burned to ashes back at the mountain. Without it, he was powerless.

He watched helplessly as Ugalino sent a surge that rattled the stones, erupting under Aaminah, Savino, and Milena. They flew up and came crashing back down. Giacomo sprinted for Aaminah and pulled her to her feet. Milena and Savino picked themselves up and together they retreated. At the back of the piazza, they all found refuge behind the side of a building.

As Giacomo caught his breath, he realized they'd ended up outside the old cultural center that housed Pietro's fresco.

Milena cradled her left arm. In the fall, her shirt had torn and the cotton bandage had come loose. She unwrapped it, revealing her Wellspring scar.

Duke Oberto's disfigured face flashed into Giacomo's mind, followed by the image of the malformed Tulpas. He began to formulate a plan . . .

"I think I might know a way to stop Ugalino," Giacomo said. "But we need to get him away from the Compass."

"Even if we could get him out of the piazza, those glowing lines are everywhere," Savino said. "There's nowhere in Virenzia he'll be weak."

"Not Virenzia. The Wellspring."

"Giacomo, no," Aaminah protested.

"I think the reason I've been able to tap into it is because I'm a Tulpa," Giacomo reasoned. "It also explains why Milena's injury was bad, but mine weren't. I don't think humans can survive in it. That's why the duke looked so beat-up. He tried to make his Tulpas using the Wellspring, but he couldn't stay in long enough to perfect one."

Milena rubbed her scarred arm. "But what about that Tulpa creature that disappeared from the obscura? You could get absorbed back into the Wellspring too."

"Not before Ugalino."

"Are you sure this'll work?" Savino asked.

"I don't know," Giacomo admitted. "But I think it's the best chance we've got. I'll create a mandorla and trap Ugalino in the Wellspring with me."

"There's one problem," Aaminah said. "You don't have your sketchbook."

Savino reached into his satchel. "Here, use mine." He handed Giacomo a bound leather book. "Just try not to get it destroyed."

"Thanks," Giacomo said.

"You'll need this too." Milena tossed him a pencil. Its lead was worn dull, but it would do the trick.

"Mico and I will wait in there." Giacomo nodded his head toward the cultural center. "I'll open the Wellspring while you three lure Ugalino inside. I'll trap him long enough for you to take back the Compass."

"Wait," Milena said. "You need two people to create the mandorla. I can help you."

"It's too dangerous," Giacomo said. "If you get hurt again . . ." A horrible image of Milena burning alive appeared in his mind. "Stay out here. I think I know a way to create it on my own." Pietro had helped him open the Wellspring once, and Giacomo had an idea of how the old master could help him again.

In the piazza, Ugalino sent another wave of light across the stones. A building on the far side collapsed in a heap of rubble and dust.

"Are we doing this?" Savino said impatiently.

Milena nodded, then locked eyes with Giacomo. "Ugalino's more dangerous than any statue or invisible creature. Be careful."

"You too," Giacomo said.

Aaminah hugged him. "I don't care if you're a Tulpa," she said. "I really don't."

Giacomo embraced her. "You always know the perfect thing to say."

The ground shook as another building crumbled. "Let's go," Savino urged.

The four looked out toward the half-destroyed piazza. In the sky, Tito relentlessly pursued Ugalino's Genius, blasting it with bursts of orange light. With each hit Ciro took, Ugalino recoiled in pain. He propelled tendrils of light up at Tito, driving him away from Ciro. On the other side of the square, Ozo and Zanobius were still in the throes of battle.

Savino held his pencil at the ready, Nero on his shoulder. "Milena and Aaminah, attack from the right. I'll flank him from the left. Try to drive him back toward the building." He patted Giacomo on the shoulder. "Good luck."

Giacomo nodded. As the others headed for Ugalino, he ducked

through the wooden doors and entered the abandoned building. Like everything outside, its walls and columns were lit up with geometric shapes.

Through the walls, he heard the distant crackle of the Compass's energy, followed by an explosion of stone. Then came the scratchy, low note of Aaminah's viol. He pictured Ugalino reeling from dizziness as Milena and Savino forced him closer. Giacomo focused his attention on Pietro's fresco.

Thanks to the Compass's web of light, its compositional structure was aglow. Lines crisscrossed, circles and triangles overlapped. Giacomo had always admired Pietro's work, but this was like looking through human skin, to the muscles and bones, to get a clear picture of how a person was built.

At the center of the fresco, Giacomo found what he was looking for—a large, illuminated circle that overlaid seven dancing figures, their outstretched arms connecting in a ring. It would serve as one half of the mandorla. All Giacomo needed to do was draw the other half. *Simple, right?*

"Ready, Mico?" Giacomo's Genius chirped emphatically and hovered next to his head.

Giacomo opened the sketchbook and held the pencil an inch above the blank page, hand trembling. *If this doesn't work . . .* Giacomo shook off the doubt and closed his eyes, focusing his imagination on the image of a circle.

He moved the pencil, arcing his hand over the page. When he opened his eyes again, Mico was projecting a circle on the wall, next to the one from Pietro's fresco.

"A little to the left," Giacomo instructed, and Mico shifted slightly, moving the red circle so it overlapped Pietro's.

"Keep it steady until Ugalino's in here." Mico chirped determinedly.

Another series of explosions rocked the building. The sounds of the battle had moved closer, which meant their plan was working.

With a sharp *crack*, the doors shattered in a burst of light and Ugalino stumbled into the room.

"He's in!" Savino shouted in the distance.

"Now, Mico!" Giacomo said.

Mico turned slightly and the edge of the red circle touched the center point of Pietro's. The almond shape of the mandorla flared and a swirling torrent of color cascaded into the room, followed by a rush of hot air.

In his periphery, Giacomo saw Ugalino raise his staff. A wave slammed into him and Mico, throwing them across the room. The sketchbook and pencil flew out of Giacomo's hands and skidded across the floor. The red circle vanished from the wall, along with the opening to the Wellspring.

Ugalino sent another attack, destroying the sketchbook. "No!" Giacomo reached feebly toward the pile of ashes.

Ugalino strode toward Giacomo and loomed over him. "An impressive attempt, especially for a Tulpa."

Giacomo stumbled to his feet, his head spinning. Mico's wings fluttered erratically as he rose off the floor.

"All these years, I believed I was the only one with the vision and courage to bring a Tulpa to life," Ugalino said. "Your creator has my respect."

"I have two. Both my parents created me."

"Yet they never told you what you truly are . . . How cruel." Ugalino raised his staff and the diamond started to glow.

Without the sketchbook and pencil, Giacomo's only hope of survival was to keep Ugalino talking. "Cruel? They created me with love and never tried to hold me back. All you've done is use Zanobius for your own selfish reasons. Are you ever planning to let him be free? Or are you going to keep him a mindless slave for the rest of his life?"

"My Tulpa is a work of art. And like any masterpiece, it can take many years of struggle and revision before it reaches its true potential." His harsh expression softened. "I'm sure your parents would agree."

"My parents are dead!"

Ugalino gave a heavy nod. "I'm sorry to hear that, I truly am. No Tulpa should have to navigate this hostile world without its creator."

"Thanks to you, I have."

"Me?" Ugalino looked offended. "I didn't know your parents, so whatever harm came to them was not my doing. I can only assume Nerezza had a hand in their deaths?"

"Yes. But if you had never created your Tulpa, Nerezza wouldn't have had any reason to start killing Geniuses."

"I see your reasoning, but it's misguided. Rarely is the world so black-and-white. Nerezza was already well on her way to becoming a tyrant. My Tulpa was merely the excuse she needed to assert total power over her subjects."

Giacomo's eyes locked on the pencil lying on the floor—maybe he still had a shot at opening the Wellspring.

"Now excuse me," Ugalino said. "There's a Supreme Creator I need to overthrow." But as he backed toward the exit, Ugalino doubled over as if struck by an invisible force. From somewhere outside, his Genius's distant cry could be heard. It was the opening Giacomo needed.

He let out a short, soft whistle. Mico snatched up the pencil with his claws and dropped it in Giacomo's hand. He raised the pencil toward Ugalino. "You're not going anywhere."

Ugalino straightened, the diamond on his staff aglow. "Your parents gave you a lot of courage, but not a lot of smarts." He thrust his staff forward and the world slowed.

I am part of the universe, and the universe is within me, Giacomo told himself.

Holding the image of a circle in his mind's eye, he swiped the pencil in a perfect arc. Mico projected a bright red circle on the wall, re-forming the mandorla. Its almond eye glowed, then powerful waves of color poured into the room, swallowing Ugalino's attack. Giacomo braced himself as the Wellspring consumed them both.

BATTLE IN THE PIAZZA

Even though the sky was dark, the glow that emanated from everyone and everything helped Zanobius see his attacker clear as day. The bloodied swordsman charged, spinning his body and whipping his blade. More than once, the steel cut Zanobius's skin, but the wounds were shallow and healed quickly.

"You remember me yet?" The swordsman hacked straight down. Zanobius jumped left. The blade whipped by.

The man seemed intent on killing him, that much was obvious. But there was something else—a haunted look in his eyes—that suggested his conflict with Zanobius might have deeper roots.

"Ozo Mori's my name!" the swordsman roared as he jabbed. "That ring a bell?"

It didn't. It dawned on Zanobius that he must have personally wronged the man in some way.

Zanobius lunged and reached with his front right arm to grab Ozo's blade, forgetting that his hand was missing. Thankfully, he still had three good fists. He swiped with his two left arms, punching Ozo in his shoulder and flank, sending him stumbling to the side.

Zanobius realized the rumble from the falling buildings had ceased. He spotted three of the children rushing across the piazza, toward the spinning Compass. With his master nowhere in sight, it was now his job to guard it.

As Ozo circled and arced his blade, Zanobius ducked and countered with a punch to the gut. Ozo staggered, dropping to one knee. Zanobius ran toward the Compass. Behind him, he heard pounding feet and crunching stones. Zanobius swung around in time to see Ozo leap off a fallen pillar, his blade coming down fast. Zanobius rolled right as the sword sparked against stone.

He grabbed three broken chunks of debris and heaved them. Ozo batted the first two away with his blade, but the third hit him hard in the shoulder and sent him sprawling.

The children now surrounded the radiant half sphere that encased the Compass. As the boy and older girl waved their brushes, the girl called Aaminah played a haunting tune that sounded familiar, though Zanobius couldn't place where he'd heard it before. Their three Geniuses hit the sphere with beams of blue, green, and yellow light.

Ozo was upon him again, this time slashing low, forcing Zanobius to leap over the blade. As he came back down, Ozo jabbed, slicing deep into his back left calf. Zanobius's leg buckled. Gray ooze sizzled as it dripped on a bright line between his feet.

A screech rang out across the piazza and a ragged-looking Ciro dove at the children. Behind him, the old man's gray-feathered

Genius was in close pursuit, firing orange spirals of light from its crown.

Ozo's sword cut Zanobius again, this time across his front left ankle. His two left legs barely held his weight now. He limped away, trying to put some distance between him and Ozo to give his wounds time to heal. But Ozo kept coming. The second Zanobius avoided one sword strike, another would come at him from a different direction.

I'm in danger. Help me. Ugalino's voice pierced his mind, distracting him long enough for Ozo to run his blade through his left shoulder.

Enraged, Zanobius screamed and dove at Ozo, tackling him into a pile of debris. He rose up, pulled the sword from his shoulder, and then flung it away. Using his one good left arm, he picked Ozo off his feet, and with his remaining right hand, pummeled his face. Teeth flew out of Ozo's mouth, followed by a spray of blood. The man went limp. Zanobius tossed him into the rubble.

In the center of the square, the kids were regrouping, making another go at the Compass. The boy named Giacomo wasn't with them. Zanobius looked around for his master. Toward the back of the piazza, streams of light and color flickered like flames through the boarded-up windows of an abandoned building. Was Ugalino in danger because of Giacomo? He wondered about the boy, who had a pattern similar to his on his body. Could it mean the boy was also a Tulpa?

Deciding to save his master instead of the Compass, Zanobius limped across the piazza. He moved as swiftly as he could, but Ozo's attacks had severely weakened him.

He had made it halfway to the building when a dust-covered

Ozo stumbled in front of him, his mouth twisted into a bloody, toothless grimace. The man was resilient, Zanobius had to admit.

"You might not remember my wife and my daughter," Ozo growled. "But the whole world's going to remember me as the man who brought down the Monster."

Wife and daughter? Zanobius searched his memory, but had no recollection of them.

The swordsman let out a howl from deep in his gut and charged, light shimmering off his blade.

UGALINO'S OFFER

Swirling colors blinded Giacomo. He crouched down, shielding Mico from the whipping winds. Out of the chaos, a white orb glowed like a beacon. An expanding sphere of light pushed the colors and the burning heat away.

Ugalino stepped out of the storm, staff held at arm's length. The diamond projected a protective shell that expanded around him.

Ugalino gazed in reverence at the maelstrom of color beating against his shield. "Incredible . . . To be surrounded by the source of all creative energy."

Giacomo trembled, realizing Ugalino wasn't going to perish inside the Wellspring. He was going to thrive in it.

"A Tulpa with a Genius and the power to summon the Wellspring . . ." Ugalino mused, moving closer. "You are a rare artist, indeed."

Giacomo took a step back and clutched his pencil. His arm shot up. Mico hovered, ready to strike.

Ugalino stopped. "That won't be necessary. I'd hoped we would speak. That's why I left the portal open."

"You . . . you wanted me to follow you back here? Why?"

"Because we shouldn't be fighting over the Sacred Tools. We should be working together."

That was the last thing Giacomo had expected him to say. "Work with you? Why would I do that?"

"Contrary to what Pietro and Baldassare may have told you, I am not your enemy. Nerezza is. After I created Zanobius, she made it her life's mission to destroy him. Once she discovers that you're a Tulpa, she'll kill you too."

He's probably right, Giacomo thought.

"With my vision, and your ability to harness the Wellspring, we could end Nerezza's reign. In the right artist's hands, the Compass and the rest of the Creator's Tools could be used to bring a renaissance to the Zizzolan Empire."

"It seems like all you want to do is destroy Virenzia and everyone in it."

"Great change often comes with a few sacrifices."

"How does that make you any different from Nerezza? You both use your Geniuses and your power to control people."

"I'm nothing like her," Ugalino snapped. "I would allow artists and their Geniuses to finally come out of hiding and create once again. Become my apprentice, Giacomo, and we will usher in a new era together."

"I already have a teacher."

"Pietro? He's a washed-up coward who won't allow true artists to flourish."

Giacomo gripped his pencil tighter. "You don't even know him!"

"I do. He was my teacher too."

A sudden coldness hit his heart. *Ugalino was Pietro's apprentice?*

"When I approached him with the idea of creating a Tulpa, I explained how I wanted to create a being that was perfectly proportioned, with unmatched strength. Someone who wouldn't be tied to the past or the future. The ideal man. And what was Pietro's reaction? He forbade me to create one. This, from an artist who was supposedly enlightened. So I pursued it on my own. When Pietro found out, he banished me from his studio. What do you think he's going to say when he discovers you're a Tulpa?"

"He'll . . . he'll understand. He'll still teach me . . ." Giacomo's voice trailed off. Was that really true? Pietro had never been that fond of Giacomo to begin with. Once he found out what Giacomo really was, he'd probably banish him from his studio too. *Or worse.*

"And Baldassare Barrolo may have harbored you in his villa, but no member of the Council of Ten can be trusted."

"Pietro's lived there for years. My other friends too. Nerezza didn't have a clue."

"Don't be so naïve," Ugalino said. "Haven't you wondered why the Supreme Creator of Zizzola, a woman with unlimited resources, didn't send out her own search party to find the Compass?"

Giacomo thought about it for a second. "She had no idea where to look," he responded.

"No. It was because Baldassare was working on her behalf. He tricked you and your friends into doing all the hard work, while he and Nerezza sat back and waited for you to return."

"That's not true!" Giacomo shouted.

"Wake up! They used you and your Genius!"

The whole point of running away from the orphanage was so he wouldn't have to serve the woman responsible for his parents' deaths. But if what Ugalino said was true, he'd been doing the Supreme Creator's bidding this whole time, without even realizing it. He began to feel dizzy. *How could I have been so stupid?*

The Wellspring's relentless pounding cracked Ugalino's protective shell. The air began to warm. Ugalino's eyes flashed fear. He raised his staff, then slammed it back down. The diamond pulsed with light and the barrier held. But judging by the nervous look on his face, Ugalino seemed concerned the Wellspring's power might overtake his.

"Guide us out of here, Giacomo. And let us begin our work together."

Back at the mountain, Ugalino could have closed the portal and left Giacomo stranded, but he hadn't. If he helped Ugalino defeat Nerezza, then he and his friends wouldn't have to live in hiding anymore. All those paintings Baldassare had locked away would be seen again. Against his better judgment, Giacomo found himself seriously considering Ugalino's offer.

"If I help you, how do I know you're not going to wipe my memory too? I won't be your slave."

The shell shook and cracked again. More color and heat streamed in. Beads of sweat ran down Ugalino's forehead. "I didn't create you, Giacomo. You're free to choose your path. But please, choose quickly."

A long seam split across the top of the sphere.

What had Pietro told him in his first lesson, when he was blindfolded? *Change your perception of reality.* He'd believed all the terrible things Pietro and Baldassare had told him about Ugalino and his Tulpa, but why? He needed to look at the situation from a different perspective to know the truth.

But it wasn't as if Ugalino was being completely honest with him either. The man was desperate now and would probably say anything if it meant he would survive. Giacomo had been told so many conflicting things, he didn't know who to trust. Even his parents had kept his true nature from him. But they must have been inspired by Ugalino and his Tulpa. *Is that why they refused to attack Ugalino when Nerezza asked? Is that a good enough reason to let him go now?*

Although Ugalino's intentions in creating Zanobius were far from pure, he'd had the courage and insight to create a living, thinking Tulpa. If he'd stopped when Pietro ordered him to, maybe Giacomo's parents would never have created a son. In a weird way, Giacomo had Ugalino to thank for being alive. *And he's the only one with the knowledge to create Tulpas. He could help bring my parents back.*

Giacomo shook off the thought. Was he really going through with this? Ugalino was a murderer. How many people like Duke Oberto and Enzio had been killed in his quest to find the Compass? How many more would be sacrificed in the search for the Straightedge and the Pencil?

"I'm the only one who understands what you are, Giacomo," Ugalino said. "Now that your friends know you're a Tulpa, they'll always treat you differently. You'll always be an outsider to them."

Giacomo had gotten a glimpse of what it was like to have friends that he cared about. But that bond had been bent, possibly beyond repair. The only thing Giacomo knew for sure at that moment was that he would never be human like them.

The Wellspring's storm intensified and Ugalino's shell buckled. The swirl of colors seeped in. He gripped his staff tighter. The diamond pulsated—bright, then dim, its light growing faint.

"Giacomo, please . . ." Ugalino held his hand out in a gesture of kindness, but also desperation. "Help me show artists a way to greatness again."

Slowly, Giacomo raised his arm and reached out. The wind screamed. The heat seared. All he had to do was take Ugalino's hand in his. Lead him out of the maelstrom.

Giacomo's hand stopped short. "I'm sorry," he said, stepping back. "But the only greatness you seem to care about is your own. I can't let you hurt Zanobius—or anyone else—any longer."

What remained of the dome broke away and the Wellspring

overtook Ugalino. His mouth opened, but his screams were lost among the Wellspring's deafening howls. The edges of his body blended into the surging colors, like oil paints smeared across a palette. Then Ugalino was gone, erased from existence.

Giacomo closed his eyes. The pelting winds died down. The heat dissipated. When he opened them again, he found himself staring at Pietro's fresco. Like Ugalino, the glowing sacred geometry lines had vanished. He looked down at his chest. The Tulpa pattern had disappeared too. A feeling of hope swelled inside him. Savino, Milena, and Aaminah must have taken the Compass back.

"Mico, come on!" Giacomo bolted out of the room, his Genius trailing him. He couldn't wait to tell Zanobius the good news—he was free.

THE CREATOR'S COMPASS

Ozo's blade came straight for Zanobius's eyes. He sidestepped and clamped his hands around the swordsman's throat. Ozo made a sharp choking sound as he was hoisted off his feet; his sword dropped with a clatter. He grasped at Zanobius's hands, trying to pry them loose. The vein in Ozo's neck throbbed slower . . . slower . . . weakening with each heartbeat.

But in his eyes, the hatred still burned. Even with his life moments from ending, the swordsman never showed a trace of fear.

His master's voice returned. *Zanobius. Zanobius!*

He wanted to shout back that he was coming, once Ozo was out of the way. But he was already too late.

Remember me, his master's voice said. Zanobius waited for more, but heard only silence.

Then an excruciating pain ripped through his head, like his skull had split open.

Through blurred vision, Zanobius spotted Ugalino's Genius

above the piazza, frantically whipping its wings and spiraling straight up into the sky. Ciro let out one last rattly shriek before plummeting to the earth.

One of the girls yelled "Watch out!" and the children dove away as Ciro crashed into the glowing dome and vanished in a blaze of crackling energy. The strings of light that shimmered across the humans and buildings retracted into the illuminated half sphere, which then faded away, unveiling the spinning Compass. It slowed and toppled, landing with a clang.

Tiles flew back onto Zanobius's memory mosaic. An image of Ozo came into view, but in it he was younger, his hair shorter, his scar missing. He stood in the doorway of a weathered farmhouse, wielding an ax. Fields of wheat shimmered in the golden light.

A woman stood behind him, just inside the house. She pulled a young girl with braids close to her. Tears streamed down the girl's face.

Ugalino stood by Zanobius's side. *Kill them all,* he ordered.

His memory jumped forward. Zanobius dropped the woman's lifeless body with a thud. The daughter lay unmoving against the wall, under a broken window, shards of glass sparkling in her brown hair. The ax was on the ground, its blade shorn from its handle. Slumped in the doorway was Ozo, bleeding from a deep gash down his cheek.

Why had Ugalino forced him to do that? What could Ozo and his family have possibly done to deserve such a brutal punishment?

A new agony lodged in Zanobius's chest. His master had built him to endure physical suffering, no matter how extreme, but he wasn't equipped to handle the mental anguish that came with the knowledge of what he'd done.

He released Ozo and the swordsman collapsed, gasping. Zanobius clutched his head and dropped to his knees, howling and writhing as more images flooded his memory.

A man's bloated body floated down a river.

Legs lay motionless, sticking out from under a toppled horse cart.

A man in a red robe with burned skin lay in a heap on a marble floor, his tongue hanging from his mouth. He was someone important. A duke, Zanobius recalled.

So many victims . . . All dead by Zanobius's hands. No wonder people had been calling him a monster and an abomination all his life. He was a scourge to the people of Zizzola, a horrible creature that should be shackled in chains and locked away in the deepest, dankest dungeon. If someone didn't put him there, he'd do it himself.

Other memories flowed. Zanobius saw himself speaking against Ugalino, trying to stand up for himself, fighting for his independence. Over and over. But every time, the diamond on Ugalino's staff glowed, the patterns on Zanobius burned bright, then . . . Nothing.

His blackouts weren't random. Ugalino had caused them in order to control Zanobius. The moment he showed a hint of free thought, Ugalino wiped it away. Zanobius had tried to rebel. He'd tried to stop the cycle of violence, but Ugalino's mental leash had been unbreakable.

Until now. The only reason his memories were flooding back was because his master was dead.

To his shock, his eyes filled with water. A drop fell to the ground, splashing in a small circle, darkening the stone. At first, he thought it was rain, but the sky was clear. Then another drop fell, followed by a third, until dark dots sprinkled the ground like a constellation of stars. Was he sad because his master was gone, or was he crying for all those lives he had destroyed?

Straining, Ozo pushed himself to his knees and crawled to his sword. He gripped its hilt. In one motion, he swung his arms, rising up and lifting the blade high.

Zanobius dropped his head and awaited his punishment, hoping his death would bring some peace to Ozo and to the rest of Zizzola. Now that Ugalino was gone, there would be no one who could revive him. Let the mercenary be celebrated as a hero alongside the great protectors of the realm. The Supreme Creator would proclaim him *Ozo Mori, the Tulpa Slayer.*

But before Ozo could bring the blade down, red light shot across the piazza, blowing up at Ozo's feet, sending him into the rubble.

Through the clearing dust, Zanobius saw Giacomo and his Genius racing toward him, a pencil in the boy's raised right hand. *Fine,* Zanobius thought. *Let it be the boy who ends me.*

But Giacomo didn't strike again. Instead, he kneeled next to Zanobius.

"Ugalino is gone," the boy told him. "I'm sorry."

"I . . . I remember. Everything." Zanobius wiped the tears from his eyes. "Why did you stop him?" he said, pointing to Ozo, who groaned weakly.

"Because he was about to kill you."

"You should have let him."

"No," Giacomo said. "You and I are the only two Tulpas in the world. We need to help each other now."

So it was true—he and the boy shared similar origins. Zanobius's life had been plagued by the fact that he was different, a freak. But Giacomo's existence suddenly made him feel less alone. Ugalino's life may have been over, but that didn't mean Zanobius's had to end too. His path was now his choice.

Another memory returned—a boy with black hair, lying lifeless in his arms.

"Enzio," Zanobius muttered. "He's still alive. I promised I'd go back for him."

"He's okay?" Giacomo said, looking relieved.

Zanobius nodded and rose to his feet. "He's probably still in the Cave of Alessio. We can use the Compass to get back to him." Saving Enzio wouldn't make up for all the terrible things he'd done, but he wasn't going to let another innocent life perish if he could help it.

"We'll save him together," Giacomo said. "Come on."

"What do we do about Ozo?" Zanobius asked, pointing to the now unconscious man covered in dust and rocks.

"We get as far away from him as possible before he comes to," Giacomo said.

They hurried over to the other three children, who eyed Zanobius watchfully. Savino clutched the Compass and raised his pencil. The Genius on his shoulder let out a harsh screech.

"Don't." Giacomo put himself between Zanobius and Savino.

With a *whoosh*, the gray-feathered Genius landed near them, carrying the old man. Zanobius remembered him as Ugalino's former teacher.

"Master Pietro," Milena said, "we have the Compass, but the Tulpa's here."

"He's not going to hurt you," Giacomo assured them.

"Everyone, away from the Tulpa," Pietro said.

The children stepped back, but Giacomo remained by Zanobius's side. "Ugalino doesn't control him anymore. He's not dangerous."

"How could you possibly know that?" Pietro said in a dismissive tone.

"Because I'm a Tulpa too."

Pietro's already pale face turned a few shades whiter. "But . . . how?"

"It's true," Milena said. "Our Geniuses couldn't free the Compass, but Giacomo could."

"Still . . . that doesn't mean . . ."

"I'll explain later," Giacomo said. "But right now, Enzio's in trouble. We can use the Compass to get to him."

Pietro dismounted his Genius. "Where is he?"

"At the Cave of Alessio," Zanobius said. "When I left him, he was still alive, but that was two days ago."

"How do we know you're not leading us into a trap?" Savino said.

"He's not," Giacomo answered, before Zanobius could.

"How can you be sure?" Milena asked.

"I just am, all right?" Giacomo grabbed one of the Compass's legs. "Give it to me, Savino. You don't have to come, but I'm going to help Enzio."

Savino pulled on the Compass's other leg. "We need to take it back to the villa."

The two boys glared at each other, waiting to see who would make the first move. But Zanobius didn't have time for their standoff. He reached between them and snatched the Compass out of both their hands.

"Enzio needs our help," Zanobius growled. Savino took a step back, pencil raised.

The clomping of boots interrupted them. Two groups of soldiers, each nearly fifty in rank, swarmed from the sides of the palace. Zanobius feared any further delay would cost Enzio his life, along with their own.

"Give me the Compass," Giacomo whispered, his eyes on the approaching soldiers.

Zanobius handed it over and Giacomo tucked it under his arm.

At the top of the palace steps, ten black-cloaked figures emerged from behind the rubble, their faces hidden by long hoods.

"The Council of Ten," Milena said nervously.

"Baldassare's with them?" Pietro asked.

"There are ten people," Savino said. "One of them must be him."

"Perhaps he has devised some way out of this," Pietro said.

"Or we've walked right into his trap," Giacomo said.

Milena looked confused. "What's that supposed to mean?"

"You all need to cover me," Giacomo said, without answering her question.

"What are you going to do?" Milena asked.

Giacomo scanned the piazza. "Find someplace a little more hidden while I figure out how to open the portal. I'll let you know when I'm ready." He whistled for his Genius and they bolted toward one of the destroyed buildings.

"Get the boy!" one of the cloaked figures hollered. "He has the Compass!"

But before the soldiers could pursue, Milena raised her brush, firing off a trail of green light that erupted in front of them. By the time the dust cleared, Giacomo was gone.

Zanobius charged the soldiers, still limping from his wounds. He crashed into the front line and punched with his two good arms, feeling metal slam against his fists. Two men went down, their swords clattering across the stones.

He dodged right, then left, avoiding jabbing spear tips. Soldiers swarmed. Black armor and metal blades filled his vision. With each punch he landed, another soldier was on top of him. Swords nicked his flesh, and a spear went straight through the back of his right leg. He roared and grabbed the soldier by the throat, hurling him into his fellow men.

Over the clanking swords and grunting, Zanobius made out the quick-tempo notes of a flute. The music was accompanied by a volley of yellow, green, and blue spirals of light that exploded around the soldiers, knocking them away. He couldn't believe the children were helping him.

With a grunt, he wrenched the spear from his calf and hurled it into the throng. Picking an abandoned sword off the ground, Zanobius rejoined the assault, slashing at anyone who came near him.

Like shooting stars, the Genius-fueled attacks rained down, forcing the soldiers into a huddle. They raised their shields, forming a dome of metal around their group.

Zanobius heard the lyrical whistle of a bird. At first, he thought it was one of the Geniuses, but they were reacting too, turning away from the fight and toward the high-pitched sounds.

They flew toward the Council of Ten, who had descended the

stairs during the battle and were marching into the piazza. One of the figures lowered his hood, revealing himself as Enzio's father. He was blowing on a small whistle, luring the Geniuses to him.

He sprinkled the ground with tiny pieces of food and the Geniuses landed, eagerly gobbling up the bait. Soldiers quickly dropped round metal cages over them, locking them inside. The Geniuses screeched and violently thrashed at the bars, but it was too late. They were Baldassare's prisoners.

It had all happened so suddenly that the children barely had time to react before they realized Baldassare's intentions.

"Drop your weapons!" Baldassare ordered.

"What are you doing?" Milena yelled.

"Let Luna go!" Aaminah cried out.

"Drop them now, or your Geniuses perish." Soldiers pointed their swords between the bars of the cages.

"All right!" Milena said, raising her hands in surrender.

Savino, Milena, and Pietro threw their brushes and pencils to the ground. Savino's sculpting tools and Aaminah's instruments followed.

"I'm sorry this is how it has to end," Baldassare said. "I had hoped you could all return to the villa peacefully, but that seems impossible at this point."

"Baldassare, how could you betray us like this?" Pietro asked bitterly.

"Coward!" Savino yelled.

The children's expressions were a mix of hurt and anger. Aaminah looked ready to burst into tears.

"Giacomo, bring the Compass to me!" Baldassare called out,

then gazed downward, smoothing his cloak. "This . . . It wasn't personal, Pietro. I . . . I want you to know that."

"Not personal? All these years, you've been lying to me. And to the children!" Pietro's voice was filled with disgust. "I was a fool to believe that you cared about the future of this city and protecting Geniuses."

"I do care," Baldassare snapped back. "That's why I had to keep the truth from you. In order to locate the Sacred Tools, we needed Geniuses, but no artist would willingly use theirs to help the Supreme Creator."

"Maybe because she was killing them all!" Savino screamed.

Baldassare smirked. "However, young minds are much easier to influence and control."

"You used us!" Milena hollered.

No wonder Enzio had rebelled, Zanobius realized. His father seemed as manipulative as Ugalino had been.

Baldassare stepped forward, calling out again. "Giacomo, come out with the Compass immediately, or your friends' Geniuses will be killed!"

"Enzio's still alive," Aaminah blurted out.

"He is?" Baldassare glanced angrily at Zanobius.

"But he's hurt," she said. "I might be able to save him, but the Compass is the only way to get to him now."

"Then the sooner Giacomo hands it over, the sooner I can send a team to bring my son back."

"Enzio doesn't want to return home," Zanobius said, following Aaminah's lead. The longer they could keep Baldassare talking, the more time Giacomo would have to devise a way out of their predicament.

Baldassare's puffy cheeks burned red. "And what would a Tulpa know about what my son needs? I am his father. Only I know what is best for him."

Zanobius seethed. "No you don't! How could you? You have no idea what he thinks or how he feels!"

Baldassare snarled, "Enough! I won't be insulted by an abhorrent monster like you."

Zanobius limped toward Baldassare, favoring his left legs. "I'm not a monster!" The soldiers leveled their weapons at him. But before another fight could break out, a bloodcurdling screech froze everyone in place. Zanobius looked up to see an enormous black Genius swooping down. Two long twisted horns sprouted from the top of its wedge-shaped head. Zanobius recalled the Genius well—Victoria was her name. He'd done battle with her many years ago. A hunched woman sat astride the Genius's neck. The children stared up in dread. Their Geniuses rattled their cages.

"The Supreme Creator . . ." Aaminah said in hushed fear.

"I was wondering when Nerezza would show her face," Pietro said. His mammoth Genius let out a growly hoot.

From Victoria's crown, a bright violet light shot forth, directly at Zanobius. He jumped away, scampering on his hands and feet, but he didn't act fast enough. The force of the blast sent him flying, along with a shower of rock. For a moment, he hovered weightlessly above the earth, then he crashed into a pile of stone.

His ears rang. His head pounded. Zanobius staggered to his feet and limped back to the children, who huddled near Pietro and his Genius.

"Any sign of Giacomo?" Savino whispered.

"Not yet," Milena said, looking around. "But he'll come through . . ."

Victoria landed in front of Zanobius, her talons clacking against the stones. The soldiers re-formed lines around their leader, blades raised like a jagged fence.

The Supreme Creator looked down with disdain. Since the last time Zanobius had faced her, Nerezza's hair had grayed and her skin showed many more wrinkles. But she still wore the same gaudy headdress. Translucent fabric draped from its padded brim, framing her angled features. Two thin brows arched above her eyes. She wore black velvet robes trimmed with gold and topped with a high, stiff collar that appeared to be the only thing holding up her ancient head. Her withered hand peeked out from an embroidered sleeve, clutching a thick wooden brush. Her piercing gaze stopped on Zanobius.

"Where's that traitorous creator of yours?" she asked.

"He's gone . . ." Zanobius said. "Killed by Giacomo. And if you don't back down, you'll be next!"

"That child is hardly a threat," Nerezza scoffed.

"There he is!" Baldassare shouted. Everyone turned toward the palace. Zanobius spotted Giacomo striding along the top of the building's fallen pediment, which now lay broken in two among the crumbled pillars. Nerezza and her Genius wheeled around to face him. Like a statue of a hero, Giacomo thrust up his arm, triumphantly raising the Compass. A few feet behind him his tiny Genius hovered, its gem aglow, bathing Giacomo in a red light.

Victoria craned her neck forward to give Nerezza a closer view of the defiant boy. "Baldassare told me of your ability to access the Wellspring," she said. "But even a boy of your incredible talents can't overpower me."

Fearless, Giacomo stood his ground. "Maybe not. But I found the Compass when you couldn't. However, I might be willing to give it to you and to help you find the Creator's Straightedge and Pencil."

"In exchange for what?" Nerezza said, sounding intrigued.

"What is he doing?" Milena whispered.

"Guess he didn't come through after all," Savino grumbled.

Zanobius didn't understand it either. When Giacomo had appeared on top of the rubble, it looked like he was going to use the Compass *against* the Supreme Creator, not turn it over to her.

"I realize my parents made a mistake by not helping you all those years ago," Giacomo continued. "I want to fix that. Let my friends and their Geniuses go, and I'll serve you."

Aaminah gasped. "Giacomo, no!"

"And the Tulpa?" Nerezza asked, glancing at Zanobius.

"He goes with them," Giacomo said.

So that was Giacomo's plan. He was going to sacrifice himself, allowing them all to go free. Zanobius had never seen such an act of selflessness from a human before.

Nerezza considered Giacomo's demands, then nodded to Baldassare. "Release the Geniuses," she commanded.

Baldassare begrudgingly unlocked the cages, and the three Geniuses flew back to Savino, Milena, and Aaminah, who were flushed with relief.

Giacomo looked down and waved them away. "Go," he said. "Trust me."

The Supreme Creator watched Zanobius, Pietro, and the children back away from the army, then she returned her gaze to Giacomo. "Now, hand over the Compass."

Giacomo took a step toward her, and for a split second, he vanished. It reminded Zanobius of the way Giacomo had appeared, then disappeared, during their first encounter.

Zanobius ushered the children in the direction Giacomo had fled earlier. "This way," Zanobius whispered, leading them behind a half-ruined wall, then circling around toward the side of the palace. The whole time, he kept an eye on Giacomo. Zanobius noticed Giacomo's form flicker again, but it happened so fast, no one else seemed to see it. "I think there's more to Giacomo's plan."

"Before I turn myself over," Giacomo said, "there is one thing I need to ask you."

"And what is that?" Nerezza asked.

"Do you know why my parents refused to help you?"

"They were too proud to share their Geniuses for the good of the empire. They were prideful and arrogant."

"That's not the reason," Giacomo said.

"Then please, enlighten me."

"Because they knew you would want to kill me if you knew the truth."

"The truth about what?" Nerezza snarled.

"They created me," Giacomo proclaimed. "I'm a Tulpa."

Nerezza jerked forward and her Genius lunged at Giacomo, its giant jaws opening to reveal a mouthful of fangs.

"No! We need him!" Baldassare protested.

Mico dodged out of the way as Victoria swallowed Giacomo in one bite.

The children shrieked and gasped, believing Giacomo had been killed. "He's all right," Zanobius quietly assured them.

When Victoria withdrew and opened her jaws, only rocks and dirt fell out. Giacomo remained atop the debris, unscathed.

"How . . . how did you know?" Aaminah asked.

Zanobius led them behind the pile of broken stones and

marble. Inside a small alcove, they found the real Giacomo, holding the real Compass, the circular pattern on its handle aglow.

Milena looked on in disbelief. "Giacomo . . . ?" she whispered.

"No way . . ." Savino uttered.

Aaminah excitedly grabbed Pietro's arm. "He's all right, Master Pietro!"

Giacomo whistled and his Genius swooped down. Without the beam, the projection of Giacomo flickered, then broke apart into tiny bits of light. The illuminated pattern on the Compass's handle went dark. Zanobius was confounded—how had Giacomo used the Compass and his Genius to project himself?

"It's not the boy!" Zanobius heard the Supreme Creator shriek. "Find him!" Clomping boots headed their way.

But Giacomo was already a step ahead. He held the Compass out in front of him, its lower leg horizontal to the ground, its upper leg angled upward.

"Ready to get Enzio?" Giacomo asked.

"But you've never been to the Cave of Alessio!" Savino said, sounding panicked.

"When I was in the duke's camera obscura, I saw it," Giacomo said. "Well enough to picture it, at least." He closed his eyes and inhaled.

Soldiers climbed over the piles of stones. Tito lunged at them, letting out an earsplitting shriek. The soldiers scattered.

"Get the Compass, you cowards!" Baldassare ordered. More soldiers clambered up the rubble. Victoria rose from behind the pile, wings heaving.

Everyone gathered near the entrance to Giacomo's hiding spot. As he turned the Compass, the pattern on its handle lit up again and a line of light trailed from its spinning leg.

Victoria landed and scrambled past the soldiers, knocking them aside. Zanobius shoved Savino out of the way and thrust out his two good arms. The Genius's massive jaws slammed into his hands. Zanobius dug his feet into the ground, his legs trembling. Saliva dripped from Victoria's fanged mouth, slathering Zanobius's arms in a thick goo; her breath stank of rotten meat. It took all of his withering strength to keep the creature at bay.

"The portal's open! Everyone through!" Milena ordered.

A glimmering white circle hung next to Giacomo in the mouth of the alcove.

Aaminah jumped through first, followed by Milena and Savino and their Geniuses.

"Pietro, come on!" Giacomo shouted.

Pietro led his Genius toward the portal, but Tito pulled back, hesitant.

"Get in there!" Pietro hollered, giving his Genius a little kick in its side. It stuck its giant head into the circle of light, then tucked its wings, wriggling through.

"You're next, Zanobius!" Giacomo said urgently.

"No . . ." he said, straining. "You go. I'll be right behind you."

Zanobius's arms and legs felt like they were about to explode. The gem on Victoria's crown bathed him in a violet light that was growing brighter by the second. "You've been a scourge upon my empire, Tulpa!" Nerezza screamed.

But as her arm swung down, a red triangle struck her hand, snapping it back. Nerezza's brush flew from her grasp.

"Zanobius warned you, I *am* a threat!" Giacomo proclaimed.

"Get out of here, Giacomo!" Zanobius urged. Victoria bore down with all her power. His knees buckled. He didn't know how much longer he could hold the Genius back.

Giacomo dove into the portal and vanished. Zanobius jumped to the side, releasing his grip on the creature's jaw. Victoria's head pitched forward, her beak smashing into the stones. The momentum threw the Supreme Creator from her Genius's neck, sending her crashing into Baldassare.

Zanobius looked out to the piazza, surprised to see Ozo lurching toward him, eyes fixed, dragging his sword across the stones. Zanobius was impressed by the man's persistence. He had no doubt they'd cross paths again.

"I'm sorry," Zanobius called out. "I truly am." Then he stepped into the light.

CONSTELLATIONS

Giacomo jetted out of the portal and tumbled across the ground, smacking into a tree. Its gnarled branches shook above him. A waterfall showered him with a cool mist. On either side of him, Savino, Milena, and Aaminah slowly rose to their feet, while Pietro climbed off Tito. The Genius shook like a giant wet dog, scattering feathers everywhere, creating some new bald spots. Giacomo collapsed with relief. By the Creator's good graces—and his Compass—they'd made it to the Cave of Alessio.

The portal ejected Zanobius, who slid face-first across the grass. He spat out a mouthful of dirt. "Close it now!" He limped up the path and disappeared into the cave behind the falls.

Giacomo grabbed the Compass and lined up its leg with the outer edge of the portal. He spun it counterclockwise and the portal shrank to a tiny dot and vanished.

Aaminah fell into him with a huge hug. "How did you project yourself like that?"

Giacomo relaxed his grip on the Compass, still reeling from the shock of everything that had happened. "I wasn't sure it would work," he began to explain as he and Aaminah separated. "I was about to open the portal when I heard Baldassare's bird whistle. Once he captured your Geniuses, I knew I had to come up with another plan. I thought about how the Compass had projected itself into Alessio's Cave and I figured I might be able to combine its power with Mico's gem to do something similar to myself."

"You made your own version of a camera obscura," Milena said. "Brilliant!"

Savino patted Giacomo's shoulder. "Thanks for getting us out of there. For a second, I really thought you were going to join Nerezza's side."

"Never," Giacomo said. "I just had to figure out a way to trick her into freeing your Geniuses. There was no way I was about to let you all become Lost Souls."

Giacomo noticed Pietro had stayed back with Tito, petting his beak, looking lost in thought. Hesitant, he approached. "Master Pietro? Are you all right?"

Pietro shook his head and scowled. "All those years . . . He pretended to care about me, acted like we were a team. It was all a lie."

"How could you have suspected Baldassare was going to betray you?" Giacomo said. "None of us did."

Pietro turned away without another word. Giacomo got the sense that Baldassare's betrayal wasn't the only thing upsetting him. This stony silence was exactly what Giacomo had feared when he'd told Pietro he was a Tulpa. *He must hate me.*

Zanobius emerged from the cave, holding a limp Enzio in his arms.

"Is he . . . ?" Aaminah asked.

Giacomo's stomach sank. *We're too late . . .*

"He's still breathing, but only barely," Zanobius said.

Relief coursed through Giacomo.

Zanobius laid Enzio under the tree and looked desperately at Aaminah. "Can you help him?"

"I hope so," Aaminah said.

"But all your instruments are back in the piazza," Savino pointed out.

Aaminah slipped a hand into her boot, pulling out a half-sized version of her flute. "I had this one tucked away the whole journey, just in case," she said with a smile. She sat by Enzio's side and began to play. A string of yellow shapes sprinkled over Enzio like drops of rain. Giacomo let the music wash over him too, soothing his nerves and calming his soul.

"One question." Milena looked quizzically at Giacomo. "You shut the portal so Nerezza couldn't follow us. Why didn't Ugalino try to stop us from showing up in Virenzia?"

"Because he wanted me to go after him."

"Why?"

"So he could convince me to join his side."

Pietro flinched in surprise when he heard that. "He did?"

"But you didn't let him out of the Wellspring," Savino said. "I guess he wasn't very persuasive."

Giacomo's heart felt heavy. Letting Ugalino die hadn't been an easy decision. But if he hadn't, Zanobius would still be under his control. And more innocent people would have suffered at his hands. "The thing is . . . a lot of what he said, I actually agreed with," he admitted.

"Then he has poisoned your mind!" Pietro shuffled over. "Let me guess, he told you artists shouldn't be bound by rules or limitations? That man was driven only by his ego. He lost his soul long ago."

"Is that why you kicked him out of your studio?" Giacomo asked bitingly.

Pietro tensed. Milena's and Savino's eyes widened in shock.

"You never told us Ugalino used to be your student," Milena said.

Pietro nodded reluctantly. "It's true. He was young and arrogant. I thought expelling him would discourage him . . . humble him a bit. Instead, it did the exact opposite. He became even more single-minded and strong-willed."

"But instead of forbidding him from creating a Tulpa, you could've guided him," Giacomo said. "Why didn't you show him a better way?"

"I tried, but he wasn't interested in hearing anything that challenged his pursuit of power. There was no getting through to him," Pietro lamented. "His intentions were misguided from the start."

Giacomo steeled himself to ask the question he wasn't sure he really wanted answered. "Do you think my parents were wrong to create me?"

Pietro's hand shot out toward him, and Giacomo flinched. Then he felt his teacher's rough fingertips graze his face, like the first time they'd met. Pietro smiled, ever so slightly. "Even though I didn't know your parents, it's obvious they created you out of love, from deep in their souls. What you did today was bold and courageous."

"So you're not going to cast me out?" Giacomo asked hopefully.

Pietro shook his head. "I believe the Creator may have bigger plans for you. And we still have a lot of work to do."

"Find the other Sacred Tools and remove Nerezza from power," Milena said resolutely.

Tears welled in Giacomo's eyes. "You . . . you can't drive Zanobius away either. He needs us. Just because Ugalino created him a certain way, that doesn't mean he can't change."

"He seems to care about Enzio's fate," Pietro remarked. "And without Ugalino's influence, he may prove to be a valuable ally."

"So he's part of our group now, like it's no big deal?" Savino asked resentfully.

Giacomo held up the Compass. "If you have a problem with it, I can send you back to Virenzia right now."

Savino held his hands up in surrender. "Okay, okay. Don't get so bent out of shape about it. By the way, can I get my sketchbook back?"

Giacomo lowered his gaze. "Yeah . . . about that . . . It kind of got destroyed. Ugalino's fault."

With a groan, Savino slumped and shook his head.

"What a loss for the art world," Milena teased. "All your sketches of nude sculptures are gone forever."

Savino blushed. "Hey, they were really good drawings!"

At the river's edge, Tito dipped his head into the water and splashed it over his body. With a playful squawk, he ruffled his feathers, spraying them all. Nero, Gaia, Luna, and Mico frolicked in the river around their huge companion.

"Sounds like Tito is enjoying being outside," Pietro said.

"I'm just happy he's finally getting a bath," Savino commented. "He's always been one smelly Genius."

Giacomo and his friends kept vigil through the night, while

Aaminah's healing music gradually coaxed Enzio back to life. They filled in Pietro on the details of their harrowing journey, trading turns recounting their adventures escaping the living statues, finding the duke's mysterious camera obscura, and surviving the Land of the Dead.

"There's one thing I still don't understand," Giacomo said to Pietro. "If I'm a Tulpa, how can I also have a Genius?"

Pietro stroked his beard, deep in thought. "That is a mystery, Giacomo. The Creator must have given you one for a reason. And how can we explain your connection to the Sacred Tools? Or why you and Zanobius are such different Tulpas? These are questions that are beyond my current comprehension."

"That doesn't really help," Giacomo muttered.

"There are no easy answers, in life or in art. You're not following anyone's path now, you're forging your own. No doubt, you will find it both lonely and scary. But no one ever said having a Genius would be easy."

Giacomo sighed. "How do you always know how to make me feel inspired and hopeless at the same time?"

Pietro shrugged. "It's my gift."

Enzio groaned and opened his eyes.

"He's awake!" Zanobius announced with relief.

Enzio weakly reached for Zanobius. "You . . . you came back for me." His words were barely more than a whisper.

Zanobius smiled and clasped his massive hand around Enzio's. "Of course. I made a promise." He pulled Enzio up and leaned him against the tree. Aaminah let the last note hang in the air before she put her small flute down.

"I thought I was never going to leave that cave again." Enzio gave Aaminah's hand a light squeeze. "Your music never sounded so beautiful. I'm sorry I ever gave you a hard time for practicing."

"It's okay," Aaminah said. "I'm glad you're feeling better."

Enzio looked across everyone's faces, his gaze stopping on the

Compass in Giacomo's hands. "You found it," he said, sounding surprised. "My father's probably thrilled. Where is he?"

They were all silent.

Enzio's brow wrinkled. "What happened?"

Realizing nobody was going to speak up, Giacomo delivered the news. "He betrayed us all. This whole time, he was only using us to find the Compass so he could hand it over to Nerezza."

Enzio's face looked blank. Was he upset? Angry? Giacomo couldn't tell.

With a dismissive snort, Enzio said, "Figures. He's always been more concerned with himself than with anyone else." His expression turned anxious. "What about my mother?"

"She was safe at the villa when Tito and I left," Pietro said. "But unfortunately, none of us can return to Virenzia right now. It's too dangerous."

"After what my father did, do you think I'd want to go back home? I don't care if I ever see him again." Enzio looked around at the group and the tension in his face eased. "I'm just glad you all came back for me."

Savino leaned in. "Oh, and one thing we should get out of the way—Giacomo's a Tulpa."

Enzio rubbed his brow. "What? A Tulpa? Since when?"

"Apparently all my life," Giacomo said. "But I only realized it a few hours ago."

"Another Tulpa, huh?" Enzio cracked a smile. "I knew there was something off about you. But don't worry, I won't hold it against you."

"Thanks . . . I guess?"

Zanobius helped them all catch and cook fish. Giacomo eagerly gobbled one down and fed Mico a small piece from his share. With all the excitement, he hadn't realized how hungry he was. Zanobius handed a cooked fish to Savino, who eyed it warily, but took it anyway. Milena and Aaminah chatted quietly with Enzio, and Pietro fed tiny bits of fish to the Geniuses. Giacomo was impressed by how quickly everyone had recovered. Despite barely escaping Nerezza with their lives, here they were, relaxing around a fire and enjoying food. He was reminded of what it felt like to be part of a family.

Giacomo nibbled the last of his fish off the bones and rinsed his hands in the river. He turned at the sound of footsteps. Milena knelt by his side.

"Here," she said, reaching into her bag. "You should keep this." She handed him the Tulpa cipher, its edges brittle and blackened from the fire. "I'm sorry I didn't trust you to have it."

Giacomo dried his hands on his tunic and took the parchment, tucking it into his pocket. "Thanks."

"You think it'll help you understand what . . . I mean, *who* you are?"

"I hope so," Giacomo said. He stared into her brown eyes, the moonlight reflected in them. He leaned forward and wrapped his arms around her. She hugged him back. His whole body relaxed in her warm embrace.

Exhaustion overtook the group, and one by one they all found places to rest their heads for the night. Milena, Savino, and Aaminah circled the glowing fire, while Pietro curled against Tito for warmth.

Zanobius sat by the river's edge, staring up at the sky.

"You like watching the stars too?" Giacomo took a seat next to him and gazed up.

"Before Ugalino brought me to life, I remember being surrounded by them. Maybe that's why they've always given me comfort."

"So did all your memories come back?"

Zanobius nodded. "Most of them. But there are still some hazy patches. I want you to know, I tried before."

"Tried what?"

"To break Ugalino's hold on me. But every time, he wiped my memory and I went back to being a mindless monster."

"You're not a monster. That's only what Ugalino wanted you to believe."

"I should be glad I can remember my life now. But it also feels like a curse. I hurt so many people. Ended so many lives. Did you know Ozo used to have a wife and daughter?"

"He did?"

"They'd still be alive if it wasn't for me. That's why Ozo tried to cut me down. He wanted revenge. I don't blame him."

Giacomo was silent for a moment as he took this in. "No wonder he wanted me dead too. He saw any Tulpa as a threat."

He thought about Ugalino and how he had pleaded for his life. A stomach-churning feeling took hold. Giacomo told himself Ugalino's death had been necessary to save himself and Zanobius, but it didn't change the facts of the matter. *I'm a murderer.*

Zanobius tapped him softly on the arm. "Are you all right? You look like you're going to be sick."

"Do you think I'm a bad person?" Giacomo asked.

"Of course not," Zanobius answered. "But unfortunately, not everyone will see the good in you. Once word gets out that you're a Tulpa, there will be a lot of people like Ozo coming after you. They won't care what *kind* of person you are, just *what* you are."

The warning gave him chills. For most of his life, he'd protected himself by hiding away. But by taking the Compass and telling Nerezza he was a Tulpa, Giacomo had made himself a target. The only way to survive now was to keep moving forward on his new path. But it felt like holding a candle in a tunnel; he was blind to the twists and turns that lay ahead.

Zanobius and Giacomo gazed up. The night sky hung like a canvas, painted with so many dots, to count them all would take a thousand lifetimes. For now, Giacomo felt content with the life he'd been given. Two stars sparkled brighter than the others. Giacomo imagined they were his parents, winking at him from above, letting him know he was going to be all right. *I have my Genius, I have my friends, and I'm safe, at least for tonight.*

"Good night," he said to Zanobius.

"Good night."

Giacomo curled up by the fire, where the last burning embers fought to stay lit against the cool air. He checked to make sure no one was looking, then pulled out the charred piece of parchment from his pocket. The illustration of the eight-limbed man stared back at him from the cipher; there was no mystery about where Ugalino had gotten his inspiration for Zanobius's appearance. But could the cipher tell Giacomo why he and Zanobius were so different? Why eating and sleeping came naturally to him, but not to Zanobius? Why Zanobius couldn't feel physical pain, but Giacomo was acutely aware of even the tiniest scratch? In time, he was confident he could uncover the secrets that the parchment held, and possibly discover a way to return his parents' souls to this world. But Giacomo knew they wouldn't be the same. It would be like making a copy of a master painting. Similar in appearance, but never the real thing.

He crumpled the parchment in his hand and held it over the fire, hesitating for a moment. He looked back up at the two

sparkling stars. *I love you,* he thought. He cast the parchment into the embers, where it went up in a burst of flame.

Giacomo lay down and Mico hopped toward him, tucking his feathered body into the crook of his arm. He realized something was different about his Genius. "You seem bigger . . ."

When Mico had first showed up, he easily fit in the palm of Giacomo's hand. Now, he was at least twice the size. Mico softly trilled and closed his eyes.

Giacomo stared at the ashes, where one final ember refused to die out. Sometime later, he drifted off to sleep. When he awoke, the dawn sky glowed pink, and the same ember still burned.

Giacomo Ghiberti

Author's Note

The book you hold in your hands began with a concept: art is magic. But it took over a decade and many false starts to figure out how to tell an exciting and entertaining story that expressed that idea.

See, the challenge of writing a story where art is magic is that something *magical* needs to happen. So even though I was drawing on the history and art of Renaissance Italy for inspiration, I wanted the world I was creating to have elements of fantasy. In my early brainstorming notes, I wrote about sculptures that came to life, but I had yet to figure out how to visualize the artistic process in a magical way.

Then, in doing research for the book, I read Fritjof Capra's *The Science of Leonardo*, where I came across the term *genius*. I discovered that the word implied something very different during the Middle Ages and the Renaissance than it does now. In Latin, a *genius* meant a guardian spirit, either of a person or a place, and was credited with an artist's remarkable creative powers. Nowadays, when we talk about a gifted person, we say they *are* a genius; long ago, we would have said a talented person *had* a genius. I loved the idea of my story's hero having a real-life muse that guided and protected him. Thus, Giacomo's Genius was born. Its birdlike appearance was inspired by Hindu and Buddhist imagery of Garuda, a divine human-bird that is often depicted with a jeweled crown.

But I still needed some magic. I had been vaguely familiar with sacred geometry, as it related to artistic design and composition, and thought it might provide a framework for how the magic in my fantasy world could work. I picked up a book by Michael S. Schneider called *A Beginner's Guide to Constructing the Universe*, which wove together the history and philosophy of sacred geometry along with practical instructions on how to create each shape. I was especially attracted to the idea that sacred geometry is a means of expressing our creative souls *and* our spiritual souls as well. As I learned how to build shapes, I began as Giacomo did, with a healthy amount of skepticism. What's so magical about a circle? I thought. But as I discovered how this seemingly simple form gave birth to every shape, I was like a kid again, excited by the hidden world that was opening up to me. Thanks to Mr. Schneider and his book for inspiring the magic of *Rebel Genius*.

The final element that brought the story together was the idea of a living sculpture that was cursed in some way. The character of Zanobius stemmed in a general way from the golem in Jewish folklore, but more specifically from the Tibetan Buddhist concept of the tulpa. This mystical being is given physical form through an act of imagination, which seemed appropriate for a book about artists. Leonardo da Vinci's drawing of the human body's harmonious proportions in *Vitruvian Man* provided the template for Zanobius's appearance, as well as for the Tulpa cipher that Giacomo finds.

When I first came up with the idea for this book, I didn't think it would amount to anything, much less be published. But my Genius spirit kept prodding me to press on, even when I thought my writing was worthless. I hope *Rebel Genius* inspires you to create something meaningful to you, in whatever form that takes.

Your Genius is out there, just waiting to find you.

Acknowledgments

I'm truly grateful to everyone who helped make my first foray into book writing a smooth and enjoyable experience.

To my editor, Connie Hsu, for your patient guidance, thoughtful questions, and brilliant insights. You've treated my characters and me with the utmost respect and care.

And the reason Connie became my editor in the first place is thanks to Mark Siegel, who believed she would champion me like crazy. Mark, you were right!

I'm confident my book and I are in very good hands with publisher Simon Boughton and the passionate team at Roaring Brook and Macmillan. Thanks to Gina Gagliano, Ashley Woodfolk, Katie Cicatelli-Kuc, and book designer Andrew Arnold for being exceedingly collaborative and considerate. Copy editor Chandra Wohleber asked all the right questions and helped fix more than a few clunky sentences.

It was a bit nerve-racking to share an early draft of this manuscript, but my readers were nothing but supportive. Brandon Huang, Kurt Mattila, Bryan Konietzko, Marie Lu, and Leigh Bardugo—thanks for your extremely perceptive and constructive feedback. I owe all of you! Bryan, Marie, and Leigh also provided very kind blurbs. Marie's and Leigh's advice was invaluable in helping me navigate the unfamiliar world of publishing as I was getting my feet wet.

Over the years, I worked on early versions of this story during workshops and retreats at Writing Pad in Los Angeles. I'm thankful to Marilyn Friedman for creating an inspiring haven for writers, and to my fellow students, who offered their feedback when I was deep in my lumpy phase.

Thanks to Lisa Wahlander for photographing me to look like a respectable author. To Nicolas Delort for his beautiful cover art. And to Jeremy Zuckerman for shedding some light on musical terms and techniques.

To my lawyer, Leon Gladstone, for making this deal and for being so enthusiastic about my work. And to Ernest Johns for keeping my business affairs in order while I focused on writing.

To Bernard Billik for our talks about consciousness and creativity and for sharing your wisdom.

To my parents, who have always supported and encouraged my creativity and artistic pursuits.

And finally, to my wife, Shoshana; I'm eternally grateful for your unwavering support and understanding, especially on those days I wasn't so supportive of myself. Living a creative life with you continues to be an honor.

REBEL·GENIUS

BY MICHAEL DANTE DiMARTINO

Turn the page
for bonus materials.

GOFISH

Michael DiMartino

What did you want to be when you grew up?
As far back as I can remember, I loved to draw and I always wanted to go to art school and become an artist.

When did you realize you wanted to be a writer?
Writing was something I did on the side while I was pursuing my artistic goals. But once I was making animated films in college, writing became more integral to my creative process.

What's your favorite childhood memory?
It's not a specific memory, but more the general feeling of freedom I had growing up in Vermont, riding my bike with friends until sunset in the summer, jumping in giant piles of leaves in the fall, and sledding in the winter.

As a young person, who did you look up to most?
I looked up to anyone who was creative—famous or not.

What was your favorite thing about school?
The friendships I made through high school and college were the most important and influential in my life.

Did you play sports as a kid?
I played baseball and soccer when I was young, but I wasn't very good at sports, so I stuck with art.

What was your first job, and what was your worst job?
I mowed lawns in my neighborhood growing up. I'm grateful that I've never had a truly terrible job. My first job in animation was in college. In the mid-'90s, I moved to New York for a summer to work as a layout artist at MTV Animation for a show called *The Head*.

What book is on your nightstand now?
I have a big stack of books waiting to be read! I have Books 3 and 4 of *My Struggle* by Karl Ove Knausgaard, the Black Panther comics by Ta-Nehisi Coates, and a nonfiction book about genetic engineering, to name a few. I try to read books in a lot of different genres.

Where do you write your books?
I write in my home office where it's very peaceful and quiet.

What challenges do you face in the writing process, and how do you overcome them?
The hardest part for me is starting out with the blank page. I outline my stories so I always have a guide for what I'm going to write next.

What is your favorite word?
I remember learning the word *antidisestablishmentarianism* in high school. It always stuck with me, but I've yet to find an organic way to weave it into a story.

SQUARE FISH

If you could live in any fictional world, what would it be?
I suppose I'm biased, but after writing stories in the Avatar universe for so long, I'd love to travel to the Fire Nation, Water Tribe, Earth Kingdom, and the Air Temples.

What was your favorite book when you were a kid? Do you have a favorite book now?
I loved Roald Dahl and still do. *James and the Giant Peach* was my favorite. *Where the Red Fern Grows* by Wilson Rawls also really stuck with me because it was so emotional.

If you could travel in time, where would you go and what would you do?
As you can tell from *Rebel Genius*, I'm fascinated by the Italian Renaissance. It would be pretty cool to visit with Leonardo da Vinci and Michelangelo.

What's the best advice you have ever received about writing?
No one ever said this to me specifically, but I've learned that becoming a writer and storyteller isn't just a natural talent that you either have or don't. It is something you can get better at through studying the craft and applying that to your practice.

What advice do you wish someone had given you when you were younger?
Don't give too much value to what other people think about you or your work. Trust yourself more.

Do you ever get writer's block? What do you do to get back on track?
It's not so much a block as writer's anxiety. Like most writers, I hit points where I'm worried what I'm writing is terrible. There's

no easy solution other than to keep working. Eventually, the words and ideas start flowing again.

What do you want readers to remember about your books?
Hopefully they come away with a slightly new perception of the world.

What would you do if you ever stopped writing?
My main hobby is photography, so I'd probably do a lot more nature and street photography if I had the time.

If you were a superhero, what would your superpower be?
Super-immunity! I hate getting sick.

What do you consider to be your greatest accomplishment?
Professionally, co-creating and making *Avatar: The Last Airbender* and *The Legend of Korra* with Bryan Konietzko is something I'm really proud of. Personally, it's the decision to start a family with my wife and the two amazing kids who followed.

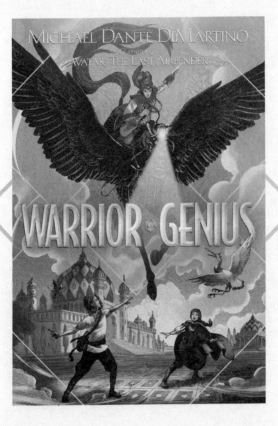

THE COUNCIL OF TEN

Giacomo Ghiberti was not long for this world.

From her throne's perch in the Salon dei Guerra, Supreme Creator Nerezza gazed down at the cloaked figures of the Council of Ten and demanded that one of her ministers explain how a twelve-year-old Tulpa, a man-made being, could have been living in Virenzia all these years without her knowing it. None of them could provide an adequate answer.

The young Tulpa had brought chaos to her city, brazenly defied her, and fled. Soon, Nerezza would make him pay for his rebelliousness. But for now, she needed to create the perception in the minds of her citizens that last night's violence had been quelled.

"Minister Monti, do you have the statement prepared?"

The Minister of Information, a woman half Nerezza's age with a frog-like face, nodded and began to read from a piece of parchment. "Loyal subjects of Supreme Creator Nerezza, let it be known that the treasonous artist Ugalino Vigano and his Tulpa,

Zanobius, returned from exile and attempted to assassinate your beloved leader. They were aided by a new Tulpa, but—"

"Stop," Nerezza interrupted. "Make no mention of the second Tulpa. We need to calm the masses, not send them into a panic."

The minister nodded and went back to her parchment. "But with the power of her Genius, the Supreme Creator repelled the attack."

Nerezza's Genius was curled up on the dais, her massive body safeguarding the throne. Nerezza reached a bony hand from under her robe to run her fingers along Victoria's long, gnarled beak, then scratched behind one of her large, pointed ears. The Genius raised her head and acknowledged her master with a groggy grumble.

"Once again, our great city is safe thanks to the leadership of Her Eminence," Monti continued. "The traitor Ugalino is dead."

And plans are already in place to deal with Zanobius, Nerezza thought.

"But make no mistake, it is a time of great strife in the Zizzolan Empire, and enemies both foreign and domestic seek our annihilation . . ."

As Minister Monti laid out the present-day dangers facing the Zizzolan people, Nerezza turned her attention to past threats, immortalized in the frescoes lining the Salon dei Guerra.

The paintings portrayed Zizzolan forces triumphing over Rachanan warriors through the ages. Some depicted ground battles with swords and spears crisscrossing amid thrashing bodies. Others showed clashes in the sky between bird-Geniuses and winged horse-Geniuses. Artists wielding brushes and pencils soared on the backs of giant bejeweled crows, eagles, and falcons, launching patterns of light from the gems in their Geniuses' crowns. Mounted warriors wielding large daggers countered with their own sacred geometry attacks, which radiated from gems on the horse-Geniuses' faceplates. The frescoes served as a reminder that Zizzola was—and needed to remain—the dominant force in the world. Nerezza wasn't about to let Giacomo and his friends threaten her supremacy.

". . . And in trying times like these, we must remain strong, vigilant, and fearless." Minister Monti looked up from her parchment.

"Good," Nerezza said. "Now go deliver the message to the people."

The minister hesitated. "But we must also address the matter of the Geniuses, Your Eminence. There may have been witnesses to the battle. What if word spreads that there is a new generation of children with Geniuses?" Monti cleared her throat, then added, "Not to mention the reemergence of Pietro Vasari and his Genius."

Nerezza's face twisted with annoyance at the mention of Pietro. She had stuffed her memories of him into a mental coffer that she kept locked, even to herself. *Especially* to herself.

"It's your job to make sure word *doesn't* spread," Nerezza ordered.

Monti bowed her head. "Yes, Your Eminence."

On one side of the vast hall, a door opened, and two armed guards entered, pulling a shackled man behind them. The rattling chains echoed through the chamber. "Here's the mercenary who was detained last night, as you requested," one of the guards said.

Ozo Mori's feet shuffled along the shiny marble and his head hung forward. Long black hair, matted with blood, covered half his face. On the other half, a scar ran from temple to jowl. As the mercenary passed the Minister of Culture, Baldassare Barrolo, the two men scowled, casting blame upon each other. Both had failed miserably in their mission to help Nerezza obtain the first Sacred Tool. But Barrolo had always been a loyal, if disagreeable, servant. The brunt of her punishment would fall on Ozo.

"For allowing the Tulpas to escape with the Creator's Compass, it is the decision of this Council that you shall be executed," Nerezza declared. "Perhaps I shall feed you to Victoria." With a long metal hook, Nerezza stabbed a piece of raw meat that had been laid out on a platter near her feet. Blood spattered across the dais as she flung the slab to her Genius. With a snap of her fangs, Victoria devoured the meal, then let out a satisfied snort.

Nerezza expected the mercenary to plead for his life, but instead, Ozo met her with an icy stare.

Barrolo strode over to Ozo and leaned in close. "You had better pray the Creator takes mercy on your soul."

Ozo let out a wolfish growl, exposing some missing teeth. Barrolo flinched.

"That's enough, Minister Barrolo," Nerezza commanded. "I'll decide who gets mercy. The Creator has no say in the matter."

Barrolo stepped back in line with the other ministers. "My apologies, Your Eminence."

"If you kill me, what I know about Giacomo dies too," Ozo remarked.

"And what is that?" Nerezza asked.

Ozo glanced at Victoria. "I'll tell you, but only if you promise I won't become your Genius's next meal."

"Very well," Nerezza said. "I don't think she has a taste for Rachanans anyway."

"Ugalino's Tulpa isn't the one you want," Ozo said. "Zanobius tried to take the Creator's Compass and failed, but Giacomo alone was able to remove it from the site."

Impossible, Nerezza thought. *How could this new Tulpa possess powers even greater than Zanobius's?*

Her Minister of War, Carlo Strozzi, stepped forward. He carried his burly frame with the confidence of a man who had survived many harrowing battles. "Don't believe a word he says, Your Eminence. He's only trying to stave off his execution. My soldiers witnessed Ugalino and Zanobius in the piazza with the Creator's Compass."

"Because they took it from Giacomo," Ozo rebutted.

Nerezza stared into Ozo's eyes, trying to discern if the mercenary was lying, then turned to her Minister of the Occult. "What do you make of this, Minister Xiomar?"

As the hunchbacked man lurched forward, his fellow Council members eyed him with long-standing distrust. At 140, he had become the oldest man in Zizzola's history. Though his bizarre regimen of imbibing foul-smelling elixirs had caused an enormous fleshy hump to grow on his back, the fact that he was still alive proved his methods were effective.

"While much has been written about the creation of Tulpas," Xiomar began, speaking between labored breaths, "very little is known about how their power manifests, or why one Tulpa differs from another. It is believed that the intention of the Tulpa's creator is somehow infused into its being."

"But is it possible Giacomo could have obtained the Compass alone?" Nerezza said, growing impatient.

"Certainly," Xiomar replied.

Nerezza clacked her red-tipped nails on the throne's golden arm. Giacomo did have a Genius, she reminded herself—impossible for a Tulpa, or so she had thought. And according to Barrolo, the young Tulpa also had been able to access the Wellspring. Clearly, Giacomo possessed great abilities. Maybe it wasn't so far-fetched to believe he was the only soul capable of acquiring the Sacred Tools. Together, the Compass, the Straightedge, and the Pencil held untold power—power that rightfully belonged to her.

Nerezza turned to her Minister of War. "Ready one of the new ships, Minister Strozzi. And assemble a crew. I want Giacomo captured—unharmed."

"As you wish," Strozzi replied. "And the prisoner? What do you want to do with him?"

"Free me and I'll help you track down Giacomo," the mercenary offered. There was a flicker of desperation in his eyes.

"The Supreme Creator already let you live; don't get greedy," Strozzi said, puffing out his chest. "My soldiers are more than capable of capturing a few children on the run."

"They'll be hard to capture with a vicious Tulpa protecting them," Ozo countered. "And from what I saw, your soldiers didn't fare very well against Zanobius. At least I was able to take one of his arms. I know his weaknesses better than anyone." Ozo turned to Nerezza. "I'm offering you my services, free of charge this time."

"What assurances do I have that you won't abandon the mission and flee to Rachana?" Nerezza asked.

"Rachana hasn't been my home since I was a boy," Ozo said. "The last thing I want is to go back there."

Nerezza considered Ozo's offer. He had provided her with vital information about Giacomo, and the reason she and Barrolo had hired him to escort the children to find the Compass in the first place was because of his reputation as a tracker. As a mercenary, he had worked for dukes and merchants throughout the empire, so he knew the lay of the land even better than Strozzi did.

"Remove his shackles," Nerezza ordered the guards.

Ozo's chains clattered on the marble, and he rubbed his wrists. "You won't regret this, Supreme Creator."

"I'd better not," Nerezza grumbled.

Barrolo stepped forward. "Your Eminence, I'd also like to join the mission. I want to bring my son, Enzio, back home."

"Very well," Nerezza said.

Ozo and Barrolo nodded begrudgingly at each other.

"We do have one problem," Ozo said. "I've never tracked anyone who had a magic Compass that can take him anywhere he wants to go."

"Not anywhere," Barrolo corrected. "The Creator's Compass will allow the user to travel only to places they've been before."

"Perfect," Ozo said. "We'll search the route I took the children on."

Barrolo shook his head. "Pietro is with them and can call upon his own memories. He's too smart to tread recent ground."

"Then where do you suggest we look?" Ozo challenged.

The Minister of Intelligence, a tall, slender man with an arrogant look about him, stepped forward. "I will send word to my spies. If anyone has seen Giacomo or his friends, we'll soon know."

"In the meantime, I'm going to contact some of my dealers in the black market," Barrolo said. "Pietro may try to seek refuge with one of them."

"Wherever Giacomo is hiding, let's find him quickly," Nerezza urged. Her heart, which usually beat weakly, began to thump. The hunt was on.

Lisa Wahlander

MICHAEL DANTE DiMARTINO,

a graduate of the Rhode Island School of Design, is the co-creator of the award-winning animated Nickelodeon series *Avatar: The Last Airbender* and its sequel, *The Legend of Korra*. He lives in Los Angeles with his wife and two children. His Rebel Geniuses series is his debut prose work.

michaeldantedimartino.tumblr.com